THE RIDGE

Also by Michael Koryta

So Cold the River
The Cypress House

MICHAEL KORYTA

THE RIDGE

HODDER &
STOUGHTON

First published in Great Britain in 2011 by Hodder & Stoughton
An Hachette UK company

1

Copyright © Michael Koryta 2011

The right of Michael Koryta to be identified as the Author
of the Work has been asserted by him in accordance with the
Copyright, Designs and Patents Act 1988.

A CIP catalogue record for this title is
available from the British Library

Hardback ISBN 978 1 444 70763 2
Trade Paperback ISBN 978 1 444 70764 9

Printed and bound by Mackays of Chatham Ltd, Chatham, Kent

Hodder & Stoughton policy is to use papers that are natural,
renewable and recyclable products and made from wood
grown in sustainable forests. The logging and manufacturing
processes are expected to conform to the environmental
regulations of the country of origin.

Hodder & Stoughton Ltd
338 Euston Road
London NW1 3BH

www.hodder.co.uk

For Tom Bernardo, whose generosity and friendship carried me through this one, and in recognition of the incredible mission and dedication of Joe Taft and the Exotic Feline Rescue Center of Center Point, Indiana. Deepest thanks.

Spirits pay rent to the basements they haunt.
Joe Pug, "Nation of Heat"

And I became a thin blue flame, polished
on a mountain range.
Josh Ritter, "Thin Blue Flame"

THE RIDGE

I

KEVIN KIMBLE MADE THE drive to the prison before dawn, as he always did, the mountains falling away as dark silhouettes in the rearview mirror. In the summer the fields below had been rich with the smells of damp soil and green plants reaching to meet the oncoming sun, but now the air was cold and darkness lingered and the scents were of dead leaves and wood smoke.

It was an hour-long trip through winding country highways, traffic almost nonexistent this early, and he could feel the familiar weight of a sleepless night as he drove. He was never able to sleep the nights before the visits.

A steady rain was falling when he left Sawyer County, but down out of the mountains of eastern Kentucky and into the fields in the north-central portion of the state the rain tapered off into a thick fog, the world existing in gray tendrils. Foreboding, but peaceful and silent.

Shattered by a cell-phone ring.

He looked at the display, expecting to see his department's dispatch number, but was instead faced with one he didn't recognize. He considered letting the call go to voicemail, but it was

5:35 A.M. and even wrong numbers deserved to be answered at such a time, just in case.

"Chief Deputy Kimble," he said, putting the phone to his ear.

"Good morning. I hope I didn't wake you. I had a feeling I wouldn't."

"Who's speaking?"

"Wyatt French."

Kimble shifted his hand to the top of the steering wheel and swung out into the next lane, away from a semi that was casting a thick spray back into his windshield as it chugged northbound, toward the Ohio River.

"How'd you get this number?" Kimble knew Wyatt French through one thing only — police work, and it was not as a colleague. He wasn't in the habit of giving out his personal number to the people he arrested or interviewed, the two roles Wyatt French had occupied in the past. Kimble had done such a thing just once, in fact, and endured eight months of physical therapy after that decision.

"I have a question for you," French said.

"I just asked you one of my own."

"Mine's a little more important." The man's voice sounded off, something coming up from beneath rocks or behind a sewer grate, someplace home to echoes and faint water sounds.

"You've been drinking, Mr. French."

"So I have. It's a legal enterprise, chief deputy."

"Conditionally legal," said Kimble, who had arrested Wyatt for public intoxication on three occasions and once for drunk driving. "Where are you?"

"I'm at home, where it's absolutely legal."

Home. Wyatt French's home was a wooden lighthouse he'd built with his own hands. When he wasn't causing trouble in the Whitman town streets, a bottle of cheap bourbon in hand or tucked into his mouth between a bristling gray mustache and an unkempt beard, the department still had to field complaints about the man. The strange, pulsing light that lit the woods in the rural stretch of abandoned mining country where he lived drew curiosity and ire.

"You're on the road," French said. "Aren't you? Early for a drive."

Kimble, who had things more personal weighing on his mind than this old drunk in the lighthouse, said, "Go to bed, man. Get some sleep. And however you got this number? Delete it. Don't call my private number again."

"I would like a question answered!"

Kimble moved his foot to the brake, tapped gently, dropping the speed down below the limit. French's voice had gone dark and furious, and for the first time, Kimble had a sense of real concern over the man's call.

"What's your question?"

"You're in charge of criminal investigations for your department," French said. "For the whole county."

"That's right."

"Which would you rather have: a homicide or a suicide?"

Kimble had a vision of Wyatt as he'd seen him last, weaving down the sidewalk outside a liquor store in the middle of the day. Kimble was on his way to buy a sandwich for lunch and Wyatt was on his way back from having attempted to buy a bottle of bourbon for the same. They bounced him out when he tried to pay with quarters, dimes, and nickels. That had been a few months ago. Since then, Kimble hadn't seen the old degenerate around any of his usual haunts.

"Mr. French," he said. "Wyatt? Don't talk like that. Okay? Just put the bottle down and get into bed."

"I'll get more than enough rest once I've had an answer. It *matters* to me, Deputy Kimble. It matters a great deal."

"Why?"

Silence, then, in a strained voice, "The question was simple. Would you rather have a —"

"Suicide," Kimble interrupted. "There, you happy? I picked, and I was honest. But I don't want *either,* Wyatt. I hate them both, and if there's some reason for this call beyond alcohol, then —"

That provoked a long, unsettling laugh, the tone far too high and keening for Wyatt's natural voice.

"There's a reason beyond booze, yes, sir."

"What is it?"

"You said you would prefer a suicide. I'm of a mind to agree, but I'd like to hear your reasoning. *Why* is a suicide better?"

Kimble was drifting along in the right lane, alone in the smoky fog and mist. He said, "Because I don't have to worry about anyone else being hurt by that particular person. It's always tragic, but at least I don't have to worry about them pointing a gun at someone else and pulling the trigger."

"*Exactly.* The very conclusion I reached myself."

"If you have any thoughts of suicide, then I've got a number I want you to call. I'm serious about this. I want you —"

"Now what if," Wyatt French said, "the suicide victim wasn't entirely willing."

Kimble felt an uneasy chill. "Then it's not a suicide."

"You say that confidently."

"I am confident. If the death was not the subject's goal, then it was not a suicide. By definition."

"So even if a man killed himself, but there was evidence that he'd been compelled to in some way —"

"Wyatt, stop. Stop talking like this. Are you going to hurt yourself?"

Silence.

"Wyatt?"

"I wanted to know if there was any difference in the way

you'd investigate," the man said, his words clearer now, less of the bourbon speaking for him. "Do you pursue the root causes of a suicide in the same manner that you would a homicide?"

Kimble drove along in the hiss of tires on rain-soaked pavement for a time, then said, "I pursue the truth."

"Always?"

"Always. Don't give me anything to pursue today, Wyatt. I'm not joking. If someone has been hurt, you tell me that right now. Tell me that."

"No one has been hurt yet."

Yet. Kimble didn't like that. "If you're thinking about suicide, or anything else, then I want —"

"My thoughts aren't your concern, deputy. You have many concerns around you in Sawyer County, some of them quite serious, but my thoughts aren't the problem."

"I'm going to give you a number," Kimble said again, "and ask you to call it for me, please. You called me early, and on a private line, and I've given you my time and respect. I hope you'll do the same for me."

"Certainly, sir. If there are two things I'd hope you might continue to grant me in the future, it is your time and respect."

French's voice was absent of mockery or malice. Kimble gave him the number, a suicide assistance line, and he could hear scratching as Wyatt dutifully wrote it down.

"Take care of yourself," Kimble told him. "Get dried out, get some rest. I'm worried about the way you're talking."

"What you should be worried about is that I'll choose to live forever. Then you'd really have your work cut out."

It was the first time any of Wyatt's traditional humor had showed, and Kimble let out a long breath, feeling as if the worst of this strange call was past.

"I've dealt with you for this long," he said. "Wouldn't be right not to keep at it."

7

"I appreciate the sentiment. And deputy? You be careful with her."

Kimble was silent, lips parted but jaw slack, and didn't realize he'd let his foot off the accelerator again until a minivan rose up into his mirror with an accompanying horn, then an extended middle finger from the driver who swerved around him. Kimble brought his speed back up and said, "Who do you mean, Wyatt?"

"The one you're going to see," Wyatt French told him. "Be very careful with her."

His voice had the low gravity of someone speaking at a wake. When Kimble finally got around to responding, offering up an awkward attempt at denial, he realized that the line was dead.

There was no time to call back from the highway, because the exit for the women's prison was just ahead, and Kimble had no desire to hear the old drunk's strange voice again anyhow. Let him sip his whiskey inside his damned lighthouse in the woods. Let his disturbed mind not infect Kimble's own.

He set the phone down and continued up to the prison gates.

2

A LONG, SINISTER BRICK STRUCTURE, the women's prison
had been built back in 1891, a hundred and twenty years
before it would house an inmate of interest to Kimble. Approved
adults could begin arriving at 6 A.M., but the parking spaces were
empty when he pulled in. Kimble was always the first one in the
door. He liked to be alone in the visiting area, and he liked making the drive in the dark.

They checked him in with familiarity and a quiet "Morning,
deputy" and then escorted him into the visitation room. He was
afforded privileges here that others were not, a level of privacy
and trust that others were not, because he was police. And
because they all knew the story.

She was alone in the room, waiting for him at the other end of
a plastic table, and when he saw her his breath caught and his
heartbeat stuttered and he felt a fierce, cold ache low in his back.

"Jacqueline," he said.

She rose and offered her slim, elegant hand. Warm, gentle
fingers in his cool, callused palm, and he found himself, as he
always did when they touched, wetting his lips and looking to

the side, as if something had moved in the shadows at the edge of the room.

"Hello, Kevin." She took her seat again, and he pulled up a plastic chair that screeched coming across the floor and sat beside her. Not all the way at the opposite end of the table, but not too close, either. Purgatory distance.

"Are you well?" he said.

"Yes."

Her voice took that distance between them and melted it like ice in a fist. It was so knowing, so intimate, she might as well have been sitting in his lap. The ache in his back pulsed.

"You look good. I mean... healthy."

Looked healthy. Shit. If all she looked was healthy, then there were starlets all over Hollywood who looked sickly. She was the kind of beautiful that scorched. Tall and lean, with gentle but clear curves even in the loose orange inmate garb, cocoa-colored hair that somehow held an expensive salon's sheen after five years of prison care, cheekbones and mouth sculpted with a master's touch. Full lips that looked dark against her complexion, which had once been deeply tanned but was now so white he could see the fine veins in her slender neck. Blue eyes that he could not, even after several years, meet for more than a few seconds.

"They treating you okay?"

"Yes, Kevin. As well as a place like this ever can treat someone."

Kevin. She said it in the sort of voice that should carry hot breath against your ear. Nobody called him Kevin. He was Kimble, had been since childhood, one of those boys who inexplicably becomes identified by his last name.

"Good," he said. He was staring at the floor to avoid her eyes, but now he saw that she had hitched those loose prison pants up slightly, so that her ankles were exposed above the thin sandals. Her ankles and a trace of legs. Long, sleek legs. She leaned back in the chair now and crossed her feet, pushing them closer toward him, which made him flush and lift his head.

"How is your back?" she said.

He was silent for a moment. His jaw worked, but he didn't speak, and this time he was able to meet her eyes.

"Fine," he said.

"I'm glad."

"Sure."

She smiled at him, rich and genuine, a smile you were never supposed to see in a place where faces were so often dark and threatening or unbalanced and psychotic.

"I'm so glad. I always worry, you know. I worry that it pains you."

"Yes," he said. "I know."

This was the game. This was the perfected exchange, performed each month as if they were rehearsing for some stage show and needed to keep sharp. Why did he drive up here? Why in the hell did he make these visits?

"I'm sorry, I don't remember," she said, and he wondered how many times he'd heard those five words now. First in a handwritten letter to him in the hospital, then in interview rooms, then at the trial and every visit that had been made since. She was always sorry that she didn't remember.

"You've told me, Jacqueline," he said, his voice stretched. "Let's not worry about that."

"You know how badly I wish I could, though. For you."

"I know."

She smiled again, this time uncertainly. "I appreciate you making the trip. I always do."

"It's nothing."

"You've been so good to me. The one person above all others who *shouldn't* be, and you're the one person above all others who *is*."

"You don't belong in here," he said.

She sat up straighter then, sat up with excitement, and said, "Didn't they tell you I get to leave?"

He cocked his head and frowned. "Leave?"

"I thought for sure they'd tell you," she said. "I mean, I'm always sure they talk to you about me. Don't they?"

If there was one date Kimble knew absolutely, knew surer than Christmas or his own birthday, it was the scheduled parole hearing of Jacqueline Mathis. She was not leaving this prison. Not yet.

"Jacqueline, where are—"

"I've been approved for work release. It might not seem like much to you, but still...you can imagine how exciting it is for me. There's not much change around here."

"What? Where?" He was embarrassed by the evident concern—check that, evident *fear*—in his voice. He liked to know where she was. He *needed* to know.

"It's a thrift shop," she said. "Some little store just down the road. I don't care where or what, though—it's not in this place! I've made the petition three times. They finally approved it."

"Why did they now?"

"Because I'm so charming," she said, and laughed. He waited, and she said, "Oh, take off the cop eyes, Kevin."

She sat up straight now, dropped her voice into a low, formal tone.

"They approved me, officer, because I've shown myself to be nonthreatening and of sound mind and character."

He stared at her, rubbing one hand over his jaw. It wasn't an abnormal decision, not at this stage of her incarceration. They'd be readying her for release, assuming she made parole. She would make parole—there had been no problems and many were sympathetic to her—but that was still a year away. He had thought he had another year to get used to the idea of her being free. Why hadn't he thought of work release?

"So you're happy," he said finally, just to say something.

She laughed. "Of course I'm happy. You think I'd prefer to stay in here?"

"Probably not."

"Probably not. Master of the understatement." She shook her head, then said, "I'll be working the mornings, though. That will change my visitation hours. I hope that wouldn't stop you, if you had to visit later in the day? I've always wondered if you're ashamed of me after the sun comes up."

"No, Jacqueline. It's just . . . well, you know, it's a long drive. If I come early, I beat the traffic."

"The Sawyer County traffic," she said. "Yes, that area around the courthouse gets pretty gridlocked for about two minutes each morning. Particularly now, with the students home for the holidays? Why, you might have to sit through one entire red light."

He didn't answer.

"You don't like the idea," she said. "Do you? Me being out of here, even for a few hours."

"That's not true," he said, and maybe it wasn't. Maybe he liked the idea an awful lot.

"Well, I like it," she said. "Out of these walls, out of these clothes. Do you know how long it's been since I wore something other than this?"

She grasped her orange shirt between her thumb and index finger and tugged it away from her body. He got a glimpse of her collarbone and below it smooth, flawless skin.

"You could drop by there sometime," she said. "You know — see me on the *outside*." She shifted her tone to a theatrical whisper and capped it off with a wink. He could feel his dick begin to stiffen, performing against his will, his own body laughing at him. He got to his feet abruptly, making his arousal evident.

"Kevin?"

13

"I've got to get started back," he said. "It's a long drive. Too long."

"Why are you leaving so early? Did I say something—"

"Be safe," he said, the same thing he always said, and walked to the door, using his hand to adjust himself within his pants, not wanting the attendant CO to see *that* development.

"I thought you would be happy for me. I thought if there was one person in the world who'd be happy for me, it would be you."

"I am happy for you, Jacqueline. Goodbye."

By the time the guards opened the door, he had his police eyes back.

It had been a long drive for a short visit. That was how it went with her. He could never stay too long.

Be careful with her, Wyatt French had told him.

Yeah, buddy. Listen to the old drunk. Watch your ass, Kimble.

Be very careful with her.

3

THE *SAWYER COUNTY SENTINEL* WAS at 122 years and counting when they shut it down. Peak circulation, 33,589. On the last day, they printed 10,000 copies. That was a bump, too, operating with an expectation that the locals would want their piece of history, so the *Sentinel* printed extras to make certain they could shake an ash out of the urn for everybody who wanted one.

The staff — nineteen members strong at the end, down from forty-eight at the start of Roy Darmus's career — blew the corks off a few bottles of champagne at five that afternoon and passed glasses around the newsroom and cried. Every last one of them. The editors, the reporters, the pressmen. Even J. D. Henry, the college intern, couldn't help it. He'd been with them all of two months, but there he was leaning on a desk and sipping champagne he wasn't old enough to drink legally and wiping tears from his eyes. Because they were a family, damn it, and it was a business that had spanned more than a century and told the stories of a community day by day and year by year longer than anyone alive could remember, and now it was gone. Who could be part of that and not cry?

When the champagne was gone, they'd all moved on to Roman's Tavern, had burgers and onion rings and pitchers of beer and told stories that had been told a hundred times before, treating each one like new material.

Sometime around midnight, as awkward silences were becoming more common than bursts of laughter, J. D. Henry commented on how strange it had been to look around the place and see all those empty desks.

"Weren't all empty," Donita Hadley said. She'd been writing obits for thirty years, and if there was anyone who wouldn't miss the details of a death, it was Donita. "Roy's got his work cut out for him yet."

How in the hell she'd known that, Roy couldn't say. He'd taken everything off the cubicle walls and cleared the surface of his desk, but he hadn't touched the drawers. Perhaps she'd opened them, snooping around. But somehow he knew that wasn't the case. Donita, she just understood.

"Really?" J.D. asked, the kid showing innocent surprise as he stared at Roy, everyone else suddenly finding other places for their eyes. They knew what the intern didn't; this was a loss for them all, but a touch more personal for Roy. He'd grown up at the paper. Literally. Had started drifting in as a kid, shoving stories onto the editor's desk. After his parents were killed in a car accident and he'd gone to live with his grandmother, the staff essentially adopted him. His first paid job was culling the morgue files for a column called "Local Lore," two-sentence recollections of the headline stories that had run twenty-five, fifty, and seventy-five years earlier. He worked his way through college at the paper, took a full-time job immediately after graduating, and never left. There were those who'd been around longer, but nobody had spent a greater percentage of life inside the *Sentinel*'s newsroom than Roy Darmus.

"Why haven't you cleared out yet?" J.D. asked.

"Lot of shit in those drawers," Roy mumbled. "Been procrastinating. You know me, always past deadline."

The truth was, he had to be alone for it. Not just alone—he had to be the last man standing. Captain of the sinking ship.

That seemed to satisfy everyone except Donita. Her eyes stayed on him for a long moment, and then Roy suggested they have another round, and the response was a collective hemming and hawing. The night had gone on too long for most now—they were an older crowd, J.D. excepted, and it had been a draining day. People began to reach for wallets, but Mike Webb, the editor, insisted he was putting it on the company tab, saying that if the owners didn't like it, they could shut the place down.

That joke landed as smoothly as a buffalo coming off a balance beam, but hell, at least the drinks were free.

Everyone walked down the steps and out into the night. December, the town aglow with Christmas lights, air biting with cold wind driven out of the Appalachian foothills, the season, quite appropriately, of death. The course had been charted nine years earlier, when a newspaper that had been family-owned since its creation sold out to a national chain. The cuts began almost immediately—first pages, then staff. There had been talk of a Web-only product for a time, but this rural Kentucky community wasn't viewed as a potential profit center, despite more than a century of profit, and eventually the terminal diagnosis was issued.

Outside of Roman's, the last of the crew shared hugs and handshakes and went off to their cars and the rest of their lives, promising to keep in touch in the way kids did at graduations, firmly and incorrectly believing it would actually happen.

That was supposed to be the last of it, the final rites administered, but Roy was back the next afternoon. He preferred to shut it down in private. It was home in a way your office never really should be, and that afternoon, when he went in alone, the building was so silent it made him feel unsteady. Newsrooms were never quiet, were always filled with a humming, delightful energy, sometimes chaotic, sometimes somber, but always present.

Today, it had all the energy of a crypt.

He had five drawers to empty — three in the desk, two in the file cabinet. It was very much like sorting through a loved one's belongings after a funeral.

The first thing to go into the recycling bin was his tips folder. He flipped it open and saw notes jotted on scraps of paper and backs of menus and napkins: *Brandon Tyler taught his blind brother to throw a tomahawk; astronomy club planning event for lunar eclipse; Evelyn Scott won national cookie recipe competition . . .*

And so on. Stories of local people and local interest. He looked at them now, feeling sorrow because their forum was gone. Determined not to wallow in that sorrow, Roy went through the crank file next, knowing it would demand a smile. It was in the bottom right-hand desk drawer, a good five inches thick, jammed with letters. He opened it up and began to read through them, and, as he'd hoped, couldn't help but smile. There was the savage critique of his story judgment from a woman who wanted to let the public know that she and her husband had caught the *exact* same smallmouth bass on the *exact* same day, and just what was the matter with him that he didn't think people would be interested in that? There was the collection of letters from a group of neighbors who had recorded sightings of a sasquatch — well, it was probably a sasquatch but potentially a wolf capable of walking on its hind legs, which was *twice* as alarming, didn't he think? There was a note from a woman who was certain her neighbor was breaking into her house to use her Jacuzzi and asserted that she had the pubic hair to prove it, and the allegation that the mayor had been sighted in Maloney Park in carnal embrace with a sheep.

He remembered them all, remembered sharing them with Donita or Laura or Stewart and sharing laughs. There would be no more crank letters here, there would be no more laughs. The smile gone from his face, he set the folder on top of his desk with a sigh and walked all the way into the break room in search of coffee, pulling up short when he saw the pot was gone. Right. He turned on his heel, and had just settled back down at his desk when the phone rang.

It was startlingly loud in the empty newsroom, which was going dark as the stormy day faded to night. Roy picked it up and said hello.

"Mr. Darmus. This is Wyatt French."

"Oh. Hot-tip time?"

Old Wyatt was a well-known figure to those in the newsroom and those in the liquor business. He didn't appear to intersect with much else, just booze and bizarre news. Roy had written about the old man's lighthouse once, and apparently Wyatt had appreciated the tenor of the piece, because he'd taken to calling every so often with what he referred to as "hot tips." They generally involved police misconduct or local bars that served watered-down bourbon. Lately the calls had been focused on the pending relocation of an exotic-cat rescue center to his isolated stretch of the woods. Wyatt did not approve of the facility, at least not across from his home. Today he'd either missed the fact that the newspaper was no longer in business or he was too drunk to remember.

"Mr. Darmus, I wanted to tell you … wanted to ask that you …"

"Buddy, we're out of the tip business, I'm afraid," Roy said, smiling, but then the smile faded when he heard French's ragged breathing.

19

"It will be very important to keep the light on when I'm gone," Wyatt French said. "Very important."

"You're leaving?"

"I'd like to say otherwise, Mr. Darmus. I would so dearly like to say otherwise."

Roy frowned. "Wyatt, what's wrong?"

"You were right about this place, you know. You just didn't look far enough. Didn't look hard enough. I don't blame you. There's more to it than I can explain, and more than a sane man would pause to hear. I'm not one who would be heard, anyhow. The mountain could tell it, if it could talk."

"I don't understand."

"Of course you don't. You haven't got the faintest notion what I'm talking about. I did more than most, though. I fought it."

"Let's slow down," Roy said. "I don't know what you're talking about."

"If I felt I could make a soul believe me, I might stay around to try. The longer I stay, though, the greater the risk. I'm getting scared of the dark coming. I'm getting scared of what I could do in the dark."

The rant faded back to ragged inhalations. The breathing of a panicked man. Roy's frown deepened.

"Wyatt, do you need help out there?"

"Oh, yes. Help is needed out here. For me? Sure. For you? Absolutely. I tried to provide it. I did what I could. You tell them that. You tell them that Wyatt French did what he could — for *them*. For everyone."

"I'm not following, and you sound —"

"They should have listened to me about those damned cats. You know how many people will come out here now? Do you have any idea what that might mean?"

"No," Roy said. "I do not. Explain it to me."

"Take a closer look," Wyatt said. "That's all I ask. If you and Kimble both do that much, then maybe—"

"Kevin Kimble? With the sheriff's department?"

"He's gone to see her, you know."

"Gone to see who?"

"Jacqueline Mathis. The woman who shot him, and he drives up there every month to pay a visit. He doesn't ask the right questions."

"What should he be asking?"

Wyatt went silent for a moment, and when he spoke again he'd gotten the harried pace under control.

"I want you to try to tell this story," he said. "You're the right one for it. You and Kimble. And somebody needs to tell it. I hope you will."

"I would if I could, Wyatt. But they've closed the paper."

"It's not a newspaper story, Mr. Darmus. But so many of the ones that really need to be told aren't, wouldn't you agree?"

"I tried to tell the ones that mattered."

"You really did, Mr. Darmus. You really did. And this one needs to be told, for you particularly. I think you need to know the character your parents showed."

Roy felt his breathing slow. His parents had died in a car accident on Blade Ridge Road, very near Wyatt's lighthouse.

"What do you know about my parents?"

"The decisions that they both made. Very brave. Very strong. And knowing what they were saying goodbye to, with a child at home, it must have been so difficult. You can be very proud of them."

"Damn it, Wyatt, I don't appreciate you talking about—"

"When you write the story," Wyatt said, "please make something clear. I didn't have to die. I could go on as long as I want."

He hung up. Roy stared at the receiver in astonishment.

Disconnected, then dialed the number that had appeared on the caller ID. It went right to voicemail. Roy hung up.

I didn't have to die.

"Oh, shit," he said, and then he took his car keys, left his boxes on the desk, and left the building.

4

Blade Ridge Road lay in the western reaches of the county, a twenty-minute drive from Whitman, though Roy did it in fifteen as dusk fell over the wooded countryside. It wasn't so much of a road—just a rutted gravel lane that broke away from County Road 200 in the foothills that had once been home to coal-mining country, making a straight line toward the Marshall River, which marked Sawyer County's western border. County Road 200 bent sharply to the left at this point, but if you missed that curve and continued straight, you'd end up on Blade Ridge, which would deliver you to the realization that you'd made a mistake and then to a sudden wall of trees.

For some people—Roy's parents among them—it was a very bad mistake. The narrow, twisting lane was treacherous, particularly in the winter, particularly in the dark. When Roy's parents died, the county was inspired to replace the original dead-end sign with two larger ones and add a warning that traffic was for residents only. Not that there were many of them. Just a lighthouse, where once a trailer had stood. And, now, a cat zoo.

Thinking about his parents made him tighten his hands on

23

the steering wheel. What had the old boozehound been trying to imply — that they'd driven off into the woods intentionally, a joint suicide?

And knowing what they were saying goodbye to, with a child at home, it must have been so difficult.

"Bullshit," Roy said aloud, his voice hot with anger. His parents had been dead for forty-six years, but even that wasn't enough time to provide a buffer against the emotions that swelled at the suggestion that they might have left him on purpose.

They were coming home from my basketball game in Jasper County, and they were looking for a shortcut and took the wrong turn. I've known that for decades, Wyatt, you prick. Don't you dare poison my memories of them, don't you dare.

Ahead of the spot where the gravel road reached its end, directly across from the fresh fencing and cages that had now been built into the woods to house a rescue center for tigers, cougars, lions, and leopards, there was a track that cut off to the right. This was the driveway to Wyatt French's lighthouse. It came in from the north side at a harsh angle and began to climb immediately. Roy made the turn, loose gravel sliding under the tires, and heard the pitch of the Pilot's engine turn harsh as it strained up the incline. It was like driving through a tunnel because the trees hung so dense and so close to the road. Then it broke to a crest and there were a few gaps that allowed you to see between the mountains and out to the Marshall River and an ancient railroad trestle.

A long fence protected the lighthouse property. The gate was padlocked; Wyatt French didn't care for visitors. Built at the base of the lighthouse was a structure that looked no bigger than a shed. It was there that the old man lived.

"Crazy bastard," Roy muttered, staring at the lighthouse as he parked the Honda in the weeds beside the fence. He hit the horn, three taps.

24

Nothing. He gave it a minute and laid on the horn again, longer this time, figuring the blaring noise would raise Wyatt's ire and call him forth.

It didn't, though. Roy shut the car off and climbed out into the rain. The fence was there, but fences could be climbed. Wyatt French hadn't added razor wire and guard towers to the property, though they were probably on his list.

There was not a sound except for the rain, but the light was flashing steadily against the gathering dusk.

I'm getting scared of what I could do in the dark.

"Just go knock on the damn door," he muttered to himself, and then he went forward. The fence was simple, six-foot chain link, and Roy was still in decent shape, cleared it easily. There was only one door. A piece of paper fluttered on it, secured with two large thumbtacks. Roy used the side of his hand to flatten the paper against the wind so he could read the message, hoping it was instructions for FedEx or a note for a neighbor.

It wasn't.

For purposes of investigation, the handwritten note read, *please contact Kevin W. Kimble of the Sawyer County Sheriff's Department.*

Roy took his hand away from the note, and the breeze slid under the paper again, rustling it against the wood. He was afraid now, plain and simple.

For purposes of investigation . . .

. Kimble was the chief deputy, a man who'd taken a bullet in the back a few years ago and still returned to the job. He was, anyone in the county would probably agree, the man you'd want on a difficult case.

But what was Wyatt's case?

Roy knocked. Nothing. He cupped his hands and shouted Wyatt's name. The rain was streaming down his neck and under his shirt collar to his spine. He tried the knob, then swore when it turned.

Unlocked. Shit. Why couldn't it have been locked? Why were the doors you knew you shouldn't open always the ones that were unlocked?

He pushed the door open and peered into the darkness. The living quarters seemed larger than they should have, but they still weren't much to speak of. There was a small bed in one corner, a desk beside it, some shelves, a kitchen table in the middle of the room. Refrigerator and range and sink. A bathroom blocked off by an old-fashioned accordion-style door.

"Wyatt? Mr. French? It's Roy Darmus."

By now he'd given up on getting an answer. He stepped into the room, and in the nickel-colored light of the rainy afternoon he could see that the walls were lined with maps. Topographic maps of Sawyer County. As he walked farther in, he saw that each map had a different year written on it in bold black marker: 1966, 1958, 1984…

Across the room was another door, also closed. This would lead to the lighthouse steps. Maybe this one would be locked. That would be nice.

It wasn't. Opened outward and revealed the base of the spiral stairs that curled up and away. Roy began to climb, one hand on the railing.

"Wyatt?" he called.

There were more steps than he'd have thought. He climbed for a long time, into progressive darkness, and then finally the top showed itself in a gray glare of daylight.

By then Roy didn't need to go any farther. The smell assured him of that — warm, fresh copper tinged the air.

He steadied himself and climbed on and at the top step his head finally broke the surface and he found himself staring at the light itself. There was one oversized bulb surrounded by a series of strange, mirror-like lenses, the light within flashing, and arranged beneath it were four odd fixtures with red lenses angled toward the cardinal directions. Roy could see no light coming from those, though.

Electrocuted himself, Roy thought. *He was doing something to the light, trying to repair it or change it, and he electrocuted himself.*

That thought lasted only until he pushed all the way up onto the lighthouse platform, turned to the right, and looked directly into Wyatt French's dead face.

He'd shot himself in the mouth, and if Roy had made a full circle around the lighthouse he would have been able to see the blood and brain tissue that was still wet on the glass. There was a gaping, grotesque hole in the center of French's face, and his long gray hair was clotted with blood. A handgun lay on his lap.

All of this Roy saw in a half-second flash, and then he turned away, turned too fast. His feet were still on the top step, and one of them slid off and his balance was gone. He fell sideways and put out a hand to steady himself, but he was dropping too fast, and knew before he hit it that he was going directly into the light. He heard a pop and felt immediate, scorching pain just before the blood began to flow. He'd landed with his palm out and his weight driving down and that was all it took for the glass lenses to shatter and bite.

"Son of a *bitch,*" he said, lifting his hand free, blood dripping onto the floor and splattering his jeans. He'd punctured not only the lenses but the bulb; the light had given a frightening spark at the moment of impact and then gone dark. Everything had; the lighthouse was soaked in shadow now.

He turned and stumbled down the stairs, grabbing at the railing with his good hand.

5

OF COURSE IT RAINED. Fate wouldn't have it any other way. Audrey Clark was moving massive, uneasy cats and it poured rain. Absolutely ideal.

She'd had a vision of this day, and it wasn't rain that spoiled that. No, rain would have been fine — she could picture David leaning down to kiss her, laughing, his wet blond hair plastered to his skull, water drops on his glasses, all of it still a pleasure to him, in charge of everything and enjoying every moment. They'd spent their first afternoon together in these Kentucky hills, when Audrey's law firm was tasked with drawing up the endowment that would fund the cat rescue center and David had capitalized on her interest — ostensibly in the rescue center, but also in him — to show her exactly what he intended to build in Sawyer County. At the time it had been fascinating, admirable, and romantic.

At that time, there'd been no cat shit on the grounds.

Her vision of the day had died with her husband in the rocks along the Marshall River six months earlier. He'd fallen forty-six feet while scouting the new home for the rescue center one evening, and although the police told her that David had died instantly, Audrey was still falling.

They'd gotten started at daybreak, the third day of moving cats and, with any luck, the last. At her side were four volunteers and the rescue center's only two paid staff members: Dustin Hall, a former student of David's, and Wesley Harrington, the preserve's manager and cat guru. She had just one transport vehicle, a large panel truck that could hold as many as eight cages at once. Getting those eight cages filled, though, took time and effort. Cats, large or small, are not fond of doing anything that hasn't been granted their express written consent. Transportation in a cage generally does not qualify.

So it became a battle of wills, with one caveat: the humans could cheat.

They started with simple coaxing. True to the cliché, the cats were curious, if nothing else. Sometimes that curiosity would be enough to lead them to inspect the transport cage. The moment they entered, Wes or Audrey would drop the guillotine gate behind them. If curiosity and coaxing didn't work, they'd stoop to the first of the cheating tactics: food baiting. Many of the reluctant animals could be lured into the cage when the right treat was offered—*Small children work well,* Wes had told her dryly—and then the gate would drop.

If the first two techniques didn't work, then they'd stoop to the ultimate cheat and use tranquilizers. Wes was adamantly opposed to that. He'd been involved in cat recoveries all over the country, and on two occasions he'd seen animals lost because of mishandled drugging. His stance on sedation was that it had to be the last measure.

After five years of working with these cats, Audrey hadn't thought they'd need to sedate any of them for the relocation, but as the day wore on she found herself in favor of the idea with

Kino, one of the male tigers, and not just because Kino sprayed her three times in the morning alone.

The big tiger was full of bad attitude on a good day, and this was not a good day. Watching all the chaos, watching his peers being loaded into cages and driven away, Kino was quite pissed off. Audrey had always made fun of the way he stalked the fence, giant shoulders rolling, giant ass swaying, a surly stare on everyone.

We need to get you a leather jacket, she'd told him once. *You can wear it with the collar up.*

He'd sprayed her almost immediately after that bit of mockery, and the plans for the leather jacket had swiftly become a promise for a tiger-skin rug for her living room.

Today he was playing the role of an antagonist, roaring and banging against the fences and trying to get the other cats worked up.

"There is *no* way we get his angry ass into a truck without sedation," she said.

"We'll get him, and we're not sedating him," Wes answered firmly. He loved all of the cats, but Audrey knew well that Kino was his favorite, simply because Kino was the most challenging.

So they worked around Kino all morning and afternoon, and it was on the last load of the day that they finally got the big tiger into the transport cage. Drug-free, as Wes had promised. In the end it came down to Wes's ingenious suggestion of totally ignoring the animal. He circled around Kino's enclosure, talking to the other tigers, reaching out here and there to scratch along their jaws or in some cases allowing them to nuzzle his face and lick his cheek. By the time he made his third pass, Kino was bellowing for attention. Wes ignored him completely. Ten minutes later, the tiger marched sullenly into his transport cage. When they dropped the gate behind him, Wes knelt beside the cage and leaned close. Kino growled. Wes said, "Yeah, I know," and held his ground, and a few seconds later the tiger's sound shifted to the chuffing noise that signified pleasure and Wes was scratching behind one of his ears.

"I can't believe you got him in that cage without tranquilizers," Audrey said, and she meant it. She was better around these cats than most people, and David had been far better than she, but Wes was something else entirely. The cats accepted him in a way that they wouldn't anyone else, and his innate understanding of them was extraordinary.

You're always worried about whether you can trust them, he told her once. *If you worry more about making it clear that they can trust* you, *you'll be amazed at the difference.*

Those lines or variations of them were constant from Wes, who spoke little except to explain things about the cats to Audrey, or, more aptly, to explain what she was failing to grasp about them. She rode an emotional pendulum between appreciation and irritation. At one moment there would be recognition that without him she could not run the preserve; in the next, deep frustration that without him she could not run the preserve.

"Kino, he's all talk," Wes said now, and then they used a forklift to put the cages onto the truck. Every time one was in the air, Audrey held her breath. She was envisioning disaster—a dropped cage, a broken door, a four-hundred-pound tiger on the loose—but Wes was calm and confident and that helped. The cages were loaded without incident, and then they were on the road, bound west across the county for Blade Ridge.

"Not many left," she told Wes as they raced the rapidly fading daylight. "I hoped we would get them all, but that was pretty ambitious. Tomorrow will be easy, though. One load of lions, and then Ira."

Ira was the preserve's prize, a black cougar, the only such creature in captivity in the world, a cat so rare that many experts still refused to believe he wasn't the product of crossbreeding.

"Hope you're right," Wes said, and she felt that she was. Despite the rain and the hard work and the weight of David's absence, she felt good. She knew also that her husband would be pleased if he could watch the cats gathering at their new home. The land on Blade Ridge Road had been his dream option. Originally part of an enormous tract belonging to one of the town's old mining families, it was so rugged that little had changed with the property in the past hundred years. It was far from any residential development and large enough for them to have plenty of room to grow, also isolated enough for the cats to have little in the way of human distraction.

Little, that was, except for the psychotic who lived across the road. Their only neighbor — the only resident on the entire stretch of gravel road, in fact — was a local drunk who had, long before David and Audrey acquired their property, made the decision to replace his trailer home with a lighthouse.

A real one. On a wooded hilltop, in the middle of nowhere.

She'd had a bad feeling the first time she saw it, only worsening when friends around town commented on their neighbor's propensity for drink and odd behavior. There was something indescribably eerie about watching the light paint the treetops with its pulsing, relentless golden flashes. She urged David to make a formal complaint. He found it amusing; she found it alarming.

It will bother the cats, she'd said. *Can you imagine how Jafar will react to that thing? It's so damn bright.*

Jafar, a leopard, was one of David and Audrey's personal favorites, a sleek, beautiful animal with the personality of an affectionate if mischievous housecat, and in the end it had probably been Jafar's desire, not Audrey's, that tipped the scale. David called the sheriff and said the lighthouse was too bright. It turned out he wasn't wrong — a permit was required for so bright a light. Wyatt French had responded formally at first, taking down his megawatt lamps and replacing them with something that — barely — satisfied the permit standards for light pollution or air traffic control or whoever made such decisions.

For a time it had looked as if he was just an eccentric, peaceful enough. Then came the county council meetings to discuss the rescue center's relocation, and Wyatt French arrived intoxicated and angry and raving grim prophecies of doom. By the time the police finally escorted him from the room, then arrested him, Audrey was looking at David with *I told you so* eyes. They didn't have an eccentric neighbor, they had an enemy.

And a cruel one, Audrey learned after David's death. A card from Wyatt French had arrived amidst all the others, but his message was anything but heartwarming. He expressed his sorrow for her loss, yes, but then he added a few lines suggesting that David had done it to himself, and that if they had not forced him to tamper with the lighthouse, her husband would have been safe from harm.

Audrey had ripped the card into breath-mint-sized shreds, slowly and methodically, while her older sister watched in astonishment. That was the last contact she'd had with Wyatt French, who had yet to come down the hill and visit his new neighbors. He surely would soon enough, though, and that expectation just added to the strange light's malevolence. It had been flashing today even after the sun rose, and continued; with each load of cats they brought, the storm-darkened skies glittered with flashes that found her eyes and crawled behind them and took hostile refuge in her mind, leaving her with an unfocused anger.

The anger was gone, though, and the frustration. The only negatives that would remain today were the muscle aches.

That was how she felt until the sirens and the flashing lights of a police car appeared behind them. Wes eased onto the shoulder, thinking they were being stopped, but the car hummed by without pause, a trail of mist from its tires hanging in the air like exhaust from a jet.

"He's in a hurry," she observed.

It was five minutes later when they turned onto the long gravel lane that led to their new home and saw a red light in the trees. As Wes drove on, Audrey stared at it, thinking that it might be from the lighthouse, thinking that the crazy neighbor was taking it up a notch, but then they rounded a bend and she could see the police car.

Or the remains of the police car.

The vehicle was upside down in the trees on the north side of the road, across from the preserve's front gate. It looked as if it had been in the process of rolling a second time when the trees caught it, and now the car was propped at an awkward angle, the passenger side in the air and the driver's side pressed against the ground. The roof was crushed down, fractured pieces of metal and fiberglass littered the gravel, and the headlights—both still on—were pointed crazily into the trees, one angled up, one angled down. The hood was torn and the engine showed like internal organs, things you knew you shouldn't be able to see.

Audrey whispered, "He's got to be dead."

Wes didn't argue. With the look of that car, there wasn't much argument to be made.

"Call 911," he said, and then a figure emerged from the trees just behind the car, stepping out of the shadows, and Audrey almost screamed before she realized that it was Dustin Hall, her own employee. He looked up at them, then back to the car, and shook his head.

Audrey knew what he meant. The driver was dead.

Wes popped open the door and stepped into the rain while Audrey took her phone out and dialed, gave their location, and explained the situation.

"It's bad," she said. "It's really, really bad."

"Is the driver breathing?"

"I don't know. I can't imagine...the car is just demolished."

34

"Could you check? Can you get close enough to see if there's any sign of motion? We have an ambulance en route, but I need to know what to tell them."

Audrey got out of the truck. Wes had dropped to his knees by the shattered window, and now he removed his jacket, wrapped it around his fist, and began swinging at the car, trying to clear away the remaining glass from the passenger window.

"Is he alive?" Audrey asked.

"I don't know."

She walked closer, knelt in the wet gravel beside him, and peered inside the car. The roof had been crushed down to the headrest, both airbags had deployed, and the inside of the car was a cloudburst of broken plastic, glass, and fabric. The airbags had left a chalky dust in the air, the smell faintly like gunpowder. Pinned between the steering wheel and the remains of the passenger seat, which had been shoved toward him, was the deputy's crumpled body. Audrey was just about to speak into the phone again, just about to say that the man looked to be dead, when he moved his head and focused his eyes on hers.

She almost screamed. It was stunning to see him move. She jerked upright and stumbled backward as the operator said, "Ma'am, what do you see?"

"He's…um…he's moving," Audrey said, watching in astonishment as the deputy blinked, narrowed his eyes, and frowned at her and Wes as if he didn't know what they were doing there and didn't like seeing them. "He's alive. I don't know how, but he's alive."

The operator was busy telling her not to try to move him until the paramedics arrived when the deputy reached out of the broken window and placed one white palm on the gravel, dug his fingers in, and tried to pull himself clear.

"Tell him not to move," Audrey said, but Wes was already leaning forward to help.

"Give a hand," he shouted to Dustin, who had been one of David's favorite students and was always capable around the preserve but now stood pale-faced and motionless. Dustin responded to the order, though, leaned down and helped support the deputy's weight while Wes pulled a pocket knife free, opened the blade, and hacked through the seatbelt, whispering to the deputy to take it easy, not to rush. The whole time the guy was reaching from the wreckage with that one free arm, pulling at the mud and gravel, as if determined to claw out from within the car that should have been his coffin. Wes and Dustin caught him by the shoulders and lifted and then, somehow, he was out of the police car and on his back, breathing and alert.

Audrey hung up the phone. "What happened?" she asked Dustin.

"I think he missed the turn or something. All I know is one second I heard the siren and then the next he was in the trees."

Dustin's face looked bloodless, and he was weaving on his feet. She said, "Do you need to sit down?"

"Maybe, yeah." He fell heavily on his ass in the road, pushing thick dark hair back from his forehead, his chest heaving. "I've never seen anything like that."

"Help's coming," she said, patting Dustin's shoulder. "And it looks as if he's okay. I can't believe he's moving. How is he moving?"

There was blood on the deputy's face, coming from his nose and his lips, and a crisscrossing of scratches over his forehead and left cheek, but those were the only evident injuries. He was a young, fit man, lean and long, with sandy hair and blue eyes. Being young and fit didn't allow for escaping an accident like that unscathed, though. He was charmed by unnatural good luck, too, it seemed.

"Lucky," Audrey said softly, thinking that her husband had died out here in a fall. One misplaced step, one slip, one life extinguished. This deputy had driven into the trees at top speed, demolished the car all around him, and survived.

Don't think about it like that, she told herself. *Stop that. Be grateful.*

There was a murmur from the deputy. Audrey looked down again, then saw that his eyes were open and locked on hers.

"You okay?" she said. "You with us? You with us?"

Water dripped out of Wes's short gray beard and off the brim of his baseball cap as he knelt over the wounded man. Beyond, in the preserve, no more than a hundred feet away, the cats had pressed close to the fences, intrigued. One of the lions gave a low roar, and that got the deputy's attention. He swung his head up and around to face the cats, and Audrey winced when he moved his neck, sure that his spine had to be at risk. They'd been telling her to keep him still, that he would need a backboard.

"Please don't move," she said, and then, seeing how intently he was looking at her cats, she added, "They're locked up. They won't hurt you."

She turned to Dustin. "Go try to calm them, please. The last thing we need is the cats going crazy right now."

He went off to try to make peace with animals who were already restless from new surroundings and unnatural activity, and Audrey knelt beside Wes, watching the deputy.

"I hit him," the deputy said.

"What?"

"Tried to miss, but he was right there, and I was going so fast...I tried to miss, I promise you that I did."

"You didn't hit anyone. Everyone is fine."

That seemed distressing to him. He moved his head again, searching the dark woods, and this time his face split into an odd smile, blood on his teeth.

"He made it?"

"You didn't hit anyone," Audrey repeated, feeling ill at ease now. Maybe he hadn't been so unscathed after all. A concussion was likely. Maybe something worse, bleeding on the brain, who knew?

"Light's out," the deputy said, staring over her shoulder. Audrey turned and looked up to the hilltop where the lighthouse stood against the weaving bare branches. It was dark, for the first time all day.

"We've got an ambulance on the way," she said. "Just stay down. Please don't move around. They'll be here soon."

"Where were you headed, bud?" Wes asked. "Is something wrong with the cats? Did you get a call about them?"

Blood was dribbling down the deputy's chin as he shook his head.

"There's a dead man in the lighthouse," he said.

6

TEN MINUTES ON DUTY, running on frayed nerves and no
sleep, and Kimble had a corpse call. He'd poured a cup of
coffee but hadn't taken a sip yet when he heard the news. Gunshot victim, they said.

"Active shooter?" he asked.

Probable suicide, he was told.

"We know the vic's name?"

French, they said. Wyatt French. Maybe he remembered —

"Yes," Kimble said. "I remember Wyatt French."

He felt cold guilt in the pit of his stomach. All those questions,
all that talk about suicide. Why hadn't he sent someone to check?
He'd hoped Wyatt was just drunk, the way he usually was. That
last joke, too, the threat that he might just decide to live forever —
it had suggested that he wasn't in too dismal a state of mind.
Hadn't it?

Kimble swallowed some coffee for warmth, kept his face impas-
sive, and, after a moment's pause, asked that they send Nathan
Shipley. He didn't want to go out there himself, not after the
morning call, and Shipley, though young, was one of Kimble's

favorite deputies, quiet and calm and tough. He'd seen worse than a suicide, and he'd be fine out there in charge of the scene.

They dispatched Shipley, only to come back for Kimble a moment later, just as he'd settled behind his desk.

It seemed Kimble's presence had been requested at the scene. "By Shipley?"

By the victim, he was told. There was a letter on the front door, asking that for purposes of investigation the case be handed to Kevin W. Kimble. Dispatch thought he'd like to know that.

First the predawn call to his private number, now a letter on the door? What did Wyatt French want from Kimble?

He pulled on a baseball cap and went back out into the rain, tired and confused and wondering what else he could have said, should have said.

What he should have done.

Roy stood outside the lighthouse as darkness gathered and the rain pounded down on him and blood dripped off his palm and into the grass. He felt a tingle in his elbow. That wasn't good. He'd probably cut right through the nerves in his hand.

Explaining this to the police was going to be a treat. Tell them that a man was dead and Roy's own blood just happened to be splattered all over the scene? Somehow he had a feeling that wouldn't go over too smoothly.

Where in the hell *were* the cops, though? He'd heard a siren that sounded as if it were just below him, but then it had stopped.

The pain in his hand had ebbed away to a dull ache, but he was continuing to drip blood all over his pants. He considered taking off his shirt and wrapping it around the wound, but then he looked through the open door into Wyatt French's strange living quarters and saw the dishtowels hanging from the stove. It wasn't as if Wyatt would miss them.

He stepped back inside, feeling an uneasy sensation the moment he reentered, knowing damn well now what waited at the top of those steps. His first stop was the sink, where he ran warm water over his hand until the pain ratcheted up a few levels, and then he switched it to cold, hoping to numb things down. The water mixed with the blood and swirled down the sink. He felt lightheaded watching it, so he looked away and took one of the dishtowels from the stove, soaked it in cold water, and then wrapped it tightly around his palm.

The dizziness was still with him. He blinked and took a few deep breaths and stared around. When he'd first entered, his focus had been on finding Wyatt, but now he had a chance to register the room itself. Wyatt had never finished the walls — two-by-fours climbed like latticework, pink insulation showing between them, no drywall pinning them in. His focus, it seemed, had been on speed as he built. He wanted to get to the top and get that light going. The same one he'd asked Roy to keep on before he'd eaten his gun. The same one Roy had promptly shattered.

Like it matters, he told himself. *Like the crazy thing really matters.*

He stepped farther into the room, looking at the maps Wyatt had pinned to the exposed wall studs. There were a lot of them, names written across in red ink. Beside the maps, and all around the room, photographs were held in place with thumbtacks. Ancient pictures, sepia-tinted relics of another time, men with old-fashioned mustaches and women standing beside cars with wide running boards. Roy stepped closer, saw that each photograph was labeled. A few with names, but most — almost all of them, it seemed — with one scrawled word: *NO.*

It was eerie, standing here in the darkened room, a dead man upstairs and all of these faces from times gone by watching him. He shot a glance at the door, wondering again about the police.

One picture caught his eye — more recent, a color shot, and the woman in it was breathtaking. He crossed the room and stared into her crystal eyes and realized he was looking at the booking photograph of Jacqueline Mathis.

What in the hell went on in that man's head? Roy thought. *What was he looking for?*

He wanted to see it all better now, but it was dark inside and the light switch by the door did no good. He thought of the popping sound he'd heard when he broke the bulb, that harsh snap. He'd taken the power out. Question was whether it was a blown fuse or a circuit breaker.

The positive side of Wyatt's sparse home was that it was hard for anything to hide. Roy found the electrical panel easily enough — its metal door stood just over the head of the narrow cot Wyatt had used for a bed, almost as if he'd wanted it as close by as possible while he slept. Roy opened the door and saw that several of the breakers had snapped down. He reset them, and when he tried the light switch at the door again, it worked.

He wandered, studying the old photographs and the maps with the names in red ink, wondering what they meant, wondering what had happened to the police car down below and whether he should head out and take a look, wondering if he'd seriously damaged his hand, wondering why the dead man upstairs had pulled the trigger and why, above all else, he'd had to call Roy before he did it.

To keep the light on. And you broke it. Somewhere, his ghost is shaking his head at you now, Darmus.

His mind was like that, uneasy and adrift, until his eyes focused on a map tacked up just above the small kitchen table.

The year was 1965, and there were two names written in red: Joseph Darmus; Lillian Darmus.

The blood seeping from his palm no longer felt warm as it met the damp towel.

It was then that Roy understood the significance of the names written in red ink.

Red was for the dead.

7

THERE WAS A TOUCH OF ICE in the rain by the time Kimble got to Blade Ridge, just enough to sting even as it soaked him. He was hardly the first responder: there was a volunteer fire unit and an ambulance already there, along with what remained of one of the department's cars. It wasn't much. Kimble, who'd heard the radio traffic as he neared the scene, knew that Shipley had wrecked but was awake and uninjured. He hadn't been expecting so much damage.

He paused at the accident scene, watching as they strapped one of his best deputies into a backboard, then went over and put his hand in Shipley's and squeezed it.

"You all right, brother? You coming back to fight another day with us?"

"Fine," Shipley said. "Just fine." But he was clearly shaken by the wreck, his typically cool blue eyes darting all around, taking in the cats on one side of the road and the lighthouse on the other. Bad wrecks were terrifying things, and one in a place like this? Had to be distressing, to say the least.

44

"Thought there was somebody here," Shipley told him. "Right in the road. He didn't move out of my way, so I swerved."

One of the paramedics caught Kimble's eye with a little hand motion, then shook his head. There'd been no one in the road. Kimble turned his attention back to Shipley, thinking that he didn't like the look of the man's face and eyes now, and when the paramedics told him they had to get on the road, he wasn't disappointed. He wanted Shipley out of here.

"Make sure he gets a full round of concussion tests," Kimble said. "He seems out of it."

"We've got good doctors waiting."

He nodded. "You take care, Nathan," he called as they slid the deputy into the ambulance. "I'll be in touch soon."

Shipley didn't respond before they swung the doors shut.

Kimble paused briefly at the wreck scene, where a tow truck was arriving, but he didn't want to get caught in the mill of taking statements about the accident when his interest was in the lighthouse. Another car was responding to the wreck, and he'd let them deal with it. For now, he needed to focus on Wyatt French.

The entire drive out here the phone conversation had played on repeat in his mind, growing darker and more disturbing with each recalled word. He should have done more than just offer up the suicide toll-free line. If he'd done that much, then he'd clearly heard enough to be concerned, and he shouldn't have settled for so little effort. But there'd been that odd remark about Jacqueline...the knowledge, first of all, that he'd been on his way to see her, and then the warning to be careful with her. After that, he hadn't wanted to call anyone about Wyatt French. Hadn't wanted to *think* about Wyatt French.

How did he know that? he thought as he drove up the steep, slippery drive. *How did an unemployed alcoholic know that I was going to see Jacqueline?*

45

He parked outside the fence, and when he got out of the cruiser he saw Roy Darmus, the newspaper reporter, standing in the yard on the other side of the fence. This was the true first responder, the man who'd found the body.

"Interesting that the gate is locked but you're on the other side, Darmus."

"I climbed over. Be glad I did, and not some kids. He's a mess."

"Yeah?" Kimble studied the padlock, then returned to the cruiser, rooted in the trunk, and came out with a pair of bolt cutters. The gate would need to be opened at some point, and Kimble's back didn't make climbing fences any easy task. He snipped through the chain that held the padlock, then swung open the gate.

Below them, the trees were lit with flashing lights from the accident. Darmus, a guy of middling size with salt-and-pepper hair and perpetually intense eyes, waved a hand in their direction.

"What happened down there? I was going to go check, but they'd told me to stay here until someone showed up. Took a while."

"One of my deputies had a little trouble navigating the road. He's all right. Now what exactly brought you out here, Darmus? And don't tell me you're working on a story. Aren't any stories left."

"There are always stories left. I just don't have a place to tell them at the moment."

"You think that qualifies as an answer?"

"I was closing up shop at the office today when I got a call from him," Darmus said. "From Wyatt French. I'd written about the lighthouse when he first built it. I took it at face value, quoted him accurately, didn't make a joke of it. He said he was building it because the place was dangerous, and I just put that in and let it sit there. I got a lot of eye rolls for that story, but I guess Wyatt appreciated the way I treated it. Him. He started calling me with tips, time to time. Once in a while there was actually some decent information. Most of the time there wasn't. But today...today he was just frightening. Talking in riddles, breathing hard, saying that he was scared of himself, of what he could do. I wasn't sure if he was suicidal or homicidal or just drunk. I drove out to see."

"You wanted to *see* if he was homicidal?"

"I wanted to see if anyone needed to be worried about him. The answer, clearly, is no. Not anymore."

"What time was this?"

"Maybe an hour ago."

So Wyatt had still been alive, and working the phones, long after he'd called Kimble. He'd seen it through almost another day. Hadn't been willing to let the sun go down, though, hadn't seen it through another night.

"He talked about my parents," Darmus said. "I didn't exactly appreciate that. Then I walk in there and I see he's got their names on a map. He's got a lot of names on maps, a lot of old photographs."

Kimble frowned. "Your parents?"

Darmus nodded, and the usually friendly eyes had a hard sheen to them now. "Yes. The old tosspot suggested that they killed themselves out here. Wanted me to know how *brave* they were, making a decision like that and leaving a child behind."

"Out here?"

Darmus waved a hand down at the flashing lights in the trees below them. "Right about where your deputy wrecked, I'd assume. They missed the curve on the county road back in '65, ended up on Blade Ridge, and ended up in the trees. I was fourteen years old."

"I'm sorry."

"It was a long time ago," Darmus said, trying without success to be dismissive. Then he took a deep breath, nodded, and said,

"Thanks, Kimble. I'm not going to let the guy get in my head. He was not a well man. And he's in mighty worse shape now."

Kimble said, "I'll go have myself a look."

"There's blood up there," Darmus said, "and it's mine." He held up his hand, which was wrapped in a towel but still showing blood.

"How'd that happen?"

"Wyatt doesn't look good. Looks pretty ghastly, in fact. When I saw him, it scared me. I fell and put my hand through the bulb."

"The wound serious?"

"Not too bad. But I'm glad that you ended up here, because —"

"Because you broke the law by trespassing and then proceeded to bleed all over the death scene?"

"The door was open."

"And the gate?"

Darmus was silent. Kimble said, "All right, let me go on up and have a look. There's an ambulance on the way. They can look at your hand. If he's as you say, isn't going to be much need to hurry him out of here, is there?"

"No," Darmus said. "There surely isn't. But you didn't let me finish. I called for you because, well...Wyatt French did, too. There's a note on the door."

"So I've been told."

"What do you know about him?"

"Less than you, I expect," Kimble said. "But he sent for you, too. Sent for both of us. And you know what that tells me?"

"What?"

"That even crazy men can read the papers."

Kimble left Darmus standing in the rain and walked to the lighthouse. He stopped at the door and studied the note. A simple, oddly polite request to contact him *for purposes of investigation*. He read it, remembering the hiss of the tires on the pavement and the look of the fog in his headlights as he'd answered Wyatt's questions that morning.

Do you pursue the root causes of a suicide in the same manner that you would a homicide?

Kimble had told him that he pursued the truth. Always.

Now, in the freezing rain outside the dead man's door, Kimble turned back to Darmus.

"I suppose I should wait for someone else now," he said. "I'm probably a suspect, what with my name stamped on the damn door. And he called me this morning, too. Probably said about the same things he did with you. Maybe he called half the town, I don't know. But since my deputy just flipped a cruiser on his way here, and I'm the only officer on scene, I guess I'll count on Wyatt having taken himself out of this life nice and simply and leaving me no trouble. Did he do that much for me?"

"He did it thoroughly," Darmus said. "That much I can assure you."

Kimble went in. The room was small but functional, with unfinished walls and bare-bones furnishings, the look and feel of a hunting cabin except that the walls were lined with maps and old photographs. He gave them a brief glance, then turned to his left and walked up the steps. He didn't cover his mouth or nose, just climbed to the top, high enough to see all that he needed to see. Wyatt's unkempt gray beard was matted with blood, and his eyes — he'd always had good-natured eyes, you could tell even when he was drunk and you were putting him in handcuffs that he wasn't likely to take a poke at you — were locked in a death stare, facing east, away from the fog-shrouded river and toward the high peaks.

"I'm sorry," Kimble told the corpse softly.

Now what if, Wyatt had said, *the suicide victim wasn't entirely willing.*

What had been going on in this man's life? So far as Kimble knew, his life was an empty one. There was never anyone who showed up to post his bond, never anyone who waited for him outside the jail when they kicked him loose on another public intox charge. He'd just been the sort who drifted along alone except for the booze, and you couldn't help but feel sorry for such people, particularly when they weren't hostile and when they didn't stand to do much harm to anyone except themselves.

"Damn it," Kimble said, and then he stepped away and went back down the stairs. He needed to get Darmus out of here, and the coroner on the way. It was time to begin processing the death scene, and he would, as he'd promised Wyatt, pursue the truth.

When he came back downstairs, he found that Darmus had stepped inside.

"Hit the road, Darmus. I'll call you when I need to get an official statement. Go get that hand checked out, okay?"

"You see the other lamps he's got in there?" Darmus said. "Those things pointed in every direction below the main light?"

"I did."

"What in the hell are they?"

"Infrared illuminators. Security camera lights. But I've yet to see the cameras, so why he installed them, I have no damn idea." Kimble looked at the steps and shook his head. "A *lighthouse*. Who builds something like that in the mountains? Though you can see the river from the top."

"Right," Darmus said. "I'm sure it has prevented dozens of shipwrecks down there. Why, I can't recall the last time I had to report on a ship foundering at Blade Ridge. Any chance you can issue a posthumous medal of valor to him?"

The reporter was still plenty angry. His final exchange with Wyatt French had gotten under his skin, and that was understandable. It was a hell of a thing to hear suggested of your own parents.

Kimble moved around the room, looking at the old photographs and maps, but then he heard a scribbling sound behind him and turned to see that Darmus had a reporter's pad out and a pencil in his hand.

"What are you doing? Don't write any of that shit down. This isn't a public scene. And there's not even a newspaper anymore."

"Did you look at these maps?" Darmus said, as if he hadn't spoken. "It's like he was charting accidents, but there's no way there have been this many accidents out here."

"Give me that," Kimble said.

Darmus stopped scribbling and looked up.

"The list," Kimble said. "You can't walk out of here with it. This is an investigation, not a sporting event, Darmus. Give me whatever you've written."

There was something deeply wrong with reporters. A corpse was sitting upstairs, and Darmus had willingly come back inside and was now taking notes?

"Come on," Kimble said, and stretched out his hand. Darmus sighed, tore a handful of pages free, folded them, and passed them over.

"You see whose picture he has on the wall?" he said, tapping on one with his pen. "Maybe there *is* a reason he called both of us. My parents, and her."

Her. Kimble followed the tip of Darmus's pen and saw that it was pointing at a color photograph of Jacqueline Mathis. Her name was written beneath it.

For a moment Kimble just stared, but he saw Darmus watching him and was unsettled by it, felt as if he were suddenly exposed. "What did I just tell you? I've got a death scene to deal with. Get out of here."

"Wyatt told me about you making those visits up to see her," Darmus said.

"Why in the hell were you talking about that?" Kimble snapped.

51

"I don't even know. He just told me that you went to see her every month. I was having trouble following the—"

"Well, it's none of anybody's damned business. I tell you, there's some good things about that paper being shut down, too. Tough that you lost your job, but you know what? There are some things people do in private that should *stay* private. Now listen to what I told you and get the hell out of here."

Darmus looked at him curiously, then nodded and turned and walked out into the dark and the blowing rain. Kimble watched until the car's taillights had vanished down the hill, wishing he'd been alone up here, wishing he'd been the first to find the body. He looked down at the folded pages in his hand, torn from the reporter's notebook, and unfolded them.

Blank. Every one.

"Son of a bitch, Darmus," he said.

Good trick. A lot better than whatever Wyatt was playing on Kimble from beyond the grave.

He looked up again, at the maps and the photographs. All those old pictures, looking as if they'd been copied out of history books, and then Jacqueline, staring at him with those endless blue eyes.

Why did Wyatt have her picture up?

Kimble reached up, pulled the thumbtacks from the wood, removed Jacqueline's picture, and put it in his pocket with the blank pages from Darmus.

8

IT TOOK A FEW HOURS for the medical folks to finish their work in the lighthouse. Kimble stood around in the rain and waited for them, spoke to the deputy coroner, and then watched as they finally removed the body, which wasn't an easy or pleasant task, coming down those steep, narrow stairs.

Kimble had another deputy on scene now, Diane Mooney, and he discharged her, said he was shutting it down for the day. It wasn't a bad move; every element pointed to a straightforward suicide.

Except for those maps. And that phone call. *What if the victim wasn't entirely willing...*

As he'd waited for the coroner's people to do their work, Kimble had perused the maps, reading the names. When he saw Joseph and Lillian Darmus, he felt a pang over the way he'd snapped at the old reporter for mentioning Jacqueline. It had surprised him, that was all. And he'd lashed out because... because it was his own damned business. Personal, private.

After Diane Mooney left, Kimble stepped back inside the lighthouse, armed with a Maglite now, and went to the electrical panel. He didn't want to leave the busted light with live current going to it. Last thing he needed was a fire. He snapped the main breaker off, plunging the room into darkness.

He turned his flashlight on, checking for last precautions before locking this place up, and around him the old pictures picked up the glow, dozens of dead eyes watching him. He paced with the flashlight held at shoulder level, taking them all in. With only a few exceptions, they were turn-of-the-century photographs. A few, such as Jacqueline's, had names, but most were tagged simply with the word *NO*. What did that mean?

Kimble slipped on a pair of plastic gloves, then moved around the room, carefully removing every photograph and every map.

It was a suicide, nothing else to it. No call for investigation. Still…

If there are two things I'd hope you might continue to grant me in the future, it is your time and respect.

"Why did you do it, Wyatt?" Kimble whispered. "And what is all *this* shit about?"

There was no suicide note, no explanation or farewell. Beyond the maps and photographs, there was nothing except a handwritten sheet of paper taped to the electrical panel above Wyatt's bunk. Behind that panel existed everything that the man seemed to care about — the circuits that controlled his lights, the power that fed them — and Kimble leaned over the bed to read it more carefully. Lyrics to some poem or song titled "Lantern."

It's a hungry world out there
Even the wind will take a bite
I can feel the world circling
Sniffing round me in the night
And the lost sheep grow teeth
Forsake the lambs and lie with the lions

The story of the song, which seemed to be a defiance of human darkness, of an evil world, and the significance it might have had to Wyatt French, became vividly clear by the end:

So if you got a light, hold it high for me
I need it bad tonight, hold it high for me
'Cause I'm face-to-face, hold it high for me
In that lonesome place, hold it high for me
With all the hurt that I've done, hold it high for me
That can't be undone, hold it high for me
Light and guide me through, hold it high for me
And I'll do the same for you, hold it high for me

I'll hold it high for you, 'cause I know you've got
I'll hold it high for you, your own valley to walk
I'll hold it high for you, though it's dark as death . . .

Kimble stopped reading, saddened, and turned away. Wyatt had certainly held a light high, but for what? Kimble thought of him living up here in total isolation, listening to the wind work over the ridge and watching from behind the glass as his lighthouse illuminated the night woods. What had it meant to him? These words, that light? He felt the weight of sorrow on him as he always did soon enough with suicides, a hard tug of personal connection that he'd never dare put into words. *I want out, too.* A person was more than twice as likely to kill himself as to be killed by another, and yet people feared murderers far more than what lurked within themselves.

"Poor bastard," Kimble said, and then he turned away. As some odd temple of loneliness the lighthouse made sense to Kimble, almost perfect sense — *You're right, Wyatt, it's too dark too often here* — but the maps seemed to suggest something more than that.

55

He had been a lonely man, certainly, but there was more than loneliness here, and perhaps Kimble should be grateful that he'd not harmed anyone else. Another year or two of living in this place and brooding over whatever the hell he brooded over and he might have picked up the same gun and ventured out. It happened sometimes. Chief Deputy Kevin Kimble had been around long enough to know that terrible things happened sometimes, strange things, things that you couldn't even say out loud . . .

With every passing minute the place felt smaller and colder, and Kimble found himself thinking of the infrared illuminators, that ring of lights below the main bulb. What in the hell was he using those for? He moved away, leaving Wyatt's treasured song lyrics where they belonged, on the front of the electrical panel, and returned to the stack of photographs and maps he'd placed on the desk. After a moment's pause, he reached into his pocket, withdrew the photograph of Jacqueline Mathis, unfolded it, and added it to the collection. For a long time he stood above the desk, staring down at her face.

One in the hole, he found himself thinking numbly. *Rookie fucking mistake. Inexcusable error. It was your own fault.*

He'd taken the gun from her without incident. Ejected the magazine, slipped it into his pocket, and then, as her husband wheezed on the floor, he'd set the gun on the coffee table and turned to the dying man. Never pulled the slide, never checked the chamber. It was his own fault.

She crossed the room for it, Kimble. That wasn't your fault. She moved like a shadow, moved fast and silent, and she came ten feet across that room to grab the weapon and then she pointed at you and fired. That was your fault?

She'd been scared. She'd been terrified, and he had to remember that.

No. She was *terrifying. There's a difference.*

He could still remember the way she'd moved, remembered it

so damn vividly that it made his whole body tense. It had been a feeling more than anything else, an instinct — he didn't remember hearing her or seeing her. There'd just been some flutter of recognition in his brain, some primal warning, and then he'd glanced back and seen her in the darkness with the gun in her hand and a smile on her face.

Well, no, she wasn't smiling. That was just how he —

Yes she was! Yes she was, don't lie to yourself, she was smiling.

Kimble remembered it, caught in his own trauma. Surely she hadn't been smiling. She'd been frightened. Thought she was shooting at her husband again, thought she was protecting Kimble.

Yes, that was it. She'd wanted to help him. Not kill him.

He took the gun from her without incident initially. She didn't fight, didn't say a word, appeared to be in shock. They knew each other by then; he was surprised by her silence, but his oath to protect and serve covered the son of a bitch on the floor, too, and he had to attend to him. The house was in total darkness except for a patch of living-room floor illuminated by the flashing lights of Kimble's cruiser. It had stopped raining, but there was still thunder on the other side of the mountains. She handed the gun, a Glock, over to Kimble calmly. Her eyes weren't even on him, but rather on her husband, who lay on the floor in his own blood. He was still breathing, but there was an awful lot of blood. Later Kimble would find himself wishing that the man hadn't been breathing. It was the breathing that rushed things along, the breathing that forced Kimble to handle the situation the way he did. The man was dying, and Kimble had to try to do something about that.

It was just him, though, no backup yet, no ambulance. Everyone was en route, but en route was awfully damn different from being there, and it was just him and the dark house and the silent woman with the gun. He took the Glock and asked her what had happened and she did not answer, but she did not need to; he could see the bruises even in the shadows. He'd been in this house before. He knew what happened here.

She was trembling, and she was glassy-eyed, and she was silent and passive, so passive. Even with the gun in her hand she hadn't appeared threatening, and once it was out of her hand, what was there to fear? She'd called Kimble for help. The man on the floor was breathing, too, he was breathing and needed attention and Kimble had to move fast.

So he didn't cuff her. He told her to sit and stay, as if she were a dog, and she had lowered herself onto the floor with her back against the wall. Kimble was standing there with two guns in his hands—her Glock and his own, which he'd drawn upon entering the home—and the man on the floor was bleeding and breathing and Kimble had to move fast. He'd holstered his own weapon and put hers down on the coffee table. Before he did it, though, he released the magazine and put that in his pocket. He was not wearing gloves and he was tainting all of the evidence, but such concerns did not seem important right then, alone in the dark house with the bleeding and breathing man on the floor.

He'd had just enough time to turn his head before she fired. Turned and saw her...

...*smiling! Absolutely delighted, she was so happy to shoot you, she was so happy...*

...with the gun and couldn't even lift his own. The bullet caught him low in the back and drove him down into her husband's blood. Jacqueline Mathis laid her Glock down, calmly, and walked toward him, knelt, and pulled his gun out of its holster. Then, while he tried to get his mouth to work, tried to tell her not to do it, she'd leveled the muzzle at his forehead.

He remembered wishing she'd just squeeze the trigger. Just finish it, not draw it out in such a way. But the smile turned to a frown and then she'd leaned toward him. Leaned toward him

58

and down, her hair swinging from her face and close to his own, and it had been almost as if she were going to kiss him. The motion that gentle, that intimate.

Until the muzzle touched his skin.

She'd pressed the gun directly to his forehead, and her finger was tight on the trigger, and out in the driveway the lights on his cruiser flashed on the two of them there on the floor and in the blood, and she kept blinking against the glare. When the red caught her face the blink turned to a wince, and she took a sharp, harsh inhalation, as if struck by a sudden pain. Looked back at him, and the lights flashed again, and again, and she suddenly removed the gun and crawled backward, into the darkness. Then there was another car in the driveway and Kimble got the words out.

"Put it down."

So she did. She laid his weapon on the floor and said, in a confused voice, as if she had just stepped into the room and interrupted his attempt at a quiet death, "I'm sorry. I just don't know —" and right then the backup deputy turned the cruiser's spotlight on, piercing the front window with an explosion of light. Jacqueline Mathis lifted her hands and covered her face, and Kimble realized he might live, and then he fainted.

Now he looked at her photograph and felt lightheaded again.

"What were you doing up here, Wyatt?" Kimble muttered, and around him the lighthouse creaked against the force of a strengthening winter wind.

9

THE CATS ALERTED WESLEY to the blue light that was not a light at all.

When they turned out in unified fury on the night after Wyatt French died at the top of his lighthouse, it was the first time Wesley had seen anything of the kind. And Wesley Harrington had spent forty-five of his fifty-seven years around cats. He'd been born in Wyoming in a place so far out in the mountains that there would be weeks at a time when he was unable to make it to school because the roads were impassable due to snow. His father had a sixth-grade education with books and a doctorate as a woodsman. He hunted, fished, and trapped, all for two things: food and money. There was only one exception to that approach: mountain lions.

Wesley went along on his first lion hunt when he was twelve. Some folks called them cougars, some mountain lions, others pumas, but in the Wyoming mountains there were just "lions." There was, as Wesley's father regularly explained to him by the fire that provided the sole heat source in their cabin, nothing finer than hunting lions. They were the only animal in America that could truly outthink a man. Oh, bears and deer and wolves had their instincts, but lions were *crafty*.

They were also, he often said, the only American animal that would stalk a man. He'd heard that polar bears would do such a thing, but there were no polar bears in the lower forty-eight. Lions would stalk, though. He'd seen it done, and heard tell of many other occasions. They were faster, more agile, more deadly, and far smarter than any other creature, and for those reasons a lion hunt had nothing to do with food or money and everything to do with the thrill of battle.

Those hunts outlasted almost all of Wesley's childhood memories. The frigid air, the deep snow, the howling sounds the wind made as it worked through the mountains. An expanse of wilderness completely empty except for Wesley and his dad and the three Plott hounds. They'd find a track, measure it, estimate the size of the cat, and then they'd be off, off through some of the most unforgiving terrain in the area, because the cat's first instinct when dogs were at its heels was not, contrary to popular belief, to tree. Cats were too smart for that. So first they'd run, and they would run toward territory that favored them. A mountain lion could cover twenty miles or more in a day.

Some of the locals had calling stands, and they'd sit up in the trees and call for the big cats, and sometimes it worked. Bill Harrington had no patience for such approaches. Lion hunts were supposed to be *chases*.

When Wesley was fifteen, he and his father had the greatest hunt of both their lives, scrambling through crusted snow and treacherous canyons, the hounds hoarse-voiced and with torn, bloody pads on their feet. They watched the lion — a massive cat, a true trophy — swim a frigid river to escape them and then, just as twilight was settling, they treed it on a rocky ledge. Bill Harrington gave his son a chance.

That was the first and last cat Wesley ever shot.

It was while they were preparing the body for transport back home that they found the cubs. The lion had led them on a merry chase away from the den at first—a wise instinct, carrying the threat away from those she loved—but in the end she'd decided to go back, maybe hoping to take refuge, maybe thinking she needed to stand and fight, but more likely confident that she'd lost the dogs in the river.

She hadn't.

There were two cubs in the den, and Bill Harrington told Wesley that they would not survive on their own and should be put down fast and painlessly. Wesley, feeling tremendous shame, had refused, and Bill had relented. They took the cubs back down and called the state to come get them. That same night a screaming blizzard blew in, and it was four days before someone with the state arrived to inspect the cubs. By then one had died in Wesley's arms; the other was alive. He'd bottle-fed it, slept with it, never left it. Those four days shaped a life.

He never hunted cats again. He tracked them, but with only a camera in his hands. After high school he worked with a group in California that studied the cougar populations. From that he met a woman who was headed to Africa to work with lions. He spent two years there. Then it was South America for jaguars, then back to the States to work for the USDA as an investigator on cases where tigers were being raised and slaughtered for their pelts, then on to one private preserve, then to another and another.

He'd spent far more time around cougars, lions, tigers, cheetahs, and ocelots than he had around people. The only people he knew well, in fact, were cat people. Big cats were his world, his life. He knew them well.

And he knew this: the cats at Audrey Clark's rescue preserve did not like their new grounds.

Wesley lived at the preserve. He'd joined them years earlier, when David was getting it started, and he'd expected it would be a temporary gig. But they were wonderful people, the Clarks, and their mission — providing rescue, then homes and safety and pleasure, for abused exotic cats — was one he believed in deeply. So Wes had stayed, living on the grounds in a well-equipped trailer and surrounded by cats that he loved as family, happy both because he knew he was needed and because he liked the idea of the planned expansion at Blade Ridge.

Liked it until tonight, at least, when a cacophony of roars, hisses, and screams broke out just as he was about to get some sleep.

He'd never heard them all join in like this. Sometimes the tigers would excite the lions and most of those groups would get to roaring — a sound that seemed to make the very earth upon which you stood tremble — but as Wesley grabbed a flashlight and stepped out of the trailer, they were *all* going. He could even hear the low hisses from Tina, a serval, the smallest of African cats, whose cage was very close to the trailer door. He shone his light down at her and saw that she was standing with her back arched and tail stiff, staring away from him, out toward the road. Out toward the lighthouse. But it was dark and nobody had come down the road, so what in the hell . . .

He saw it then. A strange blue light was working its way around the face of the lighthouse. Every cat in the preserve was staring it down, and they usually didn't give a damn about light.

"Hello?" Wesley shouted. He wasn't a large man, but working with cats for years had taught him how to use a mighty large voice when he needed it. "Who's there?"

No response came, and the light didn't stop moving. It just bobbed around the outside of the lighthouse, and Wesley stared at it in fascination. The thing was no ordinary light, and that went beyond the blue color. It had the flickering, undulating motion of a flame. Yes, that's exactly what it looked like — a blue torch.

It drifted around the hilltop and disappeared and for a moment Wes relaxed. Then he noticed that the cats had not.

Every single animal was upright and pressed to the fence, watching and snarling. Wes stared at them, truly at a loss, and then looked back just in time to see the blue light reappear at the top of the lighthouse.

"Son of a bitch," he whispered. Whoever was out there had gotten inside. But Wyatt French was dead, the police had told him that, and he knew for a fact that the last officer on the scene had left hours before.

The torch reflected off the glass and filled the lighthouse with an ethereal blue glow. Wesley suddenly felt both exposed and frightened, and he clicked his own flashlight off and stepped back into the shadows, close to Tina's cage, the serval still making those low, warning hisses.

After a time the blue light vanished again, then appeared outside the lighthouse, and the cats went wild. The roar of a tiger could always make a newcomer tremble, but Wesley couldn't remember the last time the sounds had made *him* uneasy. The cats were enraged, and it was at this blue light.

Do something, he told himself.

But what? Chase down the source? That didn't seem like such a good idea. Because that light...there was something strange about it.

He was still standing there debating when the light vanished over the crest of the ridge, and the cats began to fall silent and settle back down. Some — Kino in particular — continued to pace and voice displeasure, but the unified response was done.

"What was that, Kino?" Wesley said, walking out into the preserve, where his favorite tiger was placed in a central location. "What was that, buddy?"

The tiger continued his restless patrolling. Wesley watched him, then looked back at Tina, the always-docile serval, who'd risen in such aggressiveness, and found himself recalling all of the legends that said cats could sense spirits.

And a man just died up there, he thought. *The lighthouse keeper himself. Maybe he intends to remain on duty after all.*

"Stop it," he said, and while he directed the harsh command at Kino, it was intended for himself. He didn't need to indulge such foolish thoughts. The cats, who had never united in aggression like this before, were simply responding to the new grounds, to unhappiness with the change, to . . .

"To that light," he whispered.

And whoever carried it.

10

IT APPEARED THAT WYATT FRENCH had died intestate, no family or guardian in line to step up and handle the proceedings. That made it the county's problem. If no will or heir was found, the dead man's property would go up for auction. That one, Kimble wanted to see. Who in the hell would bid on a lighthouse in the woods?

In the course of working the phones that morning, he was beginning to develop a picture of Wyatt French. French had been an extraordinarily gifted carpenter, one of the finest in the area, and in his youth seemed destined for good things. When a big parcel of land at Blade Ridge—holdings of the Whitman Company for generations, back to the mining days—was released for sale, Wyatt mortgaged himself up to the ears to acquire it, intending, apparently, to develop it into a neighborhood of log homes that would embrace the region's beauty.

Not a single log had ever been laid.

Times got tougher, Wyatt's drinking habit worsened, and the grand plan faded from his conversation. Eventually he put a trailer on the choicest grounds of his property, telling friends—

66

or, by that point, bartenders — that he'd soon replace it with the first of his custom log homes.

Instead he'd replaced it with a lighthouse.

By then his alcoholism was a crippling thing, and no contractor in the area would hire him, no matter his skills. Too much risk. He made a living through odd jobs and people with great patience — if you could wait for him long enough, he did fine work — and lived a solitary, bourbon-soaked existence out in his lighthouse. When the bank finally went after him, he'd lost the rest of his land and declared bankruptcy. All they let him keep was the ground on which he'd built his bizarre home. The rest sat untouched for a few years — it was so far from everything that no developer was interested — and then David and Audrey Clark came along and purchased it from the bank that had held it for so long.

Now they were moving in, and Wyatt was dead by his own hand.

Kimble had been working the phones for a full hour, trying to track down next of kin, when three plastic bags were delivered to him: the items that had been removed from Wyatt French's pockets by the medical examiner.

There was a wallet, a cell phone, and a pocket knife. Kimble set the knife aside and started with the wallet. There wasn't much to study: eleven dollars in cash, an ancient set of business cards that identified Wyatt as a "skilled tradesman," and a driver's license that had been revoked years earlier. When Wyatt came to town, he walked or hitchhiked. He did not come to town often.

Kimble put the wallet back in the plastic evidence bag, then turned his attention to the cell phone. It would be the only phone — no landline had ever been extended to Blade Ridge. Wyatt could have requested one when he moved out there, though it probably would have required a substantial payment, but he never did. The cell was a cheap thing, the sort you could pick up at a gas station or drugstore with cash and no contract. It held a log of calls, though. Kimble scrolled through, wincing a bit as he saw his own number, and then put the others into a computer search, looking for matches.

The most recent call was, of course, the last — the *Sawyer County Sentinel,* where he'd reached Roy Darmus. Before that, Wyatt had called Kimble. The previous eight calls had all gone to the same number, and when Kimble ran the reverse search, it returned to the office of a Dr. Kaleb Mitchell in Whitman.

Kimble frowned. That was a lot of calls. He picked up his own phone, dialed, and got the receptionist. After he identified himself and said that he was investigating a death, he had Dr. Mitchell on the line pretty quickly.

"Of course you'll need a subpoena for medical records," the doctor said before Kimble could even get warmed up.

"I'm well aware of that. But before you get too worried about protecting your patient's rights, understand that your patient is dead. He committed suicide yesterday, Dr. Mitchell."

"Oh, my."

"Yes. I'm not interested in his medical records, I'm trying to investigate the circumstances of his death. There are some questions around it, and I'd appreciate your help."

"Within proper limits, of course."

"Do you know if there's anyone I should contact on this matter? It doesn't appear that he has any family. Are you aware of any?"

"There is no one," Dr. Mitchell said with quick confidence. "I just had that discussion with him. He told me he was very much on his own."

"You just had this discussion."

"That's right. You want to know if there was a medical reason that might have motivated him, don't you?"

"I'm curious, yes."

"Absolutely. In fact, I'm sorry to say that I'm not surprised to hear this news. Mr. French was dying, deputy. He had liver cancer."

Kimble felt an odd sense of relief. It was a sad situation, certainly, but this brought a clarity that had not been there before.

"I see," he said. "That's very helpful. You'd informed him of this recently?"

"Last week. The prognosis was not good. Very grim. He did not seek regular medical treatment, and I believe he lived in a fashion that was quite abusive to the liver. Quite abusive."

"You're correct."

"I was worried about him, frankly. Beyond the illness, I mean. I don't mind telling you that I'm a little relieved to hear that the situation is what it is. I know that sounds terrible, but—"

"You were afraid he might be a threat to someone besides himself?"

The doctor hesitated. "Yes, that's exactly it."

"Why?"

"I've given a number of terminal diagnoses over the years, deputy. It's always sad, and the reactions are always varied. Mr. French's stands out, though. He asked the standard question— how much time. I told him specialists would be more certain, but it was likely that he was down to six months to a year. He responded by telling me that if he had only six months, then that meant someone else had less time. His words, I believe, were, 'If my clock's winding down, then somebody else's is spinning faster. I can't leave this world without settling that.' I asked him what he meant by that, and he declined to elaborate. I don't mind telling you that it was...somewhat chilling. I had the distinct impression that he meant it as a threat. Not to me. But to someone."

The sense of understanding and relief that Kimble had just felt was fading. He said, "I appreciate your telling me that. It could be quite important, doctor. It could be more important than you know."

The doctor's voice changed, a note of alarm in it now. "I thought you said it was a suicide, and that was all."

"I know it was a suicide," Kimble said. "And I hope that was all."

11

THE DOCTOR HAD PUT FIVE STITCHES in one incision on Roy's palm and six in the other, given him some pain pills, and sent him on his way. When he woke the next morning his hand throbbed dully, and he washed another round of pain pills down with coffee and then stared out at the street, looking at his neighbors' front porches and thinking that it was the first time in more than a century that they'd awakened on any day but Christmas and found no newspaper to greet them.

He did not know what he should be doing with his day. Everyone else at the paper had completed résumé and cover-letter tasks months ago, and most of them had jobs. That wasn't an option for Roy. At sixty, he was hardly the commodity a newspaper wanted to add to the staff, but he didn't want to leave his home anyhow. The newspaper buyout had been larger than most, though it was hardly something to shout about from the rooftops. If he lived with a miser's eye, he'd be fine. But finances weren't his concern. Identity was. For almost forty years he'd been Sawyer County's storyteller. It was a role he cherished, and now it was gone. His own name felt hollow to him if not part of a byline.

He had one story left, though, one final assignment issued. Wyatt French had asked him to tell it, but Roy's interest was not in Wyatt French. It was in his parents and all those names that had joined theirs on the maps in the lighthouse.

One more day at the paper. One more story to work on. He didn't mind the sound of that at all. He drove to the office as he always had, cutting through the Whitman College campus, beautiful brick and limestone buildings that stretched out where once the mining company houses had been. Mines had built the town, back in the late 1800s. First it had been coal, and then timber, and then there wasn't anything left to take and the town went back to sleep for a time. Roger Whitman, son of one of the early coal and timber barons, went the Carnegie route in his later years, dispensing his fortune to various philanthropic causes, and one of them—the college—had inadvertently saved the town. Whitman College had grown into a prestigious school, known for liberal arts and environmental sciences, for high academic standards and higher tuition rates. The environmental sciences bit was ironic to anyone who knew the local history. Nobody had pillaged the land with greater ferocity than the Whitman family.

Roy's great-grandfather had worked for the timber companies, his grandfather had risen to a position as vice president of one of the town's only banks, his father had gone to law school at Vanderbilt and spurned top-dollar offers to practice family law in his hometown. At fourteen, Roy had been certain he would be the first Darmus to leave the hills.

It was easy to be certain of things at fourteen.

His own house was two blocks past the courthouse and one block from the sheriff's department, prime location for a reporter. Originally the newspaper offices had been downtown, too, but they'd moved in the 1970s for more space, a larger press, and more loading docks, unaware of the digital death headed their way.

His keycard was still active, and he went through the employee door and headed for the morgue with his list of names and dates from Wyatt French's lighthouse. Most of the names went beyond the computer days and would require poring over the dusty bound volumes down in the newspaper's morgue.

He wanted caffeine but the coffeepot upstairs was gone for good, so he walked through the pressroom, with its smells of metal and oil and newsprint, and to the break room, where for decades the pressmen had gathered in the wee hours of the morning. He fed a dollar into the vending machine and came away with a Diet Coke, then turned around and ran smack into Rex Schaub, the building's maintenance supervisor. Rex gave him a cockeyed smile.

"What are you doing here?" His eyes dropped to Roy's bandaged hand and he added, "And what the hell happened?"

"Cut myself on a lightbulb."

"Damn. Hey, you know the difference between a lightbulb and a pregnant girlfriend?"

"What?"

"You *can* unscrew the lightbulb."

Roy stared at him.

"Get it?" Rex said. "If you knock your girlfriend up, you can't—"

"Brilliant," Roy said. "Who said that, Ben Franklin? Or is that Twain?"

Rex grinned. "Look, what are you doing here? Building is closed."

"Need to do a few archive searches."

Rex's smile was slipping away. "Roy...the building is closed. I'm not trying to be a dick about it, but nobody is supposed to be in here except the clean-out crew. I should have deactivated all the keycards by now, but I haven't gotten around to it. The owners gave me real clear instructions, though, that nobody —"

"The owners can kiss my ass," Roy snapped. "I've spent more than forty years in this building, making money for them. If I want another day in this place, I'm going to take it."

Rex, who'd had a gig as a maintenance supervisor for an apartment complex in place within a week of the *Sentinel*'s closing announcement, dropped his gaze to the reel of cable in his hands.

"Okay, Roy," he said. "I get you. Do what you need to do."

"Thanks," Roy said, and walked past him, bristling with anger that had less to do with Rex and more to do with the way they were dismantling the office. He'd known it was going to happen, of course, but seeing it, watching all the artifacts of the newspaper that had been his life scooped up and put into boxes, hit him harder than he'd imagined it would.

The owners said, the owners said... The owners could go straight to hell. It was more his paper than theirs. He'd spent more waking hours in this building than any other place on earth. Hell, maybe more hours period. He worked long and late and never minded because he loved telling the stories. And those stories, the ones that were developing across Sawyer County at this very moment? What would become of them? Why didn't anyone think that loss mattered?

He opened the door to the morgue and slipped inside, back into that narrow room that smelled of dust and old paper. A hundred and twenty-four years of stories.

He was pretty sure some of them had mattered.

The morgue was where he'd gotten his professional start — an irony never lost on him — putting together that local-lore column. He'd kept it going over the years, which drove the editors nuts, because it seemed he always vanished into the archives at the exact moment they came looking for him with a shitty assignment. It got to the point where "If you're looking for Darmus, he's in the morgue" was a running joke.

There were microfilm readers, but Roy hated using those. You lost the tactile sense of history that the bound volumes exuded, wide, massive books that had to weigh fifteen or twenty pounds. You could stand in the middle of the morgue and see the ebb and flow of the industry — the date ranges getting progressively smaller as the newspaper economy boomed and the *Sentinel* added pages and ad circulars, delivering a doorstopper each morning and double that on Sunday. Then the date ranges widened and the papers shrank in more recent years, as declining revenue triggered page cuts.

He had every name in red ink from Wyatt's maps. The photographs he hadn't managed to study before Kimble shut him down. Most of them hadn't borne names, anyhow. He'd recognized one face — Jacqueline Mathis — and remembered another from her name — Becky Stapp — but it seemed as if ninety percent were anonymous faces from the past. That left him with the red-ink names, and after finding his parents among them, he was awfully curious about the others.

While his initial plan had been to work forward from the oldest date to the newest, he found himself going directly to the January–March 1965 volume. He'd seen the January 9, 1965, paper a thousand times, had stared at it for countless hours, but it had been several years since his last look. Too many years? You didn't want to drown in grief, but you needed to remember the dead, too.

He dropped the bound volume onto the old, scarred desk — it had been the editor's desk during World War II — opened it, and flipped through the pages until a familiar headline and photograph caught his eye. A single car smashed into the trees amidst a fine dusting of snow. They'd been predicting a big one, but it had never hit. Just a little freezing rain, an inch of powder, and two dead in a one-car accident. Minor storm. Minor.

75

Roy ran the back of his hand over his mouth, adjusted the light over the desk, and began to read.

Two people were killed Saturday night in a single-vehicle crash on Blade Ridge Road in the southwestern reaches of Sawyer County.

Joseph Darmus, 41, and his wife Lillian Darmus, 40, of Whitman, were killed when their 1957 Chevrolet sedan apparently skidded on black ice west of the junction of County Road 200 and Blade Ridge Road, sending the vehicle into a stand of walnut trees. The accident occurred at approximately 8:45 P.M. There were no witnesses. Joseph Darmus was killed on impact, according to police, while Lillian was transported to Sawyer County Hospital and died of massive head trauma a short time later. The couple was driving home from a Whitman Junior High School basketball game in Chambers. Their son, 14-year-old Roy Darmus, was on the bus with his teammates when the accident occurred.

That was the end of the first article. Simple, straightforward reporting, written late in the night, pushing deadline. Roy flipped to the next day's edition to read the follow-up piece, which had altered his life when it appeared, guiding him into this very building.

It led with a quote from Roy about his father: *"He was a real good driver. He always said he was going to be the one to teach me how to drive in the snow, because it was dangerous and he didn't want anything bad to happen to me."*

Even now, decades removed, Roy felt something thicken in his throat. He looked away from the article. He didn't need to read it again. He could recite it if he wished.

Time to get back to the task, back to the story. He knew his parents had died on Blade Ridge Road, but what had sparked Wyatt's interest in the others?

He returned to the morgue shelves to find out, began hauling down bound volume after bound volume, and after hours at it he had no more sense of the truth than when he'd begun.

There were connections between the names on Wyatt French's maps—some of them, at least—but the parts simply did not fit together to make a whole. Roy had expected something more coherent, even from a mind as admittedly disconnected as Wyatt's. All the time the old man had spent laboring over the odd list suggested at a linkage that did not appear—at least to Roy's eyes—to exist.

At first he thought it was simple: they were victims of car accidents at Blade Ridge. Several others besides his parents qualified for that category.

That idea, though, vanished as soon as he tracked down one of the names, Sam Fielding, and discovered that he'd been a high-voltage repairman, electrocuted while attempting to repair downed lines in a summer storm.

That fatality had occurred near Blade Ridge, in the woods west of County Road 200, which was close enough to count, but the nature of the death blew the car-wreck theory out of the water.

So then Roy shifted, thinking that the man had been looking for any deaths, *period,* in his strange little pocket of the mountains. Fielding's case wasn't unique. In several circumstances, Wyatt had noted deaths that had occurred near Blade Ridge Road. Emphasis on *near.* Because, as Roy discovered as he went deeper into the county's history, pulling down volumes that billowed out dust when opened, the pages so stiff and yellowed that you had to turn them with infinite care or the paper would flake into pieces, the accidental deaths were certainly not limited to the road. In 1978, two boys died when they fell from the railroad trestle. In 1975, one woman drowned in a canoeing trip on the Marshall River with a friend. In 1958, a Marine who'd seen tours in Korea and the South Pacific shot himself in the head while deer hunting. That one could have been suicide — newspapers always had masked such stories in ambiguity — but Roy doubted it. In 1922, two men and a woman were trampled to death when a strange and violent panic took hold of their horses.

All of those names — they were the red-ink names — could be linked by two factors: death and proximity to Blade Ridge. The manner of death, though, those tales of trestle falls and stampeding horses and electrocutions, turned any legitimate concern about the road's safety into a bizarre raving about… what? Some sort of cursed ground? A karmic disaster zone?

"What did they mean to you, Wyatt?" he mumbled, staring at the two lists, deciding that he'd wasted enough time on this endeavor. "Why did they matter?"

It would be impossible to say. And, Roy reminded himself, the old man had been losing his mind there toward the end. Yesterday's ravings were a clear indication of that.

I'm getting scared of the dark. I'm getting scared of what I could do in the dark.

Roy was halfway to the morgue door when that thought slipped into his mind, and when it did, he stopped walking and turned to look at the rows of old newspaper volumes as if they'd just told him something.

Hell, maybe they had.

He'd been looking for parallels, the same as Wyatt ostensibly had. For connective tissue between the names, and coming up empty.

Except for one thing. They'd all taken place at night. Without exception. Every fatality Wyatt had recorded from Blade Ridge's lengthy history had occurred when it was…

"Dark," Roy said aloud.

12

KIMBLE WANTED TO FOCUS ON Wyatt French, but the sheriff interrupted him in midmorning by entering with Nathan Shipley and saying they needed to have a talk about the accident.

Shipley's cruiser was beyond any hope, so far gone that they just had it towed directly to the salvage yard where the sensitive equipment could be removed, not even bothering with a body shop. Shipley himself, however, had emerged from the terrible wreck with a few minor abrasions and bruises.

"Sore," he told Kimble and the sheriff when he sat down. "I'm sore as hell, but considering . . . well, it really could have been bad."

"I saw the car, son," Sheriff Troy Black said. "*Bad* isn't the word. Damn good thing I always see that this department has quality insurance."

The implication being that they might operate without insurance if not for his savvy management. Kimble rolled his eyes, and Shipley saw it and cracked a small smile. The department was of a unanimous opinion on "Sheriff Troy," as he insisted on being called. He excelled at politicking, handled the department's public face well enough, but when it came to actual casework he'd gone past the point of being a broad-assed desk jockey and become an almost laughable figurehead. He insisted on wearing custom-made, chocolate-brown cowboy hats with his badge affixed to the crown, he was a partner in a horse farm that had yet to produce anything better than a dead-last finisher in a small-time race, he talked like he'd just fallen off a hay wagon, and everyone in the department knew damn well that when it came to investigative work, Kimble ran the show. That was fine by Kimble — he had autonomy within the department, and he also had Troy out there doing all the work that Kimble would never have been any good at. Kimble didn't have to deal with the mayor's office or the county council or campaigns or oversee the jail. The system in place in Sawyer County worked well; Troy glad-handed his way around town, keeping the public satisfied, and Kimble and his team got the policing done.

"Yes, son, it was a mighty bad wreck," Troy continued. "That cruiser is totaled, you know. Less than a year old."

"Like you said, it's a good thing we have quality insurance," Nathan agreed, and now it was Kimble's turn to hide a grin.

"It surely is. My understanding is that you were well aware that the ten-zero was a probable suicide, that there was no shootin' or stabbin' in progress. My understanding is also that you were driving like Barney Oldfield when you flipped that car."

Kimble had not the faintest idea who Barney Oldfield was, and it was clear that Shipley didn't either, but they both kept quiet. Troy let his young deputy muse on things for a moment and then said, "Just need you to get the lead out of that foot, kid. But we also need to talk about your report."

"My report."

"That's right. I just read through it. Seems to me we could have had one hell of a problem on our hands. You say you almost hit someone out there?"

Shipley's face went uncertain. He parted his lips, closed them again, then tilted his head and said, "I thought there was someone in the road, sir. I was *positive* that there was a man in the road. I was running lights and siren and coming fast, as you said, maybe too fast, but I saw this guy in the rain and I swerved and…" He spread his hands. "That's all. A mistake, I guess. Thought I saw something in the road. Tried to swerve to adjust."

Troy looked puzzled. "So there *wasn't* anyone? I was of the impression that you damn near killed a man."

"So was I," Shipley said. "But everyone else seems to disagree."

Troy turned to Kimble. "You were out there."

"Quite a bit later, but yes."

"Is he right? Were the witnesses in agreement that he just plowed the car into the trees?"

"There was only one witness, a young guy who works out there. I think he heard more than he actually saw, though. It's quite certain that Shipley didn't hit anybody, and as for the circumstances of the wreck, there's nobody to say what happened except him."

"Well, that's a load off. I looked at that report and was thinking lawsuit. You remember that college professor asshole who sued us two years ago?"

The college professor asshole had been T-boned by a deputy doing eighty miles per hour through a residential neighborhood in response to a possible burglary in progress that turned out to be a man trying to get into his own home after locking the keys inside. Kimble found it a fair enough complaint, but it would hardly do to share that sentiment with the sheriff. He just nodded.

"I don't think we've got anything to worry about."

"That's good to hear. Tell you what, Shipley. You take a day off, all right?"

"I'm good to work."

"Not until tomorrow. Make sure there are no lingering effects. With the pictures I saw of that cruiser, there sure as hell might be."

"Yes, sir. I'm sorry about the car."

Troy nodded, then stood and looked at Kimble. "You got that suicide report wrapped yet?"

"Clearing up the details."

"Good man. I'm not disappointed that we can shut that frigging lighthouse down for good. Had enough of a hassle over it when the cat people started to complain. Tell you what, crazy runs in the water out there. You got a lighthouse in the woods, and sixty damn lions right across the street? Would have been nice if they'd all crossed the river and ended up in Jasper County, you ask me."

The sheriff left, and Shipley started to follow, but Kimble called him back.

"Hey — they check you out fully at the hospital?"

"Yes, sir."

"Concussion tests?"

"Passed them, yes. Why do you ask?" Shipley had a way of discerning extra motivation, one of the things that made him good police. His understanding of the gap between what someone said and why they said it was well honed.

"The story you tell, it's a strange one. Seems like the old brain stem might have gotten a pretty good whack."

Shipley frowned.

"What?" Kimble said.

"I didn't see a flash of something in the road," Shipley said. "It wasn't a deer, or a coyote. I saw a *man*. I locked up the brakes and swerved, and he ran the wrong way. Ran toward my swerve. Nothing I could do but hit him."

Kimble said, as gently as possible, "Son, you didn't hit anyone. Stop worrying about mistakes you didn't make."

"I saw it, though."

"You *remember* seeing it. Big difference. Particularly after getting knocked around the way you did."

"And when I came back around, when I could see again, there was a light," Shipley continued, not content to dismiss his irrational memory.

"That lighthouse was right above," Kimble said. "Would have been flashing like crazy."

Except it wouldn't have been, he realized. Because Shipley responded to the call from Darmus, and Darmus broke the light before he called. So it would have been darkness.

"Not the lighthouse," Shipley said. "This was like a blue torch. That's exactly what it was like."

"A blue torch." Kimble stared at him. "*This* is why I'm worried about concussions."

Shipley forced a laugh.

"Guess I've got a creative imagination when I'm unconscious."

"Be glad you imagined the worst and got the best."

"Yes, sir." Shipley pointed at the desk, where Kimble had spread out a full set of photocopies of the pictures and maps he'd pulled off the walls of Wyatt's lighthouse. The originals were locked away. "What's all that?"

"That," Kimble said with a sigh, "is the disturbing collection left behind by your ten-zero."

"The guy in the lighthouse?"

"Wyatt French, yes."

Shipley picked up a few of the photographs, studied them. "Who are they?"

"I have no idea."

"Strange hobby."

"Strange man," Kimble agreed. "You good, Shipley?"

"I'm fine."

"All right. Go home and take some aspirin."

"I was thinking I might run out to Blade Ridge first."

"What?"

"I'd just...I'd like to look around."

Kimble said, "You think it'll help you clear your head, okay. But don't get carried away worrying about it, Shipley. I don't need a deputy who's jittery behind the wheel, and the more you think about a disaster that didn't even happen, the better the chance of nerves catching up with you."

Shipley shook his head. "Of course not. I'm no superstitious sort, chief. You know that."

Kimble did know that. If Shipley were a superstitious man, he probably wouldn't have gone after this job. His father, Ed Shipley, a former Marine, had been in the department, too, had died in action in the summer of Kimble's rookie year. Nathan Shipley had been twelve at the time.

Sixteen years ago, Kimble thought, watching Ed Shipley's son walk out of the office. *They pass by fast, no question about it.*

Ed Shipley had beaten the fire department to the scene of a trailer fire because his car was a mile away when the call came. After he arrived, the hysterical family told him there was still someone inside. *Marlon's inside, Marlon's inside, Marlon didn't come out.* Marlon turned out to be a cat. Ed Shipley, former U.S. Marine, hadn't understood, and he went charging in after Marlon and never came back out. A day later the cat turned up at a neighbor's house. Had probably been the first creature in the house to escape the inferno.

No, if Nathan Shipley had pursued this line of work, he wasn't the sort who believed in jinxes. Wyatt French, on the other hand? He'd believed in something damn strange, and Kimble could not get a handle on it.

He flipped through the photo collection, all those ancient, sepia-tinted images of men with axes or picks or saws in hand. There were dozens of them, and across almost every one Wyatt had written the word *NO* in large bold print. Ten pictures had names, and computer searching had provided answers about just three of them.

In 1966, a Whitman restaurateur and local golf champion named Adam Estes had shot and killed his financial adviser. In 1979, an auto mechanic named Ryan O'Patrick had beaten his boss to death with a wrench. And in 2006...in 2006, Jacqueline Mathis had happened.

Wyatt kept photographs of all three in his home.

The seven other people who were named—Becky Stapp, Timothy Osgood, Ralph Hill, Henry Bates, Fred Mortimer, John Hamlin, and Bernard Snell—had left no mark on the department computer system or the Internet, but that wasn't surprising. Their photographs were very old.

Kimble ran through them again, shaking his head, then locked them in his desk drawer and went down to the jail.

A three-story concrete structure built just behind the sheriff's department, the Sawyer County Jail had been home to Wyatt French on several occasions, though never for more than a night. Kimble didn't have any questions for the corrections team about Wyatt, though. He had questions about their lights.

Just inside the jail, past the booking area and behind darkly tinted glass, was the control center. Here the security of the facility was monitored around the clock, with banks of computers and television screens ringing the room. Tyler Abel, a longtime road deputy who'd eventually moved into a position as the jail commander and answered directly to Troy, was sitting in the control center today.

"What's going on, Kimble?"

"Taking bets on the Wolverine. First race is only a few months away. Figured you're in for, what, a hundred?"

The Wolverine was the department's nickname for the sheriff's current racehorse. Troy, whose ability to name a horse was only slightly more advanced than his ability to breed a winner, had named the animal Wolf and Steam for logic that only he could follow, and his deputies had quickly altered it.

Abel smiled. "Not a jockey alive who can handle the Wolverine. But assuming the sheriff finds such a wrangler, I'm in for a thousand, of course."

"Noted." Kimble waved a hand at the monitors that showed images from every security camera in the jail and said, "Got a question for you."

"Shoot."

"You use infrared illuminators for some of these, right?"

"In some cases, yeah."

"What's their purpose?"

"Lets us see in the dark," Abel said, and smiled. "To keep a camera going, you've got to have light. The infrared illuminators provide it, but it's invisible to the naked eye. So it's not light that disturbs anyone. Perfect for security cameras, or military ops."

"The ones I saw had these lenses that were, I don't know, like...textured. Kind of speckled glass?"

"That's an LED illuminator, probably. Some of them use halogen bulbs and filters, but the more expensive, better ones are LED. Light-emitting diode. Where'd you come across them?"

"You ever see that lighthouse out on Blade Ridge?"

"I have. The thing is...curious."

"That's putting it mildly."

"But that's not an infrared light, Kimble."

"I know the main one isn't. But here's the deal: he had the main bulb, and then surrounding it this ring of infrared illuminators."

"That is bizarre. And expensive."

"Yeah?"

"If it's an LED illuminator of the sort you were telling me about, I'd say each unit went close to a thousand bucks. Could be more. Lot of scratch for a man like Wyatt French to invest in lighting."

Yes, it was. Wyatt French had tried to purchase his bourbon with scrounged change. It was one hell of a lot of money to invest in invisible lighting.

"What would those be accomplishing that the main bulb wouldn't be?" Kimble said.

"Had to be using them with cameras," Abel said confidently.

"Yeah?"

"Yeah. Security cameras are my business, Kimble. The only purpose for infrared illuminators is cameras or rifle scopes. I mean, what they would have been accomplishing was keeping the place lit, even if nobody could tell. The area within range of those illuminators would never be truly dark. It would be dark to the naked eye, but not *technically* dark. But there's no gain to that unless you've got them paired with cameras, is there?"

"I'll have to take a better look for cameras," Kimble said, more to himself than Abel. He'd given the lighthouse a cursory search yesterday, but he could have missed a concealed camera easily enough. There had been the distraction of the corpse, after all.

"To see what, unchanging images of the woods at night?" Abel asked.

"The infrared lights were in the top of the lighthouse, and that's where he shot himself. Maybe there's video of it."

"And you want to *watch* that little snuff film?"

Kimble looked at him, remembering Wyatt's voice coming at him on the dark highway. *If the victim were somehow compelled...*

"Yeah," he said. "I think I ought to."

13

THE MOVE WAS GOING far more smoothly today. The rain had let up, the cats were agreeable, and Wes was his usual precise and competent self, although unusually quiet, often seeming lost in his own thoughts. Audrey watched the old preserve empty out, this place where she had met her husband, fallen in love, and spent such happy years. Everyone from friends and family to complete strangers had urged her not to allow herself to feel obligated to follow through with the relocation when David died. She understood their reasoning: it was his passion project, not hers. What they didn't understand, couldn't understand, was that the cats were all she had left of David. They had no children — that part of the five-year plan would never be completed — and now the remnants of her marriage were memories and sixty-seven exotic cats rescued from a variety of terrible circumstances. They were the legacy. And, oh, how he had loved them.

She'd had other options. One of David's dear friends, a man named Joe Taft, ran a cat rescue center in Indiana. He'd been David's mentor, and he'd offered to take the animals, all of them.

Audrey couldn't agree to it. Canceling on the relocation would have been the ultimate failure to David, who'd been determined not to be chased away, although plenty of attempts had been made. There were multiple reasons for the move, but they all boiled down to one fundamental issue: proximity to people. Ironic, of course, because that problem was the reason all of these cats needed care to begin with. The age-old territory battle never stopped, and the cats would never win. When the preserve had first been built, the locals had regarded it with a mixture of curiosity and amusement, but there'd been hardly any objection. Over the following three years, though, development had overtaken the nearby fields. First came a seventy-home complex called Eden Estates, then talk of a golf course. The good people of Eden Estates moved into their homes, heard the occasional cougar scream or lion's roar in the night, and began to fear for their children. Complaints began, alleging that the rescue preserve was too close to residential property and the cats presented a danger. True to form in the human-animal history, nobody seemed concerned with the idea that the cats had been there first.

Audrey's legal background had a real use then, as she defended the preserve, pointing out that no cat had ever escaped from the property and no human had ever been bitten or clawed or hurt in any way, but even as she was making the arguments, David was eyeing new locations. He wanted space and he wanted distance from people. They found plenty of both at Blade Ridge.

Now all of his cats were there. Well, all except for Ira. He'd be moved alone.

There were dozens of cats on the preserve that nobody cared about, and then there was Ira, the subject of intense debate, his photographs and vital statistics being shipped back and forth from cat experts around the globe. The reason: he was living, breathing proof that the mountain lion of so many legends existed. While the term *black panther* was tossed about casually by the public, it was inaccurate. There were *melanistic* jaguars who exhibited a genetic quirk that turned their fur black — or, rather, black on black, since the cats were spotted — but no proof existed for a black North American cougar.

Until Ira.

And he'd come to the preserve of his own accord.

They'd been in operation for five weeks when he made his first appearance, and Wesley had been the only one to spot him. Even David had scoffed, sure that Wes was seeing things, but their manager was adamant: a cougar had come down out of the hills and surveyed the cages. A black cougar. The kind that didn't exist.

For a time Audrey had believed Wes was enjoying a practical joke. But as the man spent more and more time in the woods around the preserve, leaving food bait behind and trying to rig a trap camera to obtain evidence of the creature, she realized he was serious, and she worried about what it meant. There was no such thing as what he'd claimed to have seen, and still he pursued it with absolute conviction. It was disturbing to watch.

And then, nine days after he'd first spotted the cat, Wesley wheeled it into the preserve in a transport cage. The cat had entered, he said, and then chosen to ignore the bait that was inside. The guillotine gate hadn't been tripped by his entrance, though; he'd somehow gracefully avoided triggering it. Rather than retreat, he remained inside and watched Wesley as if daring him to come close enough to lower the gate himself.

"I had a moment of doubt," Wes admitted.

He'd done it, though. Approached and lowered the gate, and for a moment the cat could have struck, but he did not. Then the gate was down and he was trapped and the Kentucky preserve had the only melanistic cougar in recorded captivity.

David considered that a stroke of luck unlike any other in his life — *Thanks a lot,* Audrey remembered telling him dryly when he'd informed her of that news. He believed the cougar had been drawn out of the deep woods by the presence of the other cats, by curiosity over his own kind. Wes never seemed convinced of that; cougars were not pack animals, they were isolated, territorial creatures. He would grant David the animal's curiosity, but he didn't believe the cat wanted anything to do with his peers, either — a belief that was rapidly borne out by Ira's behavior. He was surprisingly docile around people, but he *demanded* solitary confinement. Many of the cats were happy to socialize with the others. Ira wanted his own space.

The chaos built quickly. David's fellow experts disagreed at first, claiming that Ira was the product of crossbreeding, but DNA tests supported Audrey's husband: Ira was a North American puma, or cougar, or mountain lion. Wes had disregarded the controversy — *Told you from the start he was a mountain lion,* he'd said, and then gone on about his business. The cat, everyone except Wesley agreed, could certainly not have been wild. He was too good with people, too comfortable. Clearly he'd escaped from some private owner, and clearly that person had been involved in something illegal, or he would have reported him missing. Would have reported him, period.

Wes disagreed, but he didn't like to be in the spotlight, and he refused to give any interviews when curious media folks came calling. David handled that. All Wes would say was, "The cat came out of the woods. Right now, that's all you know. Don't presume a damn thing when that's all you know."

It was, though, the most uncertain Audrey had ever seen him with a cat. Wes spent hours studying Ira, and she was convinced that he was wondering the same thing: where in the world had he come from? If he was wild, why didn't he act like it? And if he was not, then how was he an unknown?

They researched for endless hours and came up with nothing but legends. According to Native American folklore, the black cat was a symbol of death. According to scientific history, the black cat didn't exist. Put the two together and you generated a lot of excitement.

"He's ready to go, you can tell," Wes said when they arrived back at the now-empty preserve to collect the cougar. "We've moved everyone else, and it's making him edgy, being the only cat left. He didn't like watching the others go away. He's ready to see where we're taking them."

Audrey hadn't been able to perceive the slightest change in the cat's countenance, but she knew better than to argue with Wes. If he suggested what a cat was feeling, he was probably right. He seemed to live inside their strange feline brains. It was, frankly, a source of irritation for her. In the months since David had died, she'd tried to think of the cats as her own, but at her core she knew that they did not trust her in the way they had trusted David, trusted Wes. Could she have even handled them without Wes, could she have kept the preserve going at all? It was a question she didn't like to ponder, because she felt the answer was all too obvious.

She looked at him now and nodded, recalling again the intensity of David's excitement upon finding Ira. He had knelt in front of the cage, staring in at the black cat with a wide smile, and said, "They're real. Every wildlife biologist in the country would tell you that if they ever existed, they don't anymore. But you're looking at one. And you know what else? This cat's roots don't go back to Africa or the Amazon. They go back to these mountains. I can *feel* it, can't you? Look at him: he belongs to this place."

Now, months removed, Audrey watched the cat swish his long black tail and nodded. "Let's get him out there."

There were no problems. In fact, no sooner did they have the transport cage placed in front of the enclosure gate and opened than Ira unfolded to his full length and stalked over to it, eyes on

Wes and not the cage. It was as if he knew exactly what was desired and saw no reason to fight it.

The drive, too, was problem-free, Wes going slow and sticking to the back roads. They'd just gotten onto the rutted gravel of Blade Ridge Road when they saw an unfamiliar truck parked ahead. A moment later, as they continued to approach, the door opened and a police officer stepped out.

"It's him," Audrey said. "The guy from the accident."

Wes slowed at the gates, and Audrey put down her window. The deputy regarded them with a nod and a slight smile.

"Hi there."

"Hi," Audrey said. "How are you?"

"Just fine. Shouldn't be, by the look of my wheels, but I'm fine."

"You're one lucky SOB, I'll promise you that," Wes said.

The deputy nodded, giving a cursory glance toward the dark lighthouse above, and then said, "Well, thanks for your help yesterday. And I'm glad I went into those trees and not into the fences. Could have let some tigers out."

Audrey had never considered the possibility. If he'd exited the road left instead of right... She shook her head against the thought.

"All that matters is that you're okay," she said. "What brings you out?"

"Wanted to look around. Trying to get a handle on just how it happened. You're certain that nobody from your staff was in the road?"

"Not a soul," she said. "Dustin heard the sound of the wreck and came out. You were alone."

"Is he here? I'd like to ask him about it."

"He's done for the day."

The deputy nodded, but he seemed distressed. "All right." He waved a hand at the preserve. "Those cats are pretty amazing.

I've been watching them. Never seen anything like it, so many together."

"You want a look around?"

"I'd love it."

She got out of the truck and told Wes they would meet him at Ira's new enclosure. Then, on foot, she began to lead the deputy around the preserve.

"You aren't scared around them?" he said.

"Not a bit. Now, there are some who I wouldn't want to be alone with in a cage, but that doesn't mean they're marauding threats. It just means they haven't been socialized with humans as well as the others. They still can be sweet cats, and they still need a home, but you have to be a little more careful. Most of them, though? Sweet."

She went over to the leopard cage and made a chirping noise with her tongue. Jafar, a huge spotted leopard, one of the most beautiful cats in the preserve, was in his cat house. Audrey had made the mistake of referring to it as a doghouse once—it seemed the universal name for such a structure—and David corrected her indignantly.

They're cat houses, he'd said, and she'd remarked that it sounded like a whorehouse, and he'd laughed. There'd been a lot of laughs in those early days, as they acquired cats and built enclosures and dreams.

Jafar's house was a long and low L-shaped structure, open at both ends, built out of plywood and filled with straw. He was one of the cats who could be distrustful of visitors, or annoyed by their presence, and so he spent a lot of time in the house, where he could retreat into the shadows and study the situation with golden eyes.

Now, when Audrey dropped to one knee and made the chirping sound, the leopard promptly left the house, trotted up to the fence, and leaned his big head against the chain link, pressing his fur against her face, cheek to cheek. She reached through and scratched his ears.

"This guy is my baby," she said. Jafar was one of the few cats with whom she felt the same level of confidence that Wes demonstrated. "He was bought illegally by some guy in Ohio who kept him caged up in the back of a tattoo parlor. Then that guy was arrested for dealing meth—you would be amazed how many of our cats come from narcotics busts—and Jafar came here. He's a little devious, likes to play tricks, but he's a sweetheart."

She stood and continued to walk, and Jafar gave an angry growl. The deputy, Shipley, turned uneasily to look back at him.

"He's just upset because we're moving on from him," she said. "All he wants is attention."

They made their way back toward Wes and the truck, stopping occasionally so Audrey could point out specific cats. She told him that the tigers tended to be far more playful than the lions, particularly in cold weather, and particularly in the snow. Nothing—*nothing*—pleased the tigers more than a snowstorm. During a good snowfall even the most lethargic of the tigers would turn playful, chasing the others and sliding through the snow. Kino would flip his water basin upside down, then climb on top and ride it like a sled, which made for the best video Audrey had ever captured at the preserve. She'd grown to pay religious attention to the snow forecasts in hopes of seeing the cats celebrate.

"Watch this," she said, stopping by another cage. "Gabby! Hey, Gabrielle. Wake up."

A tawny lioness rolled over, faced Audrey and the stranger, and yawned. Audrey whistled, said, "Gabby!" once more, and then clapped her hands three times.

Gabby rolled onto her back and clapped her own paws together, bringing a laugh from the deputy and coos of gratitude and adoration from Audrey.

95

"See? They're peaceful," she said.

"They weren't last night," Wes muttered, coming up to join them. Audrey frowned, wishing he wouldn't say anything critical. "Last night they were anything but peaceful."

At that point a tiger approached the cage, then swung his hindquarters around. Audrey grabbed the deputy's arm and pulled him aside with her just as a stream of urine shot through the fence.

"Did he actually just try to piss on us?" the deputy said in amazement, checking his jacket.

"The bigger surprise is that he didn't succeed," Audrey said. "That's Kino. He likes to mark me every time I pass by. He is, for some reason—or perhaps for that very reason—Wes's favorite cat."

Wes smiled and shrugged. Behind the fence, Kino had dropped onto his haunches and regarded them with a baleful stare, clearly disappointed with his marksmanship.

"Okay," Audrey said, "let's get Ira out of that truck. The man of mystery can check out his new digs." She was feeling good, feeling energized despite the long days. They were almost done. Soon all of the cats would be here, and she could claim a long-fought victory.

They were now at the southwestern corner of the preserve. Through the trees, bare of leaves, the Marshall River showed, gray and swollen.

"You're going to have a river view, Ira," Audrey called to the cougar, standing beside the deputy at the gate to the enclosure as Wes backed up the truck.

"Hell of a place," the deputy said to her as Wes stepped out and walked around to the rear of the truck. "Never seen anything like it."

"There aren't many things like it," she said.

"Now this is the black cat?"

96

"Yes. The one Wes trapped. It was in the paper."

He nodded. "I've heard about it. My grandmother used to tell stories about seeing a cat just like—"

He didn't get to finish, because Wes lifted the transport cage's gate and Ira came out in a blur of fury.

He streaked into the enclosure low to the ground and snarling, then spun back to face them, flattened his ears, and curled his lips back to show his teeth.

The deputy said, "Holy shit," and took a step back.

"Ira," Wes said. "Easy, buddy. Easy."

He stepped toward the cougar, and Ira leaped. When he banged into the fencing, Audrey and the deputy shouted in unison. Audrey couldn't help it; she'd watched cats twice this size show aggression before, but there was something different here, something frightening.

Even Wes seemed uncertain. He repeated his request for the cat to relax, and Ira responded by slinking toward the center of the cage and hissing. He locked his bright green eyes on the deputy and spread his jaws wide, showing every tooth in full glory, his front paws flexing.

"I know he's behind a fence," Shipley said, "but I'm still scared of that boy."

"He's the wild one," Wes said softly. "Hasn't been moved before. He'll settle down."

When Ira sprang onto the wooden platform, the deputy dropped his hand to his gun and Audrey joined him in taking yet another step back. Wes stayed where he was, and Ira ignored them completely, turned away to stare out west, toward the river. He gazed into the gray sky for a moment, then raised his head and screamed. There was no other word for it—cougars flatout *screamed,* and Audrey had heard them before.

But she'd never heard anything like this.

"He'll settle down," Wes repeated.

"Sure," Audrey said, her arms prickling, going to gooseflesh.

Behind them, the other cats had begun to stir.

Ira swung his head around, ears pinned back, and studied them. Then he jumped back down, and they all shifted when he landed, nobody — not even Wes — able to stay completely calm after that scream. The cat stalked toward them, sleek belly barely above the grass, tail swishing, each muscle loaded with coiled energy.

"Wes," Audrey said, "maybe you should get the tranquilizer rifle."

"He'll be fine."

"Wes, please."

Wes looked from her to the cougar and then moved around the side of the truck. He opened the door and came back with the rifle, which fired sedation darts. Wes hated to use them, but right now Audrey thought they should have the option. She'd never seen any of the cats look this aggressive.

"I think we should just give him some space," Wes said as he stepped back toward them. "Just give him —"

The cougar saw the rifle in his hand then, let out another chilling scream, and spun away from the fence. He darted to his left, then cut right, dodging between the platforms they'd built for him, almost as if he was seeking a screen against any attempt to shoot, and then, at the far end of the enclosure, he crouched and sprang.

And cleared the fence.

Shipley said, "Holy fuck," and drew his gun. Wes pushed on his arm, preventing him from raising it and taking a shot, and Audrey just stared in astonishment as the cat vanished into the woods, running low and fast, a deadly shadow slipping back into the mountains from which it had come.

"It just jumped that fence," Shipley said. His voice was trembling. "How tall is that fucking fence?"

"Fourteen feet," Wes said. His voice was lower, but not all that steady either. "Fourteen feet, with a recurve at the top. It's impossible for a cat to clear that thing. I built all of these enclosures myself. They can't get out."

He'd just watched it happen, but still he was insisting.

"What do we do?" Audrey said. She found it hard to speak. Her eyes were still on the place where the black cat had disappeared. Around them, the other cats were crowding to the edges of their enclosures, well aware that something was amiss. "How do we get him back?"

"I've got to call this in," Shipley said in a stunned voice. "I've got to report this. That thing's a mountain lion. We can't just let it run around."

"It was running around before," Wes said, and he stepped away from them, went up to the fence, and ran one palm along the chain link, staring at it, this device that had betrayed him. He turned back to look at them, and his eyes were wide with wonder.

"I always told you he decided to join us," he told Audrey. "I wasn't wrong. He could have left whenever he wanted to, and he knew it."

"Well, why did he pick today?" Audrey said, and as Shipley pulled out his radio and began to report the fact that they'd just lost a two-hundred-pound predator in the woods, Wes looked at her grimly.

"It's this spot," he said. "He didn't like this spot. And you know what else? None of them do. Come sundown, you'll see just what I mean."

14

KIMBLE HAD ALREADY BEEN at Blade Ridge for two hours when he heard about the cat escape.

He'd gone there in search of the security cameras Wyatt had paired with infrared illuminators, only to confirm what he'd initially thought: there were no cameras.

Kimble scoured the grounds, the top of the lighthouse, the base. He checked the wiring leaving the circuit breaker, he tapped on the walls in search of hollow spots, he turned the desk inside out again.

There were no cameras.

Maybe they'd been part of the long-range plan; Wyatt had invested in the illuminators first, and never got around to the cameras.

But the longer Kimble searched, the more convinced he became that the infrared beams weren't about capturing an image at all. They were simply about light.

They pointed in every direction, offering unseen illumination to the road and the woods, and Kimble remembered the initial fights about the light, the complaints that it was too bright, that it presented a danger. Wyatt had toned down the bulb, and apparently added invisible lighting. His idea of a compromise.

And the point?

Well, that was anyone's guess. Kimble sure as shit didn't have one.

The only find he made wasn't a camera but another light. When he pulled Wyatt's cot out from the wall, he found that the man had built a shelf beneath the bed, near where his hands would have rested while he slept. The contents: an empty holster that would have once held the Taurus .45 he'd used to kill himself, a hunting knife, a leather strop for sharpening it, and a spotlight.

The spotlight had a pistol grip and a trigger, and the lens was outfitted with a cherry-red filter. *Two million candlepower rechargeable,* a label on the handle boasted.

One hell of a bright light, Kimble thought, and then he squeezed the trigger and got nothing. He frowned, looked directly at the lens, and squeezed the trigger again. There was the faintest of crimson glows, as if the flashlight were draining away the dregs of its battery. When he touched the lens, though, he found it very hot. In fact, he could move his palm back from the light a good distance and still feel its warmth.

"An infrared flashlight," he said aloud, turning the odd device over in his hands. Of course. If the power went out, you needed a flashlight handy. Particularly an invisible one.

He set the light back down, then inspected the knife and strop. It was a serious cutting instrument — six-inch stainless steel blade going down to a military-grip Teflon handle, and it was seriously sharp. The leather strop was worn from countless repetitions. Wyatt had spent a lot of time sharpening his knife. And, Kimble remembered from handling the suicide piece, oiling his gun. He'd wanted to be prepared, and was determined that the equipment would not let him down when the time came. This would be why a man slept each night with a gun, a knife, and a flashlight with a two-million-candlepower invisible beam within immediate reach. He wanted to be ready. The only question was, for what?

Kimble had promised him that he pursued the truth always, but maybe there was no truth to be found here, just madness. Maybe that was the truth when it came to Wyatt French.

He hit the spotlight trigger again, felt the warmth of the lens, and recalled Nathan Shipley's statement about his wreck. He'd talked about seeing some strange light. Kimble looked down at the two-million-candlepower light in his hand and wondered about it. Was the thing truly invisible to the naked eye? What if it hit you just right, found just the proper angle? Those ridiculous laser pointers could do some damage to the eye, couldn't they? Well, what about a two-million-candlepower infrared spotlight? It seemed plausible that if it were beamed just right, a flash of momentary blindness could ensue.

So what are you thinking, Kimble? That Wyatt was perched on a dead-end road, hoping for some poor lost soul to wander by so he could blind him with a flashlight? Come on.

He shoved the cot back into place, then sat on the dead man's bed and wondered what Wyatt had known about Jacqueline that Kimble didn't. Or what he'd known that Kimble *did.*

Had he known about the Bakehouse, for example?

Nobody should have. Nobody except Kimble and Jacqueline. And even between them, the coffee shop had never been remarked upon. Probably never would be.

He could remember her so well, the way she looked when she would step through the door with golden light behind her, putting a raven's shine on her dark hair. Friday mornings. She never missed one. Once Kimble found out, neither did he.

Those encounters began after their first meeting, when Kimble was dispatched to the house after a neighbor called in a domestic dispute between Jacqueline and her husband. When Kimble got there, Brian Mathis came out to meet him, told him everything was fine. Kimble said he'd like to talk to the man's wife. Mathis argued. Kimble was readying to explain that it was an argument he could make to a judge if he preferred when Jacqueline stepped out of the house. Kimble sent Brian Mathis back inside so he could talk to her alone, and he'd seen the dark look the man gave his wife as he passed. Kimble stood with her in the fading sun of a cold evening and watched the way she moved, so gingerly, one arm close to her ribs, and listened as she told him the neighbors must have been confused, there was no problem.

It wasn't the first interview of that sort he'd conducted.

When he'd asked her if she was hurt, if her husband had struck her, she gave him a wan smile and said simply that there was no problem that required his assistance, though she appreciated the offer. He was explaining that she needed to be honest with him if there'd been any violence when she interrupted to tell him that she wasn't the sort of woman he was expecting her to be, cowed and frightened and unwilling to report a husband who'd just post bond and come back home to finish the job.

"I appreciate what you're telling me," she said. "But I'm fully capable of handling this situation."

The look in her eyes then, so firm, so strong, was different indeed from what he was used to in these situations. And it had worried him.

"There is nothing about you," he'd told her, "that suggests you are anything but capable. But something else you are, when you go back in that house? You're alone, Mrs. Mathis. You're alone."

She'd put her hand on his arm, held his eyes, and said, "I'm becoming more aware of that every day, deputy."

Then she'd turned and walked inside. That was his first trip to the Mathis house.

Two weeks later he'd seen her at the Bakehouse, a café three blocks from the department. He liked to walk up there in the morning, clear his head, see the town. The coffee shop looked out on the courthouse where in the spring the lawn was lined with flowering trees, and sipping a coffee nice and slow at a sidewalk table could turn a potentially bad day into a good one, sometimes.

She was stepping in as he was stepping out on that particular Friday, and there had been an awkward moment of recognition. She smiled, said, "Hello, officer," and he told her she didn't have to call him that. She asked what she was supposed to call him then, and he said that his name was Kevin Kimble but most folks called him Kimble.

"I'll call you Kevin, if you don't mind," she said.

He didn't mind.

He sat at his table outside and she sat inside, and when she left she waved at him and softly said, "Thank you for your compassion, by the way. It helped."

Routine took over, and he began his speech again, the one urging her to come down the street with him and make a formal complaint. She held up a hand to stop him and said, "It's a beautiful morning."

After a pause, he nodded and acknowledged that it was.

"Today I just want to enjoy that. Okay?"

He told her that it was okay. Told himself not to watch her walk down the street. He was full of useless advice that morning, it seemed.

It wasn't long before he determined that her trips to the Bakehouse were consistently Friday mornings. The encounters became weekly, and they lengthened, but not by much. Five minutes, ten, maybe fifteen. Small talk. Weather and town news, mostly. He didn't ask after her home life. Then one Friday she wore a sleeveless dress, and he saw the bruise on her upper arm. The dress, he thought, worn when the mark could have been covered so easily by a sleeve, was defiance. Or a call for help. Or something torn between the two.

They spoke again, and he looked at the bruise pointedly, and then he asked her if she was all right. She sipped her coffee, steam rising across her face, and did not answer. That was when Kimble wrote his cell-phone number down and slid it across the table to her and said, like some foolish gunslinger in a black-and-white cowboy picture, "You need help handling anything, I'm one ring away."

How ridiculous. How unprofessional.

How he hoped she would call.

And then one night she did.

Kimble was still sitting there on Wyatt French's bed when his radio squawked, calling him out of the past and into the present with one of the stranger reports he'd heard in his time policing: a cougar was loose.

Shipley met him at the gates, and his face was pale.

"Son of a bitch jumped right out," he said. "One try, right over the top. If I hadn't been watching it, I wouldn't have believed it."

"All right," Kimble said. "Put your damn gun away."

Shipley looked at him, hesitated, and holstered his sidearm. He kept his palm on it, though.

"If you'd seen the way that thing could move," he said, "you'd want yours out, too."

Kimble moved away from him and over to Audrey Clark and a wiry, gray-haired man named Wesley Harrington, who held odd-looking weapons in each hand.

"What in the hell are those?"

"Air rifles. Shoot tranquilizer darts."

"Can you hit him with it?"

"Sure," Harrington said. "If he's five feet away."

Kimble looked at Audrey Clark and said, "This is going to be a problem, isn't it?"

Clark, who was tall and good-looking but too thin—she'd lost a lot of weight since her husband died, it seemed—said, "Not if it's handled right."

"And how would that be?"

"Quietly," she said, and then, when he frowned, "I mean that honestly. That's not concern for my reputation, that's concern for getting him back. If you bring twenty people out here with guns and send them into the woods, we won't have a chance."

"Not the way he moves," Shipley muttered. "Could bring a battalion out here, and they still wouldn't get him."

Kimble shot him a harsh look and then turned back to Audrey Clark.

"That's a very dangerous animal," he said. "We can't just have it running around wild."

"I could point out that he was running around wild to begin with," she said, "but that's a waste of time. I want him back, too. More than you do. But I'm telling you, the more people, and the more noise, the worse our chances. The commotion will scare him."

"What are you suggesting, then?"

"I think he'll come back when he's hungry," she said, and Kimble sighed at that, the notion of letting a two-hundred-pound cougar grow hungry not one that appealed to him as a solution. "We're his home. He'll come back."

"Not here," Harrington said, and they all looked at him in surprise. He gave an apologetic glance at Audrey Clark and then said, "It's just...he had a pretty hostile reaction to this place. I don't know that he'll come back. In the old preserve, I might have agreed. But not here. Maybe he's heading back to the old place."

Audrey Clark looked as if she wanted to strangle him. Kimble said, "You're proposing that we go after him, then?"

Harrington nodded. "Ought to try, at least. I doubt we'll have much luck, but we ought to try." He looked up at the gray sky. "And we've got a short window to do it. Once it gets full dark ... that won't be a good time to be in the woods with him."

"Right," Kimble said, thinking of a black cat moving in the darkness and suppressing a shiver. "We'll want to hurry."

"Make better time at it if we split up," Harrington said. "Two by two. Work along the river, maybe, out in the open. See what we can see. I'll take Audrey and—"

"Hang on there," Kimble said, thinking that they had two police on hand and two civilians. "You and I will go down to the river together. Nathan, you hang fairly close, all right? You and Mrs. Clark can check the perimeter, but don't get far."

Having the damned cat out was bad enough; the last thing he needed was someone to be hurt by it. Harrington had the look of capability about him, and Audrey Clark appeared more shaken. He didn't need her wandering off into the woods at dusk.

"Let's go," he told Harrington, and they set off down the road and for the river as the sun settled in the west, Kimble thinking that he was really beginning to hate this place.

15

AUDREY'S THOUGHTS WERE NOT even on Ira as she and Deputy Shipley walked out of the preserve and toward the abandoned, overgrown railroad tracks that formed its southern border. They were on Wes.

She couldn't believe the way he was behaving, the things he was saying. The preserve had its share of opponents, people who didn't understand the need and knew only fear of animals that would never harm them even if they had the chance to do so, and the county sheriff was among them. Now Wes was spouting off about the place as if it *were* dangerous, and to the sheriff's deputies, no less.

"Hey," Shipley said, bringing her out of her angry fog. "Why don't we go right, not left?"

She'd instinctively started to follow the tracks to the left.

"More open view at the river," he continued. "We'll go have a look and then come on back. Like Kimble said, no need to get too far into these woods."

"Fine." She had a tranquilizer gun in her hands, and now she looked into the trees and refocused on Ira. Was he still out there?

Had he hung close by, as she predicted, or had he simply fled? And which option was preferable?

They turned around and headed toward the river, stepping over jutting timbers and stretches of iron that had once brought trains to these hills in search of fortune. With fortune never found, all that remained were the scraps of what had been laid in its pursuit, covered now by dead grass and brush and, in some cases, even trees. The legacy of the Whitman Company's efforts at Blade Ridge was becoming obscured by the very nature that it had tried to conquer. Audrey held the air rifle in her hands and swiveled her head left to right, left to right, but something deep within her whispered that it wasn't worth the effort — Ira was gone, and would not return.

The deputy, Shipley, had gone on ahead of her, expanding his lead with long-legged strides. She saw that the young man was tapping his gun with his fingers. Every second step, there he went — *tap, tap, tap.* He seemed to be humming softly, too, the sound trapped in his throat. It was the sort of thing people did to convince themselves they weren't scared when in fact they were terrified. After David's death, Audrey had found herself doing the same sort of thing: *I'm scared of what my future holds, alone in this house, so I'll hum a song and that casualness will somehow prove my confidence.*

Shipley was scared, she realized, and then, recalling the moment of Ira's escape, she didn't blame him, not one bit. Many visitors — *most* visitors, maybe — were scared of the cats at first, no matter how indifferent they tried to seem. The animals were incredible predators; there was no denying that. When people came out to see them for the first time, they were dazzled, impressed, and often afraid. Because no human stood a chance against those cats. Not without a gun in hand, at least.

Tap, tap, tap, went Shipley's fingers against his weapon.

He had seen a cat in pure, wild aggression, too. In a way

Audrey herself had never seen one before. The tigers had fights, the lions would roar with killer's rage, but never in her time on the preserve had she seen anything like *that*. And the leap that he'd made…it was impossible to believe, even after watching it happen. He hadn't laid his paws on the fence and scrambled to get over, he'd just cleared it with room to spare. Fourteen feet high, and he'd not even required a running start.

"He's never been aggressive before," she said. "What you saw back there…I don't know how to explain it, but it was an anomaly."

"I'm sure that it was," Shipley said, and his voice was steady, but his head was shifting rapidly from side to side, tracking every shadow, his hand never drifting from his gun. She had the sudden, perverse urge to tell him that Ira could climb trees, could be poised on a branch right now, ready to spring down from above. She could tell him that the cat's field of vision overlapped like a pair of binoculars, and that he could see six times better in the dark than a human could. David had named him well—Ira was Hebrew for *watcher,* and the black cat was the definitive watcher, the perfect predator. Fast and strong and blessed with extraordinary vision and sense of smell.

"This is what you do?" the deputy said.

She looked up. "Huh?"

"This is…your life. This is what you do." He waved a hand back at the tall fences, from which the occasional roar echoed through the trees.

"That's right."

"Why?" he said, and he sounded genuinely curious. "Why those cats?"

"Because I love them," she said, but she suspected she knew what he was thinking about—the way she'd reacted when Ira jumped versus the way Wes had reacted. Wes had been poised; Audrey had been terrified. So was she lying right now? She cared for the cats, certainly, believed in the importance of the rescue center's mission, but did she *love* them? Could you possibly have love in a relationship before you had trust? She didn't think so. Then different words—infatuation, obsession, enchantment—might apply, but without trust? No, love was a long step to take ahead of faith.

"They're good with people," she said hollowly. "Really."

The deputy stopped walking, looked at her uneasily, ran a hand over his mouth, and then said, "Maybe we should go back now."

"We just started—"

"Let's go back while there's still daylight," he said, and then he turned and led the way again. This time, those long strides were even faster. Audrey stumbled along trying to keep up, thinking, *First Wes, and now even the police? Am I the only one who's not scared of the dark out here?*

Blade Ridge Road died out in abrupt fashion, no circular dead end that would allow wayward drivers to turn around with ease, just a narrowing of the gravel track until it came right up to the line of shagbark hickories that ran along the top of the ridge. They were tall trees now, seeming to belong to the rest of the forest, but Wesley knew that they'd been cleared once. Probably there wasn't a tree between this lane and the trestle that was more than eighty years old. That was a good age for most trees, but not out here in the forested hills of eastern Kentucky. With the exception of that small stretch that had been cleared to make way for mining operations that never produced a fruitful yield, the trees at Blade Ridge went back centuries. They'd provided shelter for many cougars in their time, and then white men with guns came along, and though the trees still stood, the cats did not.

Or so it had been thought. Then Ira arrived, slinking out of the hills with nothing attached to him but legends and myths, and now there was Ira back in the woods again, exiting the very way he'd come in, heavy with the feel of magic.

Wesley was trying to remember if he'd ever heard a story that even resembled the one which people would now be telling about his own cat. He gave up early, knowing that he wouldn't find solace in shared sorrow. This escape was unique. What the cat did was almost preternatural. If Ira had somehow *climbed* the fence, Wesley would be stunned but able to fathom it. If Ira had somehow leaped from the top of the perch, Wesley might have been able to blame his angles, chastise himself for not creating a wider perimeter out from the top platform. Or if the son of a bitch had at least taken a running start...

But he hadn't. No, he just leaped out, and Wesley knew in that moment that he could have done so at any time. He'd come to the preserve of his own accord, and now he'd left it. He was not likely to return.

Wesley and Kimble left the road and pushed through the hickories and walnut trees and began working their way down the slope to the water's edge. There was a narrow trail of sorts here, and they made the walk in silence, stepping carefully, their footing often lost to shadow as the sun faded.

"You don't think he's coming back," Kimble said finally. They had reached the riverbank and stood with guns in hand, looking into the darkening woods.

Wesley was silent.

"Tell me the truth," Kimble said. "I've got to deal with this, and I want to do it right. For you guys, too. Not just to cover my own ass. I realize this might cause you problems, but I've got to deal with it right. Tell me what you think."

Wesley looked at him, this tall, broad-shouldered cop who walked with bad posture, canting a little to the left at all times, as though something pained him, and said, "I don't think he's coming back, no. Not so long as we're here."

"What do you mean by that?"

"I don't think he likes the place."

"You'll forgive me if I say that sounds a little wild."

You want to hear something that sounds wild, Wesley thought. *I could tell you about the ghost light that passed through here.*

He just shrugged, though. Kimble sighed and rubbed his face with one large hand, then walked to the north, splashing in puddles as he tried to step from rock to rock.

Not so nimble, Kimble, Wesley thought, and he wanted to laugh, but had the sense that if he got going he might not stop. Darkness was coming, and Ira was out, and while he didn't know what those things meant, he had an idea that it wasn't good.

"I'll give her the night," Kimble said finally, stopping and turning back to him. "I can see some logic to what she's saying, that the cat would come back only if he felt safe. Is someone going to be here all night?"

"Yes. I am."

"Just you?"

"Just me," Wesley said, and for the first time in his life that idea unsettled him. He tried to cover it by spitting into the river and scanning the low-hanging trees on the other side as if he were searching for the cat.

"Audrey doesn't stay with them?"

"No. That's a good thing, too. Audrey, she's never quite developed the trust you need with the cats."

"Seemed pretty comfortable to me."

"More comfortable than most, of course. She's great with them so long as there's a fence between her and the cats. But she won't go into the cages."

"Doesn't seem like a mistake to me."

"If you run this place," Wesley said, "there are times when you're going to *have* to go into the cages. It happens."

"You're saying she can't handle it without her husband?"

"She can handle it," Wesley said. "She's got me. If she didn't? Well, then she'd either need to find some faith with the cats or . . . or find somebody else who does, I guess. But don't worry about how she'll hold up to this. Audrey, she's got steel in her that you can't see right off. She doesn't even see it sometimes. But it's there."

"All right. Well, my understanding is that you trapped this cougar once. Can you get him again?"

Wes didn't tell him that idea was false. Ira had chosen to join them. He had gone into the trap, yes, but he'd never engaged it. Just sat there and waited for Wesley to do it by hand, daring him, challenging his courage as if it were a test that must be passed before he'd allow himself to be confined.

Only you were never really confined, Ira, were you?

"I know what I *don't* want," Kimble continued, "and that's a bunch of people out here in the dark with guns. My people, or, God forbid, civilians. The potential for a good result in that scenario isn't high, and the potential for a bad one?"

Wesley nodded. The potential for disaster was high indeed if you put jumpy, armed men into these woods in the dark and told them to keep a sharp eye out for a black cat of astonishing speed.

"So I'll give you the night to try to let him settle down and slip back in," Kimble said. "See if you can bait him, see if you can trap him, or get him with that tranquilizer rifle. Whatever. But I'm only giving you until tomorrow. If he's not back by morning, we're going to *have* to bring other people out here. The state wildlife agency might be able to help."

Sure, Wesley thought, *that cat was out here for years and they just laughed at anyone who claimed to have seen him. I bet they'll be a swell help.*

They left the river as night fell and climbed back to the road and met Audrey and the other deputy, Shipley. Then Kimble explained his decision to them.

"One night, take your best approach, and see what happens," he said. "I'll come out here at eight tomorrow. If the cat is still missing, we're going to have to make an announcement and bring some people in."

"The more activity, the more —"

"He's right, Audrey," Wesley said, interrupting her and earning a scathing look. "You don't want problems developing. We may need to get some help."

Behind them, one of the tigers struck at the fencing, a metallic ripple pulsing out from the impact point, and they all turned and stared. It was Kino, and when he saw that he had their attention, he leaned his head back and roared, fierce and furious.

"This is what I'm worried about," Audrey said. "If strangers are making them act like this, then —"

"It isn't the strangers," Wesley said. "You know that. You've seen them around people for years now."

"What is it, then?" the young deputy said.

"They don't like this spot at night," he said. "And if you stick around long enough, you might see it get a whole lot worse."

Audrey threw up her hands in disgust. "Stop," she said.

"I'd like to hear what he thinks," the young deputy began, and Audrey shook her head, and then they were all interrupted by a sudden glow of white light. All four of them looked upward instinctively, but Wyatt French's lighthouse remained dark, and then there was the crunch of gravel and they realized a car was coming down the lane. They watched it approach, a Honda SUV, and when it got all the way up to them, the driver put down the window.

"Hi, Mrs. Clark. Hi, Kimble." He was a lean older guy with short gray hair and sharp eyes, and though he was speaking to the people gathered by his car, he was watching the cats, who were making hostile circles around their enclosures, swinging their big heads from side to side. He looked familiar, but Wesley couldn't place him.

"Why are you back, Darmus?" Kimble said, and then Wesley remembered. This was the reporter. He'd written about the preserve a few times — including the day Wesley got Ira.

Darmus said, "I just wanted to see the place in the dark."

"You just wanted to see the place in the dark," Kimble echoed.

"That's right."

"Well, hang on a minute, will you?"

He turned back to Audrey and Wesley and said, "One night. Figure out what you want to try to get him back, but you've only got one night to do it. Shipley, you willing to stay on and assist?"

The deputy's brow knitted and his blue eyes drifted from Kimble and down to the road. "All due respect, sir, I'd like to head home."

This seemed to stun Kimble. He said, "Shipley, I think they could use —"

"We're fine," Audrey said. "Between Wes and me, we'll be fine."

Kimble gave a slow nod, but Wesley could see he was disappointed in his deputy. "All right. Go on and get some rest, Shipley. I know it's been a long day and you're still recovering."

Shipley, flushed with embarrassment, said, "I can come back out at sunup. See what we have."

"Sure," Kimble said, and turned back to the car. "Now, Darmus, I'm going to give you a choice, based on that stunt you pulled with the notebook yesterday. I can arrest you, or you can buy me a drink and we can talk. Right now, I could use a drink. Which will it be?"

"You know, I just noticed that I gave you the wrong pages," the gray-haired reporter said, his face suddenly full of Tom Sawyer innocence. "Silly mistake. I'll be happy to —"

"Oh, give it a rest," Kimble said. "We're going to talk. It can be an official talk pretty easily. I don't think you want that option."

Darmus grinned. "Kimble, you look parched. Could I interest you in a beverage?"

Kimble didn't smile as he said, "Roman's, twenty minutes."

Darmus put his vehicle into reverse and began the awkward trick of turning around on the narrow road and Kimble returned his attention to Audrey and Wesley.

"You're on your own, guys. Make something good happen. If you need help, call for it fast." He looked at the cats beyond and said, "Good luck."

Then they left, too, Kimble and Shipley, the latter driving away from the preserve as if he were fleeing, and it was just Audrey and Wesley in the dark.

They stood in silence until the cars were gone, and then Audrey turned to him and spread her hands.

"What is the *matter* with you? The sheriff already doesn't like us, and you're acting as if—"

"Audrey," he said, "I'm not *acting* any way. I'm not pretending. You haven't been out here at night before. Things got a little…"

"A little what?"

"Nothing," he said, because he realized that if he told her the story, she'd want to be out here herself. She'd want to see it with her own eyes. That didn't seem like a good idea. If that light—and the feline response to it—was going to continue, then Wes wanted some time to watch it and consider it, alone.

"It's just a change for them," Wes said. "They're stressed. You've moved before, Audrey. Didn't you feel any stress? Well, imagine being picked up and moved, no consultation, no understanding. How would you react?"

"They were fine until that damned cougar—"

"No, they weren't," he said.

"What?"

He sighed. "They get agitated at night. Sorry I bothered you by bringing it up in front of the police. But they were pretty wild last night."

"They seemed fine this morning."

"I'm sure they're adjusting," Wes said. He was thinking about the blue light and looking at Lily. Lily was a gorgeous white tiger. Lily was also blind. She'd been rescued from a traveling animal show where she'd been kept in a tiny cage and fed dog food. Now she was almost four hundred pounds of beauty, but the terrible care of her youth had left her blind. If the blue light came back in the night, Wes wanted to see if Lily reacted to it. If she did...if she did, it would tell him something. Not what he was hoping, but what he feared.

"Can we get Ira back?" Audrey asked.

"Ira's gone, I'd say. I'll put a trap out there, but the way he took off didn't seem to indicate he had plans for a return."

"I still can't believe he did that. What scared him so much? He was *terrified*."

"Audrey? Go on home. Get some sleep. I'll make sure the cats are safe."

"Maybe I should stay here tonight instead of you."

"Why?"

"Well, we've never seen anything like this before!"

"And you're more qualified to deal with that than I am?"

"I'm not saying that. But it's my preserve, my responsibility, so..."

"Audrey." Wes shook his head.

"It's my responsibility," she repeated.

"No," he said mildly. "It is not. When you and David hired me, you made me the preserve manager, and one of the stipulations was that I live on site. I believe it is *my* responsibility. I take that seriously. Now, it's been a long day. Hard on everyone. The cats, you, me."

"I know."

"So let's not get to tangling with each other, okay? Let's not do that."

"I'm sorry."

"I'll be here tonight, and I'll make sure everything is fine," he said. "Like I always have, Audrey. Every night since I've worked for you."

"I know you will, Wes. I'm sorry for being bitchy about what you told the police. I'm just . . . I guess I'm just scared of what will come next."

He looked away from her and out at the rows of glittering eyes in the night and said, "That seems to be a consensus."

16

ROY SAT IN A BACK CORNER BOOTH at Roman's Tavern and waited for Kimble with a mixture of apprehension and curiosity. The chief deputy's insistence on talking with him was interesting, because it suggested that more than a lecture was at hand. If anger was driving Kimble, they wouldn't have recessed to a local pub. There was a reason that this conversation was happening outside the sheriff's department, and Roy had a feeling that reason was named Jacqueline Mathis.

He'd been waiting for about ten minutes when Kimble stepped inside with a folder in his hands. He paused and scanned the room and then nodded when Roy lifted a finger to catch his attention. Most of the bars in downtown Whitman were avoided like the plague by locals unless it was summer, winter, or spring break. Roman's, on the other hand, had managed to create a perfect delineation over the years — the kids went upstairs, where the bartenders offered specials on terrible shots and massive speakers loomed in every corner, and anybody over thirty stayed downstairs, tucked into scarred wooden booths or on backless stools at a small, shadowed bar. Now, in the heart of winter break and on a weeknight, the place was nearly empty. Kimble sat down across from Roy, and when the waitress asked what he'd like, he said, "A glass of...um, just a Budweiser. Thanks."

She left, and Roy said, "So are you going to arrest me?"

"Don't laugh, old-timer. I could. You were tampering with a crime scene."

"Technically, I think I was just *observing* it."

Kimble said, "You've spent some time on those names, haven't you?"

"Why do you think that?"

"Because if you went through the effort of swiping them from the lighthouse, then you'd check them out. So? What did you find?"

Roy hesitated. The waitress returned with their drinks, and he took a long swallow of his beer and said, "You weren't down there tonight because of names on a map, Kimble. What's up?"

"Unrelated matter."

"Really? Blade Ridge is a hotspot for local law enforcement needs?"

Kimble looked at him with an expression that was torn between resentment and resignation, then tugged his department baseball cap off and ran a hand through his sandy hair. Emotion didn't often show on Kimble's face, but tonight the weariness had leaked through.

"One of the cats got out," he said.

"There's a *tiger* loose out there?"

"Cougar," Kimble said, and sighed. He accepted the beer that was dropped on the table, then lifted the cold glass to his forehead as if it were a scalding summer day and not a December night. "The black one."

"You're kidding me."

"I look like I'm laughing? Frigging thing jumped right over a fourteen-foot fence, with one of my deputies watching."

"I remember when they caught that cat," Roy said. "I'd written probably ten stories over the years about black panther sightings around here, and ignored maybe a hundred more tips. Then word got out that they'd caught one, and I didn't believe it, but I went out to check. Ended up putting the picture of it front page and above the fold. Wire services ran it all over the country. Made CNN and even the BBC."

"Good as you are at this sort of game, Mr. Darmus," Kimble said, "I've played a few of them myself, and I haven't forgotten that I'm not here to give *you* information. It's the other way around. Tell me — what did you find in that lighthouse?"

"Nothing but the names on the maps."

"And you checked them out?"

Roy gave a hesitant nod. "In the newspaper's morgue, yeah."

"What did you find?"

"All accident victims. Is there some connection? Surely is. They all died close to Blade Ridge. But it's too haphazard to make any sense. Fourteen people have died in the general area. Some on the road, some in the woods, some in the river. If that had happened last year, okay, it's indicative of a problem. Or even in the last decade. But it ranges from David Clark's fall off the trestle to people being killed by their horses in 1927. Fourteen deaths sounds like a lot until you spread it out over eighty or ninety years."

"Why was he using maps? Any ideas?"

"I would have to see them again to be sure, but my suspicion is that he was charting the locations of the deaths."

Kimble nodded. "You said you wanted to see the place in the dark. Why?"

"Everyone who died out there died in the dark."

"At night?"

"That's right."

Kimble frowned. "It's a spooky place at night, I'll admit that.

Shit, my best deputy is gun-shy about it. Now, maybe that's the cougar, I don't know." Kimble took a drink of his beer, seeming not to enjoy the taste, and said, "What did Wyatt tell you about me and Jacqueline Mathis?"

Now came the real reason for this meeting. Kimble's anger at the mention of her name in the lighthouse ran deep. Interesting.

"Not much," Roy said, "and that's the truth. He started out by raving about what the mountains could tell me if they could talk. Then he made the remark about my folks. Now, a lot of years have passed, but still..."

"It upset you."

"Of course it did. When he started complimenting the bravery of their decision, and how hard it must have been, with the child at home, I was getting a little hot under the collar, yes. He hung up before I could really get going on that, though. Now as for *you*? All he said about you was that he hoped we'd work together on telling the story."

"What story?"

"His, I suppose. The one the mountain could tell if it could talk? Hell, I don't know. But he said he was counting on the two of us, and then he told me that you make drives up to see Jacqueline Mathis."

Kimble tried to hide the bristle with another swallow of beer. It didn't work; his eyes had gone cold and angry. Roy said, "Why did that matter to him? Any idea?"

"I don't even understand how he knew about it," Kimble said. "It's nobody's damn business. I go up there because...because there's nobody else who will. She's alone, Mr. Darmus. And yes, she shot me, but it was because of that bastard husband and a lot of confusion. If that prick hadn't been beating her up, there would never have been a gun in her hands, and when I came in she was still in shock and he was still breathing and it was..."

"What?" Roy said.

"It was pitch black," Kimble said thoughtfully. "There'd been a bad storm that night. Power was out all over the county. I remember that when I pulled into the driveway I could still hear thunder on the other side of the mountains."

"Maybe that's why Wyatt latched on to her story, then," Roy said. "The man had one hell of an interest in darkness. Does it make sense? Of course not. Does a lighthouse in the woods make sense, though?"

Kimble gave a nod of acknowledgment, and then seemed to hesitate. He finally said, "Listen, Mr. Darmus—"

"Would you please call me Roy? Or better yet, just Darmus? I've worked around police for forty years, and when I start hearing politeness come out of their mouths, I know I'm getting old."

Kimble smiled. "All right, Darmus. You muckraking son of a bitch."

Roy laughed. "There you go, there you go."

Kimble turned serious again and said, "I wanted to apologize for the way I ran you out of there yesterday. My temper got away from me."

"Not a problem," Roy said. "You know what's funny, though? Both of our tempers got away from us that day. Why? Because Wyatt French knew just what buttons to push. Telling me that my parents made a brave *decision* on the day they died in an accident, that was a sharp call. Cruel, maybe, but sharp. It got a reaction. And then he poked you pretty good with Jacqueline Mathis."

"He sure did. Wonder why?"

"Well, he seemed to want our attention. He got it, didn't he? We're sitting down together now, talking about him and the artifacts he left behind, instead of just moving on through the night minding our own affairs."

After a long pause, Kimble picked up the folder he'd brought in with him and slid it over the table.

"Speaking of the artifacts he left behind — these are copies of the photographs he had on the walls."

Roy opened the folder, saw the browning images, most featuring lanky men with harsh expressions and tools in their hands. With a few exceptions, they all seemed to be from the distant past, and from a specific group of men. Laborers on some unknown project.

"Why does he have so many labeled *NO?*" Roy asked.

"I haven't the faintest idea. Most of them are that way, but there are ten with names. I've made the list there."

"I see it." Roy was scanning the names.

"Any chance you could help me figure out who they were, exactly? I know what three of them did. I don't need any more information on O'Patrick, Estes, or . . . Mathis."

Roy looked up and met his eyes. "All right. I'll see what I can do. What did you find on O'Patrick and Estes?"

"No connection to Blade Ridge."

There was more there. Roy frowned and said, "Come on, Kimble."

Kimble sighed. "They both killed people. In different ways, in different decades, in different places. I don't know how in the hell Wyatt discovered them, or why he kept their pictures, but that's the story."

"And Jacqueline," Roy said. "So of the ten here, you already know that three were murderers."

"That's right."

"If these other seven prove to —"

"If they prove to be, I won't be surprised. Murder seemed to fascinate Wyatt. I'm trying to understand why. You can help me by telling me about them."

"Why do you care, Kimble? It was a suicide."

Kimble drained the rest of his beer.

"Wasn't it?" Roy said, the first time any other possibility had crossed through his mind. He'd seen the corpse, had seen the gun in the dead man's lap. But guns could be placed in a way to suggest suicide. Kimble would be well aware of the forensic response to the scene by now, and maybe there was something in it that Roy hadn't anticipated.

"He did a lot of talking about how I would investigate this," Kimble said slowly. "When he called me that morning, he kept talking about the differences between suicide and homicide. Made the outright suggestion that someone could be compelled to kill himself by another, and then it shouldn't be considered a suicide at all."

Roy was astonished. He said, "You think somebody else is involved in this?"

"I have no idea. But it's my job to find out. And listen—you had an inordinate amount of time alone at that scene before I reached you. Would have been shorter, but Shipley flipped his cruiser."

Roy held up his hands, palms out. "I didn't tamper."

Kimble gave him a measured stare, then said, "You'd understand why I might be skeptical of that, considering the stunt you pulled with the notepad."

"I was walking around that crazy place and saw the names of my own *parents* written on one of those maps. Forgive me for a bit of curiosity."

"I understand curiosity. I also understand that I gave you a direct order, asked you to turn over the notes you'd taken, and you gave me a handful of blank pages, then chose that time to mention Jacqueline and take my mind away. Not a bad play on your part, and it's my fault for falling for it, but if you came across other things of interest in that place, I need to know."

"All I left with was the names."

"You didn't find any cameras?"

"Cameras?"

"That's right."

"No, I did not."

"A question of timing that I need answered: when you busted the bulb, that tripped the breakers and knocked out the power, right?"

"Yeah. I flipped the breakers back so I could see my way around to stop the bleeding." He held up his bandaged hand.

"All right. How long was the power out?"

"Hell, I don't know. Ten minutes? I'm not certain."

"You heard the sirens, then heard the wreck. That's what you told me yesterday. Correct?"

"Correct. I was going to go down to check it out, but your dispatcher was emphatic that I remain where I was."

Kimble mulled on that, staring at the wood paneling above Roy's head, and then refocused his gaze and said, "So when the wreck took place, when you heard the sounds of it, was *any* light on?"

It was a puzzling question. Roy thought about it, wanting to be sure he had it right, and then shook his head.

"Power was out. I went back in after I heard the accident. Found the electrical panel, flipped the breakers."

Kimble was silent. Roy tilted his head and said, "Why does *that* matter?"

"Maybe it doesn't. My deputy, though…he isn't the sort who'd just shoot off a road and into the trees."

"I thought the same of my father. It happens."

"Quite often, out there."

Roy waved a hand at the waitress, signaling for another beer. Kimble shook her off, his empty bottle already pushed to the side.

"Shipley — that's the deputy who was in the wreck, the one

who was there with me today—swears he saw a man in the road. Then some kind of blue light. You never left the lighthouse after you called in the body?"

"No."

"What about the light? He had a spotlight in there, too. You use that, thinking it was a flashlight, maybe?"

"No. I didn't see any spotlight. All I did was flip the breakers back on so I could see my way around the downstairs. I made sure not to touch the switch that fed the main light, either."

Kimble nodded, then tapped the folder between them. "Let me know what you get. You'll have better luck than me. All that local history, it's your bailiwick."

"Hell, it seems somebody read my column."

"Everyone makes mistakes."

Roy grinned. "So I get to help an investigation, eh?"

"You get to look up some history, that's all. You can probably find that sort of information a lot faster than I can."

"Reassuring news to the locals who rely on your protection, I'm sure. I'll do what I can. Though I don't know what the gain could be."

"Let me worry about the gain. And keep it quiet, okay? Otherwise I might be inspired to remember your behavior at the crime scene in a different light."

"The threats begin. Didn't your mother ever teach you that you catch more flies with honey?"

"My mother liked cop shows," Kimble said, and then he slid out of the booth and walked away. When he pushed open the door Roy could see the dark night beyond, and the twinkling Christmas lights strung from the courthouse and out to the light poles across the street, a cheerful white glow against the blackness. Then the door swung shut, and he was gone.

Roy looked down at the folder Kimble had left, opened it, and stared at the century-old pictures, marred by the single scrawled word.

No.

No.

No.

It seemed as if Wyatt French had been looking for someone.

17

THE DECEMBER NIGHT WAS cloudless and cold, the rain replaced by a steady, biting wind, but Kimble ignored his car and walked from the tavern back to the sheriff's department, breathing deeply of the frigid air, hoping it would clear his head.

It didn't.

There were too many questions. There was also the cause of death, as reported by the coroner: suicide. Case closed.

So let it go, he told himself. *Get back to work on things that can help the living.*

But he wanted to know about Jacqueline. How French had known her, and why she mattered to him. It would be hard for him to move forward with that question unanswered, and Wyatt was long past his question-answering days. Jacqueline Mathis, however, was not.

He took up the phone, dialed the Kentucky state women's prison, identified himself, and asked for a check on Jacqueline's visitation logs. Had she ever been visited by a Wyatt French?

It took a few keystrokes before the voice on the other end of the line had an answer.

"Yes, sir. He came by in late October."

"This October?"

"Affirmative. October thirtieth."

Six weeks before he put the gun barrel in his mouth.

"Any other visits?" Kimble asked.

"Negative. He was a one-shot guest. Don't see too many of those except for lawyers or journalists."

"He was neither," Kimble said, and then he thanked the man and hung up the phone feeling far worse than he had before. What had taken an elderly, suicidal alcoholic to visit Jacqueline Mathis? And what had they discussed?

Wyatt French couldn't tell him anymore. Jacqueline still could.

It was just past two in the morning when the cougar screamed.

Wesley slept with his bedroom window cracked, even on the harshest nights of winter, so he could hear what was happening with the cats. He knew any species by sound, but guessing the individual cat was next to impossible. Then it came again, a keening pitch he'd heard before but only in the mountains of the West, where such cats roamed wild and always had, and he knew the precise animal.

Ira.

Wesley swung out of the bed and onto his feet, reaching for the flashlight and rifle that he had placed at hand before going to sleep tonight. With Ira loose, it seemed prudent. He'd never use the gun unless he had no other alternative, but the black cat was the kind that could put you in that situation swiftly.

By the time he reached the door the other cats were into the fray, roars echoing through the woods. Ira had sounded the first alarm, but now the rest had joined the chorus.

He came back after all, Wesley thought, amazed. *Maybe he actually went into that trap.*

He came out of the trailer barefoot, wearing nothing but the old gym shorts he'd slept in. The gravel bit into his feet but he ran ahead anyhow, ran in the direction of the trap he'd constructed for the cougar, out near the overgrown tracks that ran through the woods south of the preserve. The cat was still screaming, and Wesley didn't like that. There should be no way it could have gotten injured in the trap, but it was screaming all the same, and—

The gunshot brought him to a stunned halt.

A rifle had just been fired. There was no mistaking it.

Shooting at the cats, he thought, and there was wild, black rage in him. *If someone is shooting at my cats, I will kill him, and I won't need a gun to do it.*

Another shot, closer, and for the first time Wesley recognized the possibility that *he* was the target. The bullet had passed close, just over his left shoulder. He turned the flashlight off, and as the world returned to darkness there was the crack of yet another gunshot and the anguished bellow of one of the tigers just behind him.

A hit. The son of a bitch had hit one of the cats.

Wesley got back to his feet, screaming, and ran toward the tree line. He got past the occupied cages and opened fire blindly into the woods. He knew that there were no cats in his line, and that was his only concern. There were only three cartridges in the huge Remington Model 798 that he held, and he put all three of them into the trees. When the last shot had been fired, he could hear the sound of someone running through the woods, crashing through the timber. Wesley could not pursue, though— a cat had been shot.

He found the flashlight where he'd dropped it in the gravel and turned it back on and searched the darkness for the wounded animal.

It was Kino. The tiger was trying to fight through the fence, trying to escape this place of rescue that had suddenly turned dangerous on him. In the pale white glow of the flashlight beam Wesley could see a wound bubbling with blood. The tiger's left shoulder was broken, so he could not stand without keeping his right foreleg on the ground, which left him attempting to chew through the fence instead of using his paws.

"Kino, buddy, relax," Wesley said. His voice was shaking. "You got to relax, buddy, I can fix this, I can fix this."

But could he? The bullet had penetrated deeply. That the tiger was still up at all was astonishing.

"We'll fix this," Wesley said again, and then he set the empty rifle down beside the fence and ran back to the trailer, his bare feet leaving streaks of blood on the gravel.

Inside the trailer, he fumbled a ketamine-filled syringe onto one of the six-foot poles they used to tranquilize the cats. Tranquilizing a wounded animal could be deadly, but he'd have to do it to have any hope of stopping the bleeding and addressing the wound. If he could get the bleeding stopped, he could call for a veterinarian — there was one in Whitman who helped them regularly — and maybe Kino could be saved.

He considered making the call now, getting the vet on his way, but decided that the loss of time was too dangerous. The first priority had to be getting the cat down and the bleeding stopped.

They had a dart rifle but he trusted the pole syringes more, particularly in the dark, and the cat was close to the fence. He'd be able to reach him.

Back outside he ran, the pole in one hand and the flashlight in the other. All around cats were roaring or growling or hissing. Somewhere out there in the darkness, Ira was loose.

Who would have done this? Wesley thought. *What sick, evil son of a whore would have done this?*

When he reached Kino's cage, he saw with dismay that the

cat had returned to the center of his enclosure. He was still trying to stand. Each time he tried the left leg collapsed and he dropped drunkenly into the dirt.

Wesley looked at the pole in his hand and back at the cat inside, now far from the fence. He'd have to go in. It was that or return for the dart rifle, but that would waste more time and—

Kino tried to rise again, and this time he let out an agonized cry, and that made Wesley's decision. There was no time. He opened the combination lock on the gate—every lock in the facility had the same combination, set to Audrey and David's wedding anniversary date—and removed the chain. Kino, thankfully, was so antisocial that he had his own enclosure, leaving no other cats to deal with.

"Easy, buddy," he called, and then he removed the cap from the syringe, opened the gate, and stepped inside, his breath fogging in the cold night air.

The tiger roared. Tried to roar. The powerful sound died into a rasp and blood ran out of his mouth and onto his muzzle. Wesley Harrington, more than four decades devoted to these beautiful cats, felt the black rage again.

I will find whoever did this and tear his heart from his chest, kill him with my hands...

"Easy, Kino," he murmured. "Easy."

He was close now, about five feet away. Within range of the pole, but it would be a stretch, and he didn't want to be off-balance. Another step, then. Two more. He needed to get this in where it would count, and he knew this cat and the cat knew him and there would be no problem with this, no problem at—

He'd just pressed the syringe to Kino's rib cage when the tiger lunged. It was difficult for the cat—obscenely difficult, considering that Wesley had carefully approached from his left side, his wounded side, knowing that if the tiger did make aggressive movements, it would be harder for him to go left than right.

It was hard. His left foreleg twisted uselessly, shattered bone rolling in the shoulder socket, fresh blood pouring free, as he pushed off the ground entirely with his hind legs. For one second they were facing each other, the tiger's lips peeled back to expose massive, bloodstained teeth and enraged eyes that glittered in the flashlight glow. Wesley saw the right paw rising, saw it coming, and even in the second before it hit him he was more dazzled than terrified. What an incredible show of power. This cat was dying, but he had risen up one last time, risen bold and brave and —

The impact caught him in the chest and threw him back toward the fence. The pole syringe and flashlight fell from his hands and he felt searing warmth and then he was down on his back and the dark trees wove overhead in the endless breeze, tendrils of fog drifting through the fences and out into the woods.

It had not been a full-strength blow. Far from it. A tiger did not need to use full strength, or even half strength, to kill a man.

Wesley got his chin onto his chest and looked down and saw the source of the terrible warmth that engulfed him. Kino had torn him open. In one swift strike, the cat had laid Wesley open from midchest to abdomen. The blood pulsed and pooled around him and he was glad that it was dark and he couldn't see the wound any better.

Should've used the gun, he thought stupidly. *Not even the dart gun — the real one. Should've just ended his misery. Because that cat is dying, and he is scared, and he knows that it was a human that did it.*

Kino was up again, moving again. Coming toward Wesley. He let out a bellow, and Wesley, who knew more about cats than he did about people, understood. The cat was not coming to finish the job. The cat was sorry.

"I know," Wesley said, or tried to say, but his tongue was

leaden in his mouth and his jaw seemed locked. "Not you, Kino. Not your fault. You were scared. We were both scared."

The cat's noise had changed, shifting from the roars of agony and fear to the softer chuffing, the sound of friendship, of love, and Wesley could see that Kino was trying to reach him. Not to strike again, not to do harm. The tiger didn't want to kill him, never had. It was scared, that was all, and an animal of such tremendous size and strength could kill quite accidentally when it was scared.

Kino fell again. The white on his muzzle was stained dark with blood. He tried to stand and couldn't. Wesley said, "Not your fault, Kino. Not your fault."

Still the cat tried to rise. Wesley dug his fingers into the grass and the dirt and dragged himself. Parts of him seemed to be trailing behind, but he did not look back. The tiger had gotten so close; all Wesley had to do was close the gap.

He reached him and got his hand up, laid it on the side of the cat's massive head. The tiger chuffed again, softer, and nuzzled against the hand. Wesley tried to scratch his ears, but it was hard to make his fingers work.

The tiger turned from him then, faced the woods, and growled. Wesley looked in the same direction, and that was when he saw the blue light. It flickered through the darkness, a thin blue flame that seemed to move on its own, a dancing orb in the black night.

"Who's there?" Wesley tried to call, but he didn't have much voice anymore.

The blue light came on toward him, and Kino growled again, and now he had support, every cat in the preserve joining the chorus, standing at attention. Across from Kino's cage, illuminated in the moonlight, Wesley could see that two of the white tigers were on their hind legs, forepaws resting against the fence, snarling into the night. The blue light retreated, flickering in and out of the trees.

That's him, Wesley thought. *That's the bastard who did this. If I had the rifle right now I could get him. I could hit him from here, so long as he kept holding that light.*

But the rifle was outside the cage, and Wesley wasn't going anywhere. The man with the light wasn't coming on, though, and after a time Wesley realized that he was scared of the cats.

Kino seemed to know it, too, and though he growled again, he lowered his head, dropped his chin onto Wesley's thigh. His large eyes regarded Wesley sorrowfully.

"Not your fault, Kino," Wesley said. "He did it to me, not you. It was his fault. I'm so sorry. I'm so sorry."

The cat's head lolled down onto the ground but his eyes were still open, his breath coming in anguished gasps.

"I'll be fine," Wesley told him. "Don't you worry about me. I'll be fine."

Take him first, he prayed silently, *take this cat first, because he will understand when I am gone, and I do not want him to know that he killed me, because that will hurt him. So take him first, and Lord, take him soon.*

"You're a good cat," he said from deep in his throat, his lips thick, impossible to move. "You're a good boy."

Then he couldn't even try to talk anymore, and they lay there together in the dirt, Wesley keeping his hand against the tiger's fur and leaning his head against the same deadly paw that had struck him in the darkness. Out in the woods, the blue light continued to glow, but it came no closer. The wind blew cold and constant, but Wesley was warm there in his own blood and against the tiger's fur. He was warm enough.

Kino died first. Wesley Harrington's final thoughts were of thanks.

18

KIMBLE HAD BEEN POLICING IN Sawyer County for twenty-one years now, and in that time he thought he'd seen about every manner of death. Homicides, suicides, car wrecks, electrocutions, fires — you name it, he'd seen it.

Except for a man killed by a tiger.

Somehow, he blamed Wyatt French. He'd been on the highway for ten minutes, headed for the women's prison, when the call came. There was an uneasy moment when the ring of the phone inside the darkened car as the countryside slid soundlessly past created a sense of déjà vu so strong he was certain that he'd look down and find the call was coming from Wyatt again.

Instead, it was his dispatcher, but as she detailed the scene and its location it felt as if it had all developed at Wyatt's hand anyhow. Kimble found out that two deputies were already en route. Pete Wolverton, a veteran, always a good man in a messy situation, and Nathan Shipley, who'd been close to the preserve already, making his own morning drive to go back out and see if they'd had any luck trapping the black cat. Apparently they had not.

Kimble said that he'd be there as soon as he could, and then he turned around and put on his lights and drove back toward the mountains.

You can put another one on the board, Kimble thought. *One more dead man at Blade Ridge, Wyatt. I'll add him to your maps.*

The glass at the top of the lighthouse glittered in early-morning sun when he arrived. The wind was still and there were birds singing in the trees and one ambitious woodpecker at work somewhere up the hill. Cold, with that December chill, but beautiful. It seemed like a spot where you'd want to stop and spend some time, right up until you noticed the crime-scene tape.

When Kimble arrived, he learned that he'd beaten Audrey Clark to the scene, and he was glad of that. The fewer civilians around, the better, for his first look, and right now he had only one: the kid who'd discovered the body. His name was Dustin Hall, and though he said he was twenty-four, he looked about fourteen. With thick dark hair that needed a cut and glasses with bent frames, he had the appearance of someone likely to need rescue from the inside of a gym locker. The kid was still worked up, crying and blubbering, and though Pete Wolverton was hardly known for his soothing qualities, Kimble asked him to calm the witness down so he could look over the death scene without distraction.

"I'll show it to you, chief," Nathan Shipley said. They'd just gone far enough to fall out of earshot of Wolverton and Hall when Shipley looked at Kimble and added, under his breath, "Do you believe this? I was worried about the one who got out. Harrington was killed by one who stayed *in,* though."

"I wish I'd posted someone out here last night," Kimble said. "I should have."

Shipley fell silent then, probably remembering the way he'd turned down Kimble's request.

"There's something wrong with this place," he said. "I really think that—"

"Just show me the scene, Shipley."

The way Shipley told it, the kid, Dustin Hall, had arrived for the morning feedings, found himself alone on the property, and gone in search of Harrington, who was always up and at work by the time Hall arrived. He first checked the trailer, found it empty but with the door open, and then ventured into the preserve. He found Harrington inside one of the cages, torn damn near in half, with a dead tiger at his side.

It was an ugly scene. The first thing Kimble thought of was a corpse from a pit-bull killing many years ago. That dog had to put in some time and effort to finish the job. The tiger, it appeared, had needed one swipe.

He went into the cage and crouched down and looked at both bodies. The tiger had been shot just behind the shoulder. There was a high-caliber rifle in the dead man's hand, his stiff fingers still on the trigger guard.

"That thing on the pole, it's a syringe," Shipley was saying. "Looks like he was trying to drug the cat when he came in, but he had the rifle with him just in case, you know?"

Kimble didn't say anything, his eyes following the blood trail back from the dead man. It seemed he'd dragged himself about ten feet after suffering the wound. Toward the cat instead of toward the gate. That was damned curious. Why would he have tried to close the gap?

"Tell you something, these damned cats are killing machines," Shipley said. "When we were out here last night, I thought, *Someone is going to get hurt.* That's just what I thought. And then this poor bastard gets killed. I don't understand why anyone is allowed to have animals like this outside a zoo. It's a dangerous place, and that's not even counting the —"

"Shipley?" Kimble said. "Shut up for a minute, all right? Just shut up."

He was looking at the dead man's eyes as if they might tell

him something. It was odd, the way the victim had fallen. Curled up against the cat, almost, but there was no way the killing wound could have been inflicted from that angle. So had the cat tried to come over and finish the job and then fallen dead almost exactly as he reached the man? It didn't make sense. Unless the poor son of a bitch had been coming *toward* the cat in the end.

"I'm guessing Mr. Harrington didn't have any luck with the missing cougar before he found his way here," Kimble said.

"No. It appears he set up a trap out by the old railroad tracks, but it hasn't been touched. That's not good, because this guy was the only person who was able to get him in a cage to begin with."

"No," Kimble said, looking back down at the body. "Not good."

Audrey was usually at the preserve no later than eight, but today she'd been delayed by a call from her sister, who'd awoken at three in the morning from a terrible nightmare, one that was hard to recall in detail but somehow left the overwhelming sense that it was time for Audrey to give up the preserve.

This wasn't a new sentiment, but it was a new delivery, and one that incensed Audrey. Her older sister had been campaigning for her to abandon the rescue center from nearly the moment the minister had finished David's eulogy. While Audrey understood and appreciated her concern, she didn't need any hysterical talk of prophetic nightmares. Not now, not the way things had been going the past few days. It was too much, and she told Ellen that in no uncertain terms. She was committed to the preserve, and if Ellen would shut the hell up about it and support her instead of arguing with her, it would be great.

Afterward, standing in the shower trying to purge the argument with hot water and deep breaths, she felt bad in the way you could only when you understood the place someone was coming from. Ellen had always had a bossy streak, yes, but being in charge wasn't the issue here. Loving her sister was. Audrey leaned her head against the cool tile of the shower as the room filled with steam and thought of her family, all of them living their practical, ordered lives in Louisville while their once most practical and ordered member, Audrey, drove to the middle of nowhere each morning to feed chunks of bloody meat to cats with paws the size of her head.

Maybe they were entitled to their concern.

She stepped out of the shower and wrapped a towel around her body, which was so thin, too thin. For a time after David's death she'd been able to con herself into the idea that losing a few pounds was never a bad thing. No creature alive was more predisposed to fall for that con than a woman, after all. It was when five pounds turned to fifteen and then to twenty that she knew it needed to be dealt with. She'd used fatigue as an excuse for a lack of appetite, but fatigue didn't keep you from avoiding the dinner table. Memories of sharing that table with your late husband did.

She'd been doing better lately, though. Five pounds back in the last month. All you needed to know about appetite you could learn from a lion.

She was thinking that, and smiling, when the phone rang again. She almost ignored it, certain that it would be Ellen again, perhaps calling to apologize, perhaps not. Then she gave in just enough to check the caller ID and saw that it wasn't Ellen but Dustin Hall.

She picked up, and thirty seconds later, that snapping dismissal of her sister's nightmare seemed a dangerous thing.

Wesley Harrington was dead.

Wes had been killed by one of the cats.

She made the drive to the preserve in a horrible déjà vu daze.

Back to Blade Ridge Road, back to a place where a good man lay dead in his own blood.

The police were there when she arrived. Two cars, an ambulance, and somebody's pickup truck. She asked to see Wesley, demanded it, but they said nobody but police and his family could see him.

"I *am* his family!"

It wasn't true, though. The cats were his family.

There were three deputies standing around watching her, and two of them were the pair who'd been on hand yesterday. Kimble and Shipley. Shipley, who'd been so nervous around the cats, who'd worried about being out in the woods when the sun went down, seemed calmer today, his blue eyes meeting her gaze without difficulty. The new one was a balding guy with sharp eyes who looked as if he wanted to arrest everyone now and sort it out later. Or not. He introduced himself as Pete Wolverton.

"What happened?" she said. "What happened?"

"One of the cats got him."

"Ira," she said.

"Is Ira the name of a tiger?" Wolverton asked.

She blinked, refocused. "No. Wait, what? He was killed by a tiger?"

"It was Kino," Dustin called, face pale, eyes ringed by dark, puffy bags. "It was Kino, Audrey."

"He went in the cage with Kino in the middle of the night?" she said.

Kimble stepped forward then, took her gently by the arm, and guided her from the others. They walked along until they came to Jafar's cage. The leopard rose at the sight of her and jogged over, just as he always did. Waited with his face close to the fence, wanting her to reach in and scratch his ears, just as *she* always did. This time she hesitated.

"Seems like something happened in the middle of the night," Kimble was saying in a gentle voice. "He went into the cage with a syringe."

Jafar growled, and Kimble pivoted away from the cage and moved his hand toward his gun.

"He just wants attention," Audrey said, and then she reached in and scratched Jafar's head, the big cat preening, delighted. Kimble watched apprehensively, and she had a feeling he was thinking about what he'd just seen in Kino's cage. She was imagining it herself.

"He went in the cage barefoot," Kimble said. "Seems to imply there was some sort of chaos or problem."

Audrey slipped her hand back through the fencing, remembering the way Wes had talked about the place being different at night, remembering the way she'd chastised him for his dire warnings. She leaned against the fence, feeling sick, and Jafar reached up and braced his front legs on the fence so that he was standing with his head close to hers. He licked her ear.

"He was *barefoot?*" Audrey said. Wes always had his boots on. She would have sworn he slept in boots.

"Yes. And he entered the cage with a rifle and some sort of a pole with a needle on it. A syringe."

Something had gone wrong. The cat had been sick, or injured. That would have explained the rush into the night. If something had been wrong with Kino, that would explain everything.

"Was the tiger hurt?"

"Beyond the gunshot wound?"

She closed her eyes, and he said, "Sorry. I know they're very important to you. Beyond the gunshot wound, I see no sign of injury. Now, I'm not a vet. Obviously, the syringe suggests *something* was wrong with the cat. What it was, I can't say. There's no obvious injury, though. Could he have wanted to sedate the animal just from a behavioral standpoint?"

"Behavioral?" Audrey felt Jafar's rough tongue on her neck, then opened her eyes and moved away from the fence.

"Yeah. If it was, you know, acting up. Really going wild, for whatever reason. Might he have tried to sedate it then?"

"Wes *hated* to sedate cats except under extraordinary circumstances."

"Well," Kimble said, "it seems there must have been something extraordinary going on last night. I've got to warn you, Mrs. Clark — I think you're likely to have some trouble over this."

"Trouble?"

His face was grave, but he nodded. "It's an accidental death. We'll be clear on that. I'm in charge of the report, and I *promise* you that we will be clear on that. But you have to take the long view — you've got a man dead on this property, killed by one of your cats, and you've got another cat missing. People are going to react to that situation. You're going to need to be ready."

She stared at him, hearing the words and processing them but unable to attach any real meaning. All she could think of was Wes, running barefoot into the night with a rifle and a pole syringe. What had gone wrong?

"When I say be ready," Kimble continued, "I mean not just for the public reaction, but for a lot of tough questions. One of the toughest: will you be able to deal with the missing cougar?"

"That will be a tough question," she agreed, her voice numb and distant. Kimble looked at her and shook his head, unhappy.

"Is there someone you can go to for help? Do you know anyone who specializes in this sort of animal?"

"Yes," she said. "Wesley Harrington."

Kimble didn't say anything. She looked away from him and up at the mountains and felt her mouth go dry and chalky. She tried to remember the trick she'd devised for herself to get through the hardest days: imagining her emotions being carefully folded and placed into a tight box and tucked away in some never-opened closet, the way she'd handled all of David's clothes after the funeral.

Strength, she told herself, *you've got to show strength. Go out and find that damn cat, bring him back, and then you can grieve for Wes. Grieve for Kino. Grieve for David again, hell, grieve for yourself. You're entitled to that. But first you have to find that cat.*

"Mrs. Clark?" Kimble said. "Is there anyone who can help? Anyone who knows about these cats?"

She looked him straight in the eye. "That would be me."

Kimble regarded her with no quality of judgment. "Can you find him?"

No, she thought. She was picturing the sleek black cat, so silent, so strange. No, they could not find Ira. That was even more implausible, somehow, than the idea that Wesley had been killed by Kino.

"We'll have to," she said.

19

Roy was lost in thought when he approached the employee entrance of the *Sentinel* that morning. A harsh electronic buzz finally shattered those distractions and brought him into the moment. He had just waved his keycard in front of the receiver. No green light, no soft chime of acceptance. Instead, the loud buzz and a flashing red light.

He passed the card over the receiver a second time, even though he knew.

Rex Schaub had deactivated his keycard. Shut him down. The *Sentinel* office doors would not open for him again.

He stepped back and stared up at the silent limestone building, his home for so many years, and then, as if he simply could not understand, he reached out and tried again, and again.

Red light.

Red light.

He could hear banging near the other side of the building, and after circling around, he saw that the loading dock doors were up. The crew was hauling out office furniture and piling it inside a pair of large panel vans that had been backed up to the docks. Rex Schaub was supervising, but Roy didn't recognize anyone else. Those who were gutting his home were nameless, faceless sorts. Roy hated them on principle, but he appreciated this much: they'd left the loading dock open. He waited until they deposited a load in the truck and returned to the building, and then he followed, slipping into the pressroom, the massive machinery taking shape from shadows. He had no idea what a press like this was worth. It had been a big deal when they'd added it because the thing could print color pages on the inside, a first in the *Sentinel*'s history. Was there even a market for such equipment, or did it go to scrap now?

Your entire life, headed for scrap, Roy thought. *Not even the dusty pages remain for you — you'll never make it that far. The day of the dusty pages is done.*

He stopped at the door to the morgue, realizing that this might be it for him. The last time in the building, the last perusal of all those pages of newsprint. Thanks to Kimble — and Wyatt — he had one last assignment, one last Sawyer County story to tell. But when he left the newspaper today... well, that might be it. The clean-out crew would work its way down to the morgue eventually. The building would soon enough be a hollowed-out corpse, and then the property would be sold, the structure torn down or converted into something else, and all that would remain of the *Sawyer County Sentinel* was the impact of the stories it had told.

He sat down with his notebook, where he'd written the names from Wyatt's photographs in a column. He'd start with those, the known quantities being far easier to trace, and then deal with the mysterious old photographs, trying to put names where Wyatt had put only *NO*. That would not be an easy task.

Kimble had told him the names were likely to belong to murderers, which meant they were likely to be in the old index — murder in Sawyer County generally qualified as big news.

Tracing some of the older cases back might be tricky, but the more recent ones should move quickly enough. He didn't need to know any more about Jacqueline Mathis, and Kimble had already found out the significance of Ryan O'Patrick and Adam Estes.

Roy frowned as he looked at the list. Estes. That name snagged on something in his brain, troubled him for no reason that he could articulate.

Adam Estes. Where had he just seen that? It was down here, in the morgue. He was sure of that. But the only reading he'd done here was confirming Wyatt's list of accident victims.

"The drowned girl," he said. That's where he'd seen it. While reading about a red-ink name, Jenna Jerden. In 1975, Jerden had drowned in a canoeing accident in the Marshall River, trying to clear the swift eddies around the trestle in the dark. She hadn't been alone. Her boyfriend had survived. Adam Estes.

He found the right volume, tracked down the story, and there it was. While Jerden had drowned among the rocks and dark water, her boyfriend had made it to shore, then gone for help. It was a long run to the nearest phone from Blade Ridge in 1975, though, and the help that finally came arrived far too late. The *Sentinel* commended the man on his futile efforts, while including a police quote that reprimanded the couple for attempting to canoe the unfamiliar and often dangerous river in the dark. The survivor was Adam Estes, thirty-three, of Whitman.

In 1975, Adam Estes had survived an accident at Blade Ridge that claimed another life.

In 1976, he'd killed a man.

"They can't all be like that," Roy said. There was no way.

It was noon by the time Kimble left the cat preserve. The scene had been processed, the body removed, the photographs taken.

When he spoke to the coroner, the man said, "Damned unlucky spot these past few days, isn't it?"

It sure was, Kimble agreed. It sure was.

He then said that in addition to the confirmed cause of death for Wesley Harrington, he would need an examination conducted on the tiger.

The coroner said "You want us to do *what?*"

Kimble explained it again, patiently. It didn't appear that the bullet had come out of the cat. There was an entry wound but no exit wound, as if the shoulder bone had stopped it. He wanted the bullet.

Just due diligence, he said.

But he was thinking about more than due diligence. He was thinking about the size of the entry wound and about the range from which Wesley Harrington would have fired his high-caliber rifle. They did not match his expectation. Kimble found it patently obvious who had killed the man — the tiger. But he wasn't so sure about who had killed the tiger.

He didn't like the situation at the cat preserve at all, and when he left Shipley and Wolverton at the scene, he had private instructions for them that went beyond what he'd told Audrey Clark their purpose was, hunting for the missing cougar. While they were searching for signs of the cat, he also wanted them searching for signs of a human. Particularly, he said, shell casings.

"You think someone else shot that cat?" Shipley said. "The rifle was in that man's hand. The brass was right there inside the gate."

"I know it was. And when the coroner gives me the bullet and we find out that it came from his gun, we can close the case. *Until* we have that confirmation, though? It's an active investigation, Shipley. Treat it like one."

He left them then, resumed the drive he'd been trying to make seven hours earlier, and now there was even more on his mind than there had been then, and all of it was bad, and all of it went back to Blade Ridge.

It was the first time Kimble had ever visited her in the afternoon, but Jacqueline Mathis showed no trace of surprise.

"We've got to stop bumping into each other like this," she said, smiling. The line seemed to hurt her, though, and he understood. It was what she'd said one Friday morning at the Bakehouse, when it had become far too clear that their accidental encounters were anything but accidental. What she'd said on a bright spring morning when she was a free woman, living in a beautiful old farmhouse with a view of the mountains, young and gorgeous and far from any idea of prison.

"I'm not visiting," he said. "I'm working."

"Working?"

"That's right. I've got some questions. It worked out that I was coming by, otherwise I'd have just made a phone call, but I figured..."

He let the lies stop there. Kimble tried hard to be as honest as any man born to sin could be, but he'd told his share of lies, enough to know that they were pointless when neither you nor the recipient believed them.

"But I figured I'd rather talk in person," he finished.

"I'm always glad to see you. And the way you left the other day... well, I felt bad about it. It was as if you didn't like the idea that I'm going to get back out."

I'm going to get back out. Yes, she was. He stared at her and felt an ache along his back, down near the scar.

"You said you had questions?" she prompted when the silence had gone on too long and sat too heavy in the room.

"Yeah," he said. "Just a few. I doubt you'll be able to help, but I had to try. I'm working a suicide, trying to find someone to come forward and deal with the dead man's property, and I'm not finding anyone. Your name was written down in his things."

"Who was it?"

"His name was Wyatt French."

She gave it a few seconds. Shook her head.

"I don't know anyone by that name."

Kimble said, "I honestly don't remember you lying to me before."

She closed her eyes and let out a deep breath. "You're playing games with the truth yourself."

"No, I'm not."

"Really? You already know that he came to see me. You didn't want to admit that, though, so you waited to see if I'd tell you. But *I'm* the only liar?"

He thought that over and nodded. "Fine. We're both lying. We haven't done that before, have we? Even in the worst of it, Jacqueline, have you ever lied to me?"

"No."

"Then let's hold that pattern. Yes, I know that Wyatt visited you a couple of months ago. Now he's dead. I'd like to know what you talked about."

She said, "No, you would not."

He frowned. "Jacqueline? What's the story?"

She looked more uncomfortable than he'd ever seen her, more shaken.

"He's dead?"

"That's right. Shot himself in the mouth."

She closed her eyes again.

Kimble leaned forward. "Please, Jacqueline. I want to know why he came to see you. Why he had your picture up in his damned lighthouse. Why he —"

"He had my *picture* up?" Now her eyes were open again.

"That's right. Along with dozens of others. Many of whom . . . many of whom I didn't recognize."

A lie again. No, just a change of the truth he'd been about to tell. At the last instant he'd decided not to tell her that she'd shared wall space with photographs of other killers.

"He killed himself," she said. The words came out slowly, as if she were carefully considering the idea.

"It appears that way, yes."

She shook her head. "Sad."

"Why did he come here, Jacqueline? How did you know him?"

She thought about it, frowning. While she thought, she wet her lips. He watched her tongue glide out, tracing the curve of her lips, and then, when she answered his question, he wanted to tell her not to be in such a hurry. *Think more,* he wanted to say, *let me watch you just a little longer. Let me just sit here and be with you and not have to talk, not have to think, not have to remember how close you came to murdering me. I do not want to think about that. I want to remember you the way you were the first day, when you would never have shot me, and I would certainly have shot him for you.*

But she didn't need to think any longer; she had her answer.

"He wanted to apologize to me."

"For what?"

"For the fact that his lighthouse was not functioning on a night in June of 2005."

Kimble tilted his head back and raised his eyebrows. "You're serious."

"Absolutely."

"Why did he think this mattered to you?"

Another long pause. She reached up and pushed her hair back over her ears, carefully, one elegant hand moving at a time, and then she fastened her blue-eyed gaze on his and said, "I tried to kill myself that night."

Kimble didn't have a response. Couldn't begin to muster one. He sat and stared at her as she watched him with detached sadness.

"I've never told anyone that, Kevin. Not a soul."

June 2005. It would have been around the same time the abuse began, around the time Kimble had first gone out to the house, first met her.

"What happened?" he said.

"There'd been a . . . debate at home," she said. "You remember the kind. I left and went for a drive. There was no destination. It was just a drive, the kind you make when you need to be moving, Kevin, moving *fast*. Ever taken that kind of a drive?"

"Once or twice."

"Then you understand. There's a curve out there, on the county road. It seems like you shouldn't take it, but you have to. Go straight and you're off the pavement and on the dead end. There's a sign, but it was late at night, and I missed it."

"Okay." She'd been on Blade Ridge then, sailing right past Wyatt's lighthouse.

"The road ends in the trees."

"I know the spot."

"Well, I hit the dead end, and I stopped. It was sunset. Not quite dark yet. A very beautiful sunset, in fact. The eastern face of the rocks was all lit up red, and the water had this beautiful shimmer. I could see the lighthouse up there, and it was so surreal. Beautiful but misplaced, you know? I got out of the car to look at it. I was all alone, and the sun was going down, and the insects were coming to life. Cicadas humming all around. There's a bridge out there, an old railroad bridge?"

"The trestle. Yes."

"I could see it through the trees. And I decided to walk out on it. There's a fence that is supposed to guard it, I guess, but that was pretty well torn down. You can slip through it easily enough. I could, at least."

His mouth was very dry, and he wanted to touch her. Wanted to take her hand, pat her arm, something. Instead he folded his own hands together, squeezed them tight.

"I walked out onto the bridge as the sun dipped down and everything gave over to night. It was one of the most beautiful sunsets I've ever seen. The lighthouse was there against the trees and the rocks, but then it got dark, and I couldn't see it anymore. Then it was just me on the bridge."

She lifted one finger and slowly, carefully, wiped a tear away from her left eye. She didn't comment on it, and neither did he.

"It had been a very bad night," she said, and her voice was softer, huskier. "I sat out there and thought about what I had to go home to, and what could ever be done about it, and...and I just wanted to sit there and hold on to the night a little longer. That was all I wanted. To keep that June night going for as long as I could."

She stopped talking. No more tears came, but her breaths were shallow and unsteady. He didn't speak, didn't move. Just gave her time.

"I don't know how long I was there," she said. "The moon came up and I watched its reflection in the water for a long time. And then there was another light there. The moon on the water, it went to blue. The strangest blue light I'd ever seen. Then the blue was moving, up onto the rocks, this flame that had just crawled right out of the water. It was the most beautiful thing I'd ever seen. And I felt, I don't know the word...beckoned by it. Called. I...I decided that I wanted to try it."

She didn't specify what the *it* was, and she didn't need to. Now it was Kimble's turn to close his eyes.

"It's not as high as it looks," she said. "I thought it would be

high enough. It wasn't. The fall was very fast, and I had imagined it would be peaceful, but it was too quick to be peaceful. I
don't remember fear. I just remember knowing that it was too
fast, that I'd counted on more time and wasn't going to get it."

She took a long, deep breath, chest filling, her breasts swelling
against the faded prison uniform, and said, "There are rocks
under the water in that spot. Not too far below. I hit one of
them."

Kimble looked away. He couldn't help it. He couldn't stand to
think of her like that, falling from that bridge into the dark and
the rocks.

"It was Wyatt who found me," she said. "Late in the night."

"You didn't go to the hospital," Kimble said. "Or at least he
didn't call the police for you."

If he had, there should have been a record. There was no
record.

"No," she said. "We didn't call the police, and I didn't go to
the hospital. He brought me up, and I got into my car and drove
home. He tried to stop me from that, but I didn't listen. That
was the last time I saw him until his visit five weeks ago."

Kimble said, "Wait a second. You said you landed on a rock."

"Yes."

"How did you just drive home, then? Weren't you hurt?"

She looked away from him. "I guess I was lucky."

"Lucky?"

"Doesn't feel like it now." She waved her hand around the
room. "Not after years in here. But I guess I was lucky."

There was something in her eyes that he wasn't familiar with,
couldn't read, and he waited for more, but no words came. She
just watched him with a detachment he'd never seen from her
before.

"Jacqueline? Is that all there is to the story?"

She held her silence for a long beat, then nodded. "Yes."

He matched her nod, but it was difficult. Just as they'd discussed when he sat down, there had always been a relationship of trust, no matter how bizarre that seemed. In all these years, all these visits, in every encounter they'd ever had, even from before the trial, even when she was refusing to tell him a damn thing about her husband's violence, she'd never lied to him. Until now. How could you feel so betrayed knowing that a woman who'd once shot you in the back had now lied to you? The logic didn't track, but emotions often didn't choose to follow logic. This lesson Jacqueline Mathis had ingrained deeply in Kimble.

"So when he came here," Kimble said, "he came to apologize?"

"That's right. The lighthouse had been off that night. It seems Wyatt had done some drinking the previous night. He was arrested. You can verify that easily enough. By the time he got out and made his way home, it was dark, but the light wasn't on. He went up and got it going and then he saw me."

"So he wanted to apologize that he didn't have the light going?"

"Yes," she said. "I guess he thought it would have helped. He seems to understand the place very well. Much better than I do. He said if I spent time there, I'd understand it better myself."

"Well, I've been out there. I don't understand a damn thing."

She said, "Take me there, then."

"What?"

"That might help. If Wyatt was right, I'll be able to understand what you can't."

"Jacqueline, I can't *take* you anywhere. You're in prison."

"I'm aware of that. But you're a police officer. You can get me out there."

The thought of it was alluring and frightening. The two of them, outside these walls and alone together. No guards.

He said, "I don't think that's an option."

"Then I don't know what to tell you," she said.

He leaned forward, braced his forearms on his knees, and looked her in the eyes. It was not an easy thing for him. Meeting her eyes had a way of tightening his lungs, a way of shrinking the walls around him, making doors seem impossibly far away.

"Please," he said, "tell me what you're holding back."

"Kevin, I would like to make parole. Do you understand that?"

"Of course."

"Do you know how much my chances will be hurt if I begin telling stories that make me sound like a lunatic?"

"It's you and me in this room. Not your parole board."

"They'll ask your opinion."

"So did the prosecutor," he said.

She knew well what that meant. She remembered the details he'd chosen to forget during her trial. Some of them, at least. Others — *I'm sorry, I don't remember* — she either did not remember or had been lying about for year after year.

"I've earned this from you, damn it," he said, thinking of the months of physical therapy, the nights of insomnia, the constant ache in his back that lived within him like a draft in an old house. "This much I have *earned*."

She winced, then nodded. "Fine. That's fair enough. You want to hear the story? Wonderful. It's a ghost story."

"A ghost story."

"That's right. Still want to hear it, or shall I save us both the embarrassment?"

When he didn't answer, she said, "You asked me how I wasn't hurt, landing on a rock like that. I was hurt badly. I was dying when he came for me."

"Wyatt?"

She shook her head. "Oh, no, Kevin. Not Wyatt. Not anyone you're going to be able to find and interview. There will be no testimony from him, there will be no fingerprints. Still want me to go on?"

No, he thought, so vehemently that he almost spoke it aloud. He had the sense that if he let her go on like this, then it would all come crashing down, every hope that he'd held, that he'd somehow patched together through overstretched threads of logic and thick ropes of fantasy.

"Go on," he said.

20

HE WAITED. She looked at him with an uncomfortable level of poignancy, as if she knew she might not see him again and wanted to preserve the moment, a woman watching her lover board a troopship and head off to war. Or ordering him aboard the ship. True to form with Jacqueline Mathis, he was never quite sure of her role.

"You've been there," she said.

"The lighthouse? Yeah."

"What about the rest of the area? The ridge, the woods, the trestle. Have you walked around there at all?"

"Just yesterday. Looking for a cat."

"A *cat?*"

"Not the kind in the Friskies commercials, Jacqueline. A black panther. But yes, I've seen the place."

She nodded. "You can picture the base of the trestle. It would be on the...eastern shore, I think. Closest to the road."

"I can picture it."

"There's a fire down there," she told him calmly.

He raised his eyebrows. "There was a fire?"

"There *is* a fire. I haven't seen it in a while — I've been otherwise engaged for a few years, you know — but I can't imagine
that it's gone, either. It had been burning for a long time when
I saw it, and I think it will burn for a long time to come."

"I don't follow this."

"Of course you don't. That's why I tried not to tell you. You
had to have it your way, though, and so now I'll tell you and live
with the response, I guess. There is a fire on the rocks below the
trestle. When Wyatt made his visit, it was still burning. I can
almost assure you that it still is now."

Kimble had passed under the trestle with Wesley Harrington
at his side the previous evening. There had been nothing there.

He said, "Okay. A fire."

"Already you're giving up on me," she said. "I can see it in
your face."

"No, I'm not. But you should know that I was just down there,
and I didn't see a fire. Neither did the man I was with. So unless
we both have really bad eyes..."

"You wouldn't be able to see it," she said. "Not yet. And I hope
you never can."

Her face was grim.

"The first time I saw it, Kevin, I was in the water and the
rocks. I was dying. Make no mistake about it — I wasn't just in
pain, I was *dying*. And I knew then that I didn't want to die.
More than anything in the world, I didn't want to die. The river
was pulling me downstream, but I got hung up in the rocks and
then I could see the fire. It burns blue, and there are people all
around it. One man stepped away from it, took one of the sticks
out of the fire, and held it like a torch."

Please, stop, Kimble thought, trying to hold her eyes, trying
not to betray the sickness. He needed her to be sane. He needed
her not to belong in this place, but with every word she was vali-
dating the orange uniform.

"He waded out to me, just glided through the water, holding that blue torch. Told me that I was dying, and made me an offer."

"An offer?"

"That's right. He told me that I was dying, and I knew that I was. He told me that he could enable me to walk away, and I knew that he could."

"This man healed you."

"I didn't say healed."

"Then what did he do?"

"He bargained, Kevin. And I accepted."

He looked at her, not really wanting to hear the answer, and said, "What did he want in exchange?"

"I think you know that."

"No, I don't, Jacqueline."

"What I promised him," she said, "I provided him."

He was silent.

"You don't just walk away from the devil," she said. "Not for free."

21

IRA MELTED INTO THE HILLS and did not surface. While Audrey and Dustin worked together to complete the day's feedings and clean the cages, the two deputies who remained at the preserve took their weapons into the woods, armed with binoculars and, in one case, a rifle scope, and searched for some sign.

They didn't come up with any.

Dustin, who hadn't seemed to have recovered his strength after finding Wes that morning, who looked unsteady with every step, watched the police in the woods and told Audrey they were up to something.

"What? They're looking for the cat."

He shook his head. "No. They're going along the fence line right now, Audrey. Watch them."

She lowered the wheelbarrow full of raw meat — they kept it frozen, then thawed it each evening so it would be ready to go in the morning — and studied the police as Dustin was. They did seem to be walking along the edge of the fence, looking in instead of looking out.

"They don't expect to find Ira hiding against the fence," Dustin said. "So what are they doing?"

Looking for breaches, Audrey thought. They were looking for some indication of poor security, something that could potentially allow a cat to escape. Something that could potentially provide the sheriff with the ammunition that Kimble had hinted he would want. Well, that was ridiculous. The preserve was secure, and she knew it.

"Let them do their job," she said. "We'll do ours. Look at Lily. That girl is *hungry.*"

The blind white Siberian tiger was trotting back and forth in her cage, looking like a kitten with too much energy. She could hear them and smell the food; she knew it was close, she just couldn't see it.

They fed Lily, then moved on to the next enclosure, which held two cougars. They were siblings. At one time the cougars on the preserve had fascinated visitors. Then Ira came along, and the standard variety was no longer of interest. People like the unique specimens, even when they know nothing about the basics.

But the two cougars Audrey and Dustin were feeding now were *plenty* unique. They were two of five cats that had been rescued from what Wes had deemed the worst conditions he'd ever encountered. The cats were at a facility licensed by the USDA for breeding purposes, which was an idea that David and Audrey abhorred—the cats were not supposed to be pets, and most of them wouldn't be suffering if some jackass hadn't decided he wanted a cougar or a lion for a pet.

The place was in Georgia, and all of the cats needed rescue. The owner simply told authorities that he'd "gotten in a little over his head." Being in over his head meant forgetting to feed the animals, apparently. The cats were housed in filthy, small cages with no food or water in reach. Every bone in their bodies showed beneath matted fur. Often taking strange cats could be a challenge, even requiring sedation. In this case, the only thing that was needed to lure the animals out and into the transport cages was a bucket of clean water.

Cody, one of the cougars, was in such bad shape that he required two weeks of antibiotics just to stabilize enough so the vet could remove several infected teeth. He now had a hilariously crooked smile, which he showed often, and his ribs were no longer pushing against his flesh. His brother, Otto, had suffered frostbite so severe that his ears were mangled shreds.

Audrey looked at the two cats, healthy and happy and eager for food, and said, "Let the sheriff's department try its worst. I run one of the best facilities in the country, and I'm not closing it. The *escape* was not due to our facility. It was due to a cat that is something strange. Our fence height exceeds the minimum. If he jumped over it without help…well, good for Ira. But we couldn't stop it."

"They say those black cats are supposed to be witches," Dustin said. "I remember reading about it with David."

She looked at him and sighed. "Helpful, Dustin. I'll just call the old witch defense into play. When they're burning me at the stake, remember that it was your suggestion."

They were cleaning one portion of the cougar enclosure while the cats were isolated with their meat in another sector. Audrey always worked this way in the preserve. David and Wes would sometimes go in the enclosures, but Audrey never did. Dustin was watching the police, and Audrey looked up, too. One of them — Wolverton — appeared to have found something. He called to Shipley, who walked on slowly, carefully — every move Shipley made out here seemed cautious — and knelt beside his comrade. They turned something over in their hands, whispering.

"What did you find there?" Audrey called, walking toward them. A plastic bag appeared, the item went into it, and then the bag disappeared into Wolverton's pocket.

"Don't worry about it, Mrs. Clark. Nothing here."

She frowned and turned back to Dustin. His pale face was grim. "They found something, all right."

"What?"

"I think it was a shell."

She stared at him. "From Wesley's gun?"

"Maybe." He didn't look at her when he said it, though.

"Dustin," she said, "do you think someone else shot my tiger?"

He still didn't meet her eyes, just took his rake and returned to work.

"We'll see what the police think," he said.

Kimble had left Jacqueline abruptly, thanking her for her time like some door-to-door salesman who'd struck out badly but had to keep the false smile until he was out of sight. She hadn't even responded, just watched sadly as he stood up to go.

"You wanted to know the truth," she said as the CO opened the door for him.

Yes, he had. And the truth was that several years of his life had vanished into a fantasy image of a woman who belonged in the state hospital, not the prison.

He picked up his phone as soon as he got into the car, began to make calls about work, *real* work, determined not only to make up for lost time but to force his mind away from her and back into the world of real problems that needed real solutions. Back into his world.

His first call was to the department's evidence tech, to see whether the medical examiners had come through on Kimble's request and retrieved the bullet from the tiger.

They had.

"Looks like a .223," the tech told him. "We can of course do more specific ballistics if you need them, but I can tell you the caliber right now. That mean anything to you?"

It meant plenty.

The gun in Wesley Harrington's hand on the night of his death did not fire .223 cartridges.

Kimble thanked them, hung up, and called Shipley.

"You still out there?"

"Yes, sir. No sign of the cat. Everything's been peaceful."

"Listen, I just got a match back on the bullet that killed the cat. It wasn't fired from Harrington's gun."

Silence.

"We're looking at a very different scene now," Kimble said, "and it is important that we handle it right. This thing is not what it appears to be. Harrington did not shoot that cat. If anything, he probably went in there *because* the cat had been shot, and that makes it a crime scene, and a serious one."

"I understand."

"Good. Well, without alarming Mrs. Clark — I'll deal with that when we have to — I want you and Pete to begin looking aggressively for signs of —"

"Pete found a spent casing."

"What?"

"Not too far back from the fence line, toward the old railroad tracks."

"Is it a .223?"

"My opinion? Yes. Probably fired from an AR-15 or, more likely, one of the clones, the cheap knockoffs."

This was serious. This was *very* serious. Someone had gone down there and shot at the cats, which was a major crime on its own terms, but it had also led to the death of Wesley Harrington. You'd probably have to call it involuntary manslaughter...

Unless it was involuntary cat slaughter, he thought. *Just because the cat was hit doesn't mean the cat was the target. Shooting in the dark like that, it would be tough to hit a man. And in that place, any bullet that sailed by would have a good chance of finding a five-hundred-pound feline. In which case, Kimble, you could be looking at attempted murder.*

"All right," he said, when he realized the pause had gone on too long. "Listen — I want somebody on security out there tonight."

"Here. At night?"

"Yes, Shipley, what the hell is the problem? You act like you're scared of the dark out there. Been talking to Wyatt French?" Kimble's frustration had been massing since he walked out of the prison, away from Jacqueline's story, and now Shipley was catching it.

"I'm not scared to be out here," he said in a clipped voice. "You just tell me the hours."

"Break it up into shifts. You work until midnight, then let Pete take it. Sound fair enough? I know you've been going all day. You want it changed, or you want some relief, then —"

"I'll do it."

"Thanks, Shipley," he said, trying to ease off. "They know you out there now, and I think that will help."

"What am I supposed to tell them?"

"Tell them I've asked that someone remain on duty in case the cougar comes back. Put all the weight of it on that black cat, okay? Why not use the creepy bastard, since we've got him?"

"Yes, sir."

"Keep a sharp eye out there. It's a damn strange place."

"It certainly is," Shipley said.

Kimble hung up and started the engine, ready to get back on the road, back home, ready to get moving through a life that

he'd been treading water in since a summer night five years earlier. It was time.

He drove fast on his way out, but there was a coal train coming through and he couldn't beat it, caught the intersection just
as the gate lowered, pinning him impatiently in place, engine
idling, unable to rid the prison from his rearview mirror.

22

THE POLICE TOLD AUDREY they would keep a man on the grounds overnight. It was the young deputy, Shipley, who informed them, and Dustin Hall shook his head as if he wasn't happy with the news. Shipley caught the gesture and fell silent, staring Dustin down. There was something remarkably cold in the stare.

Audrey said, "It's fine. It's great. I appreciate the gesture. If you see the cat, please come for *me* first, though. Don't just open fire."

"If it's possible to alert you, we will," Shipley said. "Our safety will be first, the cat's will be second. You have to understand that."

"What did you find out there?" Dustin asked.

"Find?" Shipley raised his eyebrows.

"Yeah. You put something in a bag. Was it a bullet?"

Shipley looked at him for a long time, then back to Audrey, and smiled. "Didn't know you'd hired one of the Hardy Boys. He'll be good to have around."

She didn't think it was an appropriate time to joke, and said as much. The smile bled off Nathan Shipley's face and his blue eyes went cold again and he said, "Absolutely right. Someone was killed here last night. I don't find that amusing. I'm of course in no position to reveal details of police work to Mr. Hall here. Chief Deputy Kimble can decide what he wants to share, and when. In the meantime, we'll be here for your protection."

She thanked him, and he went off to his vehicle, slid behind the wheel, and picked up the radio unit.

Dustin Hall, who was suddenly her most experienced staff member, told Audrey that he would replace Wesley on the property. To say that he was a brave kid was an understatement — this morning he'd discovered a good friend's body, and tonight he was already trying to step in to fill the void. She couldn't let him stay there, though.

"Go back home and get some sleep," she said. "I'll need you early, and need you strong. Okay?"

He frowned, watching Shipley. "I'd just as soon stay out here, Audrey. I feel like that's where the need is."

"Dustin? I know what I'm doing with the cats. I've got a police officer on the grounds all night, protecting me. Nothing's going to happen."

"All right."

"We'll stick it out," she told Dustin. "We'll be fine."

Strong words. It was good to be bold, but it was dangerous, too. She was well aware of the truth: the only thing that had kept the preserve going was Wesley Harrington. Without him, she was in over her head and sinking fast.

"Sure," Dustin said. "And *you* get some sleep, too. You need it."

But around them the cats were all awake as the sun began to set, stalking the perimeters of their enclosures, eyes glittering, tails swishing, and Audrey had the feeling that sleep wasn't permitted at Blade Ridge.

*　　*　　*

Kimble stopped by the department to pick up the reports that waited for him from the morning's death scene and then went home, poured a glass of red wine, and sat on his couch. He drank wine only when he was at home. When he socialized, which was rare, he stuck to beer — a country cop drinking wine always seemed to draw attention, and Kimble preferred to float in the background — but he loved the taste of a full-bodied red, loved the hard-to-pronounce names on the labels, loved the sound of a cork leaving the bottle. These were all things that made him think romantic notions, and it had been a long time since Kimble had been with a woman. Sometimes — many times — he'd catch himself wondering if Jacqueline drank red wine. He was almost certain she did.

He sipped a glass of blended Chilean red, purchased at an organic food store near the college that stocked wines from all over the world and was a place in which Kimble was unlikely to bump into a colleague or acquaintance. He opened the report from Wesley Harrington's death scene and tried to steer his mind away from a brown-haired woman in an orange jumpsuit.

She probably likes champagne, too. That seems right. The sparkle.

He blinked, fought to focus. He would write the formal incident report himself, but it would be heavily dependent on supplemental reports from Shipley and Wolverton, who'd both arrived on scene ahead of Kimble. Tonight he had only Wolverton's account available, because Shipley was still on duty. Still out at the ridge. Pete had taken the time to provide a clipped account of the scene, and Kimble read it with no expectation of new information. But he grew curious as he reviewed Pete's brief account of his interview with Dustin Hall, the Whitman student who'd discovered the body. *Mr. Hall first noted that there was blood in the cage,* Wolverton had written. *He then moved closer, observed that the cat was not moving and that a rifle was visible. At that point Mr. Hall entered the cage, discovered the victim's body behind that of the cat, determined Harrington to be deceased, and called for help.*

It went on for a few paragraphs after that, but all Kimble needed was contained in that initial account of the witness statement.

In order, Hall recounted seeing blood, a rifle, Harrington.

Kimble had been in the cage. Had approached just as Hall must have that morning, and he had seen blood first, yes, but he had not been able to see the rifle until he saw Harrington. Hall's recollection of the man's corpse was correct — it had been blocked from sight by the cat's body. But the rifle had been in the dead man's hand.

At least when Kimble saw it.

Perhaps there'd been two rifles on the scene, which meant maybe this wasn't going to be such a pain in the ass after all; maybe the dead man had brought two guns out with him, and the killing shot had been fired with the first, not the second. Simple.

But why would he have used two rifles? Why not just reload? How had he even managed to approach the cage carrying two rifles, a syringe on a pole, and a flashlight? It was a ludicrous scenario, would have required "Send in the Clowns" playing in the background and Harrington riding a unicycle to make it believable.

So maybe the kid had been confused. Rattled. Said the wrong thing, that was all, meant to say he spotted the rifle in Harrington's hand but misspoke due to the pressure of the moment. He'd certainly been shaken up.

Wolverton's supplemental report contained contact information for Dustin Hall, including phone numbers for both a dorm room and a cell. Kimble called the dorm first, got nothing, and then the cell. The kid answered, and sounded nervous from the moment Kimble identified himself.

"We don't have a problem," Kimble said, although that was perhaps untrue. "I'm just trying to finalize the report and need to clear up a discrepancy. You have a minute, I'd appreciate your help on that."

The kid agreed, but none of the trepidation left his voice.

Kimble pitched his question then, asked him to recall what he'd seen and when he'd seen it.

"Go slow and think clearly," he said. "I need to know the order of things."

Dustin went slowly and clearly, and he recounted everything exactly as he had with Wolverton.

"All right," Kimble said, and then, gently, "I'm wondering about that rifle, son. I was there, inside the cage. We've got photographs. You can't see the gun from the angle you describe. It was hidden by the cat."

"Not when I got there." He was firm.

"You're telling me that there was a gun—"

"You might want to ask your deputy about this," Dustin Hall said.

Kimble fell silent for a moment, then said, "Was there a problem with Deputy Wolverton?"

"Not him. The other guy."

"Deputy Shipley. What was the problem with him?"

"I'm not saying there was a problem," the kid said. He was very uneasy. "It's just...look, he was there after me, right? Maybe things got moved around."

"Got moved around?"

The kid went silent, and the silence went on too long, and when he spoke again, he sounded like a chess player regretting his last move, knowing damn well where it had placed him.

"Probably not. Maybe I just remember it all wrong. I was nervous."

Kimble was certain that the kid wanted only to end the conversation, certain that his recollections had not been skewed by nerves.

"Mr. Hall," Kimble said. "Dustin, buddy? Tell me what you're not wanting to say. Tell me now, when it's not a problem. I need to hear it."

There was a pause, and then a rush of words.

"You need to talk to your deputy, not me. He made me go out of sight of the cage first thing. Like his priority was being alone there. And that guy, he was...look, I don't know how else to say it, he was scaring me. There's something wrong with him. He wanted to talk about his car accident. Was asking me all these questions that were so fucking—pardon my language—so *weird*. Asking me why I had lied about being in the road, but I *wasn't* in the road. Sir, all I know is that I was scared of him. He didn't seem right, and he was looking at me in a, well, in a hostile way, I guess. That's the best word. Hostile."

"I see," Kimble said. "Son, let me ask you one more question, and I want to assure you that the answer will stay between the two of us."

"Yes, sir."

"Do you think Deputy Shipley moved that rifle?"

"Sir? I know he did."

23

I T WAS PROBABLY BAD PRACTICE to drop in on police unin-
vited, but Kevin Kimble hadn't returned the messages Roy
had left at his office, and he needed to talk to him about what
he'd found during his day in the newspaper morgue.

He needed to talk with *someone*.

The chief deputy lived in a modest brick ranch home five
miles outside of town. Kimble didn't go to the trouble of hanging Christmas lights as his neighbors did, but there was a wreath
on the door, a concession to the season without the time investment. Roy pulled in, looked at the list he'd compiled, and shook
his head.

Yes, he needed to talk with someone.

Wyatt French had collected a slice of Sawyer County history
that bordered on the impossible. He'd found six murderers scattered over eighty years who all shared one thing: an accident at
Blade Ridge.

Well, five of them did. Jacqueline Mathis was the rogue, but
maybe Kimble would know something about that. Regardless, it
was an unbelievable pattern. And a disturbing one.

Kimble answered the door almost immediately, as if he'd heard the car come in, and he wasn't happy to see Roy.

"There are telephones, you know, Mr. Darmus."

"You don't answer yours. And I didn't have your home number."

"But you had the address?"

"I found it, yes. Listen, I'm sorry to bother you, but I've got something you need to look at. Please."

Kimble sighed but let him in. The house was sparsely furnished but incredibly clean for a bachelor's home. Roy had been divorced for twenty years now, and he knew well the condition of the average bachelor's home: he lived in one.

"I'm in the middle of work," Kimble said. "Real work. One of the cats killed its keeper. All those things we talked about last night, I can't worry about them until I've got that situation—"

"Take a look at this," Roy said, and handed him a piece of paper. It was a neat, morbid time line:

Jacqueline Mathis, killed husband, 2006
Ryan O'Patrick, killed boss, 1982
Adam Estes, killed financial adviser, 1976
Becky Stapp, killed husband, 1948
Timothy Osgood, killed sister, 1931
Ralph Hill, killed business partner, 1927

"Okay," Kimble said. "That's about what we figured. Wyatt had an unhealthy hobby. Liked to read about—"

"Now look at this one," Roy said, feeling like a magician preparing a dubious audience for his trick, and handed Kimble a new sheet of paper.

Ryan O'Patrick, April 12, 1982
Adam Estes, July 17, 1975

Becky Stapp, January 12, 1948
Timothy Osgood, October 31, 1931
Ralph Hill, May 15, 1927

"Are these the dates of the killings? No, Estes doesn't line up," Kimble said.

"These are the dates of accidents they had at Blade Ridge. Every one of them."

Kimble looked up at him. "Accidents?"

"I'm positive. I spent all day tracking them down, and I didn't believe it myself. These people are separated by decades, but they're held together by two things: killing and Blade Ridge. Every single one of them survived an accident out there *before* they did their killing. Becky Stapp was thrown from a horse. Then she put a kitchen knife in her husband's spine. Adam Estes almost drowned. Then he shot his investment guy. Ryan O'Patrick put a Camaro into the trees, then came back and beat his boss to death with a wrench. The exception is Jacqueline Mathis. Not a recorded incident. Do you know of any connection between her and Blade Ridge?"

"No."

Roy had been interviewing people for more than forty years and had heard plenty of lies. He looked at Kimble now and knew without question that he'd just heard another.

Why? he thought. *Why would he lie about that?*

"Okay," he said. "Well, then she's the one exception. All of the others survived accidents at Blade Ridge, then went on to kill."

Kimble was looking at him, but his eyes seemed to be receding.

"It's bizarre," he offered finally.

Roy gave a short, humorless laugh. "You're awfully adept with the understatement, Kimble. It is bizarre."

"Well, what do *you* have to say about it? You have some sort of explanation?"

"No, I don't. And I'm still missing four of them. There are four other men named in those pictures. John Hamlin, Fred Mortimer, Henry Bates, and Bernard Snell. I can't find anything in the newspapers about them. I think they go back too far. Those pictures are ancient."

"Well, French found them somewhere."

"I don't know where. They're definitely..."

He stopped talking, and Kimble said, "What?"

"They're microfilm printouts," Roy said slowly. "But not from the *Sentinel*. I've been trying to think of what else he could have gone through that was on microfilm and local. The college has archives of the Whitman Company. They kept a newspaper of their own. The *Sentinel* actually spun out of it, I think. A free paper instead of a company mouthpiece, that sort of thing. But maybe those names are from the company newspaper."

"Great," Kimble said, not sounding interested in the slightest, still looking at that list of dates.

"If they are," Roy said, "then whatever happened with them happened a hell of a long time ago."

Kimble was moving back toward the front door. "Listen, I've got work to do, Mr. Darmus. I appreciate the time you've put into this, but—"

"Kimble, are you just pushing that aside and saying—"

"I don't know what I'm going to say!"

Kimble's voice had risen to a shout. It was just like the day at the lighthouse. The chief deputy was mild-mannered until you found the right nerve. Before, that nerve had been Jacqueline Mathis. Roy figured it was again, but he didn't understand *why*.

"I'm just... just trying to process a whole hell of a lot right now, okay?" Kimble said. "I'm trying to get my head around all of it."

Roy nodded. "Sure. I'm not there yet myself. I don't know what it means, but you do have to admit that those connections are... rather extraordinary."

"Yes," Kimble said. "They are."

"One of them is alive," Roy said.

Kimble stopped. "What?"

"Everyone on that list is dead except for Ryan O'Patrick. And Jacqueline Mathis, of course, but she didn't have an accident at the ridge that I can find. O'Patrick did. He lives in Modesto." He extended another piece of paper, this one with an address on it. "Just in case you want to talk to him."

Kimble took the paper.

Roy went back to his car, and for the first time in his life felt relieved that his parents had died in their accident at Blade Ridge.

What if they'd survived?

It was an idea he'd considered so often, with such hopefulness, wondering how things might have been different if he'd had a family beyond the age of fourteen. Now it entered his mind again and he suppressed a shiver.

What if they'd survived?

24

AUDREY WAS MAKING THE ROUNDS, flashlight in one hand, pole syringe in the other, when the deputy stepped out of the woods and made her scream.

"What are you doing?" she said. She'd spun the syringe around, ready to lunge. "I almost put you into a coma. And you almost put *me* into a coffin."

He was wearing a jacket with the hood up, shielding his face in shadow, his breath leaving wisps of vapor. He looked from her to the syringe and smiled.

"That's for the cougar?"

"In case," she said, feeling suddenly defensive. She realized how awkward her motion with the long pole had been, how ineffective she would have been if she'd needed to use it. Against an animal like Ira, all sleek speed and fast-twitch power? No— if he sprang on her from the darkness, she wouldn't have a chance.

"What are you doing out here?" she said again, stepping back from Shipley.

"Kimble told you. I'm the night watch."

"I thought you were supposed to be here in case anything happened, not creeping around the woods."

"Sorry."

He had turned from her and was facing one of the enclosures. Home to five lions, it was one of the largest spaces in the preserve. It was rare that you could get so many to socialize well; often there was an attitude problem that led to fights. These lions, though, got along just fine. They were all on their perches now — six, eight, twelve feet in the air, their strange eyes fractured reflections in the beam of her flashlight.

"I don't know how you do it," Shipley said.

"What?"

"Live out here with them. At night."

"They're harmless," she said, though the truth was she *hadn't* lived out here with them at night. She'd spent many evenings at the old preserve, but she always went home to sleep. This was new, and yes, a little frightening. She'd been lost in thoughts of Wes when she bumped into the deputy, thinking of how it had been for him in those last moments, wondering what had gone through his mind when he realized that his favorite cat had brought an end to his life. She hoped it had been so swift that no thoughts had come at all, but that was hard to believe. He'd bled out in the cage. That took time.

"They don't seem to like me," Shipley said. "Growl when I walk by."

"Lions are the least people-friendly of the big cats. There are exceptions, of course, but as a rule they aren't like the tigers. Many of the tigers actually *want* attention. The lions are more wary, and you're a stranger."

"You ever go in the cages with them?"

It was an innocent enough question, but she folded her arms across her chest and looked away, as if he'd said something lewd.

"No," she finally said. "I don't, personally. But they're fine with people. Wes used to go in with them. And my husband."

"You just don't trust them the same way?"

She turned back to him, thinking that he'd isolated the exact reason she was doomed to lose these cats. To care for them properly, you had to trust them. She'd always had people to do that for her. David and Wesley. Their faith had been so big that she didn't need to test her own. Now they were gone. The fences between her and the cats remained, but there was no one left to cross over them for her.

"I trust them," she said softly. She could isolate them in different portions of the enclosures for cleanings and feedings, but now that Wes was gone, there would come a time when they would need her. Something would go wrong, and they would need someone to enter the cages with them.

"You really think this is the right spot for them?"

"There aren't any zoos that will take them, if that's what you mean. And yes, in every single circumstance, we are providing a better life for these animals than they had before."

"That's not what I mean. I'm talking about *this* spot. Don't you feel it?"

"Feel what?" She was taken aback.

He spread his hands, the black-gloved fingers casting shadows. "There's something different out here, Mrs. Clark. You're telling me you can't feel it?"

What she was *feeling* was an intense desire to be back inside the trailer, with the door locked. She moved the pole syringe so that it was pointed at him, then was embarrassed when he looked down at it, well aware of the motion.

"Sorry," he said. "That's just what you don't need to hear, I'm sure. All I'm saying is … there's something strange in this place. And I think the cats feel it. I'm pretty sure about that."

He left her then, walked back into the night woods, his hand tapping along the stock of his gun.

25

K IMBLE SAT WITH HIS FOOT on the brake, staring at the
mailbox — *O'Patrick, R.* — and the trailer and five-bay
garage beyond. A man was standing in one of the open garage
bays, smoking a cigar, and Kimble pulled into the drive, parked,
and stepped out of the cruiser. Ryan O'Patrick had been paroled
after serving twenty years for murder, and he'd returned to Sawyer County, moving to Modesto, which was home to the county's
consolidated rural high school. O'Patrick lived in a trailer directly
across the street from Hefron High, and according to Roy Darmus ran a cash-only mechanic's shop and was apparently capable
of fixing anything that ailed a car, boat, tractor, or other engine-
reliant item. He'd always been handy with a wrench, it seemed.
Just got a little too handy one day, upside his boss's skull.

Kimble got out of the car and walked up to the garage. A
radio was on, tuned to a sports talk station, and beside it a small
space heater blew warm air over the concrete floor.

"You Ryan O'Patrick?"

"I got a feeling," O'Patrick said, studying the police car, "that
I'm not going to enjoy this visit."

He had the look of someone who'd been jailed for a long time. A posture that made him seem bigger than he was, eyes that were somehow both challenging and resigned. He was heavier than in his old booking photographs, with an extra layer of chin partially obscured by a short graying beard. Kimble saw an open tall-boy of Old Style sitting on top of a toolbox at his side.

"Well," O'Patrick said, blowing smoke at Kimble's face, "what do you need, deputy? If anything in these cars is stolen, I don't know about it, and I don't care to know. I just fix them."

"Not here about a car. Here to ask you about Blade Ridge."

Ryan O'Patrick drew smoke in and never released it. After a long silence, he said, "Say that again?"

"Blade Ridge. You had an accident out there back in —"

"I know damn well when I had my accident and where it was. What I'd like to know is why you're interested."

"Some other people have died out there," Kimble said. "Bad accidents. Like yours."

O'Patrick reached out and clicked off the radio, the sports talk vanishing.

"I'm investigating them," Kimble said. "And I'd like to know what you remember about your own."

"Wrecked a car. Shit happens. I was young, I liked to drive fast. Burned a Camaro along the road and it got away from me."

He looked at his boots while he told this story. Kimble nodded, leaned against the garage door frame, and said, "Figured as much. Long stretch of gravel road like that, isolated place? You were dragging, weren't you? Seeing just what the car could handle, just what *you* could handle."

"Sure. That's what I was doing."

Kimble waited for him to look up. When he finally did, Kimble said, "So when did Wyatt French come by? Last few weeks, or longer?"

O'Patrick's face tightened. "Who?"

There was a moment of silence, and then Kimble said, "He's dead now. We found his body up at the top of his lighthouse."

When Ryan O'Patrick sighed, he seemed to lose something more than air.

"Fuck," he said.

"So you knew him."

"Yeah, I knew him. Or he knew *me,* more like it. Kept coming around, trying to get me to talk about something that...that just shouldn't be spoken of."

"It needs to be spoken of," Kimble said.

"You and Wyatt should have gotten together, then."

"A little late for that. I've got you, though. Tell me about the wreck."

Ryan O'Patrick stared out of the garage and over at the football field across the street, where a group of boys in Hefron High Wrestling shirts were running the bleachers, their feet pounding off the aluminum as they sprinted beneath the harsh lights. They were bright lights, glaring, and most people wouldn't have wanted to live so close. Kimble noticed that Ryan O'Patrick didn't have curtains in his trailer. Every window was exposed to the stadium lights.

"The gauges went," he said, and his voice was soft. "Speedometer, tach, everything. Just went flat. Don't know why it happened. Electrical short of some kind. I got to staring at them and took my eyes off the road, that's all. Poor driving, nothing else."

Kimble said, "Really?"

"Yeah, *really.* Sorry you wasted the trip, bud. Might have just picked up a phone instead, saved yourself the —"

"You've told two versions of it now," Kimble said, "and neither one is the truth."

"You know what I find interesting?" O'Patrick said.

"What's that?"

"You know who I am. I can see it all over your face. You know that I did twenty years for killing a man."

Kimble nodded.

"And you know what else? The questions you're asking? They're about a lot more than a car wreck. Tell me if I'm lying."

Kimble was silent. Ryan O'Patrick gave a dark smile and then bent to a mini-fridge tucked under a nearby shelf. He pulled out another tall-boy and extended it to Kimble with a question in his eyes. Kimble accepted it.

"You want to hear it?" O'Patrick said. "I'll tell it this once. Never again."

"That's all I'm asking."

O'Patrick nodded, moved to a stool, and popped the top on his beer. He took a long pull and said, "I was always a bit of a hell-raiser. I've got a temper like a damned light switch. People used to call me that, in fact."

Kimble raised an eyebrow, and O'Patrick said, "Well, if they didn't, they should have. Because I could snap pretty fast. Had my share of fights. So when I killed Joe, everyone said, *Ah, Ryan's temper got away from him.* But that's bullshit. Or maybe it isn't. The point is that I don't *remember* killing Joe. I stuck to that story all the way through trial and rode it on into prison. It wasn't a lie. That moment? It's nothing but blackness."

Every time Kimble had seen her, Jacqueline had offered the same line: *I'm sorry, I don't remember.* She never wavered.

Kimble said, "Tell me about the ridge, please. About your accident. Describe it as best as you can remember it."

"Brother, I can describe it fine. I just don't like to. Now, the accident itself? Simple. I was watching the blue light. Watching so close I couldn't have hit the brakes if I wanted to."

"The blue light?"

"You heard me. Thing was floating through the trees, glowing.

A blue flame. I couldn't mix you a paint to match, not even a pearl coat. You ever heard of Saint Elmo's fire? Shit that shows up on a ship's mast out in the middle of the ocean?"

Kimble nodded, thinking of Jacqueline's recollections of her suicide attempt and feeling sick.

"I expect that's the closest thing to it," O'Patrick said.

"The sight of it was enough to make you wreck?"

"You say that like it's hard to believe! Let's get you out driving in the dark, pal. Let's give you the wheel, take it up to fifty, sixty, seventy miles an hour, and then let that light float your way. I'd like to see how good your reflexes are then."

Kimble held up his hands. "All right," he said. "I'm not arguing. I'm asking. What happened after you crashed?"

O'Patrick paused, and Kimble let him.

"What I remember," he said eventually, his voice the most unsteady it had been, "was the man who came for me."

It was clear he wasn't talking about paramedics.

"He came down off the ridge and out of the woods. A blue torch in his hand. Cold flame. I was hurt bad, and at first I was glad to see him, because I knew I needed help. But then he came on down the road and I didn't even call out for help, because, well... he wasn't the sort of man you called out to. I could sense that much. So he kind of circled, studying me. And I remember being afraid that he would..." His voice broke and he covered it up with a long pull on the beer. "That he would take me," he finished.

Kimble was quiet. Ryan O'Patrick fumbled a cigar out of his shirt pocket, then put it back without lighting it.

"I could see my face in the mirror," he said. "Could see how busted up I was. My nose was laid over to one side, and the skin was torn right off my jaw. I could see my teeth and my jawbone, and blood was just pouring out."

He reached up and touched unmarked skin with his fingertips.

"I saw that and I knew that I was dying," he said, and his voice was one Kimble had heard before, when he had talked to witnesses of terrible crimes. Or, more often, survivors of them. There was always weight behind the words of someone who'd passed near the mortal precipice.

"The man with the torch, he knelt down, taking his time, relaxed as could be. I can't remember much of his face, just that firelight. He was shadows and cold flame to me, nothing else. He asked if I wanted help. And I had the sense that... even if he could help, it wasn't the sort of help you wanted to accept. You know? That it came with a price."

Kimble's breathing and heart rate had slowed in the way they always did in high-pressure interviews, times when he had to will himself not to press. He was listening to O'Patrick but hearing Jacqueline Mathis.

"You asked for his help?" he said finally, after he realized O'Patrick was staring at him, waiting for a response.

"I did. It wasn't something I wanted to do, but I didn't want to die out there, either."

"And what did he do for you?"

O'Patrick gave him a long stare, then said, "The EMT who put me in the ambulance took a look at my car and called me the luckiest son of a bitch he'd ever seen."

Kimble was thinking of Shipley's car, the way he'd walked into the department the next day and announced that he was a little sore, that was all.

"In that moment, though," Kimble said, "what did he do?"

O'Patrick breathed in until his chest swelled, then steadied himself and said, "He said he could heal me, but only if I was willing. He said that he couldn't reach me if I wasn't, and that I needed to understand that he was bound by balance. That was the phrase, I'll never forget it. Bound by balance. And I knew what he meant by it, I won't lie about that. But I still said yes. Then he dipped that torch down to me. That's the last of it I remember until the EMT was there."

For a long time it was silent in the garage. Out at the high school the bleachers rattled, rattled, rattled.

"This happened in '82," Kimble said. "This happened before Wyatt put up his lighthouse."

"Yeah."

Something that had been absent fell into place in Kimble's brain, and he said, "Wyatt had an accident out there, too, didn't he?"

"He did."

"When?"

"I'm not certain. Not long before he set to building the light-house. And before you ask, yes, he saw the man with the torch, and he made his bargain. Only difference is, when I shook it off like it was a bad dream, Wyatt believed in it. I guess because he was out there all the time. You go back to that place once you've made your bargain, you can see them. That's what he told me."

"So he lived with that every night?"

O'Patrick shuddered. "I can't imagine, man. I can't imagine."

"Why didn't he leave?"

"I suppose because he knew you can't run from something that's in you. So he set to work fighting against what was in him, but once you've made that bargain, it ain't something you can fight. By the time he found me, Wyatt was understanding that much."

"What was the lighthouse supposed to do?"

"The question, deputy, is what *does* it do? Everyone laughed at that thing. When I heard about it, you better believe I wasn't laughing, just because of where it stood. Anything that went on at that place ... well, I'd just as soon have nothing to do with it. But I damn sure knew better than to find it funny. Now, you ask me what it was supposed to do? I'll tell you what it did — kept people from going my way."

"You mean murder?" Kimble said. "That's what you're telling me? That some ghost light in the woods out there made you commit murder?"

"You don't like the sound of it, huh? Well, maybe you understand why I'd rather not tell the tale. Maybe you understand *that*. And if you're so damned brave, buddy, so sure that I'm wrong, then you go on and enjoy yourself at Blade Ridge. Pitch a tent and spend the night."

"Easy," Kimble said. "I'm not trying to offend, I'm just telling you that —"

"That it sounds foolish as a campfire story."

Kimble didn't answer.

"You wanted to know what the point of the lighthouse was," O'Patrick said, the heat in his voice fading to dull embers. "Well, I'll let you answer that yourself. You consider how many problems there's been at the ridge since that light went up. You chew on that."

There had been some problems at the ridge since it went up. David Clark died. Jacqueline Mathis survived. But of course the light had been out for Jacqueline. Wyatt had come to apologize to her for that reason. And then there was Shipley ... whose accident came after Darmus broke the light and shut off the power.

"You thought it was a dream," Kimble said. "A hallucination."

"Hell, yes. Most vivid dream I've ever had, but once they got me away from there ... well, it was easier to push it to the corner of my mind then. I remembered what had happened, but away from the ridge, out in the real world and daylight, it seemed impossible. So I told myself that it was. Then along comes that night with Joe, and I wake out of a damned trance with a wrench in my hand and his blood all over me, and you'd better believe I remembered it then."

"You're saying it's a trade. You got your life back but promised to take another one?"

"That's what I'm saying. When he told me he was bound by balance, I knew what was being offered, and I accepted. Days would pass when I'd think about it and get the cold shivers, but I'd tell myself two things. The first was that I'd imagined it. The second was that I could always be in control. Well, I bet wrong on both counts."

Kimble sat down on an overturned bucket by the door. The strength had left his legs. Left his mind. He leaned back against the wall and stared at Ryan O'Patrick.

"You believe me," O'Patrick said. "That's a mighty surprising thing. I wasn't one for telling the tale, and I surely never expected to have anyone believe me. Not unless they'd gone the same way."

"I've already heard it once today," Kimble said. "I didn't do such a good job of believing it then. Now it's getting easier."

O'Patrick nodded and lifted the beer to his lips, then realized the can was already empty and tossed it. They both watched it roll across the concrete floor.

"What are you trying to do?" he asked.

"Fix the problem," Kimble said.

O'Patrick laughed. *"Fix the problem?"*

Kimble set the beer down, unable even to go through the motions of drinking it anymore. His stomach was unsettled, and his hands weren't all that steady either. He said, "I want you to go out there with me. I want you to tell me what you see."

O'Patrick shook his head. "No."

"Please," Kimble said. "I'm just asking for —"

"Not a chance, deputy. I'm not going back to that place. You'll need a warrant and a strong pair of cuffs to get that."

"Why?"

"*Why?* Because whoever was out there all those years ago still is. He's not a boy who just wanders on. I don't guess that he can. Wyatt told me that much. Something else Wyatt told me — once you belong to him, you can see him. Always. And, my friend, I do not *ever* want to see that man again."

"Wyatt could always see this...ghost?"

"That's right. He said the lighthouse kept him pinned down there under the trestle. Couldn't wander the ridge. But he's out there. And when you owe him a debt, he sees that it's paid. I spent twenty years in a cell for settling accounts."

"I've got a friend who wrecked his car out there," Kimble said. "Wrecked it bad, walked away unhurt. He talked about seeing a man in the road. Talked about a light after his accident. I'm starting to think I should be worried about him."

"Buddy," Ryan O'Patrick said, "you should be *real* worried about him."

"Well, then what can I *do?*"

"Wyatt found the only two solutions that there are," O'Patrick said. "You can tell your boy to keep himself away from people at night. That seems to work for a time, if you believed Wyatt, and I do. He'd put some study in."

"There's no way Wyatt kept himself alone at night for twenty years."

"No? Think about it — you ever see Wyatt French in town at night?"

He actually had not, Kimble realized. Wyatt was a daytime drunk. That was one of the reasons he stood out.

"That worked for him for long enough, I guess," O'Patrick said. "But you can't hide from the promise you've made. That's what Wyatt was bound to find out. There is no hiding from what's in yourself. The closer he got to the end of his time, the stronger that pull was going to be. I expect he was feeling that."

"You said there were two solutions."

"Sure. The second one is a bullet in the brain. You promised to take a life. You didn't promise whose it would be."

26

THE WAITER HAD JUST PLACED a thick steak and a fresh beer in front of Roy Darmus, and when his phone rang, he didn't have much interest in answering it. The number was unfamiliar, and though he'd made a practice of answering every call during his reporting days, whatever news this might carry wasn't going to roll out of the *Sentinel*'s presses. He ignored it, cut off a wedge of New York strip, and looked out the window at the town square, where a few stray snow flurries were drifting down from that web of Christmas lights that fanned out from the courthouse lawn.

Going to be a strange Christmas, he thought. *What does someone do on a holiday if he's not working?*

Roy had always worked Christmas Day. Nobody else wanted to — they wanted to be with their families. Having no kids waiting at home, Roy had been happy enough to take double-time pay and maintain his own tradition, working at the news desk. This year, though, he'd have to find something to do.

There had been a time when family looked like a possibility. He'd gotten married when he was thirty, to a beautiful blonde named Sarah. She was fresh out of graduate school in Lexington and filled with journalistic ambition, and theirs had been a newsroom romance.

In the end, though, Sarah's talent and ambition outgrew him, and he didn't fault her for it. They'd always talked of leaving together, going to New York or Los Angeles or, hell, leaving the country, working on a book together. To Roy, those had been idle fantasies. To Sarah, they'd been plans. He realized when they separated how dangerous it was to allow someone to think you had a shared concept of the future when in fact you didn't.

When she got the job in London, she'd been certain he'd go with her. Everyone had been. Except Roy.

He'd told her that Sawyer County was home. She was astonished. What about all those big stories they were going to tell, the ones that mattered?

He said he found plenty that mattered right here in the mountains.

She took it as a rejection of her — he didn't have any family, and how could anyone possibly be so attached to a town, so rooted to a spot in the earth? He didn't know how it was possible, he just knew that it was true, and that he was grateful for it. This place was home.

He was thinking of the way she could dance, how gracefully she moved, and trying to remember when the last time he had danced was when the phone rang again. Same unknown number. This time he answered.

"Hello?"

"Darmus?"

It was Kevin Kimble. Only he didn't sound so good. Roy swallowed his steak, took a sip of beer, and said, "You've been thinking on that list."

"I've been doing more than thinking. I just interviewed O'Patrick."

Roy pushed back from the table. "What did he tell you?"

"It's a story to be told in person, no doubt about that. But listen—you were talking about those old pictures. And about the names that went back so far you couldn't find them in the newspapers."

"Yes."

"That idea you had, something in the college newspaper, or—"

"The Whitman Company paper. The college has the archives."

"Well, if you think there's something there, please try to find it."

"All right," Roy said, watching his reflection in the window, snow flurries swirling beneath the orbs of the street lamps outside, and then, "Kimble, what are you expecting me to find?"

"I'm not sure," Kimble said. "But it might involve a fire. A torch. A lantern. I don't know, some kind of light."

Roy couldn't get any words out in response to that.

"Can you look?" Kimble said. He sounded plaintive. No, it went beyond that. He sounded desperate.

"Yes," Roy said. "I can look."

The cats were stirring, growls and sharp roars splintering what had been a quiet night. It had taken Audrey hours to fall asleep, and she fought against consciousness now, clinging to soft, sweet darkness, but the sounds didn't relent, and eventually her eyelids dragged up despite her desires. It was dim in the trailer, with only the light from one corner floor lamp. Audrey squeezed her eyes shut again, still not fully awake, but then a new sound registered: rattling metal.

They were going at the fences.

This time her eyelids snapped open, and now sleep was far from her. She sat up abruptly, a blanket sliding from her shoulders onto the floor. There was no mistaking the sound—fences all over the preserve were rattling, rippling, and the cats continued to roar.

They're trying to get out, she thought. *Please, no, don't let them get out...*

She stood and jammed her feet into the boots that lay beside the couch, then pulled on a jacket and ran down the hall and jerked open the door.

"Stop it!" she shouted. "Stop!"

Her first answer was a resounding roar from one of the male lions, a sound so powerful she took a step back, actually considering shutting the door. Then she saw them, though, and the initial fear faded to fascination.

They weren't lunging at the fences, trying to tear through them, as she'd feared. They were simply standing against them, up on their hind legs, bracing their front paws against the fences.

Every single one.

"What are you doing?" she whispered, as if expecting an answer. The sounds she had heard were more than sixty pairs of paws landing against chain link, every cat rising. For what?

She found herself wishing for David. She wanted him to see this. To tell her what it meant. David or Wes, someone who understood these animals better than she did, that was what she needed.

The voice she was hearing, though, didn't belong to David or Wes but to her sister. That morning phone call after the nightmare, Ellen telling her to abandon the preserve, near hysteria in her voice.

Audrey watched the cats and felt the flush of adrenaline that had caught her when she heard them banging against the fences fade out to a cold, damp fear.

One thing you should always remember when you're out here at night, David had told her years ago, *is that they can see in the dark six times better than a human. Think about that*—six times better. *So if they seem focused on something you don't see, pay attention.*

She'd laughed and told him that half the cats passed time by staring intently at nothing even in the daylight.

You're the one who thinks they're staring at nothing, he'd said, none of his usual humor evident. *Maybe you're wrong.*

She stepped outside hesitantly, taking a flashlight with her, and called for the police officer.

"Hello? Deputy Shipley?"

Silence except for the cats. She looked at her watch and saw that it was past two. Shipley would be gone. Who was the other one? Wolverton.

"Deputy Wolverton? Can you come here, please?"

She was out in the preserve now, and in the cage at her side Larkin gave a low growl. The lynx was *literally* at her side, too, not at her feet where she belonged but stretched out to full length, bringing her head level with Audrey's waist. Audrey stared at the cat, called for Wolverton again, and received no answer.

Some security, she thought, trying to mask fear as bitterness. *They were supposed to be here to help me, not scare the shit out of me.*

She took a step farther out and was just ready to shout for him again when she saw the blue light.

It was well into the woods, back where the ground gave way to steep stone walls, and it looked like some sort of flame. She watched it spark and flicker, then looked back and realized that every single cat was watching the light.

Call for help, she thought, but she didn't move. She couldn't take her eyes away from it. That cold, dancing glow was enchanting.

Numbing.

Jafar erupted with a harsh snarl then, and the sound jarred her back into the moment. She swung the flashlight around and fastened the beam on the spotted leopard.

"Easy," she said. "Chill out, buddy."

He looked at her but did not drop down to all fours. None of them did.

She swung the flashlight back out into the woods, toward the blue flame.

"Hello?"

There was no answer.

Has to be the police, she thought. *He's got some sort of special flashlight.*

That wasn't a flashlight, though. It was a flame.

There was no smoke in the air. No smoke, no crackle of fire, just that unmistakable flame.

She moved toward it despite herself, swinging the flashlight around, the beam tracing the trees and fences, catching eerie reflections when it hit on the eyes of the various cats that were watching her.

Go back inside, she told herself. *Go back inside.*

But she couldn't. If something was wrong, she needed to know. The police were gone, and the cats were anxious, and there was one person left to deal with it: her.

The wind blew along in a sudden gust that had brittle edges of December cold. Above her, branches knocked hollowly off one another, and one tree emitted a long, whining creak that seemed directed at her, seemed plaintive.

The blue light was moving toward her.

She stood where she was, and the cats fell silent but did not change position, every one of them watching the woods.

I want your eyes, she thought. *Just for a minute. Let me see in the dark like you, just for long enough to know what's out there.*

But all she could see was the silhouetted trees and the glimmering blue flame.

"Who's there?" she called, and then she began to walk toward it, her own flashlight now a moving glow. The blue light seemed to have stopped between the crest of the ridge and the edge of the preserve. She wouldn't go far. Just out past the cages, far enough to see, far enough to be heard. It was Wolverton, had to be. He just couldn't hear her. With those gusts of northern wind pushing the trees and the cats roaring, it would be hard to hear her.

And hard to see a flashlight, Audrey? He can't see a flashlight?

Maybe he was being silent for a reason. Maybe he was pursuing the source of that blue light himself, and the last thing he wanted was for her to come bumbling along, shouting and shining a flashlight and —

When the cat growled on her left, she wasn't immediately concerned. She was used to walking past growling animals, had just come out in the darkness to be greeted by a lion's roar. It registered slowly — far too slowly — that she was past the enclosures, and no cats were on her left.

No cats *should* be on her left.

She stopped walking, a sense of inevitable disaster descending over her, a soldier hearing the click of a land mine at his feet.

Ira.

There was another growl, a deep, warning note, and it was very near. The blue light ahead of her was forgotten now, irrelevant. All that mattered was this sound at her side and how to respond.

Move slowly, she told herself. *You have to move slowly.* She swung the flashlight to her left, the beam gliding over the trees like headlights coming around a curve, and found the black cat no more than ten feet away.

She saw the sparkle of his eyes first. Emerald, like pieces of an old bottle made of green glass. Then the rest of him took shape — hunched shoulders, coiled muscles, stiff tail. She was trying to say his name when she saw something pale beneath his front paws, and then the breath went out of her.

He was standing on a body.

One limp white palm extended out into the leaves. That was what had caught her attention. The rest was nearly camouflage, the brown uniform of the sheriff's department. He was face-down in the brush, and the blood that pooled around his throat looked so black that it seemed a part of the cougar, an extension of his fur.

Audrey screamed. Everything in her brain told her not to, told her that the cat would spring at the slightest provocation, but everything in your brain could fail you at the sight of something like this, and so she screamed despite herself.

The cat snarled, snapped forward, and lashed out with a paw. He didn't leave, though. He was protecting the kill.

Audrey turned and ran into the night, ran gracelessly and pointlessly, knowing that he would bring her down from behind and end her out here in the cold woods.

He didn't, though. He never moved, but even after Audrey fell onto her knees in the trailer, with the door closed behind her, she still had her hands up by her neck as if to protect her throat when he sprang.

27

WHEN THE PHONE RANG at three A.M., Kimble knew it would be bad in the way that you always knew a call at that hour would be bad, but he hadn't imagined it could be like this. He hadn't imagined that whatever had happened had happened out there.

His first, groggy thought upon hearing that one of his own was down at Blade Ridge was a perverse, horrible hopefulness.

Maybe it's Shipley. Maybe whatever madness exists out there is feeding on its own.

It wasn't Shipley, though. It was Pete Wolverton.

He hung up the phone, pressed the heels of his hands into his eyes, and cursed himself. All he'd heard about that place tonight, and still he hadn't called them off. He'd considered it, but then the thought of Audrey Clark had changed his mind. She wasn't going to abandon her cats, and he hadn't wanted to leave her alone out there.

"I'm sorry, Pete," he whispered. "Damn it, I'm so sorry."

Then he got up, dressed, put on his gun, and went to make amends.

*   *   *

The scene was bright when he arrived, four cars already there, three from his department and one from the state police, all with flashers going. Spotlights were shining in the woods where Pete Wolverton had died, brightening the night so that the evidence techs could take their photographs.

Kimble got out of his car, feeling wearier than he ever had in his life, and went to talk to Diane Mooney, who was in charge of the scene.

"Where's Audrey Clark?" he said. Around them the cats milled, bothered by all the lights and activity.

"Inside. She's shaken up pretty bad."

"She saw it happen?"

"Essentially. She found Pete with that fucking cat still on top of him."

The venom in Diane's voice was something Kimble had never heard from her. She wasn't facing him, was instead looking out at the preserve, where dozens of massive cats stared back at her.

"Be a pro," Kimble said, gentle but firm.

"I'm trying, chief. But that was Pete out there. That was *Pete*."

"I know it. You talked to Shipley?"

"No. Why?"

"He was here until midnight, when Pete relieved him. I want him…" He hesitated, about to say that he wanted Shipley out to tell them what he'd seen, but now thinking that he didn't want Shipley out here at all. "We need to know if he saw or heard anything during his shift," he said. "But I'll run him down tomorrow. We don't need him at the scene. We got enough people out here as it is, and since they were working together on this, it might hit him harder than any of us."

"I don't think there's a sliding scale on the way this one hits."

Kimble nodded. "Was it you who interviewed Audrey Clark?"

"Yes. We'll need to take another run at her, though. She wasn't making a whole lot of sense."

"How so?"

"Well, she's hysterical, for one thing. But when she *does* talk, she claims that all those damned cats were dancing around on their hind legs, that someone with a blue torch guided her to the body, that—"

"Hang on. Hang on. A blue torch?"

"Like I said, she's hysterical. Talking nonsense."

Kimble looked up at the lighthouse and wet his lips. "Right. You've seen the body? You've seen Pete?"

She nodded.

"Any chance he wasn't killed by the cougar?"

"Sure," Diane said. "If there's a wolf on the loose."

He followed Diane through the woods and out to the place where Pete Wolverton lay in the wet leaves. A ring of spotlights had been set up around him as if a film crew were readying for a shoot, and yellow tape was strung between the trees. Everyone was hushed. Death scenes were always grim places, but this was different. This was one of their own.

Kimble ducked under the tape, approached the body of his friend of fifteen years, and dropped into a crouch. He felt something thick in the back of his throat and tight behind the eyes, drew in air through clenched teeth and then let it out slowly.

"No sign of the cat?" he said.

"None," Diane answered. "With all these people around, he won't show himself again. But when it was just Pete out here alone . . . he showed himself then, didn't he?"

Kimble looked up at her, and she turned away. It had been Kimble's decision to run a one-man rotation in these woods, and his deputies would not forget that. He wouldn't either.

He cupped his hands to shield his eyes from the glare of the lights and focused on Pete's body. There were tears in his uniform across the back, some blood showing through them, but not much. Obvious claw marks, but not the killing wound. He'd bled out from the throat.

"You ready to turn him over?" Kimble asked the lead evidence tech, who was with the state police, a topnotch guy. He'd rolled out fast. That was the way it went when a police officer was killed.

"Yeah. Waiting on you."

"All right. Let's turn him."

Two of the technicians reached out with gloved hands and gently, with utmost care, rolled Pete Wolverton's body over. The head didn't roll in sync with the rest of him — there wasn't much muscle left tethering skull to torso.

Someone whispered an oath, someone else a prayer. Kimble slid closer.

Pete's throat had been laid wide open, and the cords of muscle showed white against the dark blood, which had spilled in enormous quantity, saturating Pete's uniform shirt and all of the leaves around him. Kimble brought a hand up to his face and squeezed the flesh between his eyes with his thumb and index finger. He squeezed long and hard, concentrating on the pressure. Nobody spoke.

When he took his hand down again, he looked right at the wound. Not at Pete's face, not at his eyes, not at the blood-soaked uniform that bound him in brotherhood to the men and women here. Just at the wound.

It was a very straight incision. An end-to-end slash that had cut remarkably deep, severing not just the arteries but the strong cartilage of the throat that people referred to as the windpipe.

Kimble said, "We think a claw did that?"

For a moment it was silent. Then the head evidence tech, from

206

the state police, who was closest to the body, said, "Well, if it had used its teeth, everything would be torn. Chewed up. So that slash, yeah, that must have been a claw."

"It's very clean."

Above him, Diane said, "There are claw marks all over his back, too."

"I saw them. Not nearly so clean. Not very deep at all."

Everyone was staring at him now. The evidence technician looked thoughtful. He turned back to the wound and said, "It is very clean."

Diane said, "What are you thinking, chief?"

"I'm thinking that I've seen six people whose throats were cut with knives," Kimble said. "One cut with a sword, one with an ax, one with a barbecue fork. I've never seen anyone's throat opened up by a cat. I don't know what it looks like."

"Like *that*," she said, her voice unsteady. The evidence technician, though, was meeting Kimble's eyes, and there was a glimmer of understanding and agreement there.

"Autopsy will tell us, won't it?" Kimble said, speaking to him.

"Yeah. We'll be able to tell."

"Tell what?" Diane said.

Kimble straightened, dusting leaves from his jeans. "Whether the cougar killed him," he said, "or found him."

28

THE IMAGE AUDREY COULD NOT get out of her mind was a Valium bottle. There was one at home, in the medicine cabinet, a prescription she'd filled in the weeks after David's death. The pills had carried her through the funeral, through the softly spoken sympathies and the offers of help and the sight of him in the casket, but then she'd tucked them in a far corner of the medicine cabinet. Not because they didn't help, but because she didn't want to have to rely on that kind of help for too long.

Now she wanted that kind of help again. Wanted to take a handful of them, wanted the world to go cloudlike, soft and distant. Very distant.

She'd spoken to two different police officers, one woman who was harsh, almost accusatory, and one older man who hadn't said much at all, just kept telling her to get comfortable, as if he were the awkward host of the world's worst party. She'd gotten the tears and the trembling under control and was just beginning to feel some strength return when the sheriff himself stepped through the door. He wore his Stetson with the badge affixed to the crown, as if he'd just ridden in from Tombstone, and he looked at her with undisguised fury.

"Mrs. Clark," he said, "I intend to let my department handle this investigation in the standard fashion. It's not my job to interview you, and I won't, though I'm damned tempted. I'm here for two reasons. The most important is out of respect for my deputy, who's being zipped into a body bag right now. The other? I want you to know that this property is going to be closed."

"What does that mean?" Audrey said. *"Closed?"*

"It means I will see this place shut down and your cats gone."

She stared at him. In her hands was a cup of tea the other officer had insisted on making for her. He was looking at the floor now.

"I've tolerated this circus when I shouldn't have," the sheriff said. "I'll carry that guilt for a long time, believe me. But in the last two days, two men have died because of your damned cats. If you think I won't respond to that—"

"Someone shot Kino," she said. "Your own officers found a bullet. They didn't want to talk to me about it, but I know what it means. Someone came out here and shot one of my cats, and my best friend left in this world died trying to help. I know you just lost one of your own, and I'm sorry. But you need to remember that I've lost one of mine, too!"

Her voice was shaking, and the sheriff looked at her without a trace of emotion. When he spoke again, his voice was flat.

"It's my understanding that the USDA handles your permitting."

"That's right," she said. "And the permits are in order. They approved the new facility before—"

"They'll be coming back out," he said. "Along with some folks from the state wildlife agency. Along with whoever the hell else I need. I'll find whoever it takes, and I'll come with them."

The door opened again, and another cop stepped through.

She recognized this one. Kimble. The sheriff glanced at him, then turned back to Audrey.

"You can't shut it down," she said. "There are more than sixty cats who need—"

"I have no interest in the needs of your cats. I have interest in the public safety of Sawyer County. You have every right to object, and I'm sure you will. I'm just telling you the score. Don't say you were blindsided. I intend to get these cats out of my county."

She didn't respond.

"As for the missing cat," he continued, "I intend to find it. I'm having poisoned bait traps placed along the riverbed right now."

"You can't *poison*—"

He held up a hand. "You lost him, Mrs. Clark. You couldn't handle him. When he was on your property, he was yours to care for. When he's loose? He's *mine*. I'm not worried about the cat's health. I'm worried about the public's."

"Good luck getting him," she said softly, and he flushed with rage, was halfway to a blustering response when she said, "No— I mean it. Good luck."

He stared at her, then turned away. Said something low to Kimble and banged open the door and went outside.

"He's hurting," Kimble said, crossing the room to sit beside her. "We all are."

"I understand that."

"He's also not wrong. Things are getting out of hand here. Do you have anyone you can contact, Mrs. Clark? Anyone who can come out here and lend some...some expertise? Experience?"

"Joe Taft," she said. Joe owned an enormous rescue center in Indiana, the model for her own facility. Joe was as good with cats as anyone other than Wesley Harrington.

"How soon can he get here?"

"I don't know."

"Well, find out. And in the meantime, who can you have here that you trust? Really trust."

My husband, she thought. *Wes,* she thought. Gone, and gone. She blinked back tears and said, "Dustin Hall is the only person qualified. Dustin and I can keep things going alone. It won't be easy, but we can do it. I have volunteers who usually help, but right now... right now it's probably a bad idea to have too many people out here."

"I won't disagree," Kimble said, and then looked up at the older deputy and said, "Rick, can we have a minute?"

The deputy nodded and left and then it was just the two of them. Kimble waited until the door was closed, then said, "I'd like to hear about the blue light."

She stared at him. When she'd told the story the first time, all she'd seen was loathing and pity from the listeners. Why tell it again, to another person who wouldn't believe her?

"I thought I saw one," she muttered, and was ready to leave it at that until he spoke.

"Was it a torch? A flame?"

She set the tea down. "Yes. It was a flame. Not just a light, but a *flame*. How did you know?"

He didn't answer that, just asked another question.

"You thought it led you to the body, is that correct?"

"Not exactly. I saw it and was walking toward it. I wanted to see who it was. I hadn't made it far before I heard Ira."

Kimble nodded. "You didn't see the cat attack him, though. Or hear anything that sounded like that?"

"No. I was asleep. I woke up because the cats got agitated. I came outside and they were all standing up against the fences. Watching something. Watching that light."

"When you saw the cougar, Pete was already dead."

"I think so. There was so much blood. And he didn't move. Yes, he was dead."

"Was the cat showing interest in the body?"

"Interest?"

He nodded.

"Ira was just...standing over it. On it. The way they do when they're protecting a kill."

"All right." Kimble reached out and touched her leg gently. "I'm sorry for your loss, too. It's easy for us to forget about that, tonight. Please understand."

"I do."

He stood up. "I'll be handling the investigation. *Both* of the investigations. If you need anything, ask for me directly, would you?"

"Yes."

"I think it's very important that you get someone out here," he said. "Right now there are police all over. But when they leave, you're alone?"

"I'm fine."

"When they leave, you're alone?" he repeated. He looked extremely concerned at the idea.

"Yes," she said.

"And you can't leave, yourself," he said, almost as if he were thinking aloud. "You can't leave the cats."

"Someone has to be with them. At this point, I'm it."

He nodded sadly. "All right. Who can you call to be with you? Someone you trust. A friend, family. I'm asking you, please, not to be here alone."

His voice was so grave that it frightened her. She said, "I'll call Dustin in the morning. He can be here with me."

"Please do."

He went to the door, then stopped with his hand on the knob and stared out the window. He was looking, she realized, up at the hill across the road, where the lighthouse stood in darkness.

"You had some altercations with Wyatt French, didn't you?"

"Altercations?"

"Disputes. I know he was arrested for disrupting a meeting about this place."

"That's right."

"Did he ever make it clear why he didn't want you here?"

She frowned. Why in the world were they talking about Wyatt French?

"He couldn't make anything clear. When he wasn't drunk, he was crazy."

"Sure. But what did he offer? What reasoning?"

"He said it was a dangerous spot," she said. "That was about it. When we complained about the light, he wasn't very happy. Then David died, and he wrote me a letter proving his point."

Kimble turned. "A letter?"

"It was a Hallmark sympathy card, came in with all the others. Just not so sympathetic. He said how sorry he was, but then said that we'd brought it on ourselves. How very kind, don't you think?"

Kimble looked thoughtful. He said, "When you complained about the light, he had to change it, didn't he? Reduce the brightness."

"Yes. It was terrible before that. These blinding flashes."

"When your husband died ... where in the process was that?"

"What do you mean, process? Why are we even talking about this?"

"I'm just trying to understand which light was up then. The old or the new."

"Neither of them."

He looked at her in an odd way. "Neither?"

She shook her head. "That was when he was changing to the dimmer lamp. I guess it required wiring changes, because he wanted us to pay for that. We declined. For a few days there, it was dark. He didn't waste much time, though."

"No," he said in a detached voice. "He went as fast as he could."

29

THE SHERIFF WAS WAITING for Kimble outside. He'd taken the Stetson off and was rubbing his eyes. When Kimble came down the steps, he put the hat back on. Kimble could see that his hand was wet with tears.

"Pete Wolverton," Troy said, "was one of the best we had."

"None better."

"Long time with us, too. Lot of good years. Lot of good work."

Kimble nodded.

"Nobody's called Julie," Troy said. Julie was Wolverton's wife. They had two children, both teenagers, and Pete was one of those dads who liked to show you pictures of the kids.

"I'll go see her," Kimble said.

"No. That's my job." Troy took a deep breath, spat, and shook his head. "I was hard on that woman in there, and maybe I ought not to have been. I'm standing out here looking at these cats and thinking that she's all alone with them."

"She is now," Kimble said. "Lost her husband a few months back. Lost her friend, who was the man who kept this place going, yesterday. She's hanging in there and taking punches the likes of which we never have. Or I never have, at least. Be a worthy thing to remember."

Troy nodded. "I know it. I came out here, I was just feeling sick, you know? Empty sick, the useless kind. And I got worked up telling myself that I wouldn't be useless. I'd answer for him somehow. The only idea I had was to clear them out of here, every last one of them, and thought that would be worth something. I still think that it is."

"I don't," Kimble said.

Troy looked at him with surprise.

"They've had this preserve going for a long time," Kimble said. "Never an incident. Not until they came here."

"Been a lot of incidents since."

"There have been. I intend to find a way to handle it, Troy. I do. But let's not allow ourselves to blame the wrong party. I was with her most of the morning. That's a brave woman."

"I don't blame *her,* Kimble. It might have sounded as such, but I don't blame her. I blame that damned cat. And while I don't like any of them here, the one that's free is the one we're going to need to deal with first. Going to need to find that cat and kill it. That's the only thing. I'm thinking poison bait traps. Spread 'em out all along the river down there."

"And what if somebody's dog gets into them, or, hell, a kid?"

"A kid's going to eat a bloody piece of raw meat? Any kid that does that is one I'd put on the scorecard as points in our favor. Won't have to arrest him for some fucked-up shit ten years from now."

Kimble couldn't help but smile at that.

"We'll figure out a way to get him," he said. "But even if the cat did kill Pete, you've got to remember that it was recently a wild animal and still has a hunter's blood. Not much Audrey Clark, or anyone else, can do about that."

Troy tilted his head and stared at Kimble. "Did I hear you say *if?*"

Kimble glanced to his left, where the crime-scene lights glared in the woods, and said, "Troy, I've seen the body. I'd wager my last dime that when the medical examiner is done, he'll say Pete's throat was cut."

Neither of them spoke for a long time. When Troy finally broke the silence, he said, "She saw the cat with him, Kimble. She saw it."

"After Pete was dead. She did *not* see it bring him down."

"You're telling me you think someone came out here and cut his throat tonight. You're serious."

"I am. We'll see what the autopsy says. The tiger that was shot out here yesterday? That was not a case of the property manager trying to put down a wild cat. Someone else took that shot."

"I know that, Kimble. I read your report, and Mrs. Clark was in there carrying on about it just a minute ago. I understand it's a crime. But there's a damned big difference between someone taking a pot shot at a tiger and someone cutting a policeman's throat."

Kimble took a breath, looked Troy in the eye, and said, "I'm going to ask you for some leeway on this."

"What do you mean, Kimble?"

"Give me twenty-four hours on my own with it. No reports, nobody riding with me, no meetings. Just give me a day of space to work."

"If you've got notions on who did this," Troy said, "I need to hear them."

"Twenty-four hours," Kimble repeated. "You give me that, sir, and I'll give you every notion I've got. If you don't like them, and you probably won't...well, we'll deal with that then. But let me run with it, sir."

Troy looked at him for a long time, and then he said, "We've been working together for too damn long, Kimble, for you to call me sir."

"I know it. But this just feels a little different, doesn't it?"

"Yes," Troy said. "It sure as shit does."

They walked together back to Troy's car, and Kimble put out his hand and squeezed the sheriff's shoulder and wished him luck. There was nothing false in the gesture. They had their differences, in demeanor and approach, but Kimble did not envy the man the trip he was about to make to see Julie Wolverton, and he was proud of him for making it.

When the sheriff was gone, Kimble waited until they removed Pete's body. He stood with head bowed as they carried it past, and then, when the others were either gone down the road or back in the woods, he got into his own car and drove across the gravel and up the winding lane until he reached the top of the hill and the lighthouse rose like a menacing specter in the night, white paint and glass picking up the pale moon glow and holding the tower stark against the night sky. Kimble parked outside the fence and left the car running, the headlights aimed at the front of the building, then found the keys to the property. He stepped out of the car and unlocked the gate and went up the path to the lighthouse, opened the door, and stepped inside the cold room. The walls were bare wood now, unadorned by the maps and photographs. All that remained was the thumbtacks, which protruded in all directions, tilting like gravestones in a forgotten cemetery.

"Okay," Kimble said. "I've heard enough and seen enough to give it a shot, Wyatt. I'll give it a shot."

He crossed to the bed, leaned over it, and opened the electrical panel. There was a series of metallic snaps as he flipped the breakers. No lights came on, but he heard a hum.

He closed the panel door, looked at the words that covered it, those song lyrics:

And the sky's so cold and clear
The stars might stick you where you stand
And you're only glad it's dark
'Cause you might see the Master's hand...

He turned away, then used the flashlight to find his way up the stairs. There he dropped to one knee, reached out, and laid a palm over the lens of the infrared lamps. Warm. They were back on, casting their invisible beams into the woods.

He straightened, turned off the flashlight, and looked at the fractured glass panel left from the killing bullet. He thought of a line he'd read long ago: It was no accident that most people who committed suicide with a gun chose to shoot themselves in the head and not the heart. It was there that they were plagued, haunted, tormented.

He stared out at the dark hills through the wide glass panes, thinking of all the stories he'd heard today. Even in the night, you could see the outline of the railroad trestle, spindly silhouettes over a river that shimmered beneath the moon.

Twenty-four hours, he'd told the sheriff, and then he'd share his thoughts. They were thoughts that might well cost him his badge. What he was coming to believe was likely impossible to prove.

But he'd be damned if he wouldn't try.

30

THE WHITMAN COLLEGE LIBRARY was open until Christmas Eve, but with classes already out of session for the semester there was hardly a student or faculty member to prowl the shelves. Roy met the librarian at the door as she unlocked the building, and his presence gave her a start. It was well past dawn but barely light, the sun hidden by layers of leaden clouds. They were predicting snow, the season's first chance of accumulation.

Roy was vaguely acquainted with the librarian who greeted him — her name was Robin and she'd helped him out with a few bits of research over the years — and that was both reassuring and a little troubling. She'd be good to him, he knew, but she might also have questions that he wasn't prepared to answer.

She led with a question, in fact. As Roy showed her the photographs and explained that he was hoping to find the source, she asked immediately what he was working on, now that the newspaper was closed.

"Looking for that next step," he said. "You know, maybe a book or something."

"I think that would be just great," Robin said in the tone of voice you used when a toddler announced his intention to learn to fly a plane. Or, in Roy's experience, when damn near anyone announced their intention to write a book. "We'd hate to lose you from town, you know."

"I don't think it's in me to leave, even if I wanted to. Still stories to tell, too. I suppose I'll turn into an old man sitting on a liar's bench, passing my news along that way."

"You could start a blog," she said cheerfully and seriously, and the word stirred bile in Roy's stomach.

"I could," he said. "Now, it looks to me like these are microfilm printouts. But they aren't from my paper." Even now, he couldn't get that out of his system. *My* paper. "I was thinking that there was a predecessor to the *Sentinel*. Very old: Back when the town was still in mining-camp days."

Robin nodded. "The *Whitman Company Chronicle*. Your *Sentinel* was a rival and eventually the last one standing. They took issue with the controlled voice during some labor disputes. For a while there were two newspapers. The *Whitman Company Chronicle* became the *Whitman Chronicle* to hide the obvious ties, as if they could be hidden, but within a few years the *Sentinel* had rendered it irrelevant."

"That's what I recalled. You do have the *Chronicle* on microfilm?"

"A lot of them. Some have been lost to history, I think, but we've got most of them." She frowned at the photographs he had in the open folder. "Who are you looking for?"

"Just names."

"Why are so many labeled *NO?*"

That one hung him up for a second, because he didn't understand the truth well enough to lie about it.

"I guess I wasn't the only person who didn't know who they were," he said finally.

"Okay. So you just want to match pictures? That's going to take a while. Maybe a very *long* while."

"I've got four names, too. Just no dates."

"Do you know who they were? What they were involved with?"

"I'm afraid not."

"How did you get the names, then?"

Roy thought for a second and then smiled sadly. "It was a hot tip."

She gave him a curious look but didn't push it. "Well, give me the names and I'll see what I can find. We've got pretty good indexing of the company records, so if they had anything to do with the Whitmans, I should be able to generate something."

The family archives were housed in a private, locked room at the rear of the library. You couldn't spend time there without supervision, and you couldn't check anything out. There was a reason: this collection held the most precious recorded elements of the town's history. Robin unlocked the door and led Roy into the room, which featured glass cabinets displaying certain historical relics, one long and ornate reading table, and, everywhere you looked, the austere faces of Whitman family members watching from portraits and photographs along the walls. It was not unlike being in Wyatt's lighthouse.

"I'll get you the microfilm and let you start where you like," Robin said. "Then I can run a search on those names you have. It's a shame you don't have a clearer starting point in time. Are there no indications in the photographs?"

"Well, it's a work crew of some sort," Roy said. "Not miners, either. Looks like they're timber men, probably. Or builders."

He set the folder down on the table and rifled through the photographs, pulling out a few as indications. "See, there's a group of men holding a timber saw, and here we've got —"

"Oh," Robin said, "they're building the trestle."

Roy turned away from the pictures and looked at her. She smiled in perfect confidence.

"The one that's still standing. The wooden one, out west of town?"

"At Blade Ridge."

"That's right."

He looked back down at a photograph of men holding a large log over their shoulders and said, "How in the hell can you be so sure?"

She laughed. "I'm not clairvoyant. I've already been through this routine once. Someone else was researching the trestle itself, and we went through a lot of those old company papers."

"Wyatt French?"

She nodded, indifferent, neither surprised that he knew about this nor sharing the troubled sensations that Roy was feeling.

"That's right. He owned most of the property at one time. He was very interested in the history."

He certainly seemed to be, Roy thought, and then he said, "Well, that can cut some time down. Maybe I should start with the trestle. I think that makes a lot of sense."

"It's a sad story," she said, moving toward a row of locked cabinets at the back of the room.

"I know that the mines didn't pan out for the company."

"I mean the trestle itself," she said over her shoulder, unlocking a drawer and running her index finger over canisters of microfilm. "A lot of people died while it was being built."

"Died how?"

"Sickness, first. Murder, later." She withdrew two canisters and said, "This should do it. Should give you a start."

"Sickness, first," Roy echoed, "murder, later?"

"That's right. There was some hostility between the company and the laborers. The Whitmans tried to force sick men to work

222

to get their bridge done on time. They got it done, but there was a bit of uprising toward the end. You know, one of the stories that were all too common out here."

Labor disputes turned violent were perhaps all too common in eastern Kentucky's history, but Roy had a feeling that the Blade Ridge story might prove to be a little more unique.

"I might be wrong," Robin said, feeding one of the microfilm reels into the reader in the corner of the room, "but I think if you start with the end of 1888 and go through the beginning of 1889 you'll get a clear idea of it. But who knows if that's even what you want. I can try some other —"

"Let me start there. That sounds right. Thank you."

"Of course. We're short-staffed because the students are gone, so if I can leave you to it, that would be a help. Just let me know what else you need."

"That's fine," Roy said. He wanted to be alone to read this.

She left the room, and he sat down and snapped on the projector and saw an image of a 124-year-old newspaper. She'd started him in September, and he flipped through the pages quickly, looking for news of the trestle. The style of journalism was opinion stated as fact, and the stories themselves were focused on either braggadocio about the company's successes or the mundane day-to-day of the mining town life. A local minister missing a service because of illness was front-page news. Obituaries were given prime placement as well, and the phrasing used to describe the deaths was colorful, to say the least. "The Reaper Calls upon Reginald Holmes," one headline read.

The dominant figure of the news in Whitman in 1888 was the town's namesake, Frederick Whitman Jr. His mining investments were just getting under way. In an early October issue, Roy found a match of one of his own photographs. Five men standing with a timber saw, smiles all around. The article announced that work on the trestle over the Marshall River was coming along nicely and would be finished, as promised to investors, by the new year. The next picture featured the bridge's Boston-bred designer, Alfred H. Tremley, a stern and bespectacled man who seemed quite pleased with the idea that the camera was preserving his image.

Roy had gotten all the way to late October before he saw another article that gave him pause.

"Trestle Work Lags as Fever Strikes," announced a boldface headline. Three days later came the report of a death, and a week after that the news that the construction crew had been quarantined in camps beside the river, no longer allowed to return home. The decision, according to Frederick Whitman Jr., was made to safeguard the health of the townspeople. A short notation at the end of the article indicated that work at the trestle continued, and Whitman remained wedded to his promise of completion by year's end.

After the quarantine, the company newspaper stopped reporting on the condition of the crew but continued to follow the trestle itself. On December 19, it was noted that only three bents — Roy understood those to be the bridge supports — had gone up in the past two weeks, and the writer predicted that the opening of the mines by 1889 was in jeopardy.

The next mention was on December 27, when it was observed — with clear astonishment — that all of the bents were in place and work had begun on the rails. On New Year's Eve, the entire front page was devoted to the trestle, which was completed as promised. Amidst the proud remarks, a brief comment on the illness:

> The bridge is a testament to endurance, completed despite the fever that infected the crew. Sixteen men were lost.

It seemed an impossibly short mention for all those lost lives, but Roy understood. The *Chronicle* was a mouthpiece, nothing

224

more. The reality of the way that bridge had been pushed toward completion despite the ravages of illness was probably quite unflattering to the company. It was in the midst of this era that the *Sentinel* had been born, and the significance of its name became all the more clear. It was a targeted move to balance the forces of the company. One paper identified itself as the chronicle of the town's new power structure; the next chose the watchdog approach.

And now they're all gone, Roy thought. *What happens when you remove the watchdog from the grounds?*

Frederick Whitman Jr. had been the company voice in the *Chronicle* until December of 1888. By the time the bridge was completed, however, he'd been replaced as spokesman by his younger brother, Roger, who closed out 1888 by boasting that the family had done exactly as promised, spanning the river with rails by year's end, and plans were made to christen the trestle on New Year's Day. Roger Whitman was quoted as saying he looked forward to crossing his bridge.

Roy loaded another canister of microfilm, feeling the familiar and beloved tingle of adrenaline that he'd enjoyed so often while working on a story, and was rewarded almost immediately by the first big news of 1889: true to his word, Roger Whitman had crossed his bridge.

Once.

On January 1, Whitman and fifteen assorted executives and investors piled into a single boxcar to celebrate "a glorious new year for the company, the community, and the country." The locomotive crossed the Marshall River, cleared the trestle, and derailed upon reaching Blade Ridge, where an obstruction had been placed over the tracks. At that point, four men emerged from the woods and opened fire. By the time it was done, eleven of the men aboard the train had been killed. Roger Whitman survived.

Four men were arrested for the sabotage and murder: John Hamlin, Fred Mortimer, Henry Bates, and Bernard Snell.

But Wyatt already had those names; they were new only to Roy. The question of whom he'd been searching for in all those photographs remained. Why had so many been dismissed with a *NO*?

Investigators of the day had been looking for a man named Silas Vesey, based on an anonymous tip. The arrested men refused to comment on Vesey and said they acted alone. All four, the *Sentinel* reported, had been involved in the construction of the trestle, believed that the Whitmans had caused death by forcing sick men to work, and readily confessed to their crimes. They hid neither guilt nor motive, and one, Mortimer, explained that Roger Whitman was never intended to be the target of the bullets.

"We wanted him to live with the price," Mortimer said. "To see our faces, and to remember who we were and what he'd done. The blood we took is on his hands. It won't end here."

Whitman had no response.

Justice was swift. In February the four men were found guilty of murder, and in March they were hanged. A hundred operatives from the Pinkerton detective agency joined local police to enforce order on the night of execution. They feared a riot, particularly after Mortimer's ominous pledge that the vengeance had not reached its end. Nothing happened, though. Nooses drew tight, lungs emptied, hearts stopped, and the violent controversy at Blade Ridge began its move from breaking news to historical footnote.

Missing from the execution and the trial was Frederick Whitman Jr. It seemed very odd—he had, after all, been the dominant voice in the early stages of the trestle's construction—but some explanation was offered in a piece that followed the executions. The *Chronicle* reported that the endeavor at Blade Ridge had put "a powerful strain upon Frederick, and the stress has been temporarily damaging to his well-being. He is in a sanctuary for restoration, and the family and company look forward to his return."

The jargon was delicate, but it would have been clear enough to anyone who read it at the time, and it still was. On the day that four of his former employees dangled lifeless at the end of their hanging ropes, Frederick Whitman Jr. had been in an asylum.

31

Nathan shipley still lived in the rambling farmhouse that had once belonged to the grandparents who raised him after his father was killed. His mother — nineteen when she had Nathan, twenty when she left town — had been a beautiful girl with a softness for sweet talk and malt liquor, a combination that had brought down many a beautiful girl before. She'd left Sawyer County without a word the same year Ed Shipley returned home from the Marines and joined up with the sheriff's department. No one had heard of her since. The story was common knowledge in the sheriff's department, where the Shipley name had long represented two things: courage and tragedy.

Kimble pulled into the driveway, shut off the engine, and sat for a time, looking at the house. After a few minutes, the door cracked open and Nathan peered out, having heard his visitor arriving, and then Kimble could delay the talk no longer. He did the oddest thing as he left the car — he blessed himself. Kimble had not been in a church for many a Sunday, and even when he had attended he had never been the sort for such gestures, but still he found himself doing it.

"Hey, there, chief," Nathan said as Kimble approached. "I just heard."

There was a hitch in Kimble's stride then, but Shipley was watching, so he came on anyhow, no longer sure of how the conversation was going to go. He'd planned to come out here and break the news himself, felt as if in so doing he would be able to read the man well, to gauge whether he was really breaking any news at all.

"Who called you?"

"Troy."

Damn it. Kimble could have asked him to keep a lid on the news at least for a little while.

But could he really have? No. Because to ask that such a thing be kept from Shipley would be to disclose his suspicion of Shipley, and then he would need some grounds, and what he had so far, well, it wasn't the sort of thing that would play well with the sheriff. With anyone.

"We haven't lost a man in the line of duty since your father," Kimble said. He was standing on the porch, just past the front steps, hadn't closed the distance or approached the door. His hand hung close to his hip.

"I know it. And if we made that shift change a couple hours later?" Shipley ran a hand over his face, had his eyes screened from sight when he said, "Then it's like father, like son, chief. And you know the damned thing about it? Would've both been due to cats."

It took Kimble a moment to understand that, but then he realized it was true. Ed Shipley had run into that fire looking for a cat that he misunderstood to be a person. He'd never run back out.

"Mind if we have a seat?" Kimble said.

"Come on in."

"If it's all the same, let's sit outside. I like to watch the fog come off those hills. You have one hell of a view for it."

Shipley gave him a curious look, it being a chill December morning with the threat of snow in the air, but he nodded. "Aren't many better views in the county," he said. "Maybe Wyatt's lighthouse."

The reference froze Kimble up. When Shipley said, "Come on in, best view is from the back porch," Kimble couldn't say a word, just followed him into the house, which was clean enough but smelled of trapped grime and the ancient sweat of people long departed, the sort of odors you could never clear out of an old home with a mop and Lysol. The place was outfitted the way you'd expect an eighty-year-old's home to be, but as far as Kimble understood, Shipley had been alone in it for nearly a decade now. The television set in the living room was one of those bulky things mounted into a heavy wooden cabinet, had to be twenty years old at least, and the screen was covered with a thick film of dust.

They went out to the back porch, which did indeed offer a fine view of the distant mountaintops covered in their trademark smoky fog.

"Sun's hardly up," Shipley said. "But it's never too early to toast a comrade, is it?"

"I suppose it never is."

Shipley nodded, went inside, and returned with a bottle of Jim Beam. "To Pete Wolverton," he said, and took a pull. His hand was trembling. His face was pale and his blue eyes rimmed with dark circles. Kimble thought, *He looks like he hasn't slept in days,* but then realized that he himself couldn't look much better. Hell, Shipley *hadn't* slept much in days.

Shipley passed the bottle to Kimble.

"To Pete," Kimble said, and then he tasted the bourbon and found it an unsatisfactory substitute for the morning's coffee. His stomach roiled, but maybe that wasn't because of the whiskey. Maybe that was because of what he was thinking of Shipley, who stood there in his jeans and sweatshirt with somber face, looking every bit the same young man in whom Kimble would have once entrusted the future of the entire department. Now he was looking at him as a murder suspect.

Bound by balance, Ryan O'Patrick had said. Anyone who bargained at Blade Ridge was required to take a life. And Wesley Harrington would have settled no debts for Nathan Shipley. In the end the cat got him, not the bullets. If Shipley had fired the bullets, they had cleared no debts for him. The ghost with the torch, Kimble believed, was not interested in the blood of animals.

They sat on cold plastic chairs as the breeze blew down off the peaks with frosty teeth, and Kimble said, "Tell me about last night, would you?"

Shipley blew out a long breath and said, "It wasn't a fun one."

"Excuse me?"

"I don't like it out there, chief. Don't hardly feel like myself."

"Explain that."

"Ever since the accident," Shipley said. "I just don't care to be back out there. Get odd memories. You were right about things getting stuck in my head. So I just don't care much for the place. As for the cougar? If he was out there, I didn't know it."

"Why don't you care for the place?"

"Same things I told you before. What I remember compared to what I was told happened, you know? What I remember, it—"

"Feels vivid?" Kimble said. "Real clear, but you still know it couldn't have happened that way? Don't trust your own memory, your own mind?"

"Exactly," Shipley said, and he jutted his chin, looking at Kimble with a hard, thoughtful stare. "Pretty good summary, chief."

He couldn't have killed one of our own, Kimble thought. *There's no way he could not have put a knife to Pete Wolverton's throat.*

But so many of the ridge survivors *had* killed one of their own. Friends, husbands, business partners, bosses. When that blackness rose up, it seemed decision-making and control were not possible. Shipley wouldn't have known what he was doing. If O'Patrick and Jacqueline were to be believed, he wouldn't have recalled a thing but blackness until he was done, like some sort of eclipse of the soul. He would know that he'd done it, though. He would know that by now.

"You saw Pete at, what, midnight?" Kimble asked.

"Ten till. He came out early. You know Pete."

"Sure. And you hadn't seen anything on your shift that was cause for concern? No sign of the cat or . . . or of anything else?"

Shipley looked away from him, out where the fog was rising in wraiths and then fading into the gray sky of a cold, bleak day.

Kimble said, "Nathan? What did you see?"

"Nothing of that black panther. But I hung pretty tight to the preserve, too. I'll tell you something, if you watch those cats enough? They're unsettled. It's a strange thing, but I feel like they get it. They don't like the place either. They understand some things about it. That could be bad."

"Bad for who?"

Shipley's eyes shifted back to Kimble. "Anyone who's out there."

There was a long pause, Kimble considering the various tracks that he could pursue, considering how many of his cards to show. In the end, he decided to hold them tight for now. He would need more facts and better understanding before he'd chance confronting Shipley with the knowledge that he'd been gathering about the bloody history of Blade Ridge.

"So when Pete came on shift, it was ten till midnight, and you spoke?" he said, returning to the procedural realm, his supposed reason for being here.

"Just a quick update. Told him things were cool, and then I bailed. Got home, went to bed."

"Yeah? You look awfully tired."

"I haven't been sleeping all that well. Not since the accident."

"How you feeling, though?"

"Lucky. Damned lucky. You saw the car, and now you see me." Shipley waved both hands over his chest, indicating the specimen of unscathed strength that had crawled out of that demolished cruiser.

"Yes," Kimble said very softly. "I saw it, and now I see you."

For a time it was quiet, and then Kimble said, "You're scheduled today?"

"Yes. Was expecting to be back at the preserve, though. That was what you'd told me."

"Not anymore. Property is closed. And I'd like you to take the day off."

Shipley's eyes hardened briefly. One flicker, then gone. "Why?"

"I might need you," Kimble said. "As I work through this thing with the cat, I might need you. I want you handy."

"I've got a cell phone and a radio. I can be handy from anywhere."

"I know it. All the same, just stick tight to the house, get some rest, okay?"

Shipley cocked his head. "Chief, is there something else on your mind?"

"Yeah," Kimble said. "Pete Wolverton. I was out there, Shipley. I saw him. He'll stay on my mind for a while. Now, I'd like you to hang close by and wait until you hear from me today. I may be needing you."

"All right. Just say the word."

"Appreciate it, son." Kimble got to his feet, and when Shipley extended his hand, he didn't want to take it. He did, though, feeling a ripple of displeasure at the touch, and then he followed Shipley back into the old farmhouse and toward the front door. He made sure to keep the younger man in front of him. They were halfway to the door when Kimble pulled up, listening. He could hear water moving through the old pipes, then a hiss and churning in a nearby room.

"Damn, kid," he said, "you don't waste time before starting your laundry in the morning, do you?"

Shipley smiled. "Most times it's a pile halfway to the ceiling. I just needed the uniform washed."

Kimble got a smile out to match. It wasn't easy.

32

As the morning wind picked up and a few stray snow-flakes drifted down off the ridge, Audrey called Joe Taft in Center Point, Indiana. Joe had been David's inspiration. His facility in rural Indiana was the nation's largest, and he'd rescued cats of every species. Joe was the man the federal agencies called on for help seizing cats from terrible situations and was the only man David had ever admitted might be better with cats than Wesley Harrington.

He'd also been the only man who had offered to take the cats off her hands when David died.

"I thought you'd just relocated all of them, Audrey," Joe said when she asked if his offer still stood.

"That's right."

"It's not working out?"

Audrey looked out to the woods where she'd seen one of her cats crouched over a blood-soaked body and said, "No. It's not working out."

"I don't know what to tell you," Joe said. "When we talked before, I had some options for you, but you were so firm... said

235

they were your cats and you weren't going to let that change, and I respected that. So the plans I had, well, they've been long dead, Audrey."

She'd had one rule for the call — don't cry. It didn't take long to determine that was a foolish rule. She couldn't have cried if she wanted to. Her voice had all the emotion of stainless steel as she told Joe about Wesley, and the cop named Wolverton, and Ira.

"They're looking for a way to get rid of us, Joe. The villagers coming with their pitchforks and torches. But I've been thinking about it all night, and I won't fight them. This place...this isn't a good home for these cats."

"I see," Joe said. "So you're asking me —"

"I'm auctioning off my heart," she said. "And you get an early bid."

"Excuse me?"

With that the stainless steel melted, and she thought *I'll be damned — I can cry.* The tears fell soundlessly down her cheeks, and on the other end of the line Joe Taft waited as if he understood.

"They need homes," she said finally, when she could speak. "David brought them here so they'd have good homes. You said you could do it once, and I'm asking you to say it again. We have funding. There's an endowment. Financially, they'd be cared for. I just need someone to actually *provide* the care. I can't do it, Joe. I tried, and I can't."

He was silent.

"Will you do it?" she said. "Will you take them?"

"There are sixty of them," he said slowly.

"Sixty-five. We had sixty-seven, but Kino is dead and Ira is gone."

"That's a lot of cats."

"We have a strong endowment. The financial support is there."

"I'm glad to hear it, but finances aren't the only concern. I've got the acreage for them, but I don't have the enclosures built. That takes time."

"I know it does. But when the sheriff comes back here, I'd like to be able to tell him I have a transition plan."

"Well, you can tell him that, I guess. I'll need to build, and I'll need to hire more staff. I can't take sixty-five in addition to the cats we already have without making some changes. But here's the more important question. With Wesley gone, can you hold out long enough for me to get this thing in motion?"

She stared out at the trees surging in the wind across the top of the ridge.

"I hope so."

By the time Dustin Hall arrived, the police were gone, and it was just Audrey and the cats. She met him when he pulled through the gates, and the first words out of his mouth were, "What's the matter?"

"I look that good, eh?"

He didn't smile. The wind blew her hair across her face and she pushed it back with one hand and said, "Ira killed a police officer last night, Dustin. The sheriff has promised to shut us down. Plenty of things are the matter."

Dustin got out of his battered Honda and went to her and hugged her. She accepted it, but the embrace was awkward and stiff, doing little to warm either of them.

"I've called Joe Taft," she said.

"He's coming down to help?"

"He's coming down to take them, eventually."

Dustin looked more stunned at this news than he had been about Ira's killing.

"Take them?"

"I don't see another choice," Audrey said. "I can't run it alone.

Together, we'll be able to feed them today. Working hard, we'll be able to handle the feedings. But long term, Dustin? I just don't see another choice."

He took his glasses off and rubbed them clean with his shirt-tail, looking out at the lions, who were massing near the fences.

"They're hungry now," he said. "I guess we'd better get to work."

He walked past her and toward the barn, and Audrey watched him go and felt a crushing sense of failure. Dustin had been one of David's protégés, a student who fell deeply in love with the rescue center and its mission and its cats. He was disappointed in her, just as David would have been. But what else could she do?

She saw Lily, the blind white tiger, sitting upright and looking directly at her. The cat couldn't see a thing, but still Audrey felt as if she were being watched. And judged.

"I'm sorry," she told the tiger. And then, more softly, "David, I'm *sorry*."

Robin, the librarian, smiled when Roy came out to her desk.

"Get what you need?"

"A start on it," he said. "I'd like to know a little more about Frederick."

"Most of what we have begins with Roger."

"Frederick is my interest. He seems to have disappeared from the family pretty abruptly."

"A suicide, you know."

"I did not. I just saw that one day he was a prominent spokes-man for the family and the company, and the next he was being, um, restored?"

Robin nodded. "Unsuccessfully. As I recall, he really came off the rails."

"Can I read about this somewhere?"

"We have correspondence between the two brothers. That's

the closest you'll get. The family didn't disclose much about Frederick after his instability began. He was the dark secret then, I guess. Always in sanitariums of one sort or another, but rarely mentioned. I've had students pull the letters before for research work on the family, but I don't recall anything else." She led the way back into the family archives, used a big set of keys to open locked drawers at the far end of the room, and withdrew several binders.

"Those are photocopies of the family correspondence from the era you're interested in. I can't let you handle the originals, I'm afraid."

"As long as they're legible, they'll do just fine."

She nodded and left and then it was just him in the large, empty room with many generations of Whitmans gazing over his shoulder from sepia-tinted photographs. He opened the first binder and set to work.

There were letters from Frederick Sr. to his son during the Civil War. The Whitmans, originally of Boston, had sided with the North, and Frederick Jr. was a West Point graduate who'd left the war with the rank of lieutenant, then abandoned the army to take over his role as obvious successor to the Whitman Company's throne. Always involved in land acquisition, going back as far as the fur-trading days in the upper Midwest, the company focused after the Civil War on timber and ore. Coal, specifically. The Whitmans saw the railroads for exactly what they were—the key to the industrial future of not just the nation but the world—and they wanted in early.

Roy scanned through one tedious letter after another detailing the prospects in the mountains that would soon be home to a town and a university bearing the family name, afraid to miss any reference to Blade Ridge. By the early 1880s, most of the letters preserved in the university's collection were in the pen of Frederick Jr. and not his father, who was clearly in ill health.

Some were from his mother, others from Roger, the younger brother, who was serving the company from its Boston head-quarters, but the core of the family's story in this time was told by Frederick Jr., who in 1882 had assumed the role of company president.

The first reference to the potential of the mines along the Marshall River appeared in 1887, and by a year later excitement over them was evident in Frederick's letters. His exasperation at the success of rivals in West Virginia was clear, and he deemed the holdings along the Marshall to be capable of triple the yield of any competitors. "Blade Ridge, the locals call it," wrote Frederick, "the name earned by the way the stone cliffs glimmer like a knife's edge in the right moonlight."

In the spring of 1888, he wrote to Roger demanding that he secure one Alfred H. Tremley for design and supervision of a railroad bridge that would allow coal to be removed from the hills by the beginning of the next year. Roger responded with good news — Tremley had agreed to their price and was headed west.

For a moment, Roy considered that Tremley might have been the source of Wyatt's continuing search. But Tremley's photograph had appeared in the newspapers, and Wyatt hadn't selected it.

For several months, the exchanges between the Whitman brothers were buoyant, filled with predictions of great wealth. Then came November, and a letter from Frederick that was a good deal bleaker: "David Watson awoke in the night shivering and soaked in sweat, and by dawn he was unable to stand, lying huddled in blankets while the others left camp. Our physician warns of a possible contagion, which we cannot afford at our current pace. Hopefully, he is wrong."

"He wasn't wrong," Roy muttered. "It was contagious, Frederick, old boy."

Future letters confirmed the diagnosis. The illness was spreading, and with it dissatisfaction among the workers, whom Frederick feared would abandon the project entirely. His younger, brasher brother responded with firm words, suggesting that the crew be quarantined along the river and saying that work could not cease, as the company's investors had been guaranteed functioning mines by the new year.

Correspondence quickly took on a grim tone — Watson had perished, and a second and third man succumbed soon after. The camp doctor told Frederick Whitman Jr. that he would have to hope the fever didn't spread through the crew.

Hope, that winter, did not seem a powerful tool. By the first week of December, seven men were dead. Frederick Whitman Jr., while holding the men to quarantine at the work site, made his own camp across the river, telling his brother that he feared "sharing in the conditions of the men."

In other words, he wanted to crack the whip from a safe distance.

Roger wrote to his brother to suggest the threat of jailing all workers who did not hold to the letter of their contract: "They were hired to build a bridge, and a bridge they shall build."

Frederick responded with caution.

"Our deadline may no longer be attainable, as I've been tremendously disappointed in our physician's abilities to handle the epidemic," he wrote. "The locals are an astoundingly superstitious people, given to beliefs in conjuring, charms, and the handling of snakes. I had long refused such foolishness be permitted in the camp, but as it seems to give them some comfort, I've since allowed the practices despite my disapproval. Well, today, brother, my disapproval has grown. A gentleman by the name of Mr. Silas Vesey arrived on foot at the camp several nights ago. He is an odd man, and I distrusted him immediately. He is clean in appearance and yet carries a quality of purest revulsion in a manner that I cannot properly articulate. There is an odor to him, almost that of cooling ashes, and he speaks in a voice that somehow distresses the soul. He told me that he understood we had health troubles, and that he was capable of offering assistance. I told him that our finest doctor was unable to handle the problem, and I doubted he could do any more. Mr. Vesey responded that he was quite certain he could assist those men who were willing. I was unsettled by the man and sent him away. He made camp not far from us, though, and I wish he would return to whatever forsaken hollow from which he came."

Soon there was another letter about Vesey, who apparently had not left his camp but stayed within range, tending to a small bonfire and watching the progress — or lack thereof — on the trestle.

"Our foreman, Mr. Mortimer, is among the gravely ill. Yesterday I saw him nearly out of his head with fever, and I feared that when the men lost their leader, our hope would perish with him. Last evening, I observed as he rose, wrapped in blankets, and went to see Vesey. I was troubled by it, but the man appears nigh his end, and I wished to make no move to stop him.

"Mr. Mortimer returned after many hours in a state of remarkable good health. I was so astonished, watching him work today, that I inquired. He has encouraged me to consider Vesey's offer, believing firmly that the man is capable of healing, and while I do not, it is worth noting that these people are deeply superstitious and perhaps others would respond to Vesey as did Mr. Mortimer."

Roger's response was swift and firm: "Allow them any fool's cure they desire so long as it encourages them to work."

Reading the letter more than 120 years later, Roy Darmus felt a chill ride up his spine.

That's who Wyatt was looking for, he thought, *a picture of Silas*

Vesey. If he was starting with pictures, that meant he could see people out there — lots of them. And if he never named Vesey, then he never found a photograph.

That wasn't impossible to believe. Photographs of people from that era were scarce. But then of course there were other possibilities, the folktale kind about those whose image couldn't be captured by a camera at all...

Roy found himself staring back at the ancient photographs that Wyatt had collected. The Blade Ridge dead were just names on maps in Wyatt's lighthouse. The murderers, though? They were names on pictures.

He could see them, Roy thought.

He returned uneasily to the letters, discovering without much surprise that Frederick had taken his brother's advice and gone to meet with Silas Vesey, who still lingered along the ridge.

"I told him that the delays were unacceptable, and that if he was capable of aiding the sick, I bid him to do so. He asked if I wished him to see that the men were bound to the bridge. I responded that if he was, indeed, capable of healing, that is exactly what I wished. His response was most unusual. He put forth a smile that chilled me more than the wind and the snow and what he told me made no sense at all. He said that it might be far easier for him to bind the most gravely ill of the men to the bridge. I denounced the claim as preposterous, but Vesey said that he could heal only the willing, and sometimes desperate men were more willing. At that moment, I had a distinct and abiding sense of fear, and wished deeply that I had not made the trip to see him at all. He seemed to sense my doubt, and told me that he could promise the bridge shall be completed, and said that I was fortunate because he was the only man in the region who could see to such a thing. There are others capable, he said, but none in these mountains. I said I had no time to send for anyone else, and he told me that if I wished the crew bound to the bridge, then he would need to be of them. I was not surprised that he should try to extort a wage, but I said not a dime would pass into his palm until I saw proof of his abilities. He then told me that dollars were not his concern, that he simply wanted me to know that once he agreed to help, he'd be required to remain with the crew for a long while, and then asked whether I believed Blade Ridge will be a prosperous and well-traveled region for years to come. I assured him that it will be, though the idea of his wishing to linger among us did not appeal in the slightest. I wished no dealings with him at all, but I know well that our time is short and our investors impatient, and so I sent him on to try. I doubt he will be of help despite his assurances, and I look forward to the day of his departure."

The next letter was a great deal shorter, and far more optimistic.

"I have counted more men working on the bridge each morning than the day before. There is an odd quality to watching them work — never have I seen a more silent group of men — but the construction is sound."

Then came his final letter, written on Christmas Eve 1888, and Roy read it with astonishment.

"My concerns about Mr. Vesey have been growing immensely, and last evening I endeavored to put them at ease by observing the men in the night. Their silence during the day, which is when I typically visit, has unnerved me, and well it should. Our bridge, brother, is a creation of an evil I have never believed possible. The nails are being driven by dead men. At night, Vesey visits the sick with a torch in hand. Sometimes he moves on, and the next morning those men have passed. But on two occasions last evening, I watched with my own eyes as he lowered the torch to a dying man. The flames turned to coldest blue, and then the man rose. I watched this happen, Roger. There is no mistaking what I saw."

It was the last letter Frederick Whitman Jr. wrote, or at least the last that the family had preserved. Roy flipped through several pages of business-related correspondence with frustration, hoping for more, and finally hit upon an exchange from May 1890, between Roger, by then located in Sawyer County, and his wife, who was still in Boston. It was the first mention of his older brother.

"We are moving him again, and I maintain hope that the plagues of his mind will soon abate. I've heard numerous accounts of the miraculous restorative powers of the mineral springs of French Lick and West Baden, Indiana, and have been assured that time spent at rest amidst those healing waters may well be what my brother requires."

The next appearance of Frederick Whitman Jr. in the college archives was his obituary, published in 1892. It said that Frederick, an ill man, had perished in Indiana. The formal language of the time did not succeed in entirely obscuring the fact that he had died by his own hand.

33

THE HONORABLE DOUG GRAYLING, Sawyer County Circuit Court judge, was presiding over his morning docket when Kimble arrived, so Kimble waited in his office, pretending to flip through an *Outdoor Life* magazine so he didn't have to make conversation with the judge's clerk and explain the purpose of his visit. The issue he picked up included a feature detailing mountain lion attacks in Montana and California. Just what he wanted to read about today.

When Grayling finally wrapped up his docket, it was nearly eleven in the morning, and Kimble had an ache down low along his spine from sitting so long.

"Kimble, hey there."

He stood and shook the judge's hand. "Hello, Doug. You have a minute?"

"Of course."

They walked into his private office, and the judge sat behind his desk, let out a soft groan, and said, "It would be nice if assholes took the holidays off, wouldn't it, Kimble? If people said, *Hey, let's take the month of December and not be pricks to one another, not get arrested, not get charged, not be arraigned.* Wouldn't that be nice?"

"It would. You'll have a tough time convincing them of the merits of the plan, though."

"Agreed," Grayling said. "What can I do for you?"

Kimble took a deep breath, looked at the judge who'd sentenced Jacqueline Mathis to ten years, and asked for an order on jailer to be issued. It was a simple bit of legalese granting the sheriff's department temporary custody of an inmate. Usually this was done for court proceedings of some kind, when the inmate was required to travel for a hearing. Today Kimble requested it for purposes of investigation, and Grayling went silent.

"She's in a minimum-security facility," Kimble said, "and she's recently been approved for work release. There's no reason we can't borrow her for a few hours."

"No reason we *can't,* okay. But I need to hear the reason we *should.*"

Kimble gave him the pitch: active investigation and a delicate one. Based on evidence found in Wyatt French's lighthouse, he said, it was possible that a series of accidents that had occurred over the years at Blade Ridge might have been initiated.

"Initiated?" Grayling said. "What in the hell does that mean? Caused by French?"

Kimble had expected this jump, and while he felt a pang of guilt at allowing the misconception to flourish, he figured Wyatt would have approved. He'd wanted Kimble to pursue the truth, not polish his reputation.

"Possibly. There have been many deaths out there, Doug, and survivor accounts are uncomfortably similar. People report the accident being initiated by a man in the road."

"You think he was *causing* car accidents by running out in the road?"

"I don't think it's anywhere near that simple. But he kept track of the dead, and of the survivors. I'll tell you this in total honesty: I've never been more disturbed by discovery of evidence than I am by what I found in that lighthouse."

"Homicide investigation," Grayling echoed. "That's what you're saying?"

"Absolutely."

"The man is dead. We can't prosecute."

"That does not remove the need for answers," Kimble said, "and there's the distinct possibility — probability, actually — that he was not working alone. One of our deputies died last night, Pete Wolverton, and that demands —"

"I've heard. I understood that he was killed by a cougar."

"Autopsy results are pending, Doug, but I just got off the phone with the medical examiner. He says those results will confirm what I suspected when I saw the body last night — the cougar might have found Pete, but it did not kill him."

"You're saying that Pete Wolverton was murdered last night."

"Yes. I think that's what happened. I may be wrong, and I hope to be. But I don't think that I am, and neither does the ME."

"Tell me again why we need Jacqueline Mathis *released* for this?"

"She's one of the survivors who reported activity on the road."

"Well, interview her then. Get a statement."

"I have. That's why I'm here. I want her to walk me through it. I can't overstate the importance of seeing the way she recreates the scene, Doug. I simply cannot overstate that."

"You have a distinctly personal relationship with that woman, Kimble."

"No, sir, I do not."

"She *shot* you. That constitutes a —"

"I am well aware of who she is and what she did," Kimble said. "I'm asking for a little latitude here."

"It's not my job to give you latitude, it's my job to uphold the law."

"That's both of our jobs," Kimble said. "How long have we worked together, Doug? How many cases? You know me, and you know my word. I'm asking you to let that count for something."

"Always has, always will. But I've got to understand *how* she can help!"

"Her recollection of the scene is special."

"Special."

"Yes." Kimble leaned forward and said, "Doug? I have never worked another case that feels as threatening to the people of Sawyer County as this one. Never."

Grayling looked at him with alarm. "Car accidents that were really homicides. We're actually talking about this. Based on evidence you found in a *lighthouse*."

"We're actually talking about it, yes. And I need her at the scene. It's critical."

"Someone else should handle her testimony."

"It's my investigation. And that was my deputy who died last night. I'm not turning it over to anyone else, Doug. You have a problem with that, you can call the sheriff himself. Troy will approve it."

The Honorable Doug Grayling swore under his breath and ran both hands through hair that glistened with dye that left it an impossibly radiant shade of black.

"She shot you," he said.

"I recall that, yes."

"And you want me to issue an order on jailer to turn her over to you."

"Twenty-four-hour release. This thing is big, Doug. It's worth it. No, check that—*demands* it. I have to know what she can recreate at that scene."

Grayling pushed back from his desk and stared at him for a long time. Kimble, who understood the value of silence, let him stare and didn't press.

"I can't give her to you alone," Grayling said finally. "Not with your personal history. And I need a female officer there. Is that clear?"

"Diane Mooney will be with me," Kimble said, and it was the second time he'd ever lied to a judge. The first time had also been with Grayling, only Kimble had been on the witness stand then. Not so much a lie back then as an omission. The prosecutor hadn't asked *specifically* if, after the supposedly accidental shot that had dropped Kimble to the farmhouse floor, Jacqueline Mathis had leaned down, smiling, and pressed the muzzle of his own gun to his forehead.

"Do me a favor on this," Kimble said. "Do the people of your county a favor on this. Keep it quiet, all right? You give me twenty-four hours and I hope to have the answers for you. You might not like them, or even believe them, but I intend to have them."

"I'll issue it. But I don't like the way it feels."

"Neither do I," Kimble told him, and it felt good to speak the truth again.

34

Roy sat in a booth at the Bakehouse, wondering why Kimble would possibly want to meet to discuss something so dark, so wildly implausible yet thoroughly documented, in a brightly lit coffee shop. It felt like a discussion for a dim and private room, where even whispers wouldn't be overheard, where two men could talk about madness and not fear the consequences.

Kimble had been firm, though. He wanted to meet at the Bakehouse.

When he came through the door, Roy was taken aback by just how exhausted he looked. The chief deputy had always walked with a touch of a limp after the shooting, and stood with a posture that suggested more years than he had, but today you could have said he was fifty and no one would have blinked.

"I've got a story," Roy said. "But it's not one you're going to want to hear, and the source is hardly reliable. It's not just more than a century old, it was also left to us by an insane man. I don't even know that it is going to be worth hearing."

Kimble said, "It'll be worth hearing. And maybe we shouldn't judge the man's sanity just yet."

It was an odd thing for him to say, this man who was so painfully practical that extracting colorful quotes from him for a newspaper story had been almost impossible. Roy shrugged, said, "Okay," and then he told him the story.

When he was through, Kimble didn't respond right away. He sipped his coffee and looked over the notes Roy had taken in the archives, studied the pictures Wyatt had already found there, and did not speak.

"Like I told you," Roy said, "this is probably wasting time that you can't afford to waste. It's a good chiller, I'll grant that, but the idea that it has anything to do with what's —"

"I think he was looking for Vesey," Kimble said. "All those pictures labeled *NO?* I think you're right. He must have been looking for Vesey."

Roy sighed, lowered his voice, and said, "I hit on the same idea. Then I hit on one that's even more absurd. I was wondering why he was content to write the names of the dead on the walls, but he used photographs for the murderers. It almost suggested that... that he had seen them, somehow. That what he was looking for was visual confirmation."

"I believe that's correct."

Roy stared at him. "The story I just told you was about dead men building a bridge, Kimble. Are you being this calm about it because you're waiting for someone to come take me away to a padded cell, or is there something I don't understand?"

Kimble was staring out to the patio, where in warm weather the sidewalk tables were popular. Now they'd been put away for the season, and a trace of snow was beginning to gather where they'd once stood.

"There are lots of things we don't understand," he said. "And I'm tired of it, Darmus. I can't bear it anymore. I've got an idea that might help me understand it, and it might also cost me my job by the time things are done. I think it probably will. If things go *well,* then my badge may be all that I lose."

"What in the world are you talking about, Kimble?"

"There's a ghost out there," Kimble said, turning back to him. "Or the devil? Some combination of the two? I don't know how to explain him, but this Vesey sounds just right. Now you've told me the stories you found. Let me tell you the ones I've found."

He told them, while Roy's coffee went cold and people milled around them, laughing and talking and complaining about last-minute holiday shopping and long car trips to see family in far-off places. Roy listened as the most dogmatic cop in the county spoke of specters with blue torches and bargaining that led to murder and invisible beams of light that had protected Blade Ridge for many years. He told all of this, and Roy listened, and he believed.

The time when he could not believe had passed.

"If I'm crazy," Kimble said, watching him carefully, "at least I've got company. I appreciate that."

Then Kimble told him his intention to take Jacqueline Mathis to the ridge, and Roy found himself shaking his head.

"Too dangerous for you, Kimble. Even if Grayling approved it, if something goes wrong out there and you're left with *this* explanation, you're done."

"I know it," Kimble said simply. "I've thought on that a great deal, trust me. But let me show you the other side of that coin. If I don't take her out there, and I don't do anything about it, and a hundred years from now someone is still adding names to that list Wyatt started...well, which would you rather have? Your parents died out there."

Yes, they had. And if Kimble was to be believed, they had

died by making the right choice. Roy thought back to Wyatt's words in that final phone call, those that had incensed him so deeply: *The decisions that they both made. Very brave. Very strong. And knowing what they were saying goodbye to, with a child at home, it must have been so difficult.*

He'd thought Wyatt was suggesting that they'd killed themselves. Instead, he was suggesting that they hadn't been willing to preserve their own lives at the cost of another's.

"That's why Wyatt killed himself," Roy said. "He had to take a life. He chose his own."

"It seems that way."

"When he got his diagnosis, he would have known that just waiting to die wasn't an option for him. Maybe he could feel that? I think that he could." Roy recalled the man's panicked breathing on that final phone call, recalled how he'd said that he was becoming afraid of what he could do in the dark, and nodded. "Whatever was pulling on him, it was tugging harder at the end."

"You see what I'm saying?" Kimble said, his voice mournful but determined. "Which is worse, Darmus?"

"The second option," Roy said, and then, just as Kimble started to nod, he said, "But that's assuming you could *do* something about whatever is out there. There's absolutely nothing to suggest that you can."

"Jacqueline thought she could help."

"How?"

"I don't know. But she can see them, Darmus. She can see them, and I can't. I can't fight something I can't see."

"I don't know that you can fight dead men, either," Roy said. "Maybe you can fight them, but win? How do you defeat the dead, Kimble?"

The chief deputy was silent for a very long time, and then he said, "I need to know what she sees. If there's nothing that can be done, she'll know it. If there is something…maybe she'll know that, too."

"Why would *she* if Wyatt didn't? He figured out that the light helped, and he figured out the history of the place. He did everything that could be done and still nothing worked."

"He also called on us," Kimble said, "and I don't think he did that just for his legacy. The man had hope."

"Again I'll ask — what suggests that Jacqueline can understand them any better than Wyatt did?"

"Because," Kimble said, "she's already settled her debt. He hadn't."

Roy pushed back from the table and let out a deep breath.

"It's one hell of a risk," he said.

"I understand that. I also think the time has come to be willing to take one. Something needs to be done. We can't allow it to continue. For more than a century now, good people have lost their lives to that place or because of it. That has to end. It has to."

Roy said, "You must be capable of believing in great evil to push it this far, Kimble."

"I suspect," Kimble said, "I've already brushed closer to it than most."

Roy took a sip of his coffee before remembering that it had already chilled, then pushed it aside.

"Tell me the part about Jacqueline, please. The part you don't want to tell. I can ride with you either way. I already am. But I'd like to know. Not judge. Just *know*."

"You already know all of that."

"I don't mean the details of what she did," Roy said. "I mean the reason you can't treat it like a cop."

He'd expected an argument. Resistance, defensiveness, even outright anger like the man had shown before. The walls Kimble had built and guarded so carefully, though, seemed to have deteriorated rapidly in the past few days.

Kimble turned his eyes back to that empty patio, where the wind was swirling snow.

"I had feelings for her," he said. "In a way I never had for a woman before, never will again. Used to daydream about the day she would leave that son of a bitch. A part of me was living for it. I didn't count on the *way* she'd leave him, right? Didn't count on that."

"You were in love with her before she shot you?"

Kimble nodded.

"Was there... were you having an affair?"

"No. I was just waiting. I knew the day would come, had to come. Even that was bad enough, though. I was waiting out the end of an abusive marriage. When I think about it like that, I hate myself, Darmus. This morning I was thinking about Audrey Clark. You've seen her, right?"

"Yes."

"She's everything you could possibly desire in a woman," Kimble said. "Bright, beautiful, and brave as hell. As strong as anyone I've ever seen. I think about her, and I ask myself, why can't I be in love with *her*? Why can't I sit in this coffee shop and hope that *she* walks in?"

He sighed, and his voice softened. "I just can't. I think about a woman in a cell instead. I'd like to fix that about myself, but it is beyond me."

"You really don't think Jacqueline belongs in prison?" Roy asked.

"The night she shot me, she was not herself. Okay? That's the clearest I can say it. You should have seen her that night. Because she was evil. Then the life went out of her husband, just as she put the gun to my forehead, and... and she was back. So now I'd say, you should have seen her that night. Because she was worthy of love, worthy of dying for, worthy of anything I could give."

He spread his hands. "They're both true. Now you try living with that. Try treating that like you're a cop."

"You can't decide which she is?"

"I couldn't reconcile how she was *both*. I went to see the woman every month, and I always left thinking how damned egregious it is that she's in that prison. But then I remembered the way she was that night, I remembered the fact that she *smiled* while she put a gun to my forehead, and I...I just didn't know."

Roy had covered the trial of Jacqueline Mathis. He had listened to Kimble's testimony, he had read every document. There had never been a mention of a gun put to his forehead. Only a bullet in the back, supposedly fired in error, supposedly aimed at her abusive husband. He knew that Kimble had not made a mistake in what he'd just said, though. You didn't forget something like that. So that meant he'd chosen to forget it on the witness stand.

"She wasn't herself," Kimble said. "When I say that, I don't mean that her mood changed. I don't mean that she was in shock. I mean that for a while there, the woman who is Jacqueline Mathis became something else. Then that woman came back. Put down the gun and apologized as I lay there on the floor in the blood — mine and her husband's — and it was like watching a...a soul slip back where it belonged."

He coughed, shook his head. "I know how that sounds. I know what you probably think of it."

Roy said, "Don't worry about how it sounds. I just needed to hear it."

"I could never come to peace with that night, and she couldn't help me. Claimed she couldn't remember a thing. But now I hear the stories from O'Patrick, and I see all the work you've done, and I can believe her. For the first time, I can explain it. When I walked through that door, she was just...blackness. Evil. But her husband was still breathing at that time. And when he was gone? She came back. I can believe all these stories now, because I *saw* it."

They sat together in silence, and eventually Roy nodded.

"Thank you," he said. "I wanted to know. And hearing it helps me believe a little more, myself. I'd still say you're taking one hell of a risk taking her out there by yourself."

"I know it." Kimble met Roy's eyes and said, "Do you ever wonder why you're along on this ride?"

"Because it's a hard story to sell, and I was already involved."

"Exactly. Wyatt called you out there, and you were willing to consider it longer than most, to follow it into stranger places and darker corners than most, and that's because it's *personal* to you. Well, it's surely personal to me, too. He didn't pick us by mistake."

"No. I don't think the man's approach was anything close to haphazard."

"All right. We're agreed on that. You asked me to tell you the truth, and I've done it. I've told you what I intend to do, and what really happened with her that night. You've heard my soul emptied out, and you've got the chance to walk away. I won't blame you."

Roy waited. Kimble watched him for a while, then gave a short nod, satisfied.

"I've got something else to ask of you," he said. "And please, Darmus, be careful. This one is riskier than reading old papers."

"What is it?"

"I'm worried about Shipley."

"I know that."

"Well, I can't very well put a surveillance detail on him. I start asking for that on one of my own deputies, say that he's suspected in the murder of another, and I'm going to have to defend my reasoning in ways that I simply can't right now. I can't do it. But I also can't have him showing up at the ridge when I'm there with Jacqueline. I want you to watch his house and call me if he leaves. That's it. Don't move, don't engage him, don't do a damn thing but call me. If he leaves his house tonight, I will need to know."

"All right."

"I don't want to ask that of you," Kimble said. "Bringing a civilian into a murder investigation ... well, you can add that to the pile of reasons I might lose my badge. But there's no one else I can ask."

"I'll do it, Kimble. Not a problem."

"There's an old gas station just up the road from his house. Empty for years, old Esso station. He'll have to come by it to head into town, or toward the ridge. The only way he wouldn't pass by is if he's headed north, and I'm not worried about him heading north. If you see him pass by, he'll be doing forty miles an hour, and he won't notice you. If that happens, just pick up the phone and dial. *Nothing* else."

"Okay. But Kimble? If you believe what you told me about Jacqueline and O'Patrick and all the others ... he's not going to kill again. If he did kill, he's satisfied his debt. None of the others in the Blade Ridge history have killed again. Bound by balance, that's what you told me. Shipley is balanced now."

"Right," Kimble said. "The difference? If he did kill Pete, right now he's getting away with it. The others were all arrested at the scene when they came back around from their trances. Shipley came back around alone in the dark woods. That means he might not understand *why* he killed, but he understands that he did."

Kimble put his arms on the table and leaned close. "If all that is true, Darmus, then he might want to keep improving his chances of getting away with it. Why wouldn't he? And the only evidence and witnesses are at Blade Ridge. Audrey Clark is at Blade Ridge. If Shipley did this, and he's thinking about ways to clean it up...well, I just worry that he might head that way."

"But you're getting ready to drive in the opposite direction."

"Yeah," Kimble said. "Because I can't see in the dark. But I think I know someone who can. At least out there."

35

THE DAY WORE ON, snow fell in scattered flurries, and police came and went steadily.

No one found any trace of Ira.

At noon, while Audrey and Dustin took their first break of the day, with not even a third of the cats fed yet and many of them growing annoyed with the delay, a pickup truck rolled up with four dogs in cages.

"I'd better see about this," Audrey said.

The dogs belonged to a man named Dick Mitchell, a wiry old-timer with a Mark Twain mustache, a scoped rifle, and a large pistol on his belt.

"I've come to catch the cat," he said. "I reckon you're not too happy about it, but when the police call, I've found it wise to pick up the phone. Got me out of a speeding ticket or two along the way."

She watched the dogs ranging about in the kennels, pressing their noses to the gates and staring out at her cats. Jafar emerged from his long, dark quarters, where he'd spent most of the day tucked back in the straw, bothered by the constant stream of traffic, and began to pace restlessly. Immediately one of the dogs let out a baying howl, and that triggered a response of roars.

"I thought the sheriff was trying traps," Audrey said.

"He's doing that, too. Somewhere along the way, he heard the best bet was Big Dick Mitchell. He heard right."

Big Dick Mitchell hefted his rifle and took an experimental sighting, aiming it down the road. Audrey thought of Ira's beautiful, sleek body, and somehow, even after the terror she'd felt only hours earlier, she was sad for him.

Just get the hell out of here, Ira, she thought. *Hit those hills running and don't stop. This isn't the place for you. For anyone.*

"Get your dogs out of sight of my cats quick," she said. "I've got enough headaches today without this."

"Plott hounds," Dick Mitchell announced proudly, opening the first of the kennel doors. "They've yet to run a mountain lion, but they'll catch on quick. They'll catch on."

"If you want to take them back home tonight," Audrey said, "you'd better hope they don't catch on."

He gave her an odd look. "That nasty of a boy, is he?"

"He was fine until he came here," she said, realizing that she sounded more like Wes with each passing day, and then she left and returned to her cats.

Kimble had once been a churchgoing man, and though he was no longer, he found himself in the parking lot of the one he'd once attended, detouring in there instead of heading for the highway and all that waited down the road. He sat alone in the parking lot with the engine running and thought about what Roy Darmus had said.

You must be able to believe in a great evil.

Yes, he was able to do that. He'd seen lesser evils — greed, anger, lust — too often and for too long not to believe there could be something beyond the crimes for which his department had specific names and charges. He was part of a justice system that was designed to quantify evil. There was something missing in that, to be sure.

He'd seen true evil in his time—mothers who killed their own babies, sons who killed their own mothers. The years in this job could erode your faith in good people just as the wind and water eroded the mountains. He fought it every day, but he wondered if there was a breaking point. How many child abuse cases could a man work, how many murders, how many rapes and assaults? How long could you go until you folded up under it? It was a question he thought most police considered on the bad nights. He remembered Diane Mooney asking it of him once, when they'd arrested a man who'd fractured his stepdaughter's skull with a wine bottle because she was using up the minutes on his cell phone. Diane had asked him as they'd walked out of the jail and into a spring evening so beautiful it hurt, the air alive with fragrant blooms and driven by a gentle, kind breeze, and he remembered what he'd told her: *You keep your head down, and you remember that people need you and that it's a privilege to answer the call.*

He thought he'd believed it back then. On that night? Yes, he'd believed it. That was a vivid memory. Such a beautiful night. He could still remember the smell of the flowers and the feel of the wind. He could still remember the way blood had filled that girl's eye socket.

Kimble wasn't certain what he thought of God. He knew that he should be certain—everyone of his years was supposed to have their beliefs in order by now. *I'm a Baptist, I'm a Catholic, I'm an atheist, I'm an agnostic, I'm a believer in the Church of the Weeping Willow Tree, Fourth Circle, Second Cabinet.* You were supposed to know where you lined up.

Kimble did not.

He knew this: there were times when he'd prayed to God and

times when he'd cursed Him. On the latter occasions, he chastised whatever higher power there might be for having blind eyes and deaf ears.

You have bound us, Kimble imagined saying, *to an evil world. Where's the love in that?*

And in that scenario, God always answered, *Temporarily bound you, yes. Now, during your time in that evil world, did you do anything to help?*

For that, Kevin Kimble would have an answer, firm as steel: *Yes.*

It was the only thing he would ever be able to answer firmly about this world. He'd tried to help it. He had fought evil, and how many people could say that?

He thought now of Jacqueline Mathis, behind razor-wire fencing and concrete blocks and iron bars and countless locks. Did she belong there? Was she good, or was she evil?

Kimble touched his forehead with the back of his hand. Sweat. Thirty degrees outside, and he was sweating.

If you do this, he thought, *it will be just the two of you in this car. You don't have to put her in the back; she could sit right at your side, where you could reach out and touch her. Or she could reach out and touch you.*

Why was he doing this? The answer lay both through the windshield ahead of him and in the mirror behind him. It was in the people who made up the place he called home. Whitman was a beautiful town, and, thanks to its distance from any interstate, a well-kept secret. Nestled among the Appalachian foothills and surrounded by deep forests and surging rivers, it drew people who wanted to get away. Kimble, born and raised here, often considered turning into one of those very people but heading in the opposite direction, packing his things and getting out.

But to where? And to what?

He'd never been an extrovert, but there was a time when he'd been at least somewhat social. That time had ended with the shooting. A version of Kevin Kimble had died with Jacqueline's bullet. The one left behind valued privacy above all else. He'd spent his career walking into the dark shadows of private lives to help prevent harm, or to correct harm already done. Then suddenly people were walking into the dark shadows of his own life. There was the arrest, the trial, the sentencing. Kimble was a popular media target during that time—the committed cop who nearly died in the line of duty, then rose to defend the very woman who'd put the bullet in him. Lots of attention had come his way in those days.

He'd never stopped retreating from it.

He had attended this church until the shooting. His mother had raised him there, and he kept going long after her death. Then came Jacqueline's bullet, and the next time Kimble entered the building, they prayed for him during the service. Aloud and before the entire congregation, they prayed for him.

He never went back. Sometimes he ran into some people from church and felt a need to explain but couldn't. Communication was a strength for him, until it came to communicating something about himself. Then he was utterly inept. He could not tell them how uneasy it had made him to be the personal target of pleas to God. He understood that it had been meant with the best intentions.

All the same, he'd never been back.

He hadn't been much of anywhere in the past few years. Not in a way that mattered. He'd been the work, and the work had been him, and all the rest was detached and hidden and married to something he couldn't explain and deeply feared. Something that, it seemed, began at Blade Ridge.

He was tired of letting it own him, and tired of letting it take its slow, steady blood toll from his town.

He would stand for it no longer.

He said a silent prayer then, first for himself and then,

spontaneously, another one for his mother, many years departed. Then he started the car and drove off to get Jacqueline Mathis.

Roy had the address for Nathan Shipley's house and clear instructions from Kimble: do not engage, do not so much as turn your headlights on if he passes. Just call.

He'd driven past the house, a sprawling but dilapidated place nestled in a high valley with a stunning view of the mountains beyond, and then he'd circled back and found the ancient gas station that Kimble had told him about.

Shipley's truck was still in the driveway of his home, and there were lights on inside. So far he was following the chief deputy's instructions and not wandering.

Roy settled into his car, looked at the fading sun, and hoped that Kimble knew what in the hell he was doing.

At sundown the sheriff's deputies came by to tell Audrey they'd had no luck with the cougar hunt.

"He hasn't touched the bait," said the cold female officer named Diane, who seemed to hold Audrey personally responsible for her colleague's death. She was the most intimidating of all of them, harsher even than the sheriff. Audrey couldn't help but be impressed by her. She certainly had the look of a woman who did not take any shit from her male colleagues. Or, for that matter, from anyone.

"I didn't think he would," Audrey said. Technically, Ira should have been interested. He should be hungry by now, having grown accustomed to a steady diet that required no hunting, and the presence of massive pieces of bloody, butchered meat scattered along the river should have appealed to him. She just knew somehow that he would not fall for the trick.

The watcher, David had said, and then named him Ira.

He would be watching now, she was certain. Maybe from the rocks, maybe from the upper branches of a tree, maybe from some unremembered crevice of the old mines themselves, over on the other side of the river. Wherever he was, he would be watching, and he would not easily be fooled.

"I'm guessing the man with the dogs didn't have any better luck," she said.

"He hasn't yet. The dogs can't seem to pick up his scent."

Again Audrey felt no surprise.

"You'll try again tomorrow, I assume," she said.

"Oh, yes. We'll keep at it until we get him. Tomorrow the folks from the USDA will be down, too. They're going to inspect—"

"They just did inspect. Right before we began to move. They said it was one of the highest-quality facilities in the country."

"They want to inspect and see exactly how the cat escaped," Diane Mooney said, as if Audrey hadn't spoken. "So we will deal with all of that tomorrow. But I don't want any of my people out here at night. Not after what's been happening." For the first time, the woman's coldness seemed to abate, and she said, "I don't think you should be here either."

Audrey took a deep breath and shook her head. "I don't particularly want to be, to tell you the truth. But I have to be. You see all of them?"

She waved her hand back at the cats.

"They can't be left alone," Diane Mooney said.

"No, they can't. So Dustin and I, we'll be here."

"Call for help if you need it," Diane said. "If you see him, or hear him, or just if anything seems wrong, call us, Mrs. Clark. Don't try to handle things on your own. You got very lucky last night. I don't want to see you press that again."

Audrey nodded. "I don't intend to."

36

I T WAS NOT YET DARK when Kimble got stiffly out of his
car — his back had been killing him all day — and walked
into the prison with his order-on-jailer paperwork. They'd already
gotten a call from the judge, so they were aware of the order and
prepared to see him, but all the same he could feel the curiosity
as he spoke with the supervising CO, a guy named John who'd
seen Kimble come and go on many visits.

"There were supposed to be two of you. A female, correct?"

There were always supposed to be two, and you always tried
to avoid pairing a female inmate alone with a single male officer.
Kimble said, "We're good," meeting the man's gaze with a flat
stare and eventually receiving the shrug he knew he would
receive. The procedural burden was on his department. If anything went wrong, Sawyer County would pay the price.

It took about ten minutes for them to bring her out, and she
showed no trace of surprise. That was expected; she always gave
off the air of having fully anticipated all developments. It had
worked against her during the trial. One juror admitted that
they had found her calm reactions to testimony disturbing.

The CO nodded at the handcuffs on Kimble's belt.

"You want to use those?"

"She's fine," Kimble said.

The CO shrugged again. Jacqueline was a minimum-security inmate and Kimble was police. They expected he could handle her. He hoped they were right.

"Let's go," he told her, voice cool, indifferent. This was for the benefit of the CO. Let them see nothing but professionalism. Jacqueline Mathis stepped forward—physically free, technically still in custody. Kimble's custody. As of this moment, she was his and his alone. He led the way to the door, held it open as Jacqueline stepped through. She walked at his side out to the car—he was in the cruiser now, this being official sheriff's department business, though the sheriff knew nothing about it—and he felt an absurd desire to go around and open the passenger door for her, chivalrous, as if they were on a date. Instead, he opened the rear driver's side door and she slid into the backseat, separated from him by a metal grate. Fences had held her from him for a while now.

She said, "We're going to Blade Ridge, aren't we?"

They were through the gates now and driving toward the highway. Kimble said, "They tell you that?" even though he knew they couldn't have, because they didn't know.

"I made a guess." Her voice was so soft, so gentle. "It's the right one, though, isn't it?"

Kimble flicked his eyes at the mirror, then back to the road. "Yeah. A lot of people have died out there, Jacqueline. A whole hell of a lot. And the people who didn't die..."

"What?"

"They've had problems," he said.

He drove them up the ramp and onto the highway, pulling in behind a semi that was headed westbound.

"Problems like mine?"

"Problems like yours."

"What are you hoping for from me, Kevin? What am I supposed to provide?"

"I want to know what you see," he said.

"And you think I will see something? Still?"

"Yes," he said. "There's a folder back there. Pictures inside."

She picked it up, opened it, began to sift through.

"Do you recognize any of them?"

"I'm supposed to recognize someone from photographs this old?"

"I thought you might."

She looked up, and when he looked in the mirror he could see her eyes narrow.

"You think one of them is him," she said.

"I don't know. Wyatt French had the pictures. You were among them. So were the others like you. And then there are many that I don't understand. I hoped you might."

She fell silent for a time as she went through them one by one.

"No," she said. "None of them are him."

"You'd actually remember?"

"Kevin," she said, "it's not a face that you forget."

"I think I know who he was," Kimble said. "Who he claimed to be, at least, what he called himself. Silas Vesey. Does that mean anything to you?"

"No. How did you find the name?"

He told her about it as he drove, told her about all the work Roy Darmus had done, the story of the trestle and the fever and the man who'd wandered out of the hills with breath that smelled like cold ashes and said that he might be able to bind people to the bridge as Whitman had wanted, but that it would be far easier to do so with the sick and desperate men.

"Do you believe that story?" he asked her.

"It's the truth," she said simply. He looked at her in the mirror again, saw her sitting in the backseat staring out the window like a child on a car trip.

"You can't be so sure of that."

She turned to face him. "I think I can. I've been one of them. The desperate. I've seen him. Kevin, that story is the truth."

It was full night by the time they reached Sawyer County, and Kimble was driving with caution, the roads slick with a light dusting of snow. There was more on the way tonight, the forecasters said. He stared out into the moonlit countryside of this place he'd known so well for his entire life and suddenly felt as if he did not know it at all, the beauty of rocky peaks and wooded hollows shifting on him, developing a constant, whispering menace.

They rounded the curves of County Road 200 and then turned onto Blade Ridge Road. Kimble had called Audrey Clark to tell her that he'd be making a patrol and not to be alarmed if she saw a police car — it would just be him, passing through. He didn't want to have to stop at the preserve and allow her the chance to see him with Jacqueline.

As they drove down the rutted gravel track the lighthouse came into view, and Jacqueline turned to stare at it.

"Dark again," she said.

Not completely, Kimble thought. *With any luck, not completely. If Wyatt knew what he was doing with those infrared lamps, it only looks* dark *to us.*

They passed by the gates to the preserve, and Jacqueline said, "Are those *lions?*"

"Yes."

"I don't think this is such a good place for cats like those."

"That seems to be a growing sentiment," he said. They went on past the preserve and all the way to the end of the road, where the gravel ended in trees. Kimble brought the car to a stop and turned out the lights.

"Here we are."

"Yes." She was quiet, subdued. He looked at her in the mirror and saw that she was watching the dark trees with apprehension.

"You don't have to," he said. "I can take you back and—"

"I have to, Kevin. You need me to. Don't deny that."

He shut the engine off, left the car, and opened her door. She stepped out and wrapped her arms around herself, and he realized for the first time that she had no jacket. He took off his own and held it out, and she gave him a faint smile.

"Thank you."

When she turned and slipped into it, first one arm and then the other, her hair was close to his face and he could smell her, feel her back brushing against his chest.

"Such a gentleman," she said. "Will you still hold my coat for me on the second date, or does it fade quickly?"

He opened his mouth but didn't get out a response. His tongue was wooden, his throat tight. She zipped up his jacket and smiled at him. He couldn't see the orange of the prison uniform now. Couldn't see anything but the fine lines of her face in the moonlight and the dark hair cascading over his coat.

"A romantic walk in the woods, is that the plan, sir?" she said.

"Sure," he said. His voice was unsteady.

Jacqueline looked at the outline of the mountains in the moonlit night, closed her eyes, and took a deep breath.

"Years," she said. "It has been *years* since I stood anywhere and felt free."

He didn't answer. She stood with her eyes shut and one snowflake fell into her hair. He reached out, without thinking, to brush it away. When she opened her eyes and took his arm, he stiffened. She kept her hold on his arm and tugged gently. He took a step forward, and she came in to meet him, leaned up, and kissed him. When her lips touched his, Kimble's legs trembled. The presence of her weakened him. Gloriously.

She shot you.

He stepped back, almost stumbling, said, "Jacqueline we're here to—"

"I know what we're here to do," she said. "I know that better than you do, Kevin. But I needed that moment. I'm sorry."

He said, "Thank you." It wasn't what he should have said, but it was all that came out.

She smiled again, smiled in that way that slid right through him.

Just like the bullet, Kimble? Does it slide through you just like the bullet?

"All those visits," she said. "All that faith. Thank *you,* Kevin."

It was silent, and he looked up at the trees and the path that led into blackness. "Maybe we shouldn't go out there."

She let out a breath, looked over her shoulder, and said, "It's why you brought me here. You want to know what I see, right? Well, let's have a look."

"All right," he said, and he could still taste her on his lips as he followed her into the darkness.

37

WHEN SHE HEARD THE SOUND of a car approaching, Audrey went to the window and peered out. A moment later it came into view, and she saw the now far-too-familiar sheriff's decal on the side, the light bar on top.

"Kimble," she said, and felt relieved. She liked Kimble. Trusted him.

Behind her Dustin Hall peered over her shoulder.

"He's not getting out, is he?" he said.

"I don't know. He told me he would be making some patrols tonight. That was all."

"Well, after last night, I hope he's not intending to walk around alone."

"I know," she said. Dustin's presence had been Kimble's idea, but Audrey was beginning to think it was a bad one. As competent as he'd been during the day, he was jittery at night. Then again, maybe he was just picking that up from her. She'd been pacing nonstop, making regular trips to the window, matching the restless behavior of the cats. They were peaceful tonight, though — no roars, no rattling of fences, no stretching upright and craning to see into the darkness.

Please, let it stay that way, she thought. *One night of peace. That's all I'm asking for.*

But of course it was not. She would need more than one night. It would take time, Joe Taft had said. How much time, she wasn't sure. But it would be much more than one night.

When it was done, though? When whatever amount of time Joe needed had passed and the cats she'd devoted the past several years of her life to were gone? What then?

Back to the legal world. She'd been thrilled to get away from it. The idea of returning to Lexington or Louisville and working in an office every day, drawing up wills and endowments and business mergers and handling corporate disputes, felt so wrong. She could go somewhere else entirely, of course, pass the bar in a new state and find a new city and get involved with a new kind of practice.

That didn't seem any more appealing, though. Her life had become these cats. She didn't want to lose that. Part of aging was adapting, was acceptance that all the planning in the world didn't stand a chance against the fickle winds of fate, but hadn't she adapted enough lately? Did she have to turn her back on the preserve that held her heart?

Dustin said, "What are you thinking about, Audrey?"

He was wearing his Whitman College sweatshirt and looked impossibly young. She was not inclined to tell him the truth. That all the best-laid plans of youth could be shattered in a slip-and-fall, a single misplaced step in the night, and the life you thought was promised to you would begin to vanish until the very memory of your plans seemed ludicrous.

"I'm thinking," she said, "that I could use a glass of wine."

"That's the best idea I've heard all day."

"Are you even old enough to drink?"

He smiled. "I'm twenty-four, Audrey."

Of course. He was a graduate student, working toward his doctorate in biology, just as David once had. Audrey was only nine years older than he was. How was that possible?

"Well, then, we'll have a drink," she said.

She went into the kitchen, trying not to concentrate on the fact that Kimble's car had not returned up the road, that he was indeed making his night patrol on foot in the woods.

Surveillance looked a hell of a lot more exciting in the movies. This was no stunning revelation, but the understanding of just how tedious it was came as a painful surprise to Roy.

He'd been parked in the abandoned gas station parking lot for hours now, his back and legs stiffening as he stared out at a dark country road where few cars passed at all. At first he'd been worried about missing Shipley's truck because of traffic. Now he was worried about missing Shipley's truck because of falling asleep.

He made a pass down the road just to see how things looked at the home, found no sign of activity, and returned to his position. Within ten minutes, he wanted to make another pass. It was hard to just sit in the dark and stare at nothing.

He ran the Honda's engine for a while, keeping the lights off, to let the heater fill the car with warm air again, then used the radio to get a little rock 'n' roll going to help him wake up. He wished he'd thought to bring a thermos of coffee. Rookie mistake.

The heater pushed the chill from the car, but the warm air made him drowsier. He leaned back in the seat, yawned, and fought the heavy eyelids.

He hoped Kimble was making progress.

38

THEY WALKED IN SILENCE, and Kimble kept his hand on his gun, well aware of the black cat. The woods were quiet, but did that mean anything? He'd seen enough of these cats now to know that when so inclined, they could move with all the advance warning of a gust of wind.

When they reached the edge of the trestle, fog draped around them and the moonlight painted the steep stone cliffs a sparkling white. He stood beside Jacqueline, cold now that he'd given her his jacket, and watched her face as she swiveled her head slowly, taking it all in.

"Do you see anything?"

She didn't answer, just took a few hesitant steps forward, then ducked and slipped through the torn-up stretch of chain link that had once—many years and many vandals before—kept people from reaching the trestle.

"I'd like to go out onto the bridge."

He didn't particularly like that idea, not after the tale Darmus had recounted earlier today—*those last nails were driven by dead men*—but he didn't argue. Just followed her, one hand on his gun.

They walked out ten paces, the old boards creaking beneath their feet.

"All right," he said, and his voice seemed too loud. "Stop here. Let's have a look."

He turned and stared off to the south, following the river's path. *This is madness,* he thought. *You'll lose your badge for it and you should; no one who would do a thing like this has any right to a badge, has any right —*

Jacqueline said, "You're looking the wrong way."

She'd been at his side just a blink ago, had moved away in swift silence. She was five paces from him and at the other side of the bridge, facing north, looking into the rocks below the trestle. Kimble watched her stare out into the darkness and the mist and he felt afraid in a way he never had before. Or at least in a way that he hadn't been in years. Not since he was down on the farmhouse floor with his blood all around him and she was moving in the shadows.

"What do you see?" he said.

She shifted, arching her back as if for a better view, watching that spot in the rocks like a fan in the nosebleed seats of a football stadium craning to see the action. Kimble followed the path of her stare, tried to see something, anything, and could not. He still hadn't taken his hand from his gun.

"Jacqueline, what do you —"

"They're nothing to you," she said. Her voice was a whisper.

He glanced up the tracks in the direction from which they'd come, thinking of the cruiser, thinking that he wanted to run for it, slam the door and punch down the locks and speed away from this place, from her. Instead he said, "No. So tell me about them."

"They're at the fire," she said simply.

There was no fire. Kimble was aging fast, but not so fast that he was capable of missing a campfire on a dark night.

"Keep going," he said.

"You don't see it. But they see you. They see us. They're all around the fire."

"More than one? I thought there was only one."

"No," she said. "There are several."

She was staring, entranced, into the blackness. Kimble thought of the man with the blue light, the torch that Ryan O'Patrick and Nathan Shipley had reported causing their accidents, that Audrey Clark had seen just the night before, and said, "Why can't I see that blue flame? Others can."

"I think he shows it when he wants to," she said. "You never see him until you're dying. Until that point, all he will show you is his light. It's a lure, a distraction, a false guide. Right now, I don't think he wants to be seen. I feel like there's something holding him down there."

Kimble looked up at the lighthouse and thought, *I'll be damned, it does work. Wyatt's infrared lights are enough. Vesey needs total darkness to wander the ridge, and he doesn't have it.*

"If all of that is true," he said, "then why can *you* still see them?"

"Because I belong with them now."

Just as Wyatt had told O'Patrick.

She was quiet, watching whatever scene was playing out below, and Kimble was growing frustrated, scared and frustrated, because he could not see a thing.

"What can I do about them?" he said. "There's got to be something."

"There's only one you've got to worry about. I don't know what you can do. I can only tell you what he wants."

"What's that?"

"Blood," she said. And then, turning to him, her face white, her dark eyes stark against the pale skin, "Right now? He wants you."

A breeze rode off the ridge and across the river and fanned

her hair out, and Kimble looked into her face and wrapped his hand tight around his gun.

"Does he?"

She nodded.

"I need to know," he said slowly, "what to do. Do you understand that? I need to put an end to this."

"I don't know how."

"You can figure it out, Jacqueline. You can put an end to this." He was sliding his index finger back and forth along the side of the trigger, a sensory reminder: *I can end her, I can end her, I am protected because I can end her.*

"I don't think that's an option."

"Who are the others?" he said.

When she spoke again, her voice was very small. "They're the ones from the pictures," she said. "And Wyatt French."

"You can see Wyatt French?"

She nodded. "I can see them all. They're all down there with him. All the ones like me."

"You're sure," he said.

"I'm sure."

For a while it was silent. The wind pushed down off the peaks and rustled the trees along the ridge and wormed the cold of the night into Kimble.

"The one who called himself Silas Vesey is the problem," he said.

"He didn't call himself anything with me. The one I saw, though? The man who made me the offer? Yes, he's there. He's watching."

The words put a ripple through Kimble. Watching. Somewhere out there in the dark a man unseen by Kimble was watching. A man who'd caused death for more than a century, a man who'd put the blackness into Jacqueline, who'd then put a bullet into Kimble.

"Does he know you?" he said. "Remember you?"

"Yes."

"Still want my blood?"

She didn't answer.

"Jacqueline," he said, and now his finger was racing alongside the trigger, "I'm not going to stand here in the dark with you forever. I can't. You've got to tell me something that helps."

"And what would that be?" she said. She wasn't even glancing at him, was totally focused on whatever patch of shadow was home to the nocturnal activity.

"How do I know? Just answer my damn questions."

"I have been," she said.

"So there's no fixing them — that's what you're telling me?"

There was a long silence. It was so cold that Kimble could see his breath, but there were beads of sweat along his spine and across his brow. Just when he'd given up on any hope of an answer, just when he was ready to say, *Okay, enough is enough, let's put an end to this circus and get you back behind bars where you belong,* she spoke again.

"I don't think," she said, "that he has much range."

"What?"

"You're not going to *fix* him. If that's what you're hoping, I'm afraid you're out of luck. No man with a gun is going to fix him, Kevin. No man is going to do anything to him, period. He isn't bound by any of the things you want him to be bound by, not even time. But I think the place matters."

"The place."

"That's right. He wouldn't have found me if I hadn't passed this way. He needs people to pass this way."

"I understand that. He also needs the darkness. The lighthouse has hampered him. For years, it has. But there's got to be more I can do."

"You can guide some people away, maybe. That might be all."

You can guide some people away. Instead, he'd brought one here. He'd brought *her* here.

She's close, though, he thought, *damn it, she is close, she's seeing this place and understanding it.*

"He's got a weakness," he said. "He has to, Jacqueline."

"I don't know about that."

"I do. Find it. Please."

She was silent for a long time, and then she said, "In the story you told me, he promised to bind people to the trestle. Right? First came the fever, and then came Vesey, and then the bridge."

"Yes."

"Well," she said, "you could burn it down. See if he goes with it."

"I can't burn down a bridge, Jacqueline. And he *likes* fire."

"He likes his own fire. It's very different from ours." She shifted, looked back at him, and said, "We need to go."

"No."

"Yes." She stepped away, toward him, and in that moment he remembered her in the dark living room, and he lifted the gun and leveled it at her throat.

"Stand where you are."

She looked at the gun as if amused by it and said, "Scared of me, Kevin?"

"No."

"Here? You should be."

He didn't say anything. He was trying hard not to let the gun tremble in his hand, trying damn hard. It looked steady. He was pretty certain it was steady, pretty certain that —

She lifted her hand, and he said, "Jacqueline, no," and then she reached out and cupped the back of his wrist, gently.

Shoot! a voice screamed from within him, the voice of the long-departed version of him that carried no gunshot scars and did not believe in ghosts. *Do it now, shoot!*

Jacqueline applied pressure, soft but firm, pushing his hand down, and he let her. The gun swung away from her throat and down until it was pointing at the tracks. She stepped in to fill the void between them, her body meeting his, the curve of her right breast resting on his bicep, her thigh pressed against his. Her face was upturned, lips and eyes dark against her skin. For a moment, he thought she might kiss him again.

She didn't.

"I think we'd better leave."

He couldn't speak. His mouth was as useless as his trigger finger.

"You're strong," she whispered, and he could feel the warmth of her breath on his neck. "But Kevin? He's not weak."

"He doesn't like the lighthouse," Kimble said.

"Then we should go there," she said. "Fast."

39

AUDREY WAS IN THE BEDROOM, trying to get some sleep but not optimistic about the possibilities, when she saw the headlights coming east. Kimble was back in the car.

She put her hands to her temples, closed her eyes, and let out a long, relieved breath.

She didn't need to worry about him anymore. He was back in the car, and no one was in the woods tonight.

Down the hall it was silent, Dustin, hopefully, asleep on the couch, getting some rest for another day that would be long and arduous with just the two of them.

Can you hold out? Joe Taft had asked.

She wished he hadn't phrased it like that. As if she were under siege.

Are you not, Audrey? What would you call it?

She opened her eyes again, well aware that sleep would not come. Outside the bedroom window, the cats were quiet and the trees were dark. Once they would have been lit by that constant, pulsing glow. Now you had to remind yourself that the lighthouse was there.

*   *   *

As they neared the lighthouse, Jacqueline stared in fascination, bending down so she could see the top, where glass glittered in moonlight. She was in the passenger seat now — Kimble saw no point to putting her in the back this far along in the journey — and she leaned across him to get a better view, her hair falling forward and brushing his arm, her hand on his leg.

"It's the strangest thing I've ever seen," she said. "He had to have cleared so many of these trees to build it."

"He cleared the trees to build his home. The lighthouse came later."

"I want to go in," she said. "I want to see it."

"We will."

He shut off the lights and they stepped out of the car and went to the gate. She waited, arms folded across her chest against the cold, looking so small in his jacket. He opened the gate and let her through and then they went up the path, footsteps crunching on the thin layer of snow, and a moment later he had the light-house door open and they were inside.

She gazed around as he shut the door behind them, locked it, and turned on his flashlight.

"Larger room than what I'm used to," she said. "But I wouldn't want to live in it, either."

She made a slow circle, studying the thumbtacks in the walls. "What did he have up here?"

"Maps and photographs. The names on the maps belonged to people who died out here. The photographs belonged to people who didn't. People like you."

"People like me," she echoed. She twisted and looked back at him, her face split between shadow and light, just as it had been that night in the farmhouse. He didn't say anything, and after a moment she turned away again.

285

"Can we go up?"

"Sure," Kimble said, and he opened the door that led to the wooden staircase, then waited so that she could go first, and handed her the flashlight. He didn't want her standing behind him.

They reached the top and stepped up into the glass shell. A lion roared somewhere below, and the sound jarred Kimble, as it always did. Ahead of them the moon glowed, and Jacqueline turned away immediately, toward the west, where the spider-webbed glass that had received Wyatt's suicide round created a jagged sparkle against the flashlight beam. She stepped closer, reached out, and traced the shattered glass with her fingertip.

"Careful," Kimble said. She smiled, as if his warning were amusing, and then lifted her head, looking off across the treetops and over the ridge to where the night fog clung stubbornly to the trestle.

"Can you see them even from here?" Kimble asked, but she didn't answer. He watched her stand there and stare off at the horizon with her finger on the shattered glass and he realized that Wyatt had been facing away from the trestle when he pulled the trigger. He would have been facing away from whatever demons he saw there.

Jacqueline clicked the flashlight off.

As the darkness draped them, Kimble reached for his gun.

She said, "Relax, Kevin."

He hesitated, then he slipped the weapon from the holster anyhow. She turned, searched his face in the shadows, and then looked down at the gun in his hand. It seemed to disappoint her, but she returned her attention to the trestle.

"Can you see them from here?" he said again.

"Yes. I can see the fire, at least. It's too far to make out the faces. I'm glad of that. It's hard to have to see their faces. Wyatt's especially. I'd met him. I knew him. When he was alive, I knew him, and to see him now ... it's awful."

She was not lying. Kimble realized that and knew that the rest of his life would never be the same, that you could not stand in the presence of someone who saw these things and then go on about your business as if nothing had changed. He didn't know how life would go from here, but he knew that it would be different.

Jacqueline turned and studied the main light, saw that it was broken.

"I don't understand why he would have broken it," she said. "It seemed to matter so much to him that he'd leave a light on."

"He didn't break it. The person who found the body did."

"What about those lamps below? Do they work?"

Kimble looked down at the infrared lights, doing their invisible toil, and said, "No, they don't." The lie came without much thought, but he knew why he'd said it, the same reason he had drawn his gun: he still couldn't trust her completely. He wanted to, but he couldn't.

Or shouldn't.

"Turn the light back on," he said.

The flashlight clicked on, and he could see her again, and he thought that if she'd left the light on when she'd asked him about the infrared lamps, he might not have lied. When he could see her, he could trust her. When they were alone in the dark, though?

Then it wasn't so easy.

"He apologized to me," she said, and shook her head in amazement. "Wyatt French. He came all the way to the prison and apologized as if everything could have been stopped if he'd gotten back here and turned on the light."

"Maybe it could have," Kimble said, and they looked at each other in silence, considering just what that might have been like.

"Can we go back down? I don't like to see them, Kevin."

"We can go back down."

He followed her down the steps and out into the living quarters. She panned the flashlight beam around the bare walls, lined with their thumbtacks, and said, "This is where he had my picture?"

"Yes. Yours and the others."

She crossed the small room, sat down on Wyatt French's bed, and began to cry.

"Jacqueline," Kimble said, walking toward her, gun in hand. "What—"

"They're all there with him now. Everyone who accepted his help is trapped with him now, and I will be, too."

No, he wanted to tell her, *of course you won't be,* but what did he know about this? He saw no ghosts in the dark, he'd made no pact in the light of a cold blue flame, he'd killed no one in a black trance.

He reached out to her with his left hand, the one that did not have the gun in it, and wiped tears from her cheek. She reached up and took his hand and held it against her face.

"I'll be there," she said softly. "I don't know when, but I'll be there. You're going to take me back to jail now, and in time I'll get out, but where I'm headed, Kevin? It's no better. It's worse."

He knelt in front of her, looked into her eyes, and said, "There's got to be something, Jacqueline. We'll find it. I will find it."

She gave him a sad smile, tears in her eyes, and said, "Sure, Kevin."

It was quiet again then, and she tilted her head and kissed his hand. He tried to reach for her, tried to embrace her, but the hand she did not have hold of was occupied with the gun. She looked up at him.

"Put it down, Kevin."

He hesitated.

"You're going to take me back," she said. "I know that you will. It's the right thing, and you always do the right things. But does it have to be now?"

She slid her hand up the inside of his leg. "Does it have to be *now*?"

"No," he whispered. It did not have to be. And even if it did, he didn't want it to be.

He set the gun on the floor, leaned forward, and met her lips with his. She grasped the back of his head with both hands and pulled him down onto the bed. It was a small bed, narrow, and he rolled awkwardly onto his back, while she moved with total grace until she was on top of him and astride him, their lips still together. She broke the kiss and sat upright, looking down at him. Then, slowly, she unzipped his department-issue jacket and slipped out of it. Beneath that was the prison shirt. She pulled that off, too, and now he couldn't just lie there and watch her anymore. He pulled her down to him and kissed her face, her throat, her breasts, thinking that it was nothing like he'd imagined it would be.

It was better.

His phone began to ring. Jacqueline moved her lips to his ear and her hand to his belt buckle and said, "Let's not take any calls for a few minutes, all right? Haven't the two of us earned at least a few minutes by now?"

He thought that they had.

They took more than a few minutes. When it was done, Kimble lay in the dark with Jacqueline Mathis pressed against him, her skin warm on his, and he thought that he had never been crazy—this was where he belonged. With her. He'd known it when he saw her, somehow, as if the universe had whispered a secret truth in his ear, and now he could feel the confirmation of it in every breath she took, her breasts pressed to his side, swelling warm against him with each inhalation. He reached out and laid a hand gently against the back of her head, stroked her hair as she twisted, nestling against him, and thought, *It will not be that long. Her parole is not far away. She will be back with me if I am patient, and I have been patient for so long, I certainly can be again. For this feeling, this moment, I can be as patient as any man alive.*

"Kevin?" Her voice was soft.

"Yes."

"There's nothing to do about him. The ghost at the fire. There's nothing to do."

"There will be something. I'll find it."

She did not respond to that. They lay in the dark and he found himself counting her breaths against his neck.

Have to leave, he thought, *have to take her back, this has to end, and you know nothing more than before.*

"Do you believe that taking the trestle down would help?" he asked.

"In this spot," she said. "But Vesey? He was there before the trestle, Kevin. He'll be there after it's gone."

The wind buffeted the lighthouse, and up the stairs there was the whisper of sleet striking the glass, the night's snowfall beginning in earnest.

"I'm cold," Jacqueline said. "I want your jacket."

"Right. Sure." Kimble wasn't cold at all, not here with her.

When she spoke again, her voice was muffled as she turned away from him, found the jacket, and slipped her arms into it.

"I understand how I can stay away from that fire."

"How?"

She zipped the jacket up, and then the old bed creaked as she leaned forward, searching for the rest of her clothes.

"It won't be something you'll like," she said, turning back to him, leaning down, and kissing his throat. Her lips were so warm. "And I'm sorry."

"What do you mean, Jacqueline?"

The gun, when she pressed it to his throat where her lips had been a heartbeat earlier, was very cold.

"Just what I said, Kevin. That I'm sorry."

40

Two things became readily apparent to Roy as he woke with a jerk and a muffled shout, rising as if from a nightmare: he was no detective, and he was getting old.

His task had been so damn simple. Watch the road and call Kimble if he saw Nathan Shipley's truck leave. It required two eyeballs and consciousness. He hadn't been able to offer both.

The clock said he'd dozed for only ten minutes, but ten minutes was more than enough time for someone to have driven past.

"Shit," he whispered, looking up the dark road and seeing no glimmer of taillights, wondering what had woken him other than the uncomfortable sense that something bad was happening, something was going very wrong, very fast.

Guilt, nothing more. His body had wanted sleep; his mind had been lecturing him for taking it. That was all.

Still, the bad feeling lingered.

Go check, he told himself. *Just take a drive down there and make sure his truck is still in the driveway.*

It was. The same lights were on in the same rooms, and the

truck was parked in the same place and at the same angle. Fog hung in the trees that ringed the yard, and beyond it the mountains were no longer visible and the moon hung mostly obscured by cloud.

All was as it should be.

Except for that feeling.

Call him, Roy thought. *Call Kimble and just check in, let him know that everything is good out here, and make sure that it's good out there, too.*

But Kimble had told him not to call unless Shipley was on the move.

Back to the old Esso station he went. He'd just pulled in, backing up so that he had a clear view of the road, when he saw headlights approaching from the direction of Nathan Shipley's home.

It couldn't be him. Just someone else passing by in the night, nothing to worry about.

The headlights were set high, though, and as they came near he saw the squared-off grille of a truck not unlike Shipley's at all. It came closer, moving fast, and Roy reached to turn off his own headlights, had just flicked them off when he realized how stupid *that* was, because they'd surely been visible already, and then he did the only possible thing that was stupider still, and turned them back on.

Brilliant, Darmus. Your only job is to sit here and not be noticed and you flash *your damned headlights? Should have asked Kimble for a siren or an air horn to help you sneak around. Quick, set off the car alarm!*

The truck blew by him then, as he sat there in the empty gas station parking lot with his headlights aimed directly ahead, and he saw the blue side of Nathan Shipley's pickup truck and caught a glimpse of the deputy's face as he turned a curious eye toward Roy's car. Then the truck was gone, and not slowing.

Nathan Shipley was on the move.

Roy reached for his phone and couldn't find it, felt momentary panic as he patted empty pockets before remembering that he'd carefully placed it in the center console to be reached quickly.

How do people do this every day? he thought as he dialed. *It sounds so simple. And I'm not even required to follow the guy...*

Kimble's phone rang. And rang. And went to voicemail.

"Damn it!" Roy shouted, and then he called back and got the same response, and now he was faced with a decision. Did he just sit there and let time pass? Or did he follow? The road ahead was a long, winding path toward the highway or town. Shipley wouldn't turn off it for a while. Roy could catch up.

"Go for it," he decided, and he dropped the phone into the console and put the car into gear, pulling out of the lot and onto the road. If he drove hard and fast he could catch up, and then, if Kimble would just answer the damn phone, he'd be able to tell him—

He'd made it a quarter of a mile down the road when he saw the truck pulled off on the shoulder, its lights off, sitting in shadows. He registered that first, and then he saw the man standing in the middle of the road, holding a badge up with one hand and a gun with the other.

Roy put on the brakes and rolled to a stop. For one wild moment he considered pounding the gas instead, driving around the deputy or, hell, right over him. Anything seemed preferable. But he was a rational man even on an irrational night, and he trusted in his ability to bullshit. Shipley didn't know him. Roy would give him some song and dance about car trouble and then be on his way.

As Shipley approached, though, there was something in his face that suggested bullshit might not work. The gun was not being held casually. His finger was on the trigger.

Roy slipped his hand down to the console, punched redial on his phone, and then turned it over so the illuminated screen was hidden. If Kimble picked up, great. If he didn't, at least he'd get to hear a voicemail preserving whatever was about to happen.

Shipley rapped on the window with his knuckles, and Roy slid it down.

"Why are you standing in the road?" Roy said, trying to look indignant, the concerned citizen, the intrepid reporter, the man who was not scared of police because he trusted police.

Shipley leaned in, his face lit by the glow from the instrument panel, and said, "I would like to know why you're watching my house."

"What? Who are you?"

Shipley smiled. His face was very pale in the glow, and his eyes were hooded. He brought the gun up and laid it on the doorframe, pointed right at Roy's head.

"Slide over," he said.

"I'm not doing that. I have no idea what you're —"

"You've driven past three times," Shipley said. "And you're parked at an empty gas station. You're not out here to look at the stars, pal. You're watching me, and not very well."

He tilted the gun so that Roy could see how tightly he had his index finger wrapped around the trigger.

"Slide over," he said again.

Roy looked into the barrel of that gun, and then he unfastened his seatbelt and climbed over to the passenger seat. He was very careful not to hit the cell phone.

Shipley popped opened the door and got behind the wheel. There were no other cars on the road.

"We're going to take a ride back to my house and talk," Shipley said, and then he lowered his gaze, just for a moment, and looked at the phone. It lay upside down on the console, but there was a thin band of light around it. Shipley kept the gun pointed at Roy's head while he reached for the phone with his free hand, picked it up, and turned it over.

Connected, the display said. *Kimble,* the display said.

"Kevin Kimble," Shipley said. "I'll be damned." He put the phone to his ear, listened for a moment, and smiled.

"Voicemail. That's what you're leaving? Not a bad try. Not bad at all." He pressed the pound key, and now Roy could hear the faint, tinny voice giving a series of options.

"To delete your message and record again, press seven."

Shipley pressed seven, then disconnected the call.

41

ACQUELINE," KIMBLE SAID, the muzzle of his own gun sliding over his Adam's apple, "don't do this. Whatever it is you're
thinking, don't do it."

She slid off him carefully, her thighs gliding over his, the gun
never wavering. She knelt, fumbled along the floor in the darkness, and then Kimble heard a metallic clatter and knew what
she was after. Handcuffs.

"No," he said, and he started to sit up, but she rose swiftly and
pressed the gun to his heart.

"Kevin," she said, "I shot you once before. Do you really think
I won't do it now?"

He was more frightened by the emptiness in her voice than he
was by the gun. More defeated by the realization that those few
moments in which she'd lain silent and warm against his side
had been a lie, a fantasy. A dead dream.

"You can stop now," he said. "You can put that gun down and
this can go away. You've seen me put things like this away before."

She shook her head. "I can't let that happen. Not now that I've seen that fire, Kevin. You don't understand, because you can't see it. You don't belong to it. That's my future."

"It doesn't have to be."

"Yes, it does," she said, and when she straightened, his handcuffs and cell phone were in her hand. "I've seen them. Wyatt French and everyone whose picture you showed me. I don't have to join them, though."

"Exactly. We will find a —"

"He was telling me to kill you," she said.

She stood in the dark, and the faint shaft of moonlight that bled through the glass dome of the lighthouse and down the stairs pooled at her feet but climbed no higher. The rest of her, every line and every curve, existed only in silhouette, like a false promise.

"He wanted you," she said. "He wanted me to kill you. Do you know what that tells me, Kevin?"

He didn't answer.

"I was given a lifetime back," she said, "but I had to trade for it, didn't I? What he wants, it's not so simple as a soul. He wants workers, Kevin. He said that he's bound by balance. A life for a life. Once you agree to it, you can't run from it. Everyone's learned that. But balance doesn't vanish. You can keep adjusting the scales to maintain it. If I take another life for him, I'll buy more time before I have to join him. And another still. If I continue to? Well, I think then I could be like him. Eternal."

Kimble remembered what Wyatt French had told Roy Darmus on his final phone call. He wanted people to know that if he'd wanted to go on, he could have. That he didn't have to die.

"You can't kill more people," he told Jacqueline. "It's not in you. What happened before... I was there. I saw it. You were lost that night, Jacqueline, there was nothing left of the woman you are. Then you came back."

She ignored him, walked to Wyatt French's desk, laid Kimble's phone down on it, and then smashed it repeatedly with the gun. While she was breaking his phone he moved, and she spun immediately, but he'd not come closer, only gone farther away. He slid back from her in the bed, bumped into the wall.

"Stop moving, please."

He stopped, now pinned against the wall, but he could get his hand down to the other side of the bed, to the place where Wyatt French had built his strange emergency shelf to hold a gun, a knife, and a two-million-candlepower infrared spotlight.

The gun was gone. The knife wasn't.

"I will take you away from here," he said. "From him."

"You can't take me far enough. I'll be returned to him in the end."

Her voice was empty, but he saw that she was crying. Tears traced the lines of her face, shadow on shadow, before falling to the floor, plinking down like drops of blood.

"It's just like the story you told me of how it all started. He was not lying. It's easier for him to work on desperate people. After what I've seen tonight? They don't come any more desperate."

She swept the broken pieces of his cell phone off the desk and onto the floor, then said, "You didn't bring a radio, did you? I can't find one. Just in the car?"

"What are you going to do, Jacqueline?"

She stepped closer, and now he could see her better, her face a sculpted white glow in the blackness, her body slim and small beneath the bulk of his jacket. She said, "What did you feel, when we were together?"

"Home," he said.

"You could join me."

"Join you? Jacqueline, you've got to stop talking, you've got to stop, please, just —"

"If I shoot you now," she said, "he will come for you. You'll have a choice. And if you make the same one I did...we can leave here together. In a way that does not need to end."

Kimble dropped his hand down to the shelf. His fingers crawled over the wood — there was the flashlight and there was the strop for the knife and there was, yes, there was the blade. He followed it down to the Teflon handle.

"You can't see them," Jacqueline said. "If you could, you would understand what I have to do. He gave me life back once in exchange for taking another. He'll do it again. He wanted you tonight, Kevin. He'll want others. That's the idea, you know. He's bound to the ridge, and he can't carry his evil into the world. We have to do that for him."

She knelt beside the bed, leaned forward, and touched his bare chest with the muzzle of the gun.

"Tell me I can do it," she said. "Then he will come for you, just as he did for me, and you can make the same choice, and we can go on. Together."

"Killing people."

"You could help me with that. You know how to get away with it. And we could pick the right ones. We could kill the people who deserve to die, we could turn it into something good, and there would be no end to us, there would be no —"

"Stop," he said. "Please, Jacqueline, I can't hear it."

The stream of words came to an abrupt end, and when she spoke again her voice was low and measured.

"I need you to make the right choice," she said. "Will you do that?"

For a moment he was silent as the snow pattered on the glass of the lighthouse above them and Jacqueline Mathis watched him in the moonlight, and then he nodded.

"Yes," he said.

"Truly, Kevin?"

"Truly, Jacqueline." He reached out gently with his right hand and pushed her hair back from her face, used his thumb to clear the last traces of moisture away from beneath her eyes.

She smiled. "I'm so glad," she said.

"I know," Kimble said, and dropped his right hand down to the gun as he swung his left out with Wyatt French's knife in it and buried the blade in her back.

She let out a sound of soft and terrible anguish, a moan that wanted to build into a scream but couldn't. The knife had entered just under her left shoulder blade. Blood seeped from the wound and flowed hot across his hand. Kimble had been trying to get the gun from her as he swung the knife, or at least get it pointed away from him, but he didn't succeed at either task. She'd anticipated that attempt; she had not anticipated the knife. She'd cleared the gun from his grasp, though, and it was pointed at his face and her finger was on the trigger and his life was a few pounds of pressure away from an end, but she did not squeeze.

The moan came again, more pain evident now, and she tried to rise. The blade slid free from her body and his hand and fell to the floor as blood streamed down his jacket and ran over the backs of her slim, bare legs. As he watched the pain rise through her he looked at the gun and said, "Go ahead," and he meant it.

She opened her fingers and let the gun fall, looked him in the eyes with impossible sadness, and whispered, "You know what you've done to me."

"I'm so sorry," he said.

"You know," she began again, but she couldn't get all the words out this time. She shuddered and fell forward, fell against him, her face against his neck, and he reached out and caught her and held her.

"I'm scared of him," she whispered.

"You don't belong to him, Jacqueline. You don't."

He felt each of her last breaths. She lay against him just as she had before, in the one moment when everything had felt perfect.

"I'm sorry," he told her again, but there was no point to it now. Her warm breaths against his neck had ceased.

Kimble pressed his face into her hair and wept.

42

NATHAN SHIPLEY DROVE with his left hand and kept the barrel of his gun pressed into Roy's stomach with his right. Roy looked at the gun and thought of what he could do to escape, the movements he could make. Then he thought of how fast a trigger could be pulled.

He made no movements as Shipley drove them back to his home.

"Get out," Shipley said. His voice was unsteady. "Get out and walk inside."

Roy climbed out of the car and went through the yard and up the creaking steps of the porch. The doorknob turned in his hand, unlocked. He pushed it open and went in and Shipley followed.

"Sit down," Shipley barked, and Roy obeyed, sitting on an ancient and dusty couch. "Who the hell are you?"

"Roy Darmus. I worked for the newspaper." It was absurdly formal, but one of the things Roy was finding he believed deeply was that you should keep men with guns happy.

"Why are you watching me?"

Roy considered the gain in a lie, and couldn't find it.

"Kimble asked me to."

"He doesn't trust me. He came out here this morning, and it was obvious." Shipley paced, rubbed a hand across his face, and then said, "Holy shit, what am I doing? What in the hell am I doing?"

Roy was silent. He'd been more focused on the gun than the man, but now that it wasn't pressed against his stomach, he looked at Nathan Shipley's face. It was haggard, weary. It was frightened.

"I'm not going to shoot you," Shipley said.

"That's good to hear."

"I just don't know what's happening. What I'm doing, what I should be doing. I don't know anymore. I said that Kimble doesn't trust me? Well, you know what, man? I don't trust myself. I don't. That's the problem. I'm seeing things, and I can't get them out my head. My mind isn't right. People are dying out there, *Pete* died out there, and then Kimble comes out to my home and it was like he thought I did it, like he thought I was some sort of evil..."

The words were streaming from him, and he was still pacing, the gun hanging idly at his side.

"There's a bad history to that place," Roy said, trying to choose his words carefully. "I think Kimble is just worried for you."

"Well, he ought to be. Because I'm telling you, I have never been more certain of anything in my life than what I saw the night of my wreck out there, but what I saw was impossible."

"It might not be," Roy said, keeping his tone relaxed, thinking that if he could be soothing and understanding, then maybe, just maybe, he might walk out of here alive.

"What the hell do you know about it?"

"I know that other people have had the same experience. Have received the same offer. You might not have imagined as much as you —"

303

"Offer?" Shipley stared at him.

"I mean, other people have seen the man in the road. Kimble's been documenting it. I've been helping."

"That kid? Somebody else saw that kid?"

"I'm talking about the man with the torch. That's what you saw, isn't it?"

"I saw a torch, yes. A blue flame. There are others? Other people have *seen* this?"

"Yes. But they describe him differently. I think most of them see a man. Most of the people who have seen him are dead now, though, and what they saw, I'm not sure. So maybe others saw a child —"

"When I say kid," Nathan Shipley said, "I mean the one who works with those cats."

The gun in Shipley's hand was no longer Roy's focus. "What?"

"That accident," Shipley said. "I am telling you, as honest as I've ever spoken in my life, I *hit that kid.* Not somebody else, not some ghost. I hit *him,* and I did not imagine it. He walked right into the middle of the road. He was just staring off at something, didn't pay any attention to my car at all, and when he moved, I swerved the wrong way. I hit him. I know that I did. I saw it, I felt it."

Roy said, "You walked away from that wreck. Unhurt."

"I walked away awfully damn sore, and awfully lucky. But that kid, Dustin Hall? He should have been *dead.*"

Roy stared at him, thinking that he'd covered a lot of bad accidents, had taken a lot of photographs of cars that did exactly what a good car was supposed to do in a wreck — absorb the beating for you. Save you.

"But you talked about the blue flame," he said. "Kimble told me that."

"Yeah. The way it happened...the way I *know* it happened, not the way I remember it, but the way I know it did, was that I hit that kid as he stood in the middle of the road staring off like somebody in a trance. You would have to be deaf and blind to just stand there like that, but he did. And I hit him. Going fast, I hit him. He popped up in the air, and I could see him going across the windshield, and then I was in the trees."

Shipley wiped a hand over his mouth and shook his head. His eyes were wild.

"When I got my bearings back, the first thing I saw was that blue flame. It was over in the woods, just where his body should have been, just where he was flying when he went past the windshield. And then...then he was up. By the time the other people, Audrey Clark and Harrington, by the time they got there, the kid was up. I was woozy as hell, I will admit that, but I will *not* admit that I am capable of *imagining* something like that."

Shipley turned, and the gun swung toward Roy, who winced. "Sorry, sorry. Look, you want the gun gone, it's gone."

He set the weapon down on the coffee table between them. "I'm going to lose my job," he said. "I know that. But I'd rather lose that than my damn mind."

"You hit Dustin Hall?" Roy said. "And when you saw the blue flame, it was with Dustin Hall? The flame wasn't with you, it was with him?"

"Yeah. And I'll tell you something else — that kid knows what happened to him. He's the reason I can't convince myself that it was a hallucination or a dream or whatever. Maybe I could have, if not for him. But when I went back out there, the morning Harrington died? It was just me and Dustin Hall at first. Before Pete got there, it was just the two of us, and he knew what had happened, he knew that I'd run him down. I'm *sure* of it. But what was I supposed to tell Kimble? Or anyone else? Say, *Hey, this kid, he rose from the dead the other day, and now I think he's lying about it.* I'm supposed to say *that*?"

"Yes," Roy said. "You're going to need to say that. To Kimble."

"I could save us both the time and put the handcuffs on myself."

Roy shook his head. "You don't understand, Shipley. Kimble will believe what you just said, because it's true. He knows somebody escaped death out there. He just thought it was you."

"What?"

"Why do you think Kimble asked me to follow you, instead of a cop? He's chasing stories that most people don't believe are possible, just like you. He's out there at the ridge now, I think. I'm not sure. I can't get him on the phone."

"What's he doing out there?"

Roy was feeling the gravity of the mistake now, sensing all that it could mean, and there was no time to explain that to Shipley.

"We need to find Kimble," he said. "And we need to talk to Audrey Clark. Isn't Dustin Hall staying out there with her now?"

"Yes."

"That's not good," Roy said. "That could be very, very bad. Will you let me call Kimble again? Please. This is serious."

Shipley thought about it, looked once at the gun, as if that were an option worthy of further consideration, and then gave a broken man's sigh and nodded.

"Call him, man. I need to understand what the hell is the matter with that place. What's out there."

He reached in his pocket and withdrew Roy's cell phone and tossed it to him. Roy missed it—his hands were shaking. He picked it up off the couch and dialed and got Kimble's voicemail again.

"Damn you, Kimble," he said. "You told me my only job tonight was to call. Well, then yours should be to *answer.*"

Shipley said, "You want me to contact dispatch? See if they can raise him?"

Roy thought about what Kimble was doing tonight, thought

about Jacqueline Mathis and how swiftly this could end the man's career, and he shook his head.

"No. But we should call Audrey Clark. She needs to know that she should be careful with Hall."

"They're together in a trailer," Shipley said. "You want to call her and tell her she should be afraid of the guy and think he's not going to notice? He's not going to pick up on that vibe?"

It was a damn good point. Roy swore, looked at the phone and then back up at Shipley.

"We've got to go out there, then. Will you do that?"

Shipley looked sick at the prospect, but he nodded.

43

A UDREY WAS STILL AWAKE when the headlights came back on at the top of the hill, and while she was relieved once again, she was also concerned. Kimble had been up there for so long. Too long.

The lights arced away, the car leaving the lighthouse and heading back downhill, and then she lost sight of them.

Out in the living room, Dustin called for her. "Audrey? The police are here."

Kimble had pulled in to see them in the middle of the night? Why? Audrey stood up and slipped into her shoes. She'd slept — or tried to sleep — in her clothes, afraid or almost expecting something just like this, another call out into the darkness. By the time she got down the hall, Dustin was standing with the door open, and he said, "What the hell?" Before she could ask him anything, before she could even register the sound of alarm in his voice, Kevin Kimble had pushed inside. His gun was in his hand, pointing straight at her.

And there was blood all over him.

It was on the hand that held the gun, his uniform shirt, his

308

shoes. He wasn't wearing a jacket; his hair was tangled. His eyes looked fevered.

"What happened?" Audrey said, and only as she watched his face did a new option begin to form in her mind — that whatever had caused this bloodshed had happened not to him but because of him. He didn't look right, didn't have the reassuring demeanor he'd always exhibited before.

"I'll be going to jail soon," he said. His voice was dull. "But before that happens, I've got something I'd like to do, and I'm afraid you might not understand. I'm sorry about that."

Audrey was looking at the blood, so much blood, all over his clothes, and she put a hand to her mouth and took a step away from him. Dustin actually went *toward* him, as if he might wrestle the big man to the floor, but Kimble lifted the gun and leveled it at his forehead.

"Son? You're not standing in front of a man of reason. You'd do well to remember that. I will not hurt you if I can help it, but helping it isn't easy for me right now."

Dustin seemed to believe him. He backed away, sat on the couch.

Audrey said, "What are you doing? What happened?"

Kimble lowered the gun after giving Dustin a careful study. "I'm going to try to put an end to it, Mrs. Clark. This place. I doubt it will work, but I'm going to try it, and then I'm going to go to jail."

"I don't know what you're —"

"You do, though," he said. "You do. You've seen it out there. That man with the blue torch. I'm going to try to put an end to him."

Audrey remembered the blue flame, drawing her into the night woods, drawing her toward a dead man in the dark.

"You sound like you're talking about a ghost," she said.

"Don't I?" Kimble cleared his throat, gave his head a little shake, as if he'd wandered from the moment and had to bring himself back around, and then said, "There's no landline here. But I'll need your cell phones."

"Why?"

He gave her a pained look. "Please, Mrs. Clark. Audrey. I don't want to be here any more than you want me to be. But I've got to make sure I have enough time to do what I need to do."

"What is that?"

"Burn that trestle down," he said. "That trestle and all that lives with it. I'm taking it down."

He was serious. There was a rust-colored streak of blood over his cheek and above it his eyes were red and swollen, but the dark irises betrayed no trace of anything but grim determination.

"Why?" she said. "Why would you burn that bridge?"

"To keep people from dying. Or killing. Or maybe it won't do a damned thing, but it will do this much — nobody will be able to walk across it anymore. I don't think that's as small a difference as most people might."

"That's where my husband died," she said.

"I know. It's where quite a few people have died. It's a dangerous place."

He said it not in the way you'd talk about someplace where you need to be careful to avoid a slip and fall, but in the way you'd talk about a dark street with snipers on every rooftop, where all the care in the world might not help you if you made the mistake of entering it.

"You're talking as if it's evil," Audrey said.

"That is exactly how I am talking, yes. Now if you would please bring me your cell phones and car keys. Both of you."

She and Dustin stared at each other. Kimble made a small gesture with the gun and said, "Please. Nobody's going to be hurt. I just need time."

She went past him to the kitchen counter and found her cell phone, then took her keys out of the drawer. He accepted them with a polite "thank you" and then put them in his pocket. Dustin got warily to his feet and did the same.

"You thinking burning a bridge down is going to affect him?" Dustin said.

Him. Audrey was surprised by both the choice of word and by the manner in which he'd said it. There was very real curiosity in his voice.

"I hope so, son. I'm going to give it a try."

"Why would it?"

"Because he's bound to it," Kimble said, and Audrey felt as if she couldn't possibly have woken up and walked down the hall, that this was far too detached from reality to actually be happening in front of her, this blood-soaked policeman discussing ghosts in her living room.

"Why would fire bother him?"

"Light does," Kimble said.

Audrey said, "You sound like Wyatt French." She remembered Wyatt and all of his strange proclamations and dark warnings about this property, his insistence that if they had not tampered with his light, her husband would not have died. Kimble had asked after that yesterday. He'd come in here after seeing the corpse of one of his own friends, and he had asked her about the lighthouse. He believed in whatever Wyatt had believed in.

"It helped," he told her. "Still is helping. There are infrared lamps going up there right now, and have you seen that torch tonight?"

She shook her head.

"It holds him down," Kimble said. "Chases him back into the shadows. Well, I'm going to burn him out of them."

He took a deep breath, his broad chest filling, and said, "Now

I've got another favor to ask. Then I'll let you be alone for a while, and when I'm done, you get your keys and your phones back and I will give you the gun and let you call the police."

She didn't know what to say. Just stared at him.

"What do you need?"

"I noticed you drive gas-powered carts around here, when you haul things for the cats."

She nodded.

"Where do you store your gasoline?"

"In the barn. We've got several cans."

"I'd like them, please."

"I'll help you," Dustin said suddenly, and they both turned and looked at him.

Kimble shook his head. "No. You don't need any of the trouble I'm bringing around, not any form of it. There might be a lot."

"I'll help you get the gasoline down there," he said. "Then you do what you want. You're going to need help with the gasoline if you want to move quickly."

Kimble thought about it, then nodded. "Fine. Show me."

44

THERE WAS A STEADY but soundless wind that made the leafless trees sway in a gentle, hypnotic motion, and the moon was high and nearly full, snowflakes spitting against the windshield, as Nathan Shipley drove Roy along the winding roads that led west to Blade Ridge.

"I knew I wasn't crazy," Shipley said. "I knew I saw that kid, but how do you *say* something like that? How do you point to a living, breathing, uninjured human being and tell someone that you are positive he should be dead? I couldn't say that."

"Not to an ordinary audience," Roy said as they sped away from sparkling Christmas lights on the edge of town and into the darkness beyond. "But at this point, Kimble and I are not the ordinary audience."

"There have been ten others? Ten like him?"

"At least."

"And they not only healed up, but they killed people. You really believe that."

"It's not a matter of belief. It's a matter of reality," Roy said. "The easy question is how nobody noticed. But those accidents, those deaths, those killings, they were spread out over decades. Years would pass between them."

"Of course," Shipley said. "Think about it — that place is as isolated a pocket of the world as you'll find east of the Mississippi. It doesn't get a lot of traffic."

"That probably disappoints him," Roy said.

"Who?"

"Vesey. The ghost. The devil. Whatever he is. He came when the bridge was going up and prospects were high at Blade Ridge. The mines went belly-up fast, though. Poor yield. Then time and money moved everything to other places, and Blade Ridge was left empty and forgotten."

They hit a four-way intersection, and Shipley banged the right turn, Roy slid against the door, and then they were on County Road 200, almost there.

Audrey led Kimble to the storage barn where the carts and two tractors were kept. The gasoline for them was stacked neatly on fresh shelves that still smelled of sawdust, Wesley's final bit of handiwork before the new preserve had opened.

"Those four are gasoline," she said. "The other two are for the chainsaw, and they're a mixture of gas and oil."

"It'll all burn," Kimble said, and then he began to load the cans into one of the carts. Four twelve-gallon cans and two five-gallon. Fifty-eight gallons of fuel in all, and although it seemed the wrong question, Audrey asked if he actually thought it could do the job.

"I don't know," he said. "I've seen house fires started with a lot less. But that thing hasn't stood for more than a century by accident. It's strong."

"I hope it works," Audrey said, and she saw Kimble look at her in surprise.

"Do you?"

She gazed back at him, looking beyond the bloodstain on his cheek and into his eyes, and nodded.

"I don't know if I believe what you've said, but I believe something is wrong here. And it took my husband. So yes, I hope it works."

"I'll do my best," Kimble said. "And you do yours. Give me time enough to get it started. That's all I ask."

He looked at Dustin. "I'm going to go down there and soak those old planks in this gasoline, and when every drop is out, I'll put a match to it. By the time that happens, I want you both gone."

Dustin nodded. He hadn't spoken since they left the trailer. He was oddly self-possessed, though, exhibiting none of the fear that the situation seemed to dictate. He was braver than Audrey had thought he would be, but how did you ever know? How could you anticipate a situation that called for true bravery?

"What about my cats?" she said.

"What about them?"

"You're starting a fire. What if it gets into the woods and comes toward my cats?"

Kimble shook his head. "There's a good stretch of rock between that trestle and the woods. Even with a strong wind blowing, it couldn't make the woods."

He waved the gun at Dustin. "Sit down."

Dustin sat on the passenger side of the little cart. Kimble turned to Audrey and offered a bloodstained hand.

"Good luck," he said.

"You, too."

He got behind the wheel then, and the little motor bubbled to life, and then they were out of the barn and driving off into the night, down toward the trestle. Dustin didn't even look back at her.

Audrey stood alone for a moment. Around her the cats were on the move, gathering near the fences, watching with curiosity. A lion roared, one tiger responded, and then it was quiet again. Snow was falling steadily. Audrey watched the tiny headlights of the cart move toward the trestle, and then, after a hesitation, she followed.

Kimble parked the cart just outside of the torn-down fencing, turned to Dustin Hall, and looked him over. The kid gazed back with a blank face, oddly unbothered. You had to have some nerve to work around those cats, though, and after everything that had happened this week, with the deaths and the escaped cougar and the kid's dealings with Shipley, maybe he was getting a little desensitized.

"You ready to help?" Kimble said.

"Sure."

"Come on, then."

They got out of the cart and Kimble took a gas can in his left hand, keeping the gun in his right. Dustin Hall picked up a can in each hand.

"Give me a moment," Kimble said. "When I call for you, come on out."

He ducked through the fencing and went out onto the trestle. He went to the spot where he'd stood with Jacqueline, and then he dropped to one knee and stared into the shadows where the foundation bracings met the rocks and water below. Where she'd seen the ghost, and seen her fate.

There was nothing.

Kimble touched the weathered planks with his palm — *built by dead men* — and remembered the way she'd kissed him back up at the car, remembered the feel of her on top of him in the dark lighthouse, remembered that she'd had the gun pointed at his face and her finger around the trigger in the end and had not pulled it.

You know what you've done ... I'm scared of him.

"All right, friend," Kimble whispered, staring down at this demon who would not show himself. "We'll see how you like a little heat. I'm going to set your fucking house on fire."

He stood up again, called for Dustin Hall, and began to pour gasoline over the boards. He was very careful to see that the old wood drank it up and that as little as possible fell to the water below. He didn't want to waste a drop.

They worked swiftly and in concert, no sounds but their footsteps echoing on the boards and the gasoline splashing. Snow fell around them but the wind had lain down and it was a quiet night. Kimble worked on the western end of the trestle, Dustin Hall on the eastern, closest to the preserve, as instructed. Kimble wasn't sure they had enough fuel, and he thought that it would be better if he could get the fire going on both ends and let it work toward the middle. If even one end collapsed, the rest of the trestle would come down.

When his cans were empty, he discarded them and walked back across the trestle, gun in hand, to join Hall.

"It's all gone?"

"Yes."

Kimble bent and picked up one of the cans, turned it upside down and shook it. Only a few drops flew out.

"All right," Kimble said, feeling the matches in his pocket. "You need to get the hell out of here. Go on up with Audrey. I'll come up when I've seen that it's burning."

Dustin Hall didn't move. He was looking at the lighthouse.

"You say there are infrared lights in that thing? On right now?"

"Yes."

"And it bothers him."

Him. The word snagged on Kimble's ear, and he realized

Hall had used it earlier. Not in an informal, pronoun sort of way, either, but with a personal touch to it. As if he were speaking of someone he knew.

"I think it does," Kimble said slowly, and it occurred to him now that he hadn't had time to follow up with Hall about the allegation that Shipley had moved the rifle in the cage.

The kid turned back to him, snowflakes melting on his glasses, and said, "That's good to know," just before he slammed into Kimble with a lowered shoulder.

Kimble stumbled backward, his first instinct to lift the gun, his second that lifting the gun was no concern, balance was the only concern, and he was losing his fast. He reached for something to catch him, but there was nothing but snow and darkness.

45

AUDREY WAS STANDING IN the trees at the crest of the ridge, snow speckling her hair, the wind stinging her face, and the night had taken on a magical surrealism to her — she was a part of this but not, detached from it all, those sounds of footsteps and splashing gasoline on the bridge couldn't belong to her world, they represented something far too strange, and the silent snow only contributed.

Then Dustin slammed into Kimble and the deputy was off the bridge and pinwheeling through darkness and Audrey's scream shattered the dreamlike feel of the night and grounded her in reality once more.

For an instant, she started toward Dustin. She was horrified but did not *blame* him yet; her initial response was to think that he had done what he believed was right, acting out of fear of Kimble, acting in self-defense, even in defense of her. It was Dustin's response to the man's death that brought her to a stunned halt.

He showed no outward emotion, neither fear nor horror, as he knelt on the edge of the trestle and looked down to where the chief deputy had fallen into the same black water and jagged rocks that had claimed Audrey's husband, and though he surely knew she was there from her scream, he paid her no mind.

Not at first.

At first he simply stared into the darkness, then nodded his head and, as he straightened, lifted his right hand and snapped off a crisp salute.

Audrey felt the first creeping knowledge then, tendrils of memory and understanding seeping through, too fast and too vague to be grasped firmly, but strong enough for her brain to accept them and merge them into one central, critical point: Dustin was dangerous.

Even to her.

He brushed dirt and snow from his jeans casually, in no rush, and then finally pivoted toward her, searching for the place where he'd heard the scream. He found her, and then, still at a calm, measured pace, began to walk off the trestle and through the snow. Coming for her.

It was his pace and his silence that extinguished any remaining doubt, and she began to back away, not running yet, because she didn't want to turn her back on him, didn't want to lose sight of him even for an instant. It was only when she began to move that he broke the silence.

"Audrey, come down here."

His voice did not belong to the competent but socially awkward young man who'd helped her handle the cats for so long. It seemed to come from another man entirely, the voice dark and demanding and with a quality of patient threat to it, like an interrogator who wanted to make it clear that he would play the game but for only a while, and then God help you if you hadn't satisfied his questions.

She continued to backpedal. The rocks were slick with snow and she slipped once and almost went down, and for the first time she looked away from him, conscious of how close to the edge of the ridge she was, how treacherous the footing. The trees were just ten paces away, and beyond them the fences, and in the moonlight and snow she could make out only the white tigers and the eyes of a handful of others. Kimble had fallen from the bridge with her car keys and her cell phone in his pockets; it was now just her and the night woods and Dustin Hall.

And the cats.

"Audrey," he said again, and the threat in his voice was clearer now, his stride widening. "Come down here *now*."

"You shot Kino," she said. The thought had just entered her mind, and with it some shred of hope that she was making a mistake, that he was not really menacing, because Dustin would never have killed one of the cats.

"To be fair," he said, "I was aiming at Wes."

"Why?"

"Because I had to kill someone, and he was handy. Just like you are."

Now she did run.

As soon as she turned her back and began to flee, she heard his boots slapping off the planks of the trestle and then a rattle as he pushed through the fencing and she knew that he was pursuing — fast.

She was faster, though. She'd run cross-country in high school, had pounded out many road miles in the days before David's death, the days when there was time for such things, and she knew she could stay ahead of him, could keep going until she made the trailer, and then she could lock herself inside and find a knife and...

But she wasn't faster than he was. When she glanced back over her shoulder she was astonished and terrified to see how quickly he was closing the gap, and how craftily. Instead of running directly after her, he was angling to his left, understanding exactly where she was headed and determined to head her off.

He could, too. He could beat her to the trailer.

With her first option removed, she did what panicked quarry generally does and redirected without purpose, simply heading in the opposite direction.

She reached the fences, heard a roar from one of the lions—fast-moving animals excited the cats, always, they incited the predatory response—and kept angling to the right.

Behind her, Dustin called, "Stop running, Audrey. Stop it, now."

He was nearing the trailer, and once he saw that he'd succeeded in flushing her away from it, he would begin direct pursuit. Understanding that she could neither find protection nor outrun him, she made the final decision of panicked quarry: she had to hide.

She stumbled along between the enclosures, ducking and moving slower now, watching as Dustin turned away from the trailer and followed. For the first time she paused, knowing that the next choice would be critical, critical in the way a choice can be only when it might be your last.

Where to hide?

She dropped to all fours and began to crawl, but he was upright and moving quickly and would find her easily enough. Wherever she picked had to be close. She could not make the road, and to push deeper in the woods seemed hopeless, because she knew of no hiding spot and would make noise searching for one.

Dustin had paused, too. He looked in her direction but clearly could not see her, and then he walked to the trailer, opened the door, and stepped inside. For a moment she just crouched in the darkness and took deep, gasping breaths, watching him and thinking that perhaps the chase was done, perhaps he had other things on his mind.

Then the door opened again, and she saw the beam of the powerful flashlight, and she knew that the chase was hardly done.

To her right was one of the largest enclosures, home to three male lions. It was wide open and exposed space. To her left . . .

She saw Jafar's golden eyes, the leopard pacing, unsettled, and then she saw the shadowed shape of his house. He'd emerged from it, straw stuck to his paws, to see what the chaos was about, and the shelter was empty now. Empty and dark and within reach.

"Audrey!" Dustin's voice was a shout, furious, and she took one look at the flashlight beam — it was pointed the wrong way, he was expecting she'd moved toward the road when he had gone inside — and then she knew that she was out of options.

She crawled to the gate and worked the combination lock. She had two numbers in when the beam swung her way, and she dropped and pressed flat, knowing that it would find her. Jafar came to the fence, curious, and the beam passed over him instead and moved on. She lay in the snow and watched the path of the light and realized that Dustin was looking everywhere but in the cages.

Because Audrey wouldn't go in the cages. She never had before, and he knew that. Everyone at the preserve did. It was the unspoken but shared understanding they all had as to why she could never manage the place on her own: she didn't trust the cats.

She lifted her head, looked at Jafar's eyes, and whispered, "Let me in, please. I love you, buddy. Now don't hurt me."

The cat gave a low growl and flattened his ears.

Tension, she told herself, *he senses your tension and doesn't like it. That's all, Audrey. That's all.*

The flashlight beam passed close again, and she could wait no longer. When it was gone and she was in darkness, she lifted her hand and finished the combination. She did not need to fear the noise of the chain rattling; the lions behind her were roaring at full volume, and when that was happening, you could do about anything short of shooting off a cannon and not be heard. She pulled the gate open and crawled inside, and Jafar came trotting up with three loping bounds, then stopped with his back arched and tail stiff.

She almost tried to open the gate and run again, thinking that Dustin was surely going to be no worse a fate than this, but then memory whispered at her.

Playing, she thought, watching his stance, the way he was exposing his side, inviting her to chase. *He's trying to play with you.*

Audrey pulled the gate shut and clicked the lock back in place and then crawled for the animal's house. The cat stalked alongside her, and she felt the tears sliding down her cheeks. She was shaking now and would not look at him, could not, as if to meet his eyes would be to engage him in hostility.

The opening to his house was tight and narrow. She crawled in, cold straw bristling against her palms, and behind her the leopard gave a growl.

It was his territory, and she was invading it.

"Please," she whispered. "Please, please, please."

He did not strike at her as she entered. She banged her head on the plywood ceiling and then ducked lower and crawled on through the straw, crawled until she reached the bend in the wall that indicated it was making the L-turn, and then she could see the opening on the other side. There, farthest away from either end and impossible to spot unless you were inside the enclosure, she stopped moving. Her breath was coming in sobs now, and she tried to quiet them. It was a good hiding place, as long as she was quiet. A good hiding place, as long as the cat allowed it to be.

Out in the preserve, Dustin was still shouting her name, but that was good. That meant Dustin didn't know where she was.

She heard another growl, turned back to her left, and saw a pair of golden eyes at the entrance to the shelter.

Jafar.

He knew where she was.

46

JACQUELINE HADN'T BEEN WRONG in her recollection — the only thing Kimble registered about the fall was that it was far too fast.

Then he registered the pain, and all else was gone.

He struck the surface of the frigid water awkwardly and plunged deeply into it, but not deep enough. An upright, jagged stone caught him in the ribs and drove the breath from his lungs, and then another drilled into his shoulder and the side of his neck, radiant pain spreading through him as he scrambled wildly at the frigid blackness, sure now that he was dying and that it would be just as he'd always feared death would be: dark and alone.

When he broke the surface a wide, flat rock caught his body and held it, and for a moment there was nothing but the agony and the cold water and the night. Then there came a light, thin and blue and cold, and the world spread out from the light, and once more he could see.

Silas Vesey was coming for him.

He held the blue torch high, and though he waded through the water to reach Kimble, it did not appear to part for him or drag against him. He was of it, and it was of him, so no conflict existed. He just drifted on through the dark water until he was at Kimble's side. He wore dark trousers and an ancient, faded work shirt with the sleeves rolled up to his elbows, and in the flickering blue light of the torch his face was lit clearly. He had dark hair and a sharply cut, sweeping mustache, and his eyes were sunken but powerful, penetrating. The flesh of his face seemed to drink in the blue light and spread it through his skin like a cobalt sunburn.

He knelt in the water beside Kimble and rested the butt of his torch on the flat rock just inches beneath the surface, and then he gazed at Kimble and smiled. When he spoke, his voice was clear but hollow and with an odd hint of echo, like something rising up from the bottom of the deepest well.

"You're badly hurt, sir," he said. Not a sympathetic observation but a delighted one. He passed the torch over Kimble's body, and Kimble turned his eyes down and saw his own ribs, blue-white and dripping blood, the ends sheared roughly, like something cut with a dull saw. He found he could not move his head or neck, only his eyes.

"Grievous," the man said, this devil who had once called himself Vesey.

Kimble didn't speak. He was looking past Vesey, to where a blue bonfire burned, and saw familiar faces all around. Empty faces, haunted eyes. They watched him with sorrowful resignation, and he saw Wyatt French and then Jacqueline.

He wanted to cry out for her, but she was staring right at him, and there was nothing in the gaze. Just an infinite emptiness.

Silas Vesey moved, blocking Kimble's view, his shadow spreading over the rocks, blue light enshrouding him.

"You will soon perish," Vesey said. "There's no doubt. I'm familiar with the ills of men, sir, and your condition is not one that shall heal itself."

Vesey rocked back on his heels, still smiling, his lips a deeper shade of blue than his face, his eyes coal black and starkly contrasting with the ethereal glow.

"Your afflictions can be healed, though you may not believe it at this moment. I am possessed of a certain level of help that may be offered, and I am prepared to offer it. Should you so desire. Help of such a nature does not come without cost. I'm bound by balance, you see. If you wish to be healed, you shall be bound by balance as well. My kind is unable to restore life. Only able to balance it. Are you in understanding of this situation?"

Kimble tried to move his hand, but his arm was not responsive. He was aware that the fluid leaking along the side of his face was too warm to be the river water. Blood, and the source seemed to be his ear.

"The choice is yours," Silas Vesey said.

Kimble flicked his eyes from that terrible pale blue face to his own ribs, watched his blood drip from shards of bone to be swept away in black water.

"Your time is fading. I'll have to hear an answer soon. I cannot extend your time without that answer."

When Kimble parted his lips, he could hardly make a sound, but the whispered word seemed to be enough.

Yes.

Vesey came closer, sliding through the water without disrupting it by so much as a ripple.

"I understand you are accepting the offer as presented," he said. "You wish to be healed, and you will be called upon to uphold your required portion of the bargain. This is correct?"

Yes.

Vesey's smile widened, the deep blue lips curling up, black teeth beneath, and then he nodded, leaned forward, and lowered the torch toward Kimble's face. Kimble watched the sapphire sparks descend and expected that excruciating pain would follow, but it did not.

Instead, blackness flapped toward him like a visible wind, and then all was gone.

47

THE LEOPARD WAS SITTING WITH his haunches on the ground and his forepaws inside the shelter, regarding Audrey through primal eyes.

"I'm just visiting, honey," she whispered. "Don't be mad. Please, do not be mad."

There was a rustle in the straw, and his spotted face vanished from the moonlight but the yellow eyes advanced. He was coming toward her. Audrey let out a low, strangled sob.

He's your favorite, she told herself, *you touch him, you let him touch you, and if he ever wanted to hurt you he could have a million times by now.*

But there'd been a fence between them. Always.

Jafar came on through the dark, and then she could see his eyes looming just before hers, could smell his snow-dampened fur. The leopard made a soft but deep growl, almost like a purr, and then he reached for her face with his. His mouth was open, and his breath smelled of meat and blood. Every one of her muscles went warm and liquid, and for a moment fainting seemed a very real possibility.

He thumped her shoulder with his head, and she bit back a scream. He made a displeased sound, thumped her a second time, and she whispered, "Okay, baby. Okay."

She reached out with a trembling hand and touched his muzzle. There was snow melting on his fur and held in crystals on the long whiskers. If he decided to strike, from this distance, and with her unable to move...

The leopard extended his muzzle as she caressed it, then nudged the side of her face. She could feel the smooth fur on her cheek, the bristling whiskers against her neck. His head was enormous. Her fingers slid lightly down the span of his massive jaws, and she thought of all the times she'd seen them close around a piece of bloody meat, the tremendous power as his teeth snapped and shredded flesh that was far tougher than her own.

"Good boy. You're my baby, aren't you? I love you, buddy. I love you."

He licked her neck, then along her jaw. His tongue was warm and rough and beyond it were canine teeth as long as her index finger. One bite was all it would take. One bite.

He made the low growl again.

That's a friendly sound, Audrey. He is happy to see you. He is happy.

"Thank you, honey. Oh, thank you." She felt able to breathe for the first time since he'd entered, and when he nudged her again, rubbing the top of his head against her shoulder, she got her hand high enough to scratch behind his ears. That was as brave as she had ever allowed herself to be before, from behind the fence. Now, the two of them alone in the dark, the big cat was just as content.

I'm okay. I am okay. He will not hurt me, and Dustin will not find me, and as long as I stay in here I am okay.

That was when the flashlight beam passed close by, illuminating the inside of the leopard's enclosure.

"Audrey, get the fuck out here," said a voice that had once belonged to a young man she had kidded about his resemblance to the boy in the Harry Potter movies, a man who once seemed as harmless as anyone she'd ever met but who now spoke from a place of unyielding blackness. He told her to get out with such confidence that she was sure he knew where she was, almost felt an impulse to respond. Then he continued talking, and she realized from the sound that he'd turned away, was speaking in another direction, still seeking.

"You don't understand this place. You don't understand how special it is. What I can be here. What *you* can be. Kimble, even. He doesn't have to die. That's up to him. I doubt he will make the right choice. What he cannot be allowed to do, though, is burn that bridge."

He paused, searching for her in the night, and then continued.

"You're thinking about Wes. You're blaming me. Well, Wes didn't have to die, either, Audrey. I watched it happen. The cats are what kept him away, and if he'd been able to get there, then Wes might be with us now. It was going to be up to him, but the cats prevented that chance. Don't worry — I won't let that happen to you. I'll bring you to him. When you see the torch yourself, you will understand. When he touches you with that flame, you will understand."

Silence. She had stopped moving, but her hand still rested on Jafar's ears, the fur beginning to bristle, the leopard unappreciative of Dustin's tone.

"Where did you go, you stupid bitch?" Dustin called, impatience returning. "You wouldn't have gone into the cages. You're not brave enough for that, no, you're still scared of them, your own damn cats. Or did you get brave tonight?"

He was passing through the fences close to her, and he began dragging the handle of the flashlight across them, metal on metal, a loud rattling sound. Jafar heard it and growled in Audrey's face.

Peeled his lips back and even in the dark they were so close that she could see those teeth, the ones that tore through meat so easily.

"Calm down, honey," she whispered, barely audible. "Calm down."

Dustin banged against another fence, this one closer, and the leopard growled again. The next fence he hit belonged to the leopard's enclosure. He was at the gate.

"Were you brave enough to go in with your favorite?" he said, voice lower and musing, as if he found the idea plausible. She was glad she'd fastened the lock.

But the snow, she realized, *my tracks are in the snow, he will see those.*

She'd been crawling, though. Not leaving footprints. Just a messy trail through the very same snow that Jafar had trampled over himself.

The flashlight beam caught the corner of the cat's shelter. Dustin was trying to angle it so that he could see inside. The light caught the back half of the cat, illuminating the long tail and spotted hindquarters, but not finding Audrey. She'd gone far enough back that it could not reach her.

Dustin banged on the fence again, and Jafar let out the loudest and angriest growl yet. Audrey lifted her hand to her mouth and bit down on the side of it.

"Where are you, Jafar? Come out here. Come out and see me."

The shelter was too narrow to allow the cat to turn around, but he was angry about the noise, and Audrey could sense that he wanted out. When he moved toward her, she felt a rush of fear, his massive paws and their deadly claws brushing over her thighs. He was pressed against her for a moment, the length of him sliding by, and then he slunk around the corner and emerged through the other end of the little house, outside again, snarling.

"Hiding out?" Dustin said. "Scared, big boy?"

There was another rattle against the fence, but this one was different from the others. Not done just to make noise. He was, Audrey realized with rising panic, working with the lock. Opening the gate.

Coming in, she thought wildly. *How does he know I'm here? How does he know?*

Then Dustin spoke again, and she realized that he was not coming in at all. He had a very different idea, one that reduced her temporary terror but replaced it swiftly with another one.

"Come on out," Dustin said. "I'll tell you something—they don't like you down at that fire. They don't like any of you. So step on out, Jafar, and get the hell away from our ridge."

Our ridge.

"You need to go," Dustin said, "and the lighthouse needs to go. Then things will be back to the way he prefers them."

Audrey heard the sound of the gate being pushed open, and then the flashlight moved away and Dustin was at another gate, another lock.

He was opening them all. He was releasing the cats.

48

THEY BANGED OFF THE PAVED county road and onto the gravel of Blade Ridge so hard and fast that the back end of the truck jitterbugged to the left, and Roy reached out and put a hand on Shipley's arm.

"Slow down, damn it. You forget what happened to you out here before?"

"All right."

Shipley let off the accelerator and they slowed to what, after the pace of their wild ride, seemed like a tractor's crawl. Roy stared ahead, thinking of blue torches dancing through the woods, thinking of his parents out here on a wintry night just like this. He wondered how soon they realized they'd missed the turn. Early, he suspected. His father would have realized it early. And he would have continued on down the road because he was looking for a safe place to turn his beloved small-block V-8 Chevy around. Or because he'd been following the blue light, enraptured, as so many seemed to be.

"If we don't see Kimble's car," Roy asked, "do we still go in? Do we try to talk to Audrey Clark?"

"I want her away from that kid," Shipley said, and then he pounded the brake all the way to the floor, the truck sliding to a stop in the snow and the gravel, and said, "Holy shit."

There was a lion standing in the road. Majestic and with a full mane, his enormous head swung toward them, studying them, eyes aglitter in the headlight beams.

"They're out," Shipley whispered. "Why are they out?"

Roy had no answer. It couldn't be good, though.

A shadow moved ahead and to the left, and they both turned toward it. Visible for an instant, then receding, was the orange-and-black-striped side of a tiger.

"Mr. Darmus," Shipley said, "you want to tell me what in the hell we're supposed to do about this?"

"Call for help," Roy said. "It's too late to be worried about protecting Kimble. Maybe too late to worry about Audrey Clark. We're going to need a lot of people out here."

"Yeah," Shipley said softly, foot still on the brake, his eyes still locked onto those of the lion, which had not turned away. The animal lifted its head and roared then, a sustained bellow that made the steel and fiberglass shell around them seem suddenly insubstantial.

"We've got to get out of here," Roy said. "I'm afraid it's too late for them. It's not for us."

Before Shipley could agree or disagree, a figure appeared at the far end of the road, walking out of the trees near Wyatt's light-house, down toward the gates of the preserve. For a moment, Roy thought of Vesey, and wondered where his torch was.

Then he recognized him, almost simultaneously with Shipley.

It was Kevin Kimble.

He'd remained in the water for a few moments, until he was certain that what he was most aware of was the cold and not the pain. There was no pain. The ghost was gone and the blue light was gone but he knew that they were not really departed, that they remained very close.

At the top of the ridge, it occurred to him that he had not been aware that he had started to climb. Had not been aware of leaving the water. His body was whole and healed; he felt stronger, in fact, than he had in many years, stronger than he had since the day his back was pierced by a nine-millimeter bullet.

It's true, he thought numbly, *it is all true, every word I have been told about this place is true.*

He was bothered by the way he had been compelled to move, the way he had emerged from the rocks and climbed to the top without decision or conscious thought, a man on the move with destination and motivation unknown.

He needs you gone, Kimble realized. *It's just as Jacqueline said—his evil is bound to the ridge. He doesn't want to hold you here, not until you've done your work. You have to carry his torch for him into the places where he cannot go.*

And the torch was in him now. It would travel with him for all of his days.

That was just fine. Kimble would not feel the weight of the burden long. He had promised balance, he had promised to take a life, and he intended to very soon.

He'd returned to kill Dustin Hall.

There was a shotgun in his cruiser, and his cruiser remained at the lighthouse. He walked through the trees, staying well to the north of the road, away from the preserve, reminding himself to walk in the path that was illuminated by the invisible beams from the lighthouse, reminding himself that if he recalled the lessons of the dead, he could see this night through to dawn. Down below, he could see a flashlight beam and hear Hall shouting, and he thought of Audrey Clark and knew that he had to hurry. He was able to hurry now; running was not a problem for Kimble, not now, not after that single whispered word of consent.

You'll make the right decision? Jacqueline had asked.

Yes, he had. It would be the right decision, because he would kill Hall, his debt immediately satisfied, and then he would retreat from this place for many years — the courts would see to that — and when it was all done, when his days were passed, he would of course have to return here. Bound to the fire. He knew that and it saddened him but he could not think of it now, because there was work to be done, because he had to focus on running up that slippery, snow-covered slope and toward the beacon that Wyatt French had built so many years ago.

The rest of his days were not a concern, it was the rest of this night that mattered. He would use evil against itself, and in that was some level of victory, the most Kimble could yet be granted. If he was damned to that fire, so be it. Because he would be damned with her, and that felt right, that felt a long time coming. He could still remember the feel of her lips, he could still remember her blood, so hot, cascading over his hand as he worked the blade into her, seeking the heart. They'd damned one another, indeed. He'd returned her here, to the one place to which she could not be returned, and then he'd killed her. Now he would never leave.

Bound by balance.

He reached the cruiser, pulled open the door, and found the shotgun clipped in its customary position. Removed it and swung the door shut and turned back to where the flashlight beam was passing through the trees below.

Debts to be settled.

He ran down the driveway, which was too steep for running in the ice and the snow and the dark, but he did not stumble, he did not fall. When he reached the base of the hill he paused, isolating the position of the flashlight and knowing that he had to go quietly now.

337

Then, suddenly, the flashlight was gone. For an instant Kimble was puzzled, and then he, too, heard the engine and saw the headlights.

Someone was coming.

When the vehicle came to a stop, Kimble stepped out of the trees and began to move toward it, his finger resting on the shotgun's trigger, and what he saw painted against the headlights brought him to an abrupt halt.

The lions were loose.

Audrey heard the engine and then Dustin fell silent and his flashlight was extinguished. When he spoke again, his voice was low and soft.

"Visitors. I should probably greet them, don't you think, Lily, old girl? Wouldn't do to be impolite."

He'd been talking to the cats consistently as he tried to urge them from their cages. He seemed to have given up on his pursuit of Audrey or the idea that she could even hear his voice; his attention had gone instead to the cats and their release. She knew from his words of approval and their sounds that a few of them had accepted the coaxing and ventured into the night. Now she heard his footsteps crunch through the snow and understood that he was moving toward the road.

She could stay here, secure in her dark hole, hiding and waiting, but whoever had come down the road did not know what those approaching footsteps carried with them. There was a tranquilizer rifle in the trailer, and while you had to be close to use it, it would be better to try than to stay here cowering in the darkness and let him destroy whatever help had arrived, let him take more blood for the ridge.

Audrey had facilitated enough blood for the ridge.

She waited until his footsteps were inaudible, and then she

slipped out of the shelter, bits of straw hanging in her hair, and peered into the night. Across from her, in the silent snow, Lily, the blind white tiger, sat on her haunches, staring at nothing.

Only Audrey knew better than to think that. The cat's other senses more than compensated for the lack of vision; so long as Lily was watching the road, that meant Dustin was in that direction.

The trailer was not far off. She could make it. He would be occupied with the car, which appeared to be stopped in the middle of the road, and even if he heard her or saw her, he would have to make a decision. Whatever choice he made, someone would have a chance to adjust to it. She needed to force him toward that moment of decision.

There was a flourish of motion to her left, and she turned to see Jafar cross the enclosure in rapid bounds, pulling directly up to her. The terror she might have felt just minutes before was gone, though. She had lain with him in the dark and emerged unscathed on the other side, and now her fear had turned to faith. She rose to one knee, took the leopard's head in both hands, and kissed his nose.

"Thank you, baby. Thank you."

Then she got to her feet, went to the gate, and stepped through. In the distance, illuminated by the glow of the headlights, she could see one of her tigers stepping hesitantly through a yawning gate and into freedom.

Hurry, Audrey, she told herself as she began to run.

If she'd ever moved faster, she could not remember the occasion. She ran expecting blows or bullets, but none came, and she neither saw Dustin nor heard him. The trailer door was cracked open; he had not bothered to close it behind him as he came out with the flashlight. She hit the door at full speed, slammed it shut, locked it, and turned to the small closet where they had kept the tranquilizer rifle since Wesley's death.

The door was open, and the closet was empty.

Of course, she thought stupidly. *Even Dustin wouldn't have been setting them loose if he didn't have some sort of weapon.*

She turned to the window, and that was when she saw Kevin Kimble in the road near the gates and, moving just behind him, a silhouette that looked like a man.

Roy said, "He's going to shoot the lion," as Kimble walked slowly forward, a shotgun in his hands.

"No, he's not," Shipley said. "He just wants to know who the hell we are."

He picked up his own gun then, a semiautomatic handgun, and reached for the door handle.

"Wait," Roy said. "He doesn't trust you. Not yet."

Shipley stopped, looked back at him, and nodded. "Right. You tell him."

Roy opened the passenger door and climbed out as a gust of wind blew snow and ice pellets against him.

"Kimble!" he shouted. "I'm with Shipley. He's safe."

Kimble hesitated, didn't answer. The lion had pivoted to face them when Roy yelled, and the wind gusted again, harder this time, and swung the door shut.

Shit, Roy thought as the lion started forward at a trot. Roy fumbled frantically for the door handle, jerked it open, and slammed himself back into the seat. By the time he'd turned around, the big cat was at a stop again, watching them like an uncertain security guard trying to assess their credentials from a distance.

"Drive," he told Shipley. "I'm not getting out again. Not with the cats loose."

Shipley proceeded forward, and the lion roared again, the sound so furious that Roy actually lifted his hands as if he might ward it off. Shipley kept his speed steady, though, and as they approached, the lion moved away, distrusting the vehicle. It circled behind them and stepped into the shadows, and then it was just Kimble in the beam of the headlights. Roy looked to his right, saw no sign of any of the cats, and put down the window. He leaned his head out.

"Kimble! Shipley is safe! You don't need to worry about —"

Beside him, Shipley said, "Son of a bitch, there he is," and banged open the door. When Dustin Hall rushed out of the trees and into the road, armed with a strange-looking rifle, he was behind Kimble and very close. Kimble spun to meet him, but Shipley had already fired. The sound of the gunshot echoed, and Roy watched as Dustin Hall crumpled at the road's edge.

Standing beside the open door, gun still extended, Shipley said, "Let's see if we can keep him down this time."

49

KIMBLE APPROACHED THE BODY slowly, the shotgun cold in his hands, and he hoped for some sign of life. One last gasp, something. He had to be the one to end it.

He had to be.

There were no last gasps coming from Dustin Hall. Shipley's shot had caught him just behind his left eye and the bullet had blown through his brain, and Kimble knew with one look that he'd been dead before he'd fallen into the snow. All the same he knelt and put his hand in front of Hall's mouth, waited for breath, found none. Touched his neck and then his wrist, searching for a pulse.

Nothing.

Shipley and Darmus were standing above him now, and Kimble looked up to see Audrey Clark approaching. A lion, out of its cage, free, moved beside her in the night, and she saw it but did not stop.

"I got him," Shipley said.

"Yes," Kimble answered softly. "You got him."

They were all together then, everyone understanding a piece

and no one the whole, and they looked at each other in silence before Audrey Clark said, "You were dead. He pushed you... you were dead."

Kimble looked up and met her eyes. "Yes."

Silence again, but only momentarily, because Audrey Clark said, "Ira."

Roy Darmus murmured an oath and moved for the truck but then decided it was too late, and Kimble turned his head and saw the black cougar advancing through the blowing snow, slinking along without making a sound. The cat stopped not five paces from him, and Kimble moved slowly to turn the shotgun toward him.

"No," Audrey said. "Don't. He wants to see the body."

Kimble couldn't process that, had shifted his finger to the trigger, when she said, "Just as he did with your deputy."

He thought about that, thought about the way she'd described her last sighting of the cougar, the black cat standing atop Wolverton as the life bled out of him and the blue torch stayed at bay, and he finally understood.

"Like the lighthouse," he said. "The cats are like the lighthouse."

Except this one, which may have been something more than the lighthouse. Kimble rose and moved backward. They all did. The cougar waited until they had cleared enough room, and then he slunk forward, his head swaying side to side, his green eyes impossibly bright. He reached the body and paused, then circled it. He paid the living no mind at all now; his focus was on the dead.

The cat studied the corpse, and then he raised his head and looked toward the ridge.

"There won't be anyone coming for him," Kimble told the cat. "The lights are on."

The black cat watched the ridge for a long time, and then he moved on through the snow and into the night.

Nathan Shipley said, "Did I just see that?"

"Yeah," Kimble said. "You saw it." He turned to Audrey Clark. "You were right."

"Dustin knew it," she said. "And Dustin could—"

Darmus said, "The cats are *out,* Kimble. The cats are out. There is a lion right behind us. *Look.*"

"That's just Woodrow," Audrey Clark said. "He won't hurt you."

"There are others."

"Not many. He didn't manage to let many of them out. I can get them back in."

There was no waver to her voice. Kimble looked at her and he believed her.

"Well, let's do that," he said. "Quickly."

She didn't move. "I saw you fall," she said. "Now here you are."

"Yes," Kimble said, and he saw from their faces that they all understood. He pointed at Dustin Hall's body. "I came back for him."

Shipley said, "But I got him."

Kimble worked his tongue around his mouth, which had suddenly gone very dry, and drew in a breath that didn't come easy.

"I know."

50

S HE MOVED WITH AN astounding grace and confidence, talking to the cats, coaxing, at times touching them. She had
Shipley follow with the tranquilizer rifle, but he did not need to
use it. Kimble took Darmus to check the rest of the gates and
secure the ones Hall had opened before being disturbed. In four
of the enclosures, the gates were open, inviting the cats to freedom, but they had remained inside.

"It's home," Darmus said. "I guess they trust it more than they
do these woods."

They were right to do that, Kimble knew.

It took her twenty minutes to escort back inside the five cats —
one lion, three tigers, and an ocelot — that had left their enclosures. There was something different in the way she moved with
them from what Kimble had seen in her before. Something had
changed, but he did not know what. They spoke little until it
was done. The three men were afraid of the cats; the one woman,
who was not afraid, was focused on them, worried for the safety
of the animals.

"I'm not going to leave you," she told the enormous lion, the one she'd called Woodrow, as she guided him toward the open gate. "If you leave, I'll go, too. I promise you that."

The lion wandered along with that on-my-own-time pace exhibited by cats everywhere from the jungle to apartment living rooms, and finally stepped within the fence, and Audrey Clark shut and locked the gate behind him.

With the preserve secured again, the cats behind their fences and Wyatt's lighthouse casting its beams into the shadows, they walked together to the trailer and went inside, and then it was just the four of them, the four of them and the impossible truths of the night.

"We should hear it," Kimble said. "From each other first."

They told it. Inside the trailer, huddled in the living room, as the night pushed on toward dawn and the snow continued to fall, three accounts were shared, three accounts believed. They were well beyond the point of doubt with one another.

Kimble listened, and waited. He stood in front of the window, where the infrared beams would be working on him. He could not see them, of course, but he knew that they were there and he took comfort in that. Took comfort in the work they could do both for him and for the others, operating unseen but also unrelenting.

Roy Darmus was the one who finally turned to him and said, "Where is Jacqueline Mathis?"

"Dead," Kimble said. "I killed her."

He realized there were tears in his eyes then. No one spoke as he pushed them away with the back of his hand, and no one spoke as he told them his own account.

"Now it's in me," he said. "Just as it was with all the others. I won't be able to control it. To hold it at bay. That's been proven for so long. Too long."

"There will be a way," Darmus said.

Kimble held his eyes and didn't speak, and after a time the reporter looked away.

"I just saw him coming at you," Shipley said, his voice barely above a whisper. "I didn't know, I just shot, and —"

"Of course, Shipley. You did the right thing. I might not have gotten him anyhow, and then where would we be?"

But he would have gotten him.

"You were going to burn the trestle," Audrey Clark said. "You said it would work. You were sure of it."

"I wasn't sure of anything," Kimble said. "But it was the only thing she told me that seemed to have a chance."

They were quiet again, and Kimble cleared his throat and said, "We've got to call it in, you know. I killed a woman. I can't stand here forever."

"Your debt is settled," Darmus said. "You already took a life. Jacqueline's."

"I don't think Silas Vesey is one for crediting accounts," Kimble said.

Audrey Clark looked at him and said, "You told me you weren't worried about adding a few more years for burning that trestle down. Are you now?"

"No."

"There's a way," Darmus said again. "We'll find it. We were getting close. Wyatt was getting close. What did you tell me? He kept himself away from others in the dark. Kept himself alone with his lights. You could —"

"Sure," Kimble said. "There might be a way. But you'll have to find it, because I'll be in prison. The rest of you should not be. As it stands now, you won't be. Grant me this much, though — I don't want to go to prison knowing that I left that trestle standing. I won't."

*　　*　　*

They made their way to the trestle as a group, Kimble walking out front. He'd already told Shipley not to hesitate to fire.

"I might feel something," he said. "And if I do..."

Shipley nodded.

They hung back while Kimble walked out onto the bridge. Dawn was close but hadn't broken yet, and the snow still fell from a black sky. The moon was behind the clouds now, out of sight as it receded to make way for the sun.

Kimble stepped onto the boards, his boots echoing hollowly against them, the smell of gasoline strong in the air. He stopped when he saw the fire.

It was tucked just beneath the easternmost upright of the trestle, and the base had to be fifteen feet in diameter. The flames were blue. They rose up and flapped at the trestle like waves on an angry sea, and milling around it were all those familiar faces. They'd stared at Kimble from ancient photographs, most of them.

Not all of them.

He looked down at Wyatt French, the old man's face painted with flickering blue light, and then at Jacqueline, and he dropped to his knees on the bridge. She was watching him, though the blue flames would wave across her face and hide her from sight at times, only to ebb back and reveal her again.

Nathan Shipley said, "Chief?"

Kimble tore his eyes away from Jacqueline Mathis, looked back at the three who waited for him among the living, and got to his feet.

"See anything?" Darmus asked uneasily.

Kimble nodded. He couldn't speak, not right then. He walked off the bridge and back to them, and then he asked Audrey Clark for the matches. She looked at Darmus, and then at Shipley, and neither of them spoke.

"I've got to try it," Kimble said. "Anybody want to argue that?"

No one did. She passed him a book of matches, and Kimble thanked her.

"Well," he said, "I'll give it a shot, huh?"

"It will work," Audrey Clark said. Roy Darmus nodded, and Shipley didn't say anything at all. His face was pale.

"I'm sorry, chief," he said.

"Shipley, that's why you were there. Why you will always need to be there, in moments like that—to hear the right call and make the right shot. I'm sorry I doubted you. It was...it was a difficult thing, getting an understanding of this place."

He put out his hand, and Shipley shook it. Then Kimble turned to Audrey Clark and said, "You're something special, you know. The way you handled those cats..."

"I love them," she said.

"I know it."

Darmus said, "It may work, Kimble. It may work. And if it doesn't? We can find something that will."

"I know that," Kimble said.

There was a pause, and then he said, "All right. I'd like you all to go up the hill a bit, get higher than I am. I don't know what these flames will do."

They listened, starting uphill, and Kimble turned from them at first, then looked back.

"Darmus?"

The reporter turned back to him, waiting.

"When you tell it," Kimble said, "tell it right, okay? Tell it the way it happened, not the way people will want to hear it. Tell it the way it happened."

Roy Darmus stared at him for a moment and then nodded. "I will, Kimble," he said.

Kimble left them then and went back out onto the bridge. Crossed the length of it, not daring to look back at the fire, where faces of his own kind gathered over more than a century waited and watched. He got to the place on the western side of the trestle where he had emptied the gasoline, and then he removed the pack of matches from his pocket, folded it backward, tore a match free, and struck it.

The glow was small but warm and bright, and he cupped one hand to shield it from the wind and then he passed it to the planks that had once been handled by fevered men who were fading fast. It sparked, hesitated, then absorbed the glow. Began to burn, and he blew on it gently, and that fanned the small flame out and grew it and then it caught the first of the gasoline and went up fast and hot. He stepped away, backpedaling, heading toward the safety of the eastern shore, where the living waited for him with hopes, however faint.

"It's going," Audrey Clark said, and Roy nodded, watching as Kimble backed slowly toward the darkness, the fire riding the lines of fuel toward the rocky cliffs on the opposite shore, the crackle of flames audible now, the smell of smoke in the air.

"It will work," Shipley said. "It will work."

Roy didn't answer.

Kimble got to the center of the bridge, still moving backward slowly, and then he turned and faced them. Held up a hand and waved, and Audrey and Shipley matched the gesture.

Roy held up his own hand and whispered, "Good luck, Kimble. Good luck, and God bless."

When Kimble knelt on the eastern side of the bridge and struck another match, Shipley said, "What's he doing? He's going to trap himself. He's going to —"

Shipley started forward then, and Roy grabbed his arm and held. The deputy was young and strong, but Roy knew that this hold mattered, and he did not let go, not even when Shipley had dragged them both to the ground and they lay in the snow and watched as the flames rose high at the eastern edge of the bridge and roared toward Kimble, who was backing up again, into the middle of the trestle, fire coming at him from both ends now, whipped by the wind and strengthening quickly.

"Why's he doing that?" Audrey cried. "Why isn't he trying to run?"

"Because," Roy said, "this may work, but he's not sure. He wants to be sure. He needs to be."

Kimble retreated to the center of the bridge and watched his fire. Only when he was satisfied that it was going well enough did he chance a look back down to Vesey's blaze, where the cold blue flames licked at the darkness, waiting for him.

You'll get me, he thought, *but you will not get anyone else. I'll hand myself over before I hand you anyone else.*

The ghost with the torch left the blue fire. He walked away from his blaze and stood looking up at Kimble, and there was abject disappointment to his posture, but no resignation. Then he turned and headed north along the river.

He's leaving, Kimble realized with amazement. *He is not done, but he is leaving. There will be another spot for him, and another fire. But not here.*

Above the ghost, a shadow ran along the top of the ridge, tracking the blue torch.

It was the black cat. Following.

But not with him, Kimble thought. No, the cat was not a friend. He was keeping watch on him, and somehow Kimble knew that it was very good that the cat had found him. The reasons were beyond him in that moment as the fire encroached, but he understood that Silas Vesey was leaving and that it was good that the black cat trailed him.

It was important that something trailed him, and kept watch.

Kimble turned back to the cold fire then, back to what waited for him, and saw that the ghosts were all leaving. They were climbing the rocks.

For a moment, he feared for those he'd left behind, those who waited on the hilltop unaware of what was coming toward them. Then he saw that the first of the ghosts — was it Mortimer? Hamlin? one of the ancients — had detoured to the right immediately, was running for the trestle.

Coming for me, Kimble thought, and then he saw the ghost enter the flames, saw a brilliant shower of red sparks, and then there was nothing.

I've released them.

The next ghost entered, another shower of red sparked high and vanished, and Kimble's excitement grew. He remembered, finally, to call out to those he'd left behind.

"It's done here!" he yelled. "I've put an end to it here!"

He couldn't see the group he'd left on the hill, though, not now, with the flames so tall. The firelight was brilliant, the night a thing forgotten. He shouted to them again, as loud as he could, and he hoped it was loud enough. He hoped that they'd heard, and that they would understand the significance of that last word.

He wanted very badly for them to know.

The fire was near him at both ends now, and one of the trestle supports broke free. It shattered with a crack and then one of the massive timbers on the trestle's eastern edge began easing away from the bridge, as if it hated to let go, and swung down in a ribbon of golden light and met the river with a splash.

The ghosts continued their entrance — *exit,* Kimble thought, deliriously happy, *exit* — and as he was pushed farther back into the center and the trestle continued to give way around him, he saw Wyatt French coming, and he wanted to laugh, wanted to shout his thanks, but the lighthouse keeper was already gone into the warm sparks, and then there was only one left, at the top of the ridge and heading his way.

"Jacqueline," Kimble said as she stepped toward him, "I'm here."

He went forward to meet her.

ACKNOWLEDGMENTS

There was a time when I felt eternally bound to *The Ridge* myself, and I'm deeply grateful to those who cast guiding lights along the path for me (no blue torches in this group): Christine, Tom Bernardo, Vanessa Kehren, David Hale Smith.

For Michael Pietsch, I haven't the proper words of thanks. Michael, the importance of your insight, patience, faith, and unbreakable, irreplaceable enthusiasm cannot be overstated. Thanks for having confidence to spare on the days when I ran dry.

The rescue center portrayed in this book is based on a far more fascinating reality, the Exotic Feline Rescue Center founded by Joe Taft. Joe's willingness to share his time, expertise, and perspective with me enabled this story to exist, and his mission is deserving of our attention and support.

Every writer jokes about someday killing off his editor in a book. I've now done it! Felt pretty good, I have to say. But in all seriousness, I'm forever indebted to Pete Wolverton, who read my first manuscript when there was no earthly incentive to do so, then took a chance, and taught me so much about the craft through our five books together. Always, always grateful, Pete.

Josh Ritter and Joe Pug, both wildly gifted artists, graciously allowed me to use their lyrics in the book.

To Marlowe, thanks for the insight into the complex feline mind, not to mention the help with choreography. To Riley... well, you punch the time clock every day, if nothing else.

And now the list of people I'd like to thank in detail but who would take out red pens and begin cutting pages if I tried: David Young, Heather Fain, Terry Adams, Sabrina Callahan, Nicole Dewey, Amanda Tobier, Tracy Williams, Robert Pepin, Louise Thurtell, Nick Sayers, Renee Senogles, Anne Clarke, Heather Rizzo, Luisa Frontino, Miriam Parker, and everyone else involved in making the books a reality.

ABOUT THE AUTHOR

Michael Koryta is the author of seven previous novels, including *Envy the Night,* which won the Los Angeles Times Book Prize for best mystery/thriller, and the Lincoln Perry series, which has earned nominations for the Edgar, Shamus, and Quill awards and won the Great Lakes Book Award. His work has been translated into twenty languages. A former private investigator and newspaper reporter, Koryta lives in Bloomington, Indiana, and St. Petersburg, Florida.